I0744298

Blood Brothers:

Meetings

A Division One Universe Novel

by Stephanie Osborn

Chromosphere Press

Huntsville AL

Meetings
© 2023 Stephanie Osborn
ISBN # 978-1-950633-33-3 (print)
ISBN # 978-1-950633-32-6 (ebook)
Cover art © 2023 Tiffanie Gray
Fiction
First electronic edition 2023

Chromosphere Press
P.O. Box 252
56 Hughes Road
Madison, AL 35758
www.chromospherepress.com

*This book is dedicated to my lost love,
my late husband Darrell.*

*You are missed, sweetheart, more than you know,
and more than my poor words can ever say.*

Books in the Division One/Pan-Galactic Coalition Universe

Division One:

1: Alpha and Omega

2: A Small Medium At Large

3: A Very UnCONventional Christmas

4: Tour de Force

5: Trojan Horse

6: Texas Rangers

7: Definition and Alignment

8: Phantoms

9: Head Games

10: Break, Break Houston

11: Tourist Trap

12: Mega Moth

13: Byegones

14: The Bounty Game

…With more on the way!

Blood Brothers:

1: Meetings

…With more planned!

Coming Soon: The *Stellar Vistas* series, by A.G. Thompson!

Table of Contents

Chapter 1 — Hell in a Handbasket

The boy was uncertain what was happening, but he knew it wasn't good, and he didn't like it. The soldiers wearing the emblem of a strange bird carrying a half-dead spider had burst into Uncle's home, where they were visiting, late in the afternoon and forced the whole family outside, into the street, then into the back of a big truck. It had been raining heavily at the time, and they were all soaked and cold.

Now they'd been dumped from the truck into a kind of paddock, not nearly large enough for the number of people they were forcing into it. There were several gates on the far side, and the crowd instinctively began to move toward the openings, the boy and his family along with them.

But when they got to the gates, to his horror, armed soldiers standing on wooden platforms above the crowd used staves to direct the people like cattle, separating him from his family, and dividing them into several groups, herding them along…like those same cattle. Women, girls, and very small children of both sexes were herded through one gate, men between the ages of roughly sixteen to forty or fifty were herded through a second, boys and old men through a third. So when his mother and sisters were forced through the first gate, his father and brother through the second, and he was pushed toward the third, he reacted.

"Nein! NEIN!" he cried, reaching out and running to try to grasp his parents' hands. "Mamma! Abba! Nein!" (*No! NO! Mamma! Daddy! No!*)

"Nein, zun, gehorche ihnen!" his mother shouted. *(No, son, obey them!)*

"Geh, mein zun! Geh mit ihnen!" his father added. *(Go, my son! Go with them!)*

"NEIN!" the boy screamed, fighting his way to the fence separating him from his mother. "MAMMA!" He tried to shove his way through the fence wire, arms reaching for her.

Abruptly the wire became electrified, and the boy was knocked several feet backward, landing hard in a muddy puddle, barely conscious.

By the time his uncle could help him sit up on the muddy ground, the rest of the family was gone.

***

He was herded, along with his uncle and many others, along a fenced corridor and into a series of concrete buildings. Here, he was forced to strip down to skin, leaving his sodden clothing and anything in his pockets behind.

Coming out of that building, he stood in shock while his dark hair was shaved off and his still-hairless privates perfunctorily checked for vermin, then he was pushed into another building, where he was issued more clothes. He donned a coarsely-woven pair of trousers and shirt, both having vertical stripes of dark blue and a dingy, unbleached cream color. He also got a strange pair of poorly-tanned leather thong sandals. With no socks, the stiff, hard leather abraded between his toes, and his feet quickly became cold. With still-damp skin, no underwear and only a light jacket and cap, the rest of him soon followed.

Forced out the other side of the concrete building by the next group being driven into it, the boy found himself a few feet away from his uncle in another kind of human paddock. A quick, subtle motion by the elder told the boy to act as if he didn't recognize his kinsman, and still confused, he followed instructions as the group was herded into one of the drafty, poorly-made wooden barracks, which he would come to learn were called 'blocks.'

***

Inside there was but one room, and in this were rows upon rows of narrow, multi-level beds built of raw, rough lumber, supplied with basic straw-tick mattresses and one threadbare blanket each. He saw no pillows, at least in the beds around him.

When it became obvious that he would have one of the upper bunks, and that there was not enough room for all of the men and boys crowded into the narrow aisles, he clambered up to his bunk and hunkered down, out of the press of people.

When all of the beds were filled — some with multiple bodies — the guards closed and locked the one door; there were no windows, but the cold winter wind whistled through cracks between the boards in the walls. *We have fresh air, but it will be very cold,* the boy considered, worried. *And there is only one blanket here.* A sort of stove — more of a long, open fireplace — on the far side of the oblong room produced a certain amount of heat, but it didn't begin to reach clear across the barracks. And his bed was halfway along the barracks' length, so he felt little of the fire's effect.

Matters remained so until it grew dark…and even colder than he had feared. What few exposed bulbs lit the area abruptly went out. He burrowed down into the scanty straw-tick bedding as best he could, wrapping himself in the ratty old blanket, thankful that he was on the top bunk, nearly in the low rafters, and that heat rose; quite a few of the 'beds' were actually on the rough plank floor of the block.

Shortly thereafter, despite the cold and the hard bed, the exhausted boy fell asleep.

***

Many light years away, a huge and awe-inspiring representative hall was lavishly bedecked with crystal sculptures symbolizing all the species of the Pan-Galactic Coalition of what some called the Milky Way Galaxy. It was on the planet Aleancë in the star system of the same name, and it was there that the recently-elected representative for the planet Emdali, Lord Pulgey Entiyti, received thunderous applause as he was sworn in as the elected-by-representatives President of the Pan-Galactic Coalition. When the solemn swearing-in ceremony was complete, he moved to the central podium.

"Thank you, my friends," the Draconan declaimed with a wide, toothy smile. Instinctively he flexed back muscles, and the leathery gray wings on his back fluttered briefly, even as the sound system translated his words for the many different species present.

Entiyti was from one of two reptilian sentient species inhabiting his homeworld, and the burgundy tunic and trousers he wore, the formal livery of House Entiyti, set off his silver-white scales, black horns, and copper-colored eyes impressively. The fact that he stood nine feet tall helped.

"I am very honored you saw fit both to nominate me for, and elect me to, the highest office in the galaxy, moreso as I am but an annum into my elected representation of Emdali. It is true that I have some experience in such things, as I came here from heading the Council of Lords on Emdali, and am the Clan Lord for House Entiyti; still, planetary politics is minuscule compared to galactic politics. I swear to you all that I will do the best job of which I am capable! More, during the recesses of this august body, I plan to travel through its divisions and territories, meeting its people and its leaders, and determining where our help is most needed."

Another thunderous round of applause fairly rattled the representatives' consoles. When it had died down, a hand went up. Entiyti acknowledged the being.

"Lord President, what do you intend to do about the Sol system?"

"Sol system? Let me see, that…" The Draconan paused in thought, copper eyes going distant as he tried to remember the reference — a staggering amount of reading material had come with being elected to the position. A green-skinned humanoid woman stepped to his side.

"The system in Territory One, sir. The one that has been periodically petitioning us for membership, even though the majority of their populace knows nothing of us. Earth is the planet's name. They have been far more, mm, persistent, than most of their more-advanced galactic neighbors in the territory."

"Ah, yes, I recall now. Thank you, Lady Krimnet," Entiyti said with another smile. "I suppose we should go there at some point and determine more directly what should be done. But for now, and as they are not even a spacefaring species at this time, I agree with the majority of the House of Representatives: I fail to see the point in prioritizing the matter…"

***

The next morning in the camp came very early, well before dawn, with a loud gong sounding from somewhere. Everyone in the block sat up, waiting, wondering what was about to happen. When nothing did, they all laid back down and waited. Many fell back asleep. Franz fell into a light doze, but did not fall fully asleep, waiting for whatever the gong had signaled.

5

Two hours later, the single door slammed open and several Nazi soldiers entered, shouting orders for them to get up. Within moments they were all up, having slept in the only clothing they now had, the striped trousers and shirts. Then an SS officer strode through the door.

"Achtung! Bilden Sie eine Linie, die an der Tür beginnt. Wenn Sie die Kaserne verlassen, gehen Sie zum Tisch draußen, wo Ihr benenn und Geburtsort aufgenommen und ein Abzeichen an Ihrem Hemd angebracht wird." *(Attention! Form a line starting at the door. When you exit the block, move to the table outside, where your name and birthplace will be taken, your offense determined, and a badge affixed to your shirt.)*

The boy's bladder ached badly, but he didn't even know where a bathroom was — there was nothing to the block but the one big room — so there was no chance of slipping off to relieve himself before getting in line.

However, once he got outside, he spotted several of the prisoners slipping around the corner of the building to relieve themselves; the Nazi guards merely shook their heads and stood upwind. So the boy joined them, then got back in line.

This time as they were identified, they were forced to stand at gunpoint and have a number crudely tattooed onto their arms. When it came Franz' turn, he looked frantically for a way out, but there was none. The tattooing process hurt, and the skin was reddened around the fresh ink of the tattoo, but the tattoo 'artist' swiped it with something that stained the skin brown, then gestured him to move on and began on the next man.

There were a couple of hundred men in the block, but the matter was accomplished in less than two hours, and despite his protests that he was only a boy and hadn't committed any crimes, the boy found himself with a yellow star of David on his shirt.

When he saw the star, though, he wasn't confused about that: he was Jewish, and Hitler blamed Jews for all the ills of the world.

Only then were they allowed access to the latrines — such as they were; a separate building, one latrine per so many blocks — and the food line.

By the time all of the blocks for their latrine were catalogued and tattoed, the day was over.

***

The next morning began before dawn once again, with the same gong. This time, they followed instructions given the previous day: they rose, hit the latrines — they were only able to squeeze fifty at a time into the cramped, smelly space, and there were several hundred in the one block, with three more blocks assigned to that latrine, so they couldn't dawdle — after which came roll call.

Then, and only then, selected prisoners went to collect breakfast for the entire block and return it to the block to be handed out. This, it turned out, would be the means of food distribution henceforward.

There wasn't much. Mostly it consisted of a poor excuse for coffee, some sort of brewed toasted grain rather than actual roasted coffee beans, and nothing to go in it…and at his age, the boy didn't care for coffee to begin with. A very few, mostly the younger boys, got small slices of bread.

Then they fell out for work detail assignments.

***

That first day, the boy was given the job of policing the area around the block. There wasn't much to police; there was little in the way of trash to pick up, for the simple reason that the prisoners had little to throw away, and tried to hold onto what they had, even if it was broken. But they had to try to look busy, or they risked attracting the attention of the guards…which they quickly found was not a good thing.

It was a small space, not more than ten feet between the walls of the block and the fencing on all sides except the front, and that a bit more to allow for the inmates to form ranks each morning. There was little grass; this time of year, it was mostly a muddy mess.

This work lasted until noon, when he — and the rest of his work detail — was sent back to the block.

There, 'lunch' awaited.

It was a wooden bowl containing roughly a liter of 'soup.' This comestible consisted largely of root vegetables, with a scant amount of whole grains poorly hulled, a thin, watery broth made of stewed weeds and fish meal, and barely thickened with some sort of flour.

The boy took one taste and nearly threw up.

This is nasty, he thought in disgust. *I wish I had some of Mamma's vegetable soup. Better yet, her chicken soup.*

Still, he was hungry, having had nothing for breakfast save 'coffee,' so he picked out the vegetables: a scant few small, mealy potatoes, and a couple of chunks of turnips. Several had rotten places on them; he cut those away as best he was able with the wooden spoon he was given.

Then he closed his eyes, held his nose, and sipped on the broth, trying not to gag in between sips.

I hope we get more for dinner, he decided. *And something that tastes better, too.*

***

But 'more' proved to be relative.

It was late winter — it was early March, but winter was hanging on, this year — so it was after dark when they finally ceased work and returned to the block. There, they went through roll call again, en masse; it took over an hour.

Finally the hungry boy got dinner.

It was a thick piece of coarsely-ground black rye bread, with a scant spoonful of margarine — he knew it wasn't real butter by the taste — to scrape over it.

This, he was informed, was dinner AND breakfast. But everyone around him was so hungry, they ate it all at one go.

So he did, too.

It did taste better than lunch, he decided, but that wasn't high praise.

***

He had a hard time understanding how all this was going on; the suburbs of Lublin and the local villages fairly wrapped around the camp's fencing, and Franz thought the 'neighbors' HAD to know what was happening.

It turned out, he discovered as his stay extended into months and then years, that they were aware; there were several attempts by the Polish Resistance to free camp inmates, but they seldom got far. Most of the 'neighbors' either ignored the concentration camp, or actively aided it by turning in the resistance efforts to free the prisoners.

***

The next morning began the same as the one before. This time, he took a mug of the 'coffee' and chugged it. It didn't taste like coffee, but maybe it had a few nutrients to tide him over. It wasn't very filling otherwise, he thought. At least it didn't taste too bad.

When the boy, belly growling, was assigned to a work detail, he was given the job of helping to empty the 'showers.' He thought that was odd, but he'd seen what happened the day before when someone questioned their assignment, and he didn't want to be beaten like that.

So he followed the guard to the concrete buildings that housed the showers. They went behind the buildings, and a special locked door was opened.

To his horror, the naked dead bodies of women fell out.

"All right!" the guard cried in German. "Get to work!"

The prisoners formed several lines and began extracting the bodies, piling them in nearby wheelbarrows, before trundling them off to a relatively small red-brick building with a tall smokestack that stood close by. Black smoke issued from the smokestack; in all the time the boy was there, he never saw a day when the smokestack was not belching dark smoke.

The boy moved to the back of the line.

***

But when he came to the front of the line and reached for the nearest bodies, they tumbled over onto their backs, white faces looking up at the leaden sky with empty, glazed gazes.

The boy stared at the faces on the bodies in shock, paling so much his face turned a light green; abruptly he turned and bolted.

"HEY! Damn you, get back here!" one of the guards cried in German, but the boy kept running, ducking and dodging around barbed wire, quickly disappearing between nearby buildings. "Verdammt!"

"Be silent, Matthaus," the overseer — who wore the rank and insignia of an SS captain, a hauptmann, or more properly in the Nazi SS ranks, a hauptsturmführer — said, holding up a hand. "He's a boy; by the look, not even in his teens yet. Chances are, he's never seen a dead body before, and ran off to throw up. Which is better for us; we don't have to smell his filth."

"But they have to be moved to the crematorium," Matthaus protested.

"No worries; I will go fetch him myself," the overseer said. "I'm sure the other workers will not mind filling in for him for a few moments?" He raised an expectant eyebrow at the patently rhetorical question.

He looked over the group of prisoners in their blue and 'white' striped uniforms; most of them had yellow stars of David stitched to the shoulder, but a few had other symbols, mostly triangles of various colors. They all responded in the affirmative, mostly by nods; though a few seemed sullen, most had tense, worried expressions. He chewed his lip, thoughtful, then gestured to the oldest to come closer. When the man obeyed, he drew him aside. Only then did he notice the tears in the prisoner's eyes.

"Do you speak German?"

"Yes."

"Good. There is more here than I am seeing. You are worried about the boy?"

"Yes, sir."

"Why?"

"Those," the prisoner gestured at the bodies now being removed from the gas chamber, "those in particular, they were his mother and sisters…"

The overseer glanced where the elder indicated, and noted one adult female and two smaller females, the familial resemblance strong, among the group of women's bodies being stacked like cordwood for transport to the nearby crematorium. The old man continued.

"His father is likely to be in the next chamber; I don't know about his brother."

"I see. And how old is the boy?"

"He is well over a year from his bar mitzvah; he has not yet turned twelve."

"Mm. Younger even than I thought. A child, then. But his body is bigger, stronger."

"He speaks often of going with his older brother Eleazar to the boxing and health clubs; Eleazar was very much into physical fitness."

"So he is more developed physically than his years?"

"He is, sir. His father had high expectations for the boy's physique, and the mother for his intellect, until…"

"I see. Very well. I will find the boy and speak with him. Please coordinate with the other workers to ensure his family members — including anyone in the next chamber — are removed to the crematorium before I return with him. I will see that the guards are given orders to allow it. That will be easiest, I think."

"Yes, sir. And…thank you, sir."

"He is strong. He will be a good worker. But he is young yet. I think a bit of leniency may be in order. And perhaps a word to assign him to other details than this," the overseer decided. "Until he is older, or at least until he is more used to it. Back to work."

"Yes, sir."

***

Dodging between the many close-set blocks, the farther the boy ran, the more upset he became, as memories of his mother and sisters playing with him, cooking him meals, helping to teach him how to dance, and more mingled with the far more recent sight of their staring, lifeless, naked bodies. Had it only been two days before that they had been separated? What of his father, his elder brother? Were they dead, too? Was all his family dead but him?

12

Tears filled his eyes, a few spilling down his cheeks, and soon he was running blind.

So when he ran headlong into something, he bounced off and fell to the cold wet ground, even as the something let out a loud grunt.

"Beobachten Sie, wohin Sie gehen!" barked from overhead. *(Watch where you're going!)*

The boy sniffled, as the tears began to overflow despite his best efforts. He glanced upward to see a guard in a Nazi uniform. Abruptly his stomach churned, then purged itself…all over the soldier's feet.

"Es tut mir leid. Ich habe dich nicht gesehen." *(I am sorry. I did not see you.)*

"UGH! Dann werden Sie lernen, darauf zu achten, wohin Sie gehen!" *(Then this will teach you to watch where you are going!)*

And the Nazi guard drew back a fist.

***

When the overseer found the boy, another guard was beating him viciously, as he wept and cried out in pain, trying to pull away and shield himself from the blows.

"What are you doing?! Stop at once!" the overseer demanded in haughty German.

"Hauptmann! Sir, he was running, and when I stopped him, he threw up all over my uniform boots," the Nazi soldier answered in kind, pointing at the scant but aromatic detritus on his footgear. The boy crouched down nearby and sniffled softly as tears continued to trickle down his bruised, swelling cheeks.

"Of course he did. He is on my transfer detail, but due to his youth, has never dealt with dead bodies before. I was just coming to fetch him."

"But he's a prisoner, sir! His feelings don't matter!"

"He is just a boy of some eleven years' age. He is inexperienced but strong. For that, I will allow some opportunity to get used to…matters." The hauptsturmführer raised an irritated eyebrow, daring the sergeant to defy him.

"Um. Yes, sir." He turned and cuffed the boy hard with his fist. "Go with the hauptsturmführer, here, and see that you behave next time."

The hauptsturmführer saw red.

"Stay here, and do not move," he told the boy, who nodded, trying not to cringe away from both men.

The hauptsturmführer let his true nature emerge.

The guard didn't have time to scream.

***

The boy blinked, and suddenly both men were gone. He did as he was told, however; he had learned enough in the short time he had been in the concentration camp that one did as one was told, and he didn't want another beating — he was going to have a black eye and some impressive bruises as it was.   After a couple of minutes had passed, he sat on the cold ground in the narrow alleyway and leaned against the wall of the closest block to wait.

Some ten minutes later, a shadow fell across him and he looked up; the hauptsturmführer was back, but the guard was not.

"There," the hauptsturmführer said, sounding satisfied. "He will not bother you again."

"Where did you go? How do you know?"

"We…stepped outside the camp…to talk."

"You, um…you have…blood…on your mouth…"

The captain calmly took out a plain white handkerchief and wiped his lips, careful to also cover the area below the lower lip, where fluids might drip. He looked at the cloth.

"So I do," he noted. "Is it gone?"

"Um. Y-yes."

"Good. Can you keep secrets?"

The boy nodded.

"It was his," the captain said. "The blood was his. That's how I know he won't bother you again."

"Did you shoot him?"

"…No."

The boy studied him a moment. "Do you know Yiddish?"

"A little, yes. Probably not as much as you do, but a good bit."

"Are you a vrokali?"

"A vampire?" The hauptsturmführer laughed. "What do you think?"

It did cross the boy's mind — he was anything but stupid, though his youthful innocence was being rapidly stripped away — that the man had not denied it. He pondered for long moments before answering.

"I think…I think you drank his blood until he died, and that is why the blood was on your mouth, and how you know he will not bother me again — he is dead," the boy decided. "Are… you going to do it to me, too?"

"No," the man said, voice softening. "You are safe with me and will always be safe with me. Do you believe me?"

The boy studied him, taking his time, considering.

"Yes, I think so."

"Good. Now, what I am going to tell you, you must tell no one."

"Shall we go somewhere no one can hear?"

"No one can see or hear us right now. I'm taking care of that. That way, neither of us will get into trouble."

"How are you doing that?"

"Why, you know vampires have special abilities," he said with a teasing grin. "I'm not a Nazi; I'm an Allied spy. I infiltrated Majdanek—"

"Where is that?"

"It's this place."

"What? This place? I thought it was called Konzentrationslager Lublin."

"Officially it is, but its more common nickname is Majdanek. You may call me Jakob," he said. "You'll see me around here from time to time. I'll be in and out as I gather information and take it back to Allied command. But when I'm here, I'll do my best to look after you."

"What's your last name?"

Jakob drew a deep breath.

"My last name is one that's been lost to history," he admitted. "Just call me Jakob for now. I'll be here for a little while, but then I'll have to go. But when I come ba—"

"Take me with you!" the boy cried, reaching out and grasping the man's trousers legs, pleading. "Take me and my family — what's left of us — before they kill us all!"

"I can't, son. My abilities are good, but I can't manage that one, no matter how much I'd like to, and I do want to. I could take you, but not your whole family. Maybe one day in the future, but not right now, nor any time soon. Besides, if I did, the Nazis would probably kill everyone we left behind before I could bring anyone to rescue them. I'm sorry."

The boy nodded, disconsolate.

"What's your name, son?"

"Franz. Franz Levy. Of Leipzig, in Germany."

"All right, here's what I can do, Franz. I'll hunt up the rest of your family and do what I can, when I can. But I can't promise I can save them," Jakob admitted. "I can't be around all the time. Sometimes I have to leave to report back."

"I…I understand. But you will try?"

"I'll do my best."

"All right."

"Good. Here." He pulled out a bar of Belgian chocolate from somewhere inside his uniform. "It was in Georg's pocket; I found it after I, ah, 'ate' him. Eat it. You're going to need the calories. I'll try to bring something a little more substantial next time. Let's head back to work."

"Do I have to? Mamma…and my sisters…" His eyes filled with tears. "And I don't know about Pappa, or, or my brother…"

"I know, son. I had the others tend to them for you; we'll find out about your father and brother. And I have to get you back, or we're both dead. We have to make it look normal. I've already gone out on a limb for you; don't make me saw it off behind us both. Hurry and eat that, and let's go."

Franz nodded and wolfed down the chocolate, managing to keep it down somehow, and they headed back to the gas chambers.

***

By the time they got back to the work detail, the other prisoners had emptied the gas chamber containing Franz' mother and sisters, and were halfway through the next one. With the help of the elder prisoner, he eased young Franz back into the work of moving the dead from the gas chambers to the crematorium for disposal. At a gesture from Jakob, the elder sidled over. A raised eyebrow was Jakob's only request.

"Yes, sir," the elder murmured. "Mother and sisters and father are…accounted for, and already transferred. The workers in the crematorium put them at the front of the queue, just in case. It wouldn't do for the boy to see that, too. I have it to understand that most likely the grandparents came through here yesterday."

"Any other kin in the immediate family?"

"One older brother. Eleazar by name. We didn't see him; apparently he still lives — for now — elsewhere in the camp."

Jakob nodded and the elder returned to the work, moving close to young Franz and assisting him where needed.

Good, Jakob thought, watching. *That makes things a little easier, at least. For now, I suppose. Well, not good for the boy, but at least he's spared seeing their bodies any further. Maybe I can find the brother and watch out for him, too.*

***

They had been at it for about three hours and it was nearing lunch when a 'blood brother' — a human in Allied intel who had knowingly given Jakob a small amount of his blood to consume, thereby forming a bond, though few in the Intelligence Service knew of the link, let alone knew of Jakob's true nature — contacted him through the bond with instructions.

Mmph, he grumbled to himself. *Bad timing. But when is it ever good?*

He stepped away from the detail, then gestured to the elder, who broke off the grisly work and came to him.

"Yes, sir?"

"You have been a great help to me this morning."

"Thank you, sir."

"You may be of additional assistance. Are you in the same block with the boy?"

"I am."

"Good. Do you know his family?"

"I do. They are — were — my kinsmen. They were visiting me and my family in Lublin, here in Poland, from their home in Leipzig when…my home was raided and we were all taken prisoner." He grimaced. "I wish…"

"Do not trouble yourself," Jakob said, very quiet. "There was a typhus outbreak a few months ago; the workers here all died of it, so the camp had to be…'restaffed.' It was bound to happen in Leipzig as well. It may already have done so."

"Ah."

"I understand now. Listen, I need to leave the camp for a time to obtain orders, and I would like for you to do something for me while I am gone."

The old man glanced around to be sure no one was nearby, then lowered his voice.

"You are not one of them, are you?"

"What?"

"You are not a Nazi. You care. Even the nominal Nazis are not so caring as you have shown, for all you cover it well — yet you wear the uniform of an SS officer. Are you Allied? A spy?"

Jakob simply smiled, and mentally answered, *Yes*.

The old man's eyes opened wide, but otherwise he gave nothing away, so Jakob continued.

I want you to look after Franz as best you are able; I understand you are limited in what you can do, but try to keep him calm and out of trouble, especially if this damn mess of a war lasts as long as I suspect it will. Keep your eyes open for his brother as well; I'll want to find him when I come back, and try to protect him, too. If you have already spotted him by the time I return, it'll save some trouble — and potential questions — hunting him up.

Can you hear me? the old man asked mentally, seeming tentative.

Yes.

I see a small, fresh bloodstain on your collar…

Damnation. I thought I got it all. Is it noticeable?

No, and if they noticed, the guards likely think you beat the boy; he is badly bruised.

I did not. Another guard had already found him. The guard will not hurt anyone again. Ever.

Ah. I see. So the fact that the stain is in line with the corner of your mouth may be no coincidence. What are you?

Jakob grumbled to himself. *I must be more careful,* he considered. *I was so enraged at how he beat the boy, I was messier than usual.* Finally he answered the elder.

…A friend.

Mmm. The elder appeared to consider. *And the boy is under your protection?*

He is. For whatever that's worth, these days. I'm not omnipresent, and I'm sure not HaShem. But I try.

I see. And his family?

Are you part of his family? You said his family was kin…

Uncle, yes. Well, great-uncle. I am Rabbi Eitan Levy. His grandfather was my brother.

Aha. Yes, I will. As I identify you all, I will do what I can to protect you. Whatever else you consider me — and I see in your mind, you suspect several things, based on the lore of your religion — I AM a friend.

But you can do…these things. And more.

Yes. But my…less benevolent…abilities are only directed against evil ones.

Huh. Interesting. You are not human.

No. Not now. I was, once.

What was — is — was — your belief system, your faith, if I may ask?

You would probably have considered me one of the righteous among the nations. Not Jewish, but I did and do consider them to have much — most — of the Truth, and to follow the One.

And now?

I still believe that.

Were you Christian?

No. That didn't exist yet when I was human.

The rabbi's eyes widened again.

You are old.

I am, yes. Very old. Fortunately, I don't look my age. He hid the grin as he added, "I must go very soon. Do as I have said." Then he continued mentally, *And in turn, I will do what I can. We are neither of us omnipotent, but between us, perhaps we can do a good bit.*

"I shall," Eitan replied, then added, *The other boy will need to know how to identify you. As will what is left of my family, though there are only a couple more.*

We'll use a kind of password, Jakob decided. *You've seen the gate placards?*

Yes. Eitan was disgusted. *'Arbeit macht frei.'*

Exactly. Work doesn't make us free, especially in this place, but there's a song...

Ah! Die gedanken sind frei!

That's the one. Thoughts are free.

And it can be hummed without the words, and no one else the wiser.

You're a quick thinker, Rabbi. You catch on quickly. Jakob grinned again. "All right, back to work," he said. "I will be back when I can."

Rabbi Eitan Levy nodded and turned, searching out young Franz with his eyes.

When he turned back, the 'hauptsturmführer' was gone.

***

The next day, Eitan Levy was assigned to the litter detail, and he strongly suspected this was thanks to Jakob, somehow. He kept an eye out for Eleazar, even as young Franz scoured the area on the opposite side of the yard, near the closest lookout tower; the Nazi soldiers tended to think it funny to throw out their meal waste around their posts, then watch as the prisoners alternated between trying to eat the scraps and putting the inedibles into their burlap trash sacks. One perverted bastard even thought it was funny to relieve himself on whoever was below the tower on rubbish detail.

Unfortunately his latest victim was young Franz.

Franz leaped away, between the supports, up under the tower proper, and tried to wipe away the urine…

…Just as a roar of outrage erupted nearby.

"YOU DAMN BASTARD SON OF A BITCH! THAT'S MY LITTLE BROTHER, DAMN YOU!!"

And suddenly Eleazar was running toward the guard tower, as the laughing guard fastened his uniform trousers.

"Oh no," a horrified Eitan murmured to himself, too far away to do anything.

***

Franz spun when he heard the shout from a familiar voice.

"ELEAZAR!" he cried. "Oh, Eleazar! I'm so glad to see—"

What happened next happened fast.

***

Eleazar bent and scooped up something from the ground, then made a throwing motion.

The powerfully thrown rock soared upward, striking the perverse guard, who was wearing a uniform cap rather than a helmet, squarely in the temple. The guard staggered, his rifle clattering to the deck of the platform. Then he pitched over the rail, plummeting to the ground more than a story below, and laid there, his head canted at an odd angle, eyes glazing.

The other two guards swung their weapons around and opened up on Eleazar.

The young man staggered as blood spattered out from his body, but he stood upright, strong and proud, the very picture of young manhood.

"Feh! Geh in drerdt, shtikl'ch drek!" (*Eh! Go to hell, shitheads! [lit. get in dirt, pieces of shit]*)

One of the guards shifted his aim and put a bullet through Eleazar's head. A red mist exploded outward behind him.

He dropped like a stone, a round, slightly singed hole in his forehead, and most of the back of his head missing.

***

By the time Eitan could reach Eleazar's side, a horrified Franz was already kneeling beside him, in shock. It didn't take medical knowledge for Eitan to realize that Eleazar had died instantly, and judging by Franz' subdued behavior, he realized it as well. He simply held his brother's limp hand and sat beside him, silent and pale.

"YOU! Down there! Get back to work!" one of the guards shouted, waving his weapon at them.

"It is his big brother, and he is just eleven," Eitan replied. "He only says goodbye."

"He'll be lucky if he doesn't see him in hell in the next five minutes," the guard retorted, hefting his rifle. "GET. TO. WORK."

"Come, Franz," Eitan murmured, taking the boy by the shoulders. "Kiss him and let us go. You take my area, over by the fence, and I'll police this area, and see to Eleazar if they'll let me."

Numb, Franz bent and kissed the cheek of his older brother, then stood and walked away.

Eitan looked after him, worried.

***

Chapter 2 — Endurance

The first ten-annum term of President Entiyti had gone very well. He had been elected to the general representative body considerably less than two annums before becoming president, had been a duly sworn representative scarcely one, and very quickly developed a name as a fair, just leader. It had been little surprise to anyone when he was nominated, then elected, to the office of President. He was a being of honor, and did his best by all the galactic peoples, running the Ennead — the Council of Nine, charged with the high-level affairs of the Coalition, and a subset of it — and overseeing the full meetings of the Representative House. When those were not in session, he often spent his time in his personal flagship, the *Hsshthh*, or the *Winged Serpent,* visiting the various planets of the Coalition. Only when he needed a break did he return to his estate on Emdali.

By the end of his term, he was beloved by most of the galaxy.

It took no great difficulty to be re-elected, first as the Emdalian representative, then as the Coalition President. He didn't even have to do more than accept the nominations.

On Earth, a certain human boy was just being inducted into Majdanek with his family as, on Aleancë, Entiyti was sworn into his second term of office.

***

Franz did not grieve for Eleazar. Nor, for that matter, did he grieve for the rest of his family, who he now knew were all dead, except for Uncle Eitan and a few cousins.

Only a couple of months after his arrival in Majdanek, Franz celebrated his twelfth birthday.

Well, it was not so much that he celebrated it, as that he noticed when it went by, the same as any other day passed in the hellhole in which he currently found himself.

He wept in his bed that night.

He wept for his brother, his mother and father, his sisters, the way of life they had known, the home he now understood that he would never see again, and for all that he had lost. Including his birthday.

He was quiet, and did not sob openly, but he sniffled a lot. It never reached his awareness that the restlessness of his bed-neighbors meant they knew he was crying, and felt sympathy for him, but were unable to help.

The next morning, he washed the tearstains off his cheeks and stood for roll call, his face expressionless, hazel eyes hard and empty.

Uncle Eitan, watching, worried for the boy.

***

The next week, Jakob returned, once more in the SS captain's uniform. He found Eitan in the work details, and gestured to him to leave the detail. The Nazi sergeant who oversaw the detail spotted the hauptsturmführer, nodded, and gestured to Eitan to obey the senior officer.

When Eitan reached his side, Jakob said, "Come with me."

They moved away from the work detail and disappeared between the buildings.

***

Finally they stopped.

"All right," Jakob said, "no one can see or hear us now. So—"

"But there are Nazi soldiers not fifteen feet away!"

"I've taken care of it," Jakob said, then gave the rabbi a lopsided grin. "Remember, I'm, ah, 'special.' No longer human."

"Oh," Eitan recalled. "All right. What…?"

"Have you found young Franz' brother?"

"Well, yes…"

"Good. How many of your own immediate family still live?"

"At this point? Two. Out of fourteen."

"How do you know?"

"I've had reports from the transfer detail."

"Ah. Your wife?"

"No, she died some years ago. Well before all this… drek…began, thank HaShem."

"…I'm sorry. For all of it, including your wife."

"Thank you. Things do not always work out as we had planned. HaShem has His own plans, I suppose, though it is very hard to understand, sometimes."

"He does, yes." Jakob paused. "Someday we'll understand, I suppose. All right. Can you introduce me to Franz' brother?"

"I'm afraid not. I found him when he got himself shot in the skull for defending Franz from a perverted bully among the soldiers."

"Damnation."

"Something like, yes. For whatever it is worth, Eleazar did take the pervert with him."

"How?!"

The rabbi gave a wry grin.

"It seems he took a page from the story of David and Goliath…only without a sling. His throwing arm was excellent. In my considered opinion, it is a tossup as to whether the rock to the temple killed the drek, or the broken neck when he fell off the watchtower as a result."

"I see." Jakob's eyes widened. "He was a powerful young man."

"He was, yes. And a good man."

"Very well. I suppose the supplies I brought will go a bit farther than I'd anticipated."

"Supplies?"

"Yes. I was able to bring the equivalent of two small boxes of C-rations with me, tucked in various hidden pockets. They aren't crates; those were too big for me to smuggle readily, but there's enough for a couple of full meals for several people — say eight or ten meals per box, as well as a dozen small bags of chocolate candies. It isn't haute cuisine by any means, but it's nourishment you aren't getting here. Can you get any of them to your own family?"

"Unfortunately, I don't think so. They are in a different block on the far side of the camp. I have seen them at a distance, but have not been able to contact them."

"Mm. That's a problem. Well, perhaps I can locate them myself and explain."

"That would be difficult, but greatly appreciated."

"I'll give it a shot, and you're welcome," Jakob said with a smile. "Now, here." He pulled a C-ration pack from somewhere in his uniform. "Sit and eat. I'll keep watch and ensure no one can see, then do away with the waste when you're finished. Then we'll go find Franz and feed him, and you can tell me about your family members, so I can find them. And," he added, raising a grim eyebrow, "maybe we can identify the guards who shot Eleazar and I will…have a meal, myself."

***

Franz was subdued when Jakob found him, but Jakob wasn't surprised, after Eitan gave him the detailed story of Eleazar's death over his C-rations. The boy was already considerably thinner than when Jakob last saw him, his face paler.

He took the C-ration that Jakob gave him without question or hesitation and ate it ravenously.

When he was done, Jakob returned Franz and Eitan to their respective tasks, then went in search of two or three Nazi tower guards for his own meal.

His search was successful, and the Allied spy ate well that day.

***

Next, Jakob tried to find the rest of Eitan's family, but failed. Eventually he resorted to the more dangerous method of searching records files in the camp's headquarters building, where he discovered that they had been less than the docile prisoners that Majdanek's commandant wanted, and had been sent that very morning to the gas chambers, much to Eitan's sorrow.

29

"I'm sorry, my friend," Jakob offered, voice soft. "I wasn't fast enough. I'm afraid I failed you."

"No, you did not," a grieving Eitan noted, as Franz looked on, impassive. "This place, these people…it is their fault."

"I won't argue that," Jakob agreed. "I am still sorry I couldn't save them."

Franz nodded agreement as well…but said nothing.

Jakob cocked his head and looked at the boy, reaching out mentally, seeking a sense of his mood. What he got was anger, despair, and hopelessness, but he couldn't sort it all out; it was churning inside the boy and creating a jumble of Jakob's mental impressions.

"Are you angry with me?" he finally asked.

"No," Franz replied, subdued. "I am angry, very angry, but not at you."

"At who, then?"

"The Nazis. Especially the ones who killed Eleazar."

"Those particular ones won't be doing that any more."

"Did you do the same to them as you did to the guard who beat me?"

"I did." Jakob chuckled. "I had a plentiful dinner that day." Then he sobered. "They were terrified when they realized what fate awaited them, and I did nothing to assuage that fear. Not," he added, "that anyone could hear their screams. And there is a very convenient forest not far removed from the outer perimeter that makes a nice spot for a…picnic."

"Thank you for that, at least. But I do not think we," he gestured at Eitan and himself, "will ever get out of here alive."

"I'm working hard on that, my boy," Jakob said. "Keep your head down and do everything you can to stay alive that doesn't violate your personal morals, and I'll do everything I can to keep you that way. And that's how you'll get out of here alive. Deal?" Jakob offered his hand with a smile.

Franz gazed at the no-longer-human man for long moments, seeming to consider. Finally he put out his own hand and took Jakob's.

"Deal," he said, very serious.

But he didn't smile.

***

For the next several days, Jakob brought at least one C-ration can per day to Franz and Eitan — when Eitan would accept it. "No, I am old, and I have not much time left, even were I outside this camp," the rabbi protested. "Keep Franz alive. That is what is important. You can only bring so many, after all."

The C-rations were exhausted save for a couple of cans, when Jakob was summoned away again.

"Here," he said, giving the last two ration cans to Franz and Eitan in their empty block, ensuring they were unobserved. "Hide these in your bunks and eat them at night, when the others are asleep."

"But they are hungry, too," the rabbi protested.

"I know, but I can only bring so much with me, and the two of you are under my personal protection," Jakob pointed out. "I keep my word to the best of my abilities, Rabbi. I WILL protect the two of you, as much as I am able. I don't know when I'll be back, but we're working on invasion plans that could free you soon. Assuming certain things fall into place first. If not, there's no telling when."

And he was gone.

'Certain things' did not fall into place.

Franz did not see Jakob again for a long time.

***

31

That night, after everyone had gone to bed, the lights were out and the block was quiet, Franz set about creating a little nook in his bunk that would be easy to hide small items such as the cans of C-rations that Jakob had brought. He did not expect to have those frequently, but he intended to hang on to them when he did; whatever might come of this war, he had every intention of surviving it, if he could. He had made a deal, after all. And his father had taught him to keep his word.

After about half an hour of quiet work in the darkness, during which he'd only managed to carve out a small hole in one of the rough 'bedposts' with a tin mess-kit spoon he'd found in the trash and sharpened on a rock, a frustrated Franz decided that it would be better to simply hide the few cans and such under the straw-tick mattress, then scatter some additional straw over it and put his blanket over all. The guards seemed rarely to come into the block — the boy was already dealing with fleas, lice, and bedbugs, and the guards knew it; it was an unpleasant experience of which they wanted no part — so unless another prisoner found them and either stole them outright, or ratted him out to the guards, it should be safe.

Just then, his great-uncle's face loomed in the darkness right below his bunk. Silently he gestured for the boy to follow. Franz quietly clambered down from his topmost bunk and followed Uncle Eitan over to the fireplace, which was mostly embers by this point — even the firewood issued to the blocks was rationed — but still emitting heat. He sat on the warm stone of the hearth, and Eitan stiffly followed suit.

"What is it, Uncle?" Franz breathed, keeping his voice as low as possible so as to avoid annoying the sleeping prisoners, nor yet drawing attention to the conversation by those who might be spying.

"I have something for you, Franz," Eitan said very quietly, reaching into the folds of his clothing. "Your father told me where your mother intended to hide it, and that day, when… well. While the guards weren't looking, I was able to find it. I only hope she and your father can forgive me, but he told me so you could have it." He handed over a gold band inset with a ruby.

"What? That is…that is Mamma's wedding ring," the boy murmured, staring.

"Yes. She, um, she hid it…inside," his uncle tried, gesturing at his lower abdomen.

Franz would understand many years later what the old man was trying to tell him, but at the time, he did not. All he knew was that he now had a remembrance of his beloved mother. Eitan handed it to him and he took it, pressed it to his lips, then held it to his heart. It had a warm, feminine smell to it.

"What should I do with it?" he whispered. "I cannot wear it, even on a string around my neck; the guards would see it and steal it."

"Do you have a cubbyhole in your bunk yet?"

"Yes; I was working on that when you came just now. But it isn't very big."

"That's not very big." Eitan gestured to the ring.

"Ah! All right, I can put it in there and put the plug in, and no one will notice," Franz realized.

"Good. Try to remember to grab it and hide it on your body if you should be taken elsewhere."

"Elsewhere?"

"I have it to understand that sometimes prisoners may be moved to other camps."

"Oh. All right. I hope I am not." The boy sighed and looked at the ring in the dim firelight. "I am glad I do not have to carry bodies anymore."

"That might change yet, my zun. And those on the detail are called sonderkommandos."

"What? Special commandos? Why? That is a strange name."

"It is, but you can see why it is 'special,' I am sure."

"Yes. It is not a nice special."

"No, not at all. But yes, I am also glad not to be on that detail any longer." He rose. "Now, zun, run back to bed and hide that well. I will see you over breakfast."

"Yes, Uncle." The boy stood, leaned up and kissed his great-uncle, then headed for his bunk.

The next morning, as if someone had overheard the conversation in the night, the boy was reassigned back to the sonderkommandos.

***

The oberführer, the SS senior colonel, had arrived the night before last, and yesterday had been a hard one: the guards had driven them especially hard, showing off for the oberführer, who was there for 'inspections.' Even so, Franz' active mind had not stopped working. He was worried.

He had a sneaking suspicion that the Nazis very deliberately went through their sonderkommandos like water through a sieve, in an attempt to keep a secret of the mass killings. He already knew there had been some considerable upset when it was discovered that Jakob had had him reassigned to the trash pickup detail. Unfortunately that had not lasted long, and the Majdanek kommandant, a Standartenführer or SS Colonel, one Karl Koch at that time, ordered him transferred back to der sonderkommandos, though somehow his great-uncle Eitan had escaped notice; the two Levys suspected Jakob had somehow managed that much. Jakob's abilities exceeded normal humans, true, but they did not approach HaShem's; he could not work great miracles.

The boy had a hunch that the vampire wanted an adult available to watch over Franz when he himself could not be there, and for that, the boy was grateful. Vampires, he had decided, made good friends and terrible enemies, and he was glad Jakob was his friend. In the end, it had been almost exactly three months before all the confusion over his reassignment was worked out and he had returned to gas chamber/cremation duty.

One horrifying discovery he had made, however: None of the other men he remembered from that dreadful day were still there.

He found out why when they began emptying the gas chambers on his first day back on that task.

They do not want us to talk, to reveal the secret of this… this nightmare they make real, the boy realized, as he forced himself into a kind of numbness while he hauled the bodies of those former sonderkommandos unceremoniously from the gas chambers to the crematorium. *So they kill us before we can tell.*

That discovery had been two months and a bit under three weeks ago. Franz was casting about in his mind for some way to escape the certain death he knew was coming.

So far, he was coming up blank.

He had warned Uncle not to talk about the detail, and why, and Uncle had paled and promptly agreed.

But now the elderly uncle looked likely to outlive the boy, unless Franz was blessed with a miracle.

Please, HaShem, he pleaded, *I need a miracle.*

***

Since he was small but strong given his age, he was eventually assigned the specific task of pulling the bodies well into the crematorium chambers; rigor mortis meant that the bodies did not always 'want to go,' as he thought of it. The first time he had had to break bones to accomplish the task sickened him, but after a few days he began to get used to it. That realization did not do him any favors mentally, however. He did not want to become like those who had imprisoned him, heartless and unfeeling.

He hated the guard who supervised him, however — the sick bastard despised Jews, and was constantly taunting Franz with the threat of locking him inside while he worked, and burning him alive. The boy was justifiably terrified of the guard, but also afraid of being killed at the end of the three months, and generally lived in gut-melting fear.

The only saving grace was that, as a sonderkommando, he was fed marginally better than the average camp inhabitant; the C-rations had run out weeks before. It was as well that there was little food, he supposed, for it was disgusting and he was barely able to keep it down as it was.

***

Franz was headed for 'work' like the other sonderkommandos; the crematorium was on the outskirts of the camp for obvious reasons, and his path — and that of the others — took them by the mechanics' shop, though on the other side of a fence. There he paused very briefly, startled at the outbreak of heated German cursing.

"You damned ignorant peasant! Utter imbecile! What do you mean, telling me you cannot fix my automobile? I must be at Auschwitz by sundown, and we are late as it is!" It was the oberführer. (*SS senior colonel*)

"I am sorry, sir! It is likely the poor quality of the workers who made it!"

Franz recognized this as a reference to the forced labor the German automotive manufacturer had been required to use to meet quotas, after most of the German men had been placed in the military.

The driver was frantically turning the key in the ignition. The big car — it was a Benz W31 6-wheeled staff car — would crank, stutter, shudder, click, and sputter out, over and over.

"Well?" the oberführer demanded, cold.

"I don't know, sir! I'm only the driver! I'm not a mechanic!"

Franz, brain churning, moved as close to the fence separating him from the shop as he dared without touching it; many of the fences were electrified, sufficient that several prisoners had been able to commit suicide by throwing themselves against it.

"I can fix it!" he called in German. "Sir! I know what is wrong. I can fix it."

The oberführer and his driver looked up.

"You? You're a boy, AND a Jew. Go away," the driver scoffed.

The oberführer, however, stepped closer.

"How do you know what is wrong?" he asked. "Why do you think you can fix it?"

"My father used to work on cars," Franz explained. "He was a rabbi, but rabbis do not make much money unless they work in a big synagogue in a big city. He brought in extra money by fixing cars around our town. I often helped, because I liked doing it, and I could spend time with him." He paused briefly, realizing that would never happen again, before resuming. "I heard the sound just now, and I think I know what is wrong."

"What, then?"

"I think it has a bad ignition coil."

"How would you repair it?"

"Replace the coil. There is likely a spare in the shop."

"Have you ever repaired an auto without your father?"

"Yes, several. He said I was very good."

The oberführer cocked an eyebrow, then turned to the nearest guard. Gesturing at Franz, he ordered, "Bring him to me."

***

Once Franz stood before the SS oberführer, he addressed him directly.

"Boy, can you really repair my automobile?"

"Yes, sir," Franz said, polite despite his wont; his heart seethed with hatred. "If there is a spare in the shop, I think I can."

"What detail are you on?"

"I am a sonderkommando, sir."

"Mm. Very well. Be useful and repair my vehicle. Otherwise I shall shoot you where you stand and your body will feed the crematorium. Do you understand?"

"Yes, sir."

"Oberscharführer?" the oberführer addressed the driver. (*NCO; squad leader*)

"Yes, sir?"

"Take him into the mechanics shop so he can find this spare coil. Watch him. See that he does not sabotage instead of repair. You have enough mechanic knowledge for this?"

"Yes, sir; of course, sir."

"I understand that you are not trained as a full mechanic, oberscharführer. Unfortunately the previous mechanic here seems to have died in the plague that swept the camp last year, so it may prove that this boy is useful. Hang on to him if he repairs it; I can think of several ways we can use him. If he does not… shoot him."

"Jawohl, mein Herr."

Despite his confidence, Franz suppressed a shiver.

***

In the end, the driver was rather impressed. Having found a spare ignition coil inside the shop, Franz was able to fix the senior colonel's car in about thirty-five minutes. The big Benz practically purred…until the driver gunned it, and it roared.

The oberführer's eyebrows shot up.

"Ausgezeichnet!" he exclaimed. *(Excellent!)*

"He is very good, sir," the driver noted. "And he even showed me what was wrong, and what he was doing to fix it."

"Yes, it seems he is very good. Can you fix it yourself, next time?"

"Uhn," the driver grunted. "Not really, sir. Not that fast, anyway. He's smaller and can get his hands into places mine would not fit. I will, however, see to it that certain spare parts are ordered and kept in the boot. The boy told me what to get."

"I see," the oberführer said, seeming to consider. Then he turned to the kommandant, who had come out to see what the problem was. "Standartenführer Koch?" *(SS colonel)*

"Ja, mein Herr?"

"You will keep this boy available for me in future. I care not what you do with him when I am not here, but keep him alive, uninjured, and available to work on my vehicles when I am here. Under no circumstances let harm befall him until I tell you otherwise."

"Ja, mein Herr. It will be done."

At a gesture from Koch, the guard promptly led Franz to the mechanics shop, where he began familiarizing himself with the layout and the tools available.

The next morning, with the oberführer and his big auto gone, Franz was placed back on trash policing detail.

But not the crematorium detail.

***

The next year crept by in excruciating torture. The winter was especially bad, cold and wet. Many of the prisoners died outright, freezing to death. This was followed by a cool, rainy spring and a hot, stifling summer, which faded only reluctantly into a warmer-than-usual autumn.

Many of those elders in Franz' barracks did not survive the deprivation, starvation, weather extremes, and hard work. Their bodies fed the crematoria…or the mass burial pits.

Everyone grew leaner and their faces became marked with an unhealthy pallor.

From time to time, Jakob returned. But he seldom had good news; the war was dragging on, and it was difficult to make any headway against the Axis powers, especially Hitler's Nazi regime, which was surprisingly well armed…and vicious. The fact that the Allies were having a hard time agreeing on a plan of action going forward did not help.

"I suspect there is something going on with the Soviets," Jakob told them in private, "but I cannot be sure. They had that treaty with Hitler, after all. There is some discussion in my intelligence chain of command of using my abilities to infiltrate the Soviets and see what I can find out."

"Will that mean leaving us?" Eitan wondered.

"No. It will simply mean splitting my time between three places instead of two. As you may expect, I can travel…very fast."

He brought with him small amounts of nutrient-and calorie-dense food for Franz, and the boy managed to eke by on that. He tried to provide food for the rabbi, but the elder passed on most of it to Franz.

So the one-year anniversary of Franz' incarceration came and went, largely unnoticed.

From time to time, a fresh surge of prisoners was inducted into the camp, denoting some new atrocity or other that the Nazis had done in the world outside, though news of exactly what could be difficult to come by. And from time to time, entire groups of prisoners were taken to the back of the camp and shot.

But Jakob vanished and was not seen again — in Majdanek, at least — for over a year.

***

There wasn't much to young Franz' bar mitzvah a few months later. There couldn't be. There was no synagogue, no Torah, no kippah, no tallit, no tefillin. (*Old Testament scroll; Jewish skullcap; fringed prayer shawl; phylactery or leather box on straps containing Scripture verses*)

But Franz' great-uncle, Rabbi Eitan, blessed the boy and he and a few of the other Jewish men sang softly and prayed over him, and that had to do.

Three weeks later, Rabbi Eitan died from starvation.

***

Two months after Uncle Eitan died, construction began on something at the far end of the camp, next to the crematorium.

A month after construction started, it finished.

It was a new, larger crematorium.

Franz shuddered.

***

Early that November, 'Aktion: Erntefest' came to Majdanek. New prisoners from the small camps and prisons around the city of Lublin started to arrive, and shortly thereafter, they were led to the far end of Majdanek, hard by the crematorium. (*Operation: Harvest Festival*)

Abruptly music blared over the loudspeakers placed around the camp for announcements, and continued for some time; for those in barracks closest to the crematorium, however, it could not cover the sounds of shots fired. Nor did it cover the transport of hundreds of bodies dumped into mass graves, nor the quiet rumors that spread from the sondenkommandos on the burial detail: These were the insurgents involved in the Bialystock and Warsaw ghetto uprisings, being executed so they would not cause further problems.

Then the longstanding camp prisoners began to be rounded up and taken down to the area near the crematorium.

The first wave took many of what Franz privately termed the 'grumblers,' the ones who mouthed off and often got in trouble with the guards, but who had yet to do more. Once again the music blared, but did not fully cover the sounds of the gunshots. Franz, on garbage detail, watched surreptitiously between the buildings as the prisoners were shot and fell backward into a pre-dug trench, after which sonderkommandos began throwing dirt atop the bodies.

***

That night, Franz took straw from his mattress and braided a tight strand with it with nimble fingers. Extracting his mother's ring, he slid it onto the strand, knotted the strand closed, and slipped it over his head. The whole thing disappeared inside his striped shirt.

Then he lay down to sleep.

***

The next morning, before assignments for the day were handed out, he approached the guard assigned to his block.

"Sir," he said, "have you heard whether or not der Oberführer is really returning this week?"

"I had not heard," the guard said with a shrug. "What is it to you?"

"I am his automobile mechanic," Franz pointed out. "If he is to be here, I must go to the shop and make sure all is in order, should he need me to work on his auto."

"You are lying," the guard said. "Get back in line."

The other guard, however, demurred.

"No, Otto, it's true," he said in German. "I was there when der Oberführer commanded the boy be preserved for work on his automobile. He is very good, this one, and it would not do to go against those orders."

"It's true? Really?"

"Yes, my friend. Do not harm this boy. The Oberführer will be angry."

"Huh." The first guard shrugged, marked something on his papers, then waved at Franz. "Go to the mechanics shop, then. Stay there for the week. Do not return to the block. You will be assigned a new billet soon. Now go."

Franz went.

***

In all, some 42,000 Jews were killed during the 'harvest festival.'

Franz never saw the other occupants of his block again.

***

Hitler's solution to his 'Final Problem' proceeded apace, however, and soon the slaughtered inhabitants of Majdanek were replaced with more. Most had been Jewish, at least at Majdanek, though there were also members of various resistance groups, a few gypsies and homosexuals — all considered 'undesirable' by the Nazis — but mostly Jews. There were very few Jews sent to Majdanek by this point, however; there were very few to send. Now other 'unwanted' nationalities, such as Polish and Ukranian, began to show up, along with Soviet prisoners of war.

Communication became more difficult because of language barriers, and the prisoners were no longer as cohesive. Kapos, or funktionshäftlings, turncoat prisoners who worked with the Nazi guards, became more common. Franz had to walk a careful line, never sure just who he could trust. (*prisoner functionaries*)

There had been kapos before; it was the only way to maintain decent control of a prisoner population so large, and the Nazis had developed it to a fine art. But at least in Franz' block, the kapos had been benevolent and tried to help, rather than use the position for their own benefit.

Many of the kapos got preferential treatment, and these were resented by the other prisoners. Initially, when Franz was given a marginally more comfortable billet, there were accusations thrown that he, too, was a kapo…until his age was brought up. He was, at this time, still some months out from his 14th birthday, and the muscular young body he had once had was now shrunken and wiry thanks to near-starvation. He was tall for his age and sometimes mistaken for older than his years, but the few inmates who still knew him vouched for him, and for how his older brother had been shot dead in front of him. That quickly put paid to the 'collaborator' charges. Much, he considered, to his relief.

***

The automotive shop was fairly large, to accommodate several vehicles in it at once. There was a human door to one side, and a large garage door on the other, across from the hydraulic lift; pegboards and gray metal cabinets lined most of the walls. The floor was of concrete, and the overall construction was steel and brick or cinder block. There was a large washroom in the rear, with a sink, toilet, and urinal but no shower. A big rectangular shop sink stood in one corner of the main shop, however, and this would, Franz found, allow for a teen boy to clamber into it in the evenings to bathe away the grease.

Several bins stood near the sink, and these were earmarked for greasy rags, dirty coveralls, and trash — to be disposed-of, washed, and burned, respectively. While a Nazi mechanic might have been issued coveralls, however, Franz was not; there were a few leather aprons about and he tried to use those when possible, to keep his only clothing reasonably clean.

To the left of the sink was an alcove; judging by the empty hook-ups, it had been intended as a small kitchen or break room, but there was nothing installed there. Most likely, the boy considered, because an actual Nazi mechanic had never been assigned there.

Industrial gray was the overall color scheme, though the brick on the outside was, as usual in Majdanek, red.

***

Late in December, near the turn of the year, several of the new prisoners showed signs of being ill. In a matter of days, a dysentery outbreak swept the camp, and prisoners dehydrated from the diarrhea yet still forced to work often dropped dead where they stood. The guards simply ordered the sondenkommandos to fetch the body and load it into the crematorium.

Franz was an observant young man, and he saw the first victims fall, albeit from a distance. Instead of returning to his assigned billet, he holed up in the 'kitchen' alcove of the mechanics shop, managing to construct a rude bed out of clean shop cloths and some discarded car seat cushions. He used the washroom in the back as needed, washing his hands frequently. He used the big shop sink to bathe himself at the end of each day, and kept scrupulously clean. It wasn't a mikvah, but it served his purpose. *(Jewish ritual bath)*

He intended to fetch his own food from the camp kitchens…until individual cases of C-rations began to show up in the shop, tucked into the back out of sight, behind his bed alcove…while he slept. He raised an eyebrow, but there was no other sign of Jakob.

Though, equally mysteriously, the wrappers and cans disappeared in the same way, and at the same time that the new cases appeared.

He stayed well.

The dysentery outbreak ran its course, but Franz stayed in the shop, fetching his blanket from the billet he'd been assigned, washing it thoroughly in the shop sink. and hanging it up on an unused pegboard to dry completely before using it. A request to one of the friendlier kapos resulted in a cord and a coarse curtain he could hang across the door to the 'kitchen' where he slept, keeping it completely out of sight. He would stay away from the other prisoners as much as he could, and perhaps it would accomplish two things: first, the guards would tend to forget about him save in the context of the automobiles, and second, he would stay out of the way of further contagion.

When der oberführer returned two weeks later, he had Franz change the oil and check the filters on his armored staff car, and remarked on the boy's relative health and cleanliness.

***

Chapter 3 — Getting By

The year had finally turned, and with it came the snow. Lots of snow. Much more snow than the Lublin area usually got. Never mind the frigid temperatures.

It was difficult for the prisoners; the coats given to the camp prisoners were thin and did not provide a great deal of insulation. Shoes might or might not be waterproof, or even enclosed. Frostbite was a frequent danger, and the cause of lost toes, fingers, and even ears. Gangrene was an ever-present danger.

Fortunately for Franz, the shop had to be kept reasonably warm so that the various lubricants remained properly fluid. The only times he had to go out at this point were mealtimes, to fetch his food when the C-rations ran out; he generally preferred to eat in his nook in the corner of the shop. Fortunately no one had noticed that he did not come to fetch food during the dysentery outbreak. Most likely, he decided, the workers in what passed for a kind of cafeteria thought he had dysentery himself, but somehow managed to recover. He did not disabuse them of the notion.

Once in a great while, one of the guards for whom he'd repaired, say, a personal motorcycle, might bring him food, though it was rare; chocolate bars and such like were the typical gift — not long on nutrients, but caloric. One for whom he'd rebuilt an engine, seeing the crude thongs without socks that shod the boy's feet, took pity and brought him a pair of homespun wool socks and hand-me-down oxfords, which he appreciated. The shoes were too big, but the socks were thick and soft, and he tied them as snugly as they would go, then stuffed the toes with packing paper. Still, it could be hard, and he winced when he saw the starving, freezing inmates in the rude, uninsulated, drafty blocks.

He often bit his lip and felt guilty. But he had already lost everyone he had ever cared about, and he had promised Jakob he would do all he could to survive. There was no guarantee he would survive where he was — his environment tended to be dirty and greasy despite his best attempts at cleaning, and he still had far too little food when the C-rations did not miraculously appear — but his skills had at least given him a fighting chance. Still, he had lost all track of what day it was; worse, the son of a line of rabbis was completely unable to keep kosher, or to observe the high holy days, or even note when the Sabbath passed. Most of the time, he didn't even know what day it was.

But his father had taught him that HaShem in His benevolence and love of the Chosen People did not condemn those who were simply attempting to survive while following what commands they could, and that was all he could do. He prayed frequently, mostly for release from fear, privation, and this nightmarish existence. If that meant his death, as long as it was quick and relatively painless, he could accept that…though he remembered his promise to Jakob, and kept on doing what he could to survive. It was, after all, up to him to continue the family line somehow, he supposed.

Occasionally he was able to rise above it all and pray for those enmeshed in this world war, for the fall of the Nazi regime, and Hitler's fall in particular. He wasted little sympathy for the Nazi Führer; he had heard some of the Christian prisoners surreptitiously reference him as an antichrist, even possibly THE Antichrist. He'd had to ask what that meant, and eventually came to understand that it was a kind of fake messiah…which made perfect sense to Franz. So other than a consistent petition for Hitler to fall, preferably hard, he spent no other prayer time on the creature he considered evil incarnate.

***

Since Franz was currently living in the auto shop, many of the drivers brought by their trucks, staff cars, jeep-like kübelwagens, and other vehicles for checks, filter and oil changes, tune-ups, and to have help putting chains on the tires in the snow. Franz was the only actual mechanic there, and there were no assistants, so he stayed very busy.

Occasionally this proved difficult when one or another of the Nazis bringing in a vehicle decided to pull rank to get in faster, but the boy tried hard to be reasonable and point out that he could do little once another vehicle was already on the rack. If the vehicle in question was a personal vehicle rather than a military one, it went to the back of the queue, and Franz had a rote response if protest was made. The given officer usually quieted immediately if Franz invoked an SS oberführer, it seemed. Never mind the current vehicle was seldom the oberführer's; the officer trying to bully his way in did not know that.

He kept a small schedule book which had been provided to him upon lodging the request with the oberführer — about whom he still knew nothing except his rank and his task — and he tried to keep in mind what groups were considered high priority, which officers thought they were high priority, and which were not urgent, then schedule accordingly. This job was intended to get him out of trouble and avoid getting killed, not hasten his demise because someone got pissed.

*****

He sighed, despondent, when he realized how long it had been since he had seen Jakob; the C-rations had ceased shortly after the dysentery outbreak ended. He was thankful for the clean, uncontaminated, and calorically-high food, but he wondered if the vampire-person had forgotten about him, or if the espionage task was so difficult that he had no time to check on a young boy alone in a concentration camp.

After all, he considered, that was all he was — one lone boy, an orphan in a concentration camp. One among thousands, likely. There were other things, he was sure, that were much higher on Jakob's list of priorities. And no one else to care. Farkakte, there was no one else who KNEW. Jakob was currently the only living — well, sort of living — being on the whole planet who had shown the boy any caring whatsoever.

Worse, he tried not to think about the possibility that Jakob had been caught. That was a sure death sentence. They would torture him for information, then kill him. How did one execute a vampire, anyway? What few movies he had seen before the war were mostly drivel where that was concerned, according to Uncle Eitan, with whom he had had several discussions. He had never thought to ask Uncle Eitan HOW to kill a vampire, however, and now it was too late — he had seen Uncle Eitan's lifeless, emaciated body carried away to the crematorium…was it only last summer? Still, one thing the Nazis were exceptionally good at was killing, so he was sure they would find a way.

He prayed the vampire would remain safe and undiscovered.

***

The oberführer had shown back up for his periodic inspection, and dropped his big Benz off for a tune-up — the more common officer vehicles were variants on the kübelwagen, and an occasional motorcycle, but he seemed to prefer larger, more ostentatious cars, especially with heavier armor. It was time to change the spark plugs and filters and replace the oil, and Franz had gotten the filters changed and was preparing to drain the oil when a new kapo showed up in the shop.

The shop itself was no different than anywhere else in the camp in that it was partitioned off by the ubiquitous fencing, both electrified and barbed/razor wire. But it was one of the places that kapos were allowed to access, in order to fetch vehicles and have them repaired for the guards to whom they reported. It was considered a privilege of sorts; this had been one of the reasons Franz was temporarily seen as a kapo.

Casimir Kalemba was one of the new Polish prisoners, a fugitive murderer who had been caught and just another of the large group of 'undesirables' that had been increasingly dumped into Majdanek when the region had been depleted of Jews. As a new inductee — he had been incarcerated not quite a month prior — and not yet beginning to starve, he was still possessed of a relatively normal, stocky, muscular body. He was dark-complected, with a dour expression most of the time, what would come to be called 'resting bitch face' in the next century. He was also ruthless; the only person he cared for was himself.

Upon induction into the concentration camp, he had promptly volunteered to become a funktionshäftling, a prisoner functionary or kapo, both for the preferential treatment and for the ability to bully the other prisoners. A week before, Franz had seen him beating one of the longer-term — hence emaciated — prisoners for some imagined infraction, and promptly decided he was no better than the Nazis themselves. Arguably, he supposed, he was worse; the Nazis at least had a kind of credo to which they adhered, whereas Kalemba would do whatever it took to get what he wanted. Not, Franz considered, that it made much difference. Evil was evil; to compare one evil to another was like comparing a belle de boskoop to a golden delicious — both were, after all, apples.

Now Kalemba stood in the auto shop wearing a broad smirk.

"Yes, I think this will do very well," he said in heavily accented German.

"Excuse me? May I help you?" Franz asked the big man.

"Yes. You can get your things and leave," Kalemba said. "I'll be doing this job from now on."

"Well, I could use another hand," Franz admitted. "What is your experience with automobiles?"

"I said, get your things and go," Kalemba reiterated.

"I don't understand. Go where?"

"Away from here."

And Kalemba backhanded the boy hard across the face.

Startled, Franz staggered back, falling hard into the wall, and Kalemba followed, throwing punch after punch. Franz tried to block the blows and managed to deflect some, but he was too weak from semi-starvation, and the bully still had his full musculature. Within moments, Franz slumped into unconsciousness.

Kalemba grabbed him by the collar and flung the limp body through the nearby door to the 'kitchen' and onto his bed-pallet, then pulled the curtain closed. *I'll dispose of him later,* he thought. *I like the idea of a private little corner here, where no one can find me.*

Then he looked at the big Benz, up on the rack, and grinned.

***

When the oberführer and his driver showed back up late that day to get the car, Kalemba was standing beside it on the drive, wiping his hands on a rag.

"Who are you?" the oberführer demanded. "Where is young Franz?"

"He's sick," Kalemba said, shrugging. "I'm handling the shop now."

"I repeat, who are you?"

"I'm Funktionshäftling Kalemba, sir. I'm responsible for the shop now. The Jewish boy is being reassigned."

"That does not please me," the oberführer noted. "The boy is brilliant with mechanics." He shook his head. "Driver, if you please?" He waved a hand at the Benz.

The driver got behind the wheel and started up the big armored vehicle. It turned over, caught, and chugged, but it did not purr, as the oberführer had expected. Catching the driver's attention, he made a pushing motion, and the driver obediently pressed down on the accelerator.

The Benz rumbled loudly.

Kalemba beamed proudly.

The oberführer frowned.

"Where is Franz? Has he been reassigned already?"

"I don't know, sir."

"Is Franz here?"

"Yes sir." Kalemba jerked a thumb over his shoulder. "I made a pallet for him in the back. He's resting. I'll take him back to his billet later."

The oberführer raised an eyebrow; he knew from previous visits that Franz had created a small billet in the back corner, expressly to avoid the dysentery, and that he had given up his standard billet in the barracks in preference to the isolation of the shop. This had suited the oberführer, as it left room for other prisoners and kept Franz well and available to work on his vehicle. But it also meant that this man was lying, for the pallet had already existed; he did not make it himself. And if he was lying about that, what else was he lying about?

The oberführer turned and stalked toward the shop door. As he passed the Benz, he murmured to the driver, "Stay here. Keep an eye on that one. Above all, keep him HERE. I do not want him sneaking up on me while I am seeing about the boy." The driver nodded, and the oberführer entered the shop.

There was no sign of current activity inside, though there was a mess on the floor — grease, transmission fluid, and oil — that Franz would never have allowed to remain. The SS officer clucked to himself, then walked around the mess, headed for the back corner and the curtain that partitioned Franz's little bedroom from the rest of the shop.

Pulling back the curtain, he found the boy curled on his pallet, apparently unconscious. Both eyes were black, bruises were everywhere, and his jaw was badly swollen. Hissing in dismay, the SS officer crouched beside the pallet.

"Franz?" he asked, keeping his voice low. "Franz? Can you hear me? This is Oberführer Albrecht. You work on my Benz."

Franz let out a soft groan.

"You can hear me?"

A grunt, nearly a groan.

"Are you sick?"

"Nn-uhn."

"Did you fall?"

"Nn-uhn."

"You have been beaten?"

"Mm-hm."

"Was it this Kalemba who did it? The kapo?"

Franz managed to partly open one black, swollen eye.

"Sir," he whispered. "Yes, sir. The new kapo beat me. Don't know name."

"Why? Why did he beat you?"

"Not sure. Think…think he wants the shop for himself."

"Did he break your hands?"

"Um…" Franz' gaze grew distant and wandered. "Um, what?"

"Did he hurt your hands?"

"Uhhh…no. Arms bruised, though. Tried…tried to defend myself."

"Good for you. Is anything broken?"

"Uhm. Don't know. Face hurts. Side too."

Oberführer Albrecht overlooked the lack of 'sir's punctuating Franz' remarks; the boy could barely open puffy, split lips to speak at all, and appeared to be fading in and out of consciousness, which meant a likely concussion.

This consideration Albrecht gave the injured youth had nothing to do with altruism. He knew Franz was in his early teens, and knew that Kalemba made at least three of him, maybe four. And Franz was Jewish, and the Jews were to be exterminated in the end. But he also knew that this skinny Jewish boy was a positive wizard with vehicles of any sort; he had even seen the boy tune a motorcycle until it purred like a cat.

And the Benz was not currently purring, let alone roaring like a lion.

It all came down to the fact that Franz was useful.

Kalemba…was not.

"Stay here," Albrecht said. "I will see to matters."

Der Oberführer rose and headed for the door.

***

As soon as he emerged from the shop door, Albrecht pulled his Luger and calmly put two rounds into Kalemba's forehead. The heavyset man dropped like a rock, dead where he stood, a startled look on his face and the back of his head missing, splattered across the gravel of the shop yard. Then Albrecht turned to his driver.

"Oberscharführer Schmidt, you will please return to the camp commandant's office and request of Obersturmbannführer Weiss that the staff physician attend our chief mechanic at the earliest opportunity, and send a detail of sondenkommandos for this trash, who has badly injured our mechanic." He gestured at the body of Kalemba. "You will please also reiterate to Weiss the need to take good care of our mechanic. There have been a few changes of command since our last injunction, after all." He frowned, stern.

"Jawohl, mein Herr."

Schmidt hastened off.

***

In the end, Albrecht and Schmidt stayed a couple more days, until they were certain that Franz would be all right. He did indeed have a concussion, numerous hematomas, and some severely bruised ribs — he appeared to have been viciously kicked at some point — but the staff physician could find no broken bones for certain, though he strapped up the ribs just in case. Several of the boy's teeth were loose in the area of the jaw swelling, but X-rays did not show a broken jaw, and the teeth would eventually tighten back in place as the swelling went down.

Franz was still unable to put the Benz back into its optimal performance, but the boy assured Albrecht that to run the car for a few weeks in the condition Kalemba had left it would not damage it, and if they could swing back by in a month or so, Franz would put all to rights.

***

A month later, Franz was losing the last of the bruising, the Benz purred, and Oberführer Albrecht left satisfied.

***

After the incident with Kalemba, camp commandant Obersturmbannführer Weiss saw fit to place a small guard detail over the automotive shop.

There had been issues with Majdanek's management all along; Weiss was the fourth commandant the camp had had since its inception, and half of those had left the position when they'd been arrested for corruption. Since Oberführer Albrecht was the regular inspector and outranked the commandants — and had made the reports that led to the arrests — Weiss was determined to do things to suit Albrecht.

This, however, proved to be the source of Franz' next troubles, though Kommandant Weiss would never know about it.

***

Franz was still a bit stiff after his beating but had returned to his usual tasks, and the hard winter was finally breaking into a cool, wet spring. He still slept in his clothes, as did all the prisoners, but had been able to do away with sleeping in his coat, hanging it carefully on a peg he'd put on the wall in his alcove before bedding down and burrowing into the blanket.

So when he woke up with a chill to find his naked body completely exposed, it was startling.

***

"Ahhh, there you are, my little beauty," one of the guards, part of the daytime detail around the shop, murmured with a leer as he leaned over the teen. Franz recognized the face, but had never learned the names of any of the guards, not caring to know. "I have been watching you for days. You are a handsome young one, much to my taste. And here we have plenty of quiet, yes?"

"I…I don't know what you mean," Franz said, confused. "Where are my clothes? What are you doing?"

"Oh, I think you know exactly what I am doing," the guard said with another leer. "You cannot tell me, with a body and a face like yours, let alone the position you hold, you have never done this before. Oberführer Albrecht certainly prefers you!"

"I…I don't—" Franz broke off with a gasp as the man pinched his nipples and twisted them. "Stop! That hurts! Where are my clothes?!"

"You won't be needing those until morning," the guard said, reaching for the fly of his own trousers. "This will be lovely. Your privates are well developed, and you have just the beginnings of a tuft of pubic hair! And you are here and clean, and your ass does not contain the bloody flux and will be nice and tight."

Suddenly Franz remembered the sight of two of the guards raping a male prisoner behind a block shortly after his arrival in the camp, while he was on trash detail; Uncle Eitan had hastily herded him away, then sat him down and explained that night, once they were back in the block. He had also taught Franz some tactics whereby he might be able to defend himself from such an attack, though it might mean death.

Farkakte, Franz thought, growing angry, *this one figures to do the same to me.*

"No, I don't think so," he said aloud…

…And drove his bony knee as hard as he could into the guard's now-exposed and very aroused groin. It was a move calculated to cause maximum pain, and it succeeded.

The man screamed.

Oddly, Franz could not hear it.

But he saw when the guard's face twisted from intense pain into an expression of utter terror. He screamed again, but once more, Franz could not hear it.

There was a sudden rush of wind, and the guard was gone.

***

Franz rose and found his clothing nearby, where the guard had tossed them carelessly, and got dressed again. Then he fetched the biggest wrench in the shop's tool inventory and sat down on his bed, waiting to see what happened next.

***

"Well, you look all right," a vaguely familiar voice said, and Franz hefted the wrench like a club. "No, that won't work on me, son. Besides, you won't need it. It's me."

Jakob emerged from the shadows, smiling. A trickle of blood ran from the corner of his mouth.

"Jakob! You're all right!" Franz exclaimed, dropping the wrench and leaping to his feet.

The smile morphed into a grin, and Jakob opened his arms in invitation; the boy ran into a hug.

"Are YOU all right?" Jakob asked him, as he eased the boy away from him and looked him up and down. "Did I get here in time? Did he get his hands on you?"

"Only my chest," the boy admitted. "He pinched my nipples. It hurt."

Jakob stifled a snort.

"Well, you're half-starved; things probably haven't developed quite that much yet," he decided. "You'll change your mind in a few years, assuming we can get you out of this hellhole. At any rate, he won't be bothering you any more."

"I figured. You have blood on your mouth again."

"Ah. Well, damn." The vampire extracted a disposable tissue, wiped away the blood, and tossed it at the shop wastecan; Franz watched, startled, as it incinerated in mid-air — a few bits of cold ash were all that landed in the wastecan. "Thank you. I was worried about you, so I hurried the matter."

"I'm okay. I was figuring out how to put his, um, personal parts out of alignment."

"I would say from the shriek I heard when I arrived, you did a good job."

"Are you the reason I couldn't hear him scream?"

"I am, yes. And no one else could hear him, either."

"Ah, good. So did he scream again when he saw you?"

"Yes."

"Why?"

"You've never seen me like he saw me. This — how you see me now — is the appearance I usually use; it's roughly what I looked like when I was, um, turned. I tweak it from time to time; I've lived so long that periodically I have to stage my death and create a new persona, which often involves some basic changes to my looks — hair, eyes, that sort of thing. I have another appearance I call my 'monster look.' It's…not pleasant."

"And that's what he saw? The monster look?"

"It was, yes. I wanted him to shit himself."

"Did he?"

"Yes. And pissed himself, too. He fairly reeked, he was so soggy with his own waste. I had to hold him away from me while I drank him dry."

"Do any of them ever…turn into vampires when you're done?"

"Not unless I want them to. The trick is, if you want them dead, drink 'em dry. If you want 'em turned, you snack on 'em from time to time. If you only want a connection, a means of communicating, just have a little taste."

Franz snorted.

"Do we need to cover up what happened to him?"

"No. I took care of that before I came back. He'll be considered a deserter. We're fine."

"I'm glad to see you," Franz admitted. "I've been worried. I haven't seen you in a good while. Was it you who kept leaving the C-rations?"

"Yes. I didn't have time to actually stop, but I heard about the dysentery outbreak, swung by and found you, then made sure you had clean food to eat when I saw you'd effectively quarantined yourself. Smart move, by the way. And also smart that you're keeping it up. It makes you useful, so they won't get rid of you readily."

"Thank you. Yes, that was what I was trying to do. Why are you so busy?"

"I'm working several undercover espionage jobs now. I'm American these days and have been for…a couple of centuries, I guess, so my name there currently is Jake Abrams. It's not the name I was born with, but that language has been dead for millennia anyway. For now, I use my changes in personas for espionage purposes. I'm in Military Intelligence, so I can't tell you any more than that. But in Germany, I'm Hauptsturmführer Jakob Brahms; in the Soviet Army, I'm

Kapitan Yacov Abramov." He shrugged, then chuckled. "At least I know I'll answer when I'm called. Every time I have to kill myself off and adopt another persona, I have to get used to answering to a new name. Pain in the ass."

Franz snorted again.

"What if someone who knows you as one sees you as the other?"

"It doesn't matter. I can change my appearance enough to look different. Not a LOT different, but for instance, I can change my hair and eye color. Hauptsturmführer Brahms is blond with blue eyes — he's the version of me you usually see. Kapitan Abramov has black hair with brown eyes, and Abrams has light brown hair and green eyes. Well, he did have green eyes. I decided I liked your eyes, so they're hazel now."

"Oh! Is, um, is that a compliment?"

"It is. Your eyes are piercing, Franz. If we can get you out of this mess, you're going to be a handsome man one day."

"Uh…"

"What?"

"Did you, uh, were you…jealous…of the guard?"

"What? Oh. No, that sort of thing went the way of my human life, my young friend. Why? Do you lean that way?"

"I…don't think I lean at all…"

Jakob laughed.

"Well, that would go along with the half-starved thing, I expect. If we can get you fed and beefed up, eventually that's going to change. Let me put it this way: I'll be surprised if it doesn't."

Franz shrugged. He never saw any girls to know how he felt about them, and none of the current camp inmates were anywhere close to his age anyway. He changed the subject.

"Can I see the monster look?"

"No. I never let my human friends see that. It's truly horrifying, and I don't want you to have that image of me in your head. It's not what I think of as 'the real me' anyway; it's just another persona I use. Besides, I don't want YOU to be afraid of me, and you would be, if you saw — you couldn't help it. So no. That's strictly for those who deserve it."

"Oh. Well, that's fair, I guess."

"Yes. You want to be able to sleep at night, after all."

"Oh."

***

They sat and talked quietly for a time; Jakob wanted to ensure that his young friend was mentally and emotionally in decent shape after the rape attempt. But Franz seemed to have taken it in stride, partly, he suspected, because it hadn't really gotten very far. Still, he decided to stay around and keep an eye on his sleep periods for a few days just to make sure. He was stationed close, so it wouldn't be hard, and no one would be the wiser.

"Are you here to check on me?" Franz wondered then. "Is that why you are here?"

"Partly," Jakob admitted. "Any time I'm in this general area I try to at least verify you're okay, and determine where you are. You may not see me, but I do come by and see about you, however briefly. Sometimes I can get you food, and sometimes I can't, just because I might not always have access to it. I have a friend in my intel chain that provides the C-rations, but if I'm coming from Soviet territory, I won't have had a chance to get any."

"Oh, I see. If you are headed out, you can bring it with you, but if you are returning, you cannot."

"Exactly. I'm also here to get a good look at the camp. The Soviet army isn't very far away, and sometime in the next few months, they're going to make a hard push into Poland. It wouldn't surprise me if the camp is liberated by the end of the summer, if not before."

"Oh!"

"Exactly. So be ready to do what I tell you, when I tell you. Oh, and just in case, this is Kapitan Abramov." His features blurred, and suddenly the blue-eyed blond Aryan was a dark-complected Slav. "This is how I'll look when I come in with the Soviet Army. I'm here ostensibly for them on a scouting mission; they do NOT know I'm a double agent, or that I can change my appearance through anything other than makeup. Oh, and this is Jacob Abrams." The Slav was replaced by a casual American possessing light brown hair with blond highlights, and striking hazel eyes. "Got it?"

"Yes."

"Good." The Aryan was back. "Keep an eye out, and make sure you're ready. I'll seriously need you to do what I say, when I say it, if I'm to get you out of here safely."

"All right. I will be ready, and I will do as you say." Franz grinned, excited. "You are the answer to my prayers, meyn khaver."

"Aw. I'm glad, my young friend. And yes, we ARE friends, and always will be."

"Good. I like that."

***

Two months later, Franz turned 14. He had spent two and a half years of his young life in Majdanek, some of the most important years of that young life, and he had learned that life could be harsh and end quickly. He had also learned the importance of love and caring, and the frequency of unreasoning hate. He had learned, as well, that it was often best to keep one's thoughts and feelings to himself, and not let them show; one could stay alive easier, so.

These were lessons that would stay with him the rest of his life.

***

Jakob showed up on his birthday with a couple of gifts: a case of C-rations and a tiny compass.

"Keep that on the thread with your mother's ring," the inhuman being told him, indicating the compass. "When I get you out of here, I may not be able to go with you. Use it to head west, toward the American forces, if you can. You'll be better off there."

Franz nodded, but another matter was on his mind.

"How did you know about the ring?"

"I smelled the gold," Jakob noted, "then I…scanned for it, I guess you could say. You're lucky no one has found it."

"I don't know why the guard who tried to rape me didn't find it."

"That would have been me, I think," Jakob noted. "When I'm headed for Majdanek, I sometimes reach ahead and locate you, then start trying to sense if there is anyone nearby. I picked up on the guard while I was still a distance away, realized what was happening, and started trying to…I call it 'fading' where I make us undetectable to others…so I tried to fade you while I started running, about as fast as I've ever run, I think. I think it faded you enough that he didn't see the ring hanging around your neck."

"Well, that makes a certain sense, then." Franz nodded. "Thank you. It's the one thing I have left, and it was my mother's wedding ring."

"Then it's an heirloom. Hang onto that as best you can."

"I have, and I will."

"I can't stay long. I'm here on a sneaking expedition, and the Soviet commander will expect me back in a few hours, so I'll have to do some sneaking before I head back. But to start, what do you know of the camp conditions?"

"Not a lot," Franz said, thinking. "There's a new commandant; I'm not sure why, but this time the old commandant made it out without getting arrested for corruption."

"That's right; there've been four commandants so far, and two were arrested, weren't they?"

"Yes, though the whole shtick drek is corrupt."

"Well, of course it is. Hitler merely used antisemitism as a way to gain power, then fanned the flames to KEEP power. I saw it coming, but there was no way to stop it. Not just me."

"No, I understand. Eventually I ought to learn what happened, what led up to this," Franz considered. "I was too young as it was happening to really be aware of it."

"You're only fourteen now, my young friend. But I guess you HAVE to be aware of it now, eh?"

"Yes. Which is why I want to study how it happened. Never again."

Jakob pressed his lips together in concern at the boy's solemnity…and wisdom.

"That…is a good plan, son. I'll help you where I can… after we get you out of here."

"Right."

"So who is it this time? We've had…who?" Jakob began counting fingers. "Koch — he got arrested…Koegel…"

"He should have been arrested, I think," Franz grumbled.

"They all should get a taste of their own medicine," Jakob agreed. "Who came after him?"

"Florstedt. He was arrested, too. Then Weiss, but he left two weeks ago, and now there is Liebehenschel."

"Got it. Do you have a feel for him yet?"

Franz shrugged. "No different."

"Same ol', same ol', eh?"

"Yes."

"All right, Thanks for the info. I'm sorry I couldn't smuggle in a birthday cake for you."

"That's fine, Jakob. I had rather have my friend here, even if only for a few minutes, than all the birthday cakes in the world."

The vampire left the automotive shop with a warm heart.

***

Chapter 4 — Bad to Worse?

About a month after Franz' birthday, he was working on the armored car for the new camp commandant SS Obersturmbannführer Arthur Liebehenschel, when he overheard parts of a disturbing discussion between the chauffeur and one of the guards.

"Have you heard about Unternehmen Werwolf?" the chauffeur wondered.

"Das was? Unternehmen Werwolf? Vas ist das?" the guard responded in German. (*The what? Operation Werewolf? What is that?*)

The chauffeur glanced around, looking for anyone who might overhear the gossip; Franz was 'nobody,' so he wasn't worried.

"Herr Himmler is starting a new thing. Operation Werewolf. I heard der kommandant saying that Obergruppenführer Hans-Adolf Prützmann had been ordered to organize it."

"But what is it?"

"No one knows yet. It is a new kind of army. But with a name like Werewolf? You know Himmler loves der okkult."

"Hah! Would it not be just if he had found how to make these worthless subhumans fight for us?" the guard wondered. "To make them obey orders like mindless automatons?"

"It would," the chauffeur said, and laughed. "We can hope, I suppose. Kill them, then reanimate them to fight for us like fierce wolves. The Allies are pressing hard; we could use the additional manpower."

Franz began to tremble.

***

After the kommandant's car was out of the shop — it was, fortunately for Franz, the last vehicle of the day — the boy closed the shop, went into his alcove, pulled the curtain closed, and sat down on his makeshift bed.

They want to make…make…I guess it is a kind of golem… of us, he thought, mentally replaying the conversation between the chauffeur and the guard. *They are not satisfied to simply kill us. They want to violate our dead bodies and use us to fight for them!*

He wrapped his arms around himself, feeling his own trembling body, desperately wishing for a visit from Jakob.

But Jakob did not appear.

A badly frightened yet completely exhausted Franz finally fell asleep well after dark, still shaking.

***

He woke to the feeling of being strapped, nude, to a cold steel table. The staff physician leaned over him with a leer, scalpel in hand, but wearing no surgical gown.

"Hier sind wir," he said. "Und jetzt werden wir den genialen Mechaniker nehmen und ihn dazu bringen, alles zu tun, was wir wollen." (*Here we are. And now we will take the genius mechanic and make him do all as we wish.*)

"Nein," Franz cried. "Nein! NEIN!"

The physician began to wield the scalpel against his close-shaved head. The boy felt the scalpel bite, and the warm blood run down his head.

Franz began to scream.

***

"Hey! Here now! Calm down, Franz!" a familiar voice said, as Franz sat bolt upright in the makeshift bed. There were gently restraining hands on his shoulders. "What's wrong? What happened?"

"Uh, unh," the boy panted, struggling to orient himself. After a moment of staring up into by-now-familiar blue eyes, he ran his hands over his head, finding the stubble that was all the Nazis allowed in the way of hair. "It…it's not shaved. No incisions…"

"No, what hair they let you have is still there. Now what the hell happened?" Jakob demanded to know. "I got that desperate mental call all the way in London, and came here as fast as I could, to find you asleep and screaming. I faded your screams, so nobody else knows, but shit, little brother!"

Franz drew a deep breath and let it out in a shuddering sigh. He explained about the conversation he had overheard, then told Jakob about what he was coming to realize had been a nightmare based on the conversation.

"Mm. Yeah, that would tend to induce nightmares like that, I suspect," Jakob said when he was finished. "Especially given the way those idiots were interpreting it."

"You know what they were talking about?"

"Yeah. And there's nothing supernatural about it, except the name they've taken for it. It's a grass-roots guerrilla warfare operation; they call themselves the Werewolves, I guess because they usually operate at night. Evidently the SS is trying to organize them into a more effective fighting force. And maybe draft some of the other local fanatics into it."

"But they are not real werewolves? Nor, nor golems, or, um, automatons, they said?"

"No. I've known some real werewolves, and these guys are wannabes at best. And zombies don't work like that."

"Zombies?"

"Yeah. It's a voodoo thing. Started in Africa, then made its way to the Caribbean with the slave trade. Reanimated corpses. It's basically what they were talking about, only instead of using witchcraft to do it, they figured on some sort of mechanism."

"Oh. Yes, that would be it. Zombies. Are they real?"

"Sort of, but not really. More like putting someone into a suggestive state, a 'trance,' they call it, usually with drugs or psychoactive herbs, and controlling them that way. They CAN control them, at least to a point, but they aren't undead or anything. And they can't be made to do something they would really refuse to do. It's a kind of hypnosis. Does that make you feel better?"

"Yes. I will remember all of that. Thank you for explaining."

"Good."

"Wannabes. I like that word. It makes sense."

"Yeah, it's one I've used for a while now, though it's never caught on with anyone else, at least so far. So no, it has nothing to do with any experiments coming out of Auschwitz or similar, and you're in no danger from it. Only those wearing Allied uniforms are gonna be in danger from these werewolf excuses, and I'm not sure how much of that. Though I expect it's going to result in some pockets of intense resistance once we get into mopping up."

"Mopping up?"

"Yeah, Operation: Werewolf is a desperation move. The Nazis are running out of steam, men, materiel, equipment, room, and about every other commodity. The Allies are pressing hard."

"Good. Soon?"

"Very soon. I'll bring some clothes with me when it reaches that point; you don't wanna look like a concentration camp inmate any more than we can help, once you get out of here. We'll want you to blend in more."

"That would be nice. I wash these at night when it's warm enough for me to sleep without, but after the guard…"

"I understand. I'll bring two sets of clothes, then. You can wear one and wash the other."

"That sounds wonderful."

"Well, I need you to understand something," Jakob said earnestly. "Once you leave this place, it will be because the Soviets have pushed the fighting front west, past Lublin, not because the war is over. You'll still have to be damn careful. You might even have to travel east before you can go west."

"Ooo. I see. Is that what is causing the distant booming we've been hearing to the east of the camp?"

"Yes, it's the Soviet artillery hitting the German lines. The louder and closer they sound, the closer you are to your freedom. Be extra careful right now."

"Why?"

"Because the Nazis are going to be…tense. Anxious, on edge, and easily angered as a result. You don't want to get this close to getting free, then have one of 'em kill you because you looked at him funny."

"Ah. So I should keep my head down."

"Yes. There's a possibility they'll retreat — most likely, they WILL retreat from the camp — and the question becomes what they'll do with the prisoners. As I see it, and as I've reported to my various Allied superiors, there are three possibilities. One, they'll just cut and run, and leave all of you to your own devices. Two, they'll load all or some of you up and ship you elsewhere, deeper into German territory. Three, they'll kill you all and run, so there's no one to squeal on them."

"'Squeal on them'?"

"Bear witness to what they did. The killing, the mistreatment, all that. So far, nobody but a couple of us spy sorts has any real idea about the concentration camps; this one will probably be one of, if not the, first liberated. It'll be a shock to 'em."

"Oh. So I might not get out after all." Franz tried not to start shaking again, but didn't quite manage it. His emaciated body was simply too weak NOT to react to the anxiety.

"Shush, little brother," Jakob said kindly, reaching out and rubbing the youth's shoulder, offering comfort. "It's all right. I have some ideas on how to keep you safe. Is there anywhere you can hide, here in the shop, where they couldn't find you? Or any way we can MAKE such a place? A bolt-hole, it's called."

"Huh. I think we could make one, maybe." Franz eyed Jakob. "How long do you have?"

"I told my handler I got a distress call from one of my informants," the vampire explained, "and that I'd be back when I'd ensured his safety. He knows what I am, and what I can do, but he's one of the few who does. He told me to go, and he'd make sure things were where they needed to be when I got back. Given you've fed me information on the camp, you're one of my informants."

"How strong are you?"

"Really, really strong."

"Then let me show you what's under one of the tool cabinets…"

***

With a vampire's strength and speed to throw into the effort, there was soon a small hidey-hole, just big enough for a lanky teenage boy, a blanket, a couple of boxes of C-rations, and a tiny latrine tucked into the ground beneath the tool cabinet. The fact that there was no flooring under that particular cabinet and there WAS a slight hollow in the ground there had helped. It was well hidden, and easy and quick for the nimble Levy boy to access. More, unlike the barracks and other structures, the building was made of metal and masonry, and nothing about it could be burned, should the Nazis try to destroy evidence of their work. It could, perhaps, be bulldozed, but there were neither bulldozers nor tanks nearby, according to Jakob, who had already scouted out that matter.

"This will do," Jakob decided after they were done, watching as Franz quickly slipped inside, closing the cabinet door. Immediately Jakob reached over and opened the door, but there was now a false floor, covered with tools, where the opening had been. He knocked on the false floor, the signal they'd arranged, and Franz emerged. "Now, see if you can't lie down and get some sleep, little brother. I'll stay here and stand guard until it's daybreak."

It was more difficult than Jakob expected; he figured that, if Franz didn't fall asleep quickly, he'd simply use his abilities to aid the matter. But he hadn't reckoned on Franz' willpower, which was significant. It took over an hour of gentle mental nudging along with, "No more questions; go to sleep," before Franz finally yawned fit to split his head in two, then fell silent.

About five minutes later, Jakob checked him mentally; the boy had fallen asleep on his own.

An undercover Jake Abrams, thoroughly faded, sat and guarded him all night.

***

The next morning, after watching Franz eat a breakfast of C-rations, Jakob hugged the boy he had indeed come to think of as a younger brother despite the vast disparity in ages, and returned to his handler, with a final admonition to be careful.

***

A week later, the booming sounds of the bombardment grew somewhat louder. Franz thought the ground sometimes shook lightly, as well.

They must be getting closer, he thought. *Jakob will be back and help me — and the others! — get away. Soon. SOON!*

But he neglected to consider a few details.

***

A couple of weeks after that, a sudden whistling sounded, and abruptly there was an explosion in a copse of trees just outside the camp; wood splinters and leaves flew everywhere, even over the fences and into camp. Several prisoners and one guard went down when chunks of wood embedded themselves in parts of their bodies. The fleeing Nazi guards left them where they lay, alive or dead; they only cared for their own skins.

Abruptly the loudspeakers around the camp came to life.

"Achtung! Achtung! Alle Mitglieder des Lagerpersonals sollten sich umgehend im Hauptquartier melden!" (*Attention! Attention! All members of the camp staff should report to the headquarters building immediately!*)

A puzzled Franz stood just inside the door of the auto shop, wiping greasy hands on a rag, and watching as another whistling sound announced another explosion of wood shards, this time from a house in the adjacent village. Just then, Jakob's voice rang out…in his mind.

Franz! Are you in the auto shop?

Startled, the boy responded aloud. The guards had already headed for the SS building at a run, so there was, fortunately, no one around to hear.

"Yes, I am. Why?"

HIDE NOW! Close the shop NOW, lock the doors, get into your bolt-hole, and stay there until I tell you!

Franz grabbed the big garage door and pulled it closed, setting the padlock into the loop embedded in the floor. He twisted the deadbolt lock on the human-sized door next to it. Then he spun and ran to the back of the shop, flinging the now-greasy rag at the rag bin.

***

The next hour or so was a cacophony from hell, even inside the bolt-hole, as the Soviets shelled the area, and Nazi soldiers ran to and fro, shouting.

Eventually matters quieted. It felt eerie after all the racket.

Can I come out now? Franz wondered, simultaneously wondering if Jakob could hear him.

Not yet, came the immediate answer to both questions. *There's a reason I put all those supplies in there. I know it's cramped, and I know you'll eventually need to use the little latrine I dug for you. But you may have to stay in there a couple of days. Try to be patient, and try to be quiet. Very, very quiet.*

Why?

Because, damn them, the Nazis are evacuating Majdanek, and they are taking as many of the prisoners as they can load on a train with them, and shooting most of the others. The crematorium is already on fire, though since it's mostly a brick structure, I doubt they'll eradicate it very well.

Farkakte!

Exactly. If you are out of sight, you're out of mind. I can't save everyone, but I might be able to save you. Sit tight until I come and get you. I'm not far, and I can see what's going on. I'll be there as soon as it's safe for you to come out.

***

Late in the afternoon, Franz heard a racket outside his cubbyhole; he thought it was at the door of the shop, and sounded like someone trying to open both of the locked doors… or come through them. He hunkered down and tried to breathe quietly.

Moments later, he heard at least two Germans in conversation inside the shop.

"Where is he? He should be here!"

"I told you Oberführer Albrecht would have taken him already!"

"I have not seen Albrecht!"

"Just because you haven't doesn't mean he wasn't here, or that one of his agents has not."

"Look anyway!"

Franz listened, his heart in his throat, as the two Nazis banged through cabinetry, tore down the curtain covering his billet, and ripped equipment off the pegboard walls, searching for him. When the door to his cabinet crashed open, he held his breath. Seconds later, it slammed closed.

"You're right. He's not here."

"Told you. Let's get the hell out before one of those artillery shells gets us."

Jackbooted footsteps faded. The door slammed, the key jangled in the lock, and there was silence.

Franz slumped in his bolt-hole, gasping for breath.

***

The bolt-hole was a fairly tight fit, and once Franz had to relieve himself, he expected it to become smelly, but Jakob had lined the bottom of the latrine pit with something that looked like small gray pebbles; it absorbed the liquids, and kept the smell down. Franz realized that this was as much to prevent the possibility of discovery as for the comfort of not having to sit in one's own stench, and he was grateful.

But he had food and water, and a blanket, so he stayed reasonably comfortable, and slept much of the time, which was a relief, as he'd seldom had enough sleep since coming to Majdanek.

***

He had been hidden for almost a week and was starting to need to stretch his legs when he heard the special signal knocked on the tool cabinet door, the signal he had worked out with Jakob.

***

Franz? Die gedanken sind frei. Can you hear me, little brother? Are you still there? It's Jakob. I'm here to get you out. Stay quiet, and come with me, quickly. I'll keep us faded until we're safe.

A sudden upwelling of joy came through to the once-human man, and suddenly the cabinet fairly exploded open, as Franz flew into Jakob's arms.

You're here you're here you're here! Am I free? Franz wondered. *You look like your American self.*

You will be in a few moments. And yes, I'm tired of the subterfuge for now. Besides, here, no one knows the American Abrams. I won't be recognized even if someone sees me.

Jakob produced a wrapped parcel. It contained a couple of changes of clean clothing, leather shoes, several pairs of socks and boxer shorts, over a dozen cans of C-rations, a wallet with a small amount of several different national currencies, fake identification papers, and a small duffel in which to carry all of it, as well as a few personal items, including a military personal hygiene kit — a roll with toothbrush, toothpaste, safety razor, brush and soap, comb, and similar. *I know you can't use some of this just yet, but hang onto it,* he told the youth. *You'll start to need to shave soon, unless you prefer to grow a beard. And you'll want the comb once your hair grows out. Go ahead and change clothes.*

It looks wonderful, Franz said, as he stripped to skin and began to don one of the outfits Jakob had brought. *I will do as you say. I've managed to stay fairly clean, especially once I moved in here.* He gestured to the shop around them. *I even managed to get rid of the fleas and lice. It took a bit of work, though.*

I expect so, but good for you. Are you ready?

I am now, Franz said, turning to the vampire with a smile. *Oh, the shirt and trousers feel so much better than that! And I have undershorts!* He waved a hand at the threadbare, striped clothing.

Good. I'll see that gets burned for you. We're going to go now, Jakob told him, *and we're going to go at my speed. Crawl onto my back and hang on tight. Don't worry about hurting me, because you can't. Tuck your face into my back.*

Franz scrambled onto Jakob's back, riding 'piggy-back.' He got a good grip on Jakob's shoulders, Jakob got hold of his thighs…

…And they fairly vanished from the camp.

Behind them, Franz' discarded camp clothing ignited where it lay on the concrete floor. In seconds there was nothing left. Not even scorch marks marred the concrete where it had lain.

It was the evening of July 23rd, 1944.

***

Jakob took Franz as far as Warsaw before he stopped.

"Here," he said, easing the lad to the ground in the shadows of a huge cathedral in the Old Town. "I have to go back to the Soviet forces for now, but I'll stop off in the automotive shop long enough to make sure there's no sign left of you, little brother. This is the arch-cathedral, though there is currently no archbishop, for obvious reasons. On the far side of the cathedral, the monastery runs a small lodging; you'll be safe there — tell them Jake sent you — and you can take a nice long bath if you like, and sleep in a soft bed for a change. Try to head west as soon as you can. For now, stop and eat something, get your bearings, and rest if you need to. But don't stay too long — a few days, no more. The Soviet Army is headed this way, and if you thought the camp was tricky to get through, that'll be nothing to being in the middle of an invading army with the Nazi ground forces fighting back. Give me a hug, little brother; I have no idea when, or even if, I'll see you again."

Franz hugged him tightly, and received just as fervent a hug in response.

Then Jakob was gone.

Franz looked in the general direction he'd seen him depart for long moments, then hefted the duffel and walked toward the front of the cathedral.

***

On July 24th, 1944, the Majdanek concentration camp was liberated by the Soviet army during the Lublin-Brest Offensive.

There were estimated to be less than one thousand prisoners left alive inside the camp.

Only a couple hundred of those were Jews.

***

The friars in the monastery adjacent to the cathedral welcomed Franz into their small lodging.

"Come, come, if you are a friend of Jake, then we will see to you," Friar Antoni said. "You are in a safe place here. The Soviet Army is working with the Polish Home Army to liberate Warsaw. It will be soon." He eyed Franz' stubble-covered head. "You escaped a camp?"

"Does it matter?"

"No, no. But if you did, then I have no doubt you would like a hot bath and a soft bed about now."

"Those would both be very nice, yes."

"Which?"

"Which what?"

"Which camp?"

"…Majdanek."

"Ah. Very good. We will see to you, my son. Are you Polish, Soviet, Romani…"

"None of those."

Friar Antoni studied the youth, then his eyebrows shot up.

"Oh my," he murmured. "And you survived? You survived Majdanek? After that God-cursed Operation Harvest Festival?"

"Jakob. And some quick thinking."

"Ah. Of course."

"You, um, you know about him?"

"We do. We also know that he is on the righteous side. Come with me. I will put you in a special room and draw a bath for you, my son. You have more than earned it."

***

That night, Franz Levy, thoroughly and scrupulously clean for the first time in two and a half years, slept in a soft, warm bed with all the blankets he could want, and a pile of down pillows.

Already relaxed from the bath, his body became almost limp when it found itself between the sheets, gently cradled in downy softness.

He was asleep in moments.

***

It was well into the morning before he woke the next day, to a tray full of breakfast — semolina porridge, made expressly for the nigh-starved youth as it was easy to digest, cheese toast made with potato bread, and apple butter — borne by Friar Antoni.

***

The friar, upon realizing that Franz was Jewish, and hearing about the liberation of Majdanek, insisted he stay there for some few days, while he tried to put more meat on his bones.

"Because even when we are liberated here, it will still be hard," Friar Antoni pointed out. "You will need enough reserves to go on awhile."

Unfortunately, a week later, Hitler issued the Order for Warsaw.

Within hours, Nazi soldiers moved on the western suburbs of Warsaw, Poland, killing everyone they found, including the women and children, often burning the buildings around them.

Franz was trapped.

***

Chapter 5 — Warsaw

Sometime after luncheon — a British ex-prisoner would have said it was approaching teatime — Franz was exploring the cathedral with the benevolent Friar Antoni as his tour guide, when someone came to the door of the nave and held up a hand, waving and gesturing to catch the friar's attention.

"Excuse me, son," the friar murmured, and hastened to the nave.

Franz stayed where he was, watching as the newcomer spoke to the friar, whose friendly face sobered rapidly. The stranger departed, and the friar hurried back.

"Come with me, and hurry," he said, and turned toward the narthex and the door leading to the monastery.

***

As they went, Antoni issued orders to everyone he encountered on the way. The pair stopped off in his room barely long enough for Franz to grab his few things and throw them into the duffel, then continued downstairs into the wine cellar, eventually entering a hidden passage and going down a very long set of spiral stairs. At the bottom, a room opened up.

There, the other friars awaited.

***

"I was just contacted by one of our go-betweens," Antoni said without preamble. "The Nazis are moving on Warsaw."

"Good," one of the friars said in satisfaction. "Then the Home Army and the Red Army will close on them and we will soon be free."

"No, that is not what is happening," Antoni replied, grim of face. "The Soviets are not responding to the calls of the Home Army. They sit a few miles away and wait. No one knows why."

"Huh," Franz grunted. "Jakob was right; they are using delaying tactics. I wonder why."

"They are not helping because the Resistance is not communist," another monk remarked. "They are part of the Allied forces in name only, I think. They are on their own side. Remember, they originally had a treaty of cooperation with Hitler."

"That…would make sense," Antoni acknowledged, wincing. "Worse, in response to what LOOKS like an alliance between the Home Army and the Red Army, even though that isn't what's happening, Hitler has issued orders: Warsaw is to be obliterated before the Soviets can arrive. No prisoners, not even children, and nothing is to be left standing. They have advanced on the western suburbs and are already setting alight houses with people inside as they proceed. If the occupants flee the fire, they are shot. Otherwise, they burn."

Unhappy murmurs rose from the friars.

"And we have a visitor, a guest, bestowed upon us as our responsibility," Antoni reminded them, gesturing to Franz. "He is a friend of Jakob. When Jakob told me to expect him, he called him, 'little brother.' No, no, he is not like Jakob," Antoni added, raising his hands to silence the concerned murmurs. "This is Franz. He is escaping from…farther east. We need to get him out."

"What of the cathedral? The relics?" one of the monks asked.

"If they are truly doing what was reported to me, and let me note that the source was impeccable, then there is little that can be done to save the cathedral," Antoni noted. "We will fetch the relics and artwork and take them as deep into the hidden crypts and catacombs as we can get them. That should protect them from both Nazi fires and Nazi theft. Though, if we should all be killed, they will be lost to history. Still, they will remain, and may one day be found." He pointed. "Marcus, Ludwik, Jan, and Olek — fetch baskets and gather the relics and art, then take them to the north deep crypt. Put them inside and lock the door. When you have done that, get out as fast as you can. The rest of you, get only your essentials and go. It is, I think, more important that we live to assist the rebuild than to try to stop these curséd of God."

"But perhaps," one monk began.

"Jaszc," Antoni interrupted, "they have brought sturmtigers."

The monks blanched.

"What's a sturmtiger?" Franz wondered, barely above a whisper, and mostly to himself. But in the sudden silence, it was overheard.

"According to resistance intelligence, it is a kind of tank, a very BIG tank," Antoni explained, "but instead of a turret with cannon, it has a 380-millimeter rocket launcher. It has fifteen-centimeter-thick armor, and it is thought to weigh around 70 tonnes, give or take."

"Fah—" Franz began, then broke off the curse; not only were these men priests of the One as he had decided, the Yiddish curse word would be too revealing. Antoni had guessed his ancestry, but Franz had not confirmed it, and Antoni had told no one his guess, keeping Franz's secret insofar as the boy could tell.

"Exactly," Antoni said with a slight smile, apparently having mentally filled in the rest of the curse word, though the others wore blank or confused expressions. "It is nigh unstoppable, and it WILL take down any structure it comes against. If nothing else, it can simply batter it down."

"Then yes, we must go," Friar Jaszc agreed.

"Then go," Antoni said. "I will take care of our guest. Jaszc, would you kindly fetch my things with yours? I will meet you outside the Royal Castle at the usual place once I have sent young Franz, here, on his way."

"Gladly, Antoni."

The group broke up.

***

Antoni took Franz to a stash of C-rations, evidently smuggled in by a means Franz didn't know. There, he filled a small pack with the lightest weight foods, attached the duffel to the bottom in lieu of a bedroll, then handed it to Franz.

"Can you carry this, son?" he asked.

Franz shrugged into the backpack; it was heavy on his bony frame, and if he had to carry it far, his shoulders would rub, but he could manage. He nodded.

"Then this will keep you going awhile. Jakob was right; I should have sent you on sooner. I had hoped to have longer to build you up for the journey, but there it is. I pray the Lord forgives me for the error in judgement; it was well meant, at least. Let's go."

***

At a steady jog, Antoni led a breathless, panting Franz through a veritable labyrinth of dim, barely-lit underground passages — catacombs, crypts, wine cellars, ancient sewers, and more. As they progressed, the passages grew danker; in places, water dripped, and Franz realized they must be approaching the river, though the approach was slow because they doubled back frequently.

Many years later, and upon studying the maps, Franz would realize that Antoni was taking him underneath what was left of the Warsaw Ghetto. Whether he had been protecting the boy from the sight, or merely choosing an easier route, Franz never knew, though he preferred to think it was both.

Eventually Antoni put his finger to his lips, signaling Franz to be silent, and they climbed a ladder upward, emerging in a tiny cobblestoned, brick-walled mews. The sun had set while they were still meeting with the monks, and the light was fading fast; the first stars were showing in the heavens. A red glow still lit the skies to the west, however, and Franz knew that it was not from the sunset: Warsaw was burning.

Warsaw to the west of the Vistula River was largely under Nazi control, but east of the river, the Home Army controlled the city. There was a musty, rank smell in the air, and the youth realized this likely emanated from the river, which therefore must be close. There were few lights, and the shadowed streets were growing dark fast, especially on the slope leading down to the river.

Antoni led him around a corner into a street so narrow an automobile could not have traversed it. At the far end, in the cross street, several dark silhouettes passed, hopscotching from cover to cover; they all wore flanged helmets, belted uniforms, and jackboots, and all carried long guns. Antoni put his arm across Franz's chest and pushed the boy behind himself as he leaned back, deeper into the shadows of the constricted street.

Once the Nazi soldiers had passed on, and the sounds of their hobnailed boots on the cobblestones faded in the distance, Antoni moved forward, Franz close behind. Double-checking the intersection first, they crossed the wider street and disappeared into another alleyway a little farther down.

Franz glanced up the slope and saw a large structure, somewhere between a castle and a mansion, silhouetted against the glow of the fires. Ahead, between the buildings — several of which were ruined, likely by bombs or artillery — he just caught the glimmer of water illuminated by starlight.

He tugged on Antoni's robes, and the friar glanced at him. He gestured ahead, then made a waving motion with his hand, and the friar nodded.

Moments later, they emerged on the river's bank. A man was waiting in a small mud-colored boat that looked, in the scant light, the same color as the water.

"Myśli są darmowe," Antoni murmured. (*Thoughts are free.*)

"Nasze życie nie jest," came the countersign. (*Our lives are not.*)

"This is Franz," Antoni said, as he gestured the boy toward the boat. "He is a friend of Jakob."

"Ah," the ferryman said with a grin. "He is a friend of mine, then. Come. I'll get you across safely."

Franz clambered aboard, followed by Antoni.

***

Half an hour later, they were inside one of the old 19th century periphery fortresses constructed by the Tsarist Russian Empire to hold the city. It was currently occupied by the Home Army, and was one of their centers of operation in Warsaw.

"Ah, so we have someone else to get out of the city," the Polish commander sighed. "Really, Friar Antoni? You know what's happening in the west suburbs."

"I know. That is why the boy must get out now," Antoni averred. "Jakob called him, 'little brother.' And you know Jakob will not be happy if we do not take proper care of him."

"Co?! Wampyr?" (*What?! Vampire?*)

"No, no; I think the reference is in how he's cared for the boy. But Jakob is a powerful — and a staunch — ally, and it would not do to get on his wrong side."

"No. No, it would not." The commander sighed again. "All right. There are some others that we plan to send down the river tonight; I'll add him to the cargo. He's thin, and won't add much to the weight; it should be fine."

"Thank you." Antoni turned to Franz. "It is likely I will not see you again, my boy. Perhaps, if we both survive the next few days, we may, but during my prayers, I have seen you going far, far away and becoming someone who makes a major difference in this world. Take care, and always remember to trust the One in Whom we both believe." He took the lad's hand and squeezed it.

Franz said nothing; his throat was choked up. Antoni had taken good care of him in the short time they had known each other, and the thought that he might die later tonight upset him as he had not been upset since Uncle Eitan died. But he squeezed the friar's hand in return, blinked several times, and nodded.

Then Friar Antoni was gone, and Franz was in the hands of the Home Army.

***

"No, we need to go now," the local commander, whose name Franz never caught, said as he led Franz and three more men down the riverbank. All four refugees were now dressed in

91

a kind of camouflage brown; Franz had put his regular clothing into his pack for later use. It never occurred to him that, in the process, the others had been able to see the number tattoo'ed on his arm. "The Nazis are practicing scorched-earth, and moving fast as a result. If we wait, we might not get you out."

"It is damned inconvenient," one of the other three men grumbled. "I do not like being routed out of my bed in the middle of the night. Inconvenient, I say!"

"Death is worse," the commander pointed out. The man silenced.

They reached the river bank, and three more men waited there. It was very dark, and Franz could make out no more than their shadowed outlines, but there was something in the water, right on the edge of the bank.

"Here," the commander said in a low voice, ensuring it would not carry across the water. "Get in, lie down, and be still. We'll ensure you won't be seen."

"What…?" Franz wondered in a murmur, moving where the commander indicated.

"We have had to do this before," the commander explained, keeping his voice low. "We are going to float you down the river until you are out of Warsaw. You will still be in Nazi territory, but Gabe there knows the resistance members in the region; stay with him, and he will keep you safe."

"But they'll see! We'll be shot!" the complainer protested.

"Keep your voice down," the commander ordered. "You will get us all killed."

"No, you will not be shot," one of the men with the watercraft denied, his voice barely audible. "It is camouflaged. It will look like no more than debris floating in the river, especially given how the Nazis are destroying as they go. The tarp we will put over you is also camouflaged. They will not see you, especially in the dark. With any luck, you will be out of the city by daylight…if you go now."

"Put the boy over there," the commander said, pointing, and Franz moved into position. "It will cause the boat to list oddly, and it will look even more like debris."

"Why is he coming with us?" the complainer started in again. "He is a child, and a concentration camp prisoner, at that."

"What makes you say that?" the commander demanded. "And keep your voice down!"

"Did none of you see the number tattoo'ed on his arm? He is from Auschwitz!"

"Son, is that true?" the commanded asked, raising an eyebrow at Franz. In the dark, the youth couldn't be sure, but he thought there was a smirk on the commander's face.

"No, sir," he responded truthfully, "I didn't come from Auschwitz."

"You lie!"

"HEY THERE!" came a call in German from the far bank. "What's going on over there?!"

"Now you've done it," the commander breathed, adding a couple of pithy curses for good measure. "Everyone else, into the boat. Hurry. They'll have a spotlight over here from the castle in moments."

Franz scrambled into position in the strange boat and laid down, as two of the three other men joined him. Complainer stayed behind; the commander had grabbed his shoulder and held tight. Within moments the three in the boat were draped with a tarp and shoved into a small side channel of the river, where it went around an island.

Franz discovered that he was in a position to peep out from beneath the tarp in several directions without being seen.

They were drifting slowly downstream. Behind them, a spotlight began to play on the bank, as the commander called out.

In flawless German.

"Keine Sorge, mein Herr. Wir erwischten diesen Mann, der versuchte, über den Fluss zu schwimmen. Wir haben uns mit ihm beschäftigt." (*Not to worry, sir. We caught this man trying to swim across the river. We've dealt with him.*)

"Nie! Nie! Co robisz?!" the voice of Complainer cried in Polish. (*No! No! What are you doing?!*)

There was a gunshot — Franz saw the muzzle flash, and something or someone toppled backward — and a splash of water.

"I guess they won't have to shut him up any more," breathed one of the other men — he had grabbed Franz' shoulder and given it a reassuring squeeze when he'd been accused of escaping Auschwitz — in the boat with Franz. "Dupek." (*Asshole*)

Moments later, the searchlight shone on a body floating down the main channel, just barely visible over the low sandbar island.

"Ausgezeichnet," came the reply from the castle, and the searchlight went off.

They were headed downstream, out of Warsaw.

***

As they floated downstream in darkness, Franz began to feel he had, perhaps, escaped at last.

Until they reached the northwestern part of the city, and the western bank lit up in fire.

"Verdammt," Franz murmured, careful to avoid cursing in Yiddish. "The city burns."

"Hush, child," hissed the other man, who had been less than friendly if not openly hostile, "lest someone hear you."

He silenced, but watched in shocked horror from beneath the tarp as flames roared high, and men and women — sometimes in flames themselves — ran screaming until they were shot down.

Abruptly a brick house fairly exploded. Through the cloud of dust a huge, clanking machine emerged, a gigantic tank with no turret, but with a big stubby cannon barrel protruding from its front. Its position relative to the clandestine escapees was such that they looked almost straight down the cannon's maw.

"Sturmtiger," the friendly man breathed.

They all held their breaths until they were well downstream from the behemoth.

***

It was sometime before midnight when they had launched into the Vistula River, which did not flow overly fast at Warsaw, but was still somewhat faster than a man could walk. Sunrise came just before 5 in the morning, and by that time, Franz estimated they were a good twenty to twenty-five miles downstream of Warsaw and had already passed one town along the river. The river was wide and fairly heavily braided at that point, with small tributary streams entering. The surrounding land was flat, but the river itself flowed through a shallow valley, so the crude boat was reasonably well hidden.

As the day wore on, all three of the boat's occupants grew hungry, and it grew hot with nothing to shade the boat as it drifted downstream. A quick, low discussion between them around noon resulted in the decision to pull onto a sand bar between islands. They were still too close to Warsaw for comfort — only two hours as the Sturmtiger ran — but there was little along the banks at this point but forest, the islands were forested, and there was no sign of human life along this stretch of river, so they felt reasonably safe in doing so. Franz estimated that they were probably close to fifty miles out from Warsaw; the land grew flatter as they went, so the river's rate of flow had slowed, but the damage the Nazis had done to the lock and dam infrastructure as they retreated from the Soviets meant it was moving faster than it might have otherwise.

Friendly Man produced a paddle, evidently given him by the Home Army soldiers, and he slipped it through a special slot in the stern to surreptitiously steer them into one of the channels between islands. Once they were out of sight of the main channel, he rose from beneath the tarp and paddled quietly until they grounded gently on a sandbar in the shade of an old beech, likely one of the anchors that held the island in place during spring flooding. They were surrounded by brush and scrub.

"There," he murmured. "Trees on either side, and a bend in the channel hiding us upstream and down, with shade overhead. I think this will suit us for a safe meal and resting during the heat of the day."

"It'll do," Less Friendly Man said, less than gracious, if not quite rude. "Do we have anything to eat?"

"There's a small stash of German iron rations in the corner, here," Friendly said. "Looks like a little of everything. There's also a good bit of dried beef and hardtack."

"Give me one of the rations," Less Friendly said. "Water?"

"There are several canteens, and some filters for later," Friendly said. "Son? What about you?"

"Um, is there maybe chicken or lamb?" Franz wondered.

"There is," Friendly said, as Less Friendly eyed him with suspicion. "No lamb, but plenty of chicken. Here." He selected three of the packaged rations and handed them around. "We can share a canteen."

"I think not," Less Friendly said, glaring at Franz. "I would like a canteen of my own, if you please."

Franz flushed, and Friendly eyed Less Friendly in a scolding fashion.

"Here, then," Friendly said, almost snapping, as he tossed a canteen at the other man. "What's your problem?"

"Ask the boy why he doesn't want to eat the pork," Less Friendly said by way of accusation.

"It does not sit well with me," Franz offered, unwilling to admit that it was not kosher and he tried to keep kosher when he had a choice. Something about this man set his instincts on edge; he did not trust him. The question had been rather pointed, and Franz suspected the dead loudmouth back in Warsaw was not the only antisemite around.

"But you have no problems with any of the other meats, do you?"

"Actually, I do best on chicken or lamb right now," Franz confessed, "with turkey a possibility too. I have, er, been very ill. Friar Antoni has been nursing me for a bit, and he recommended those meats." It was true; the boy was nigh-starved, and while he'd eaten whatever Jakob had been able to bring him, his stomach was still easing back into having food on a regular basis — he was prone to bolting it and then throwing up. And Jakob had been considerate about what meats he had brought the Jewish boy, in any case.

"Uh-huh," Less Friendly grunted. Franz was strongly considering re-dubbing him Unfriendly, the original Unfriendly's body having apparently sunk to the riverbed overnight. If there was anything left of him by the time the deep-water wels catfish finished eating, Franz would be surprised.

"Let's introduce ourselves," Friendly tried. "I am Gabryjel, Gabryjel Elhert. My friends call me Gabe." He nodded at Franz, who thought fast.

"Franz Blutwert," he said, drawing inspiration from Jakob's 'little brother' reference and twisting it to become a surname. "I'm a friend of, of, he's known as Jakob."

"Aha! You have a good friend, then. And you?" Gabe turned to New Unfriendly Man.

"Janusz Sasinowski," he almost growled…but his eyes darted from side to side. "I've heard…things…about this 'Jakob' person."

"I'm sure," Gabe said. "He's a bit of a, mmm, a legend of sorts, I suppose. Almost more of a rumor than real. Few have met him. He is said to be a ghost among the Resistance." He threw a surreptitious glance at Franz, who looked down at his food to avoid grinning. "Is the food all right, Franz? Is it sitting well in your gut?"

"So far, yes," Franz noted. "I think it will be all right. But I am tired; I was too tense to sleep much last night."

"Weren't we all?" Janusz agreed. "It was a stressful night, and we are all lucky to be alive."

"We were, and are, indeed. I suggest we take turns napping," Gabe said. "We're in this together, so we might as well work together. You two rest, I'll stand guard for an hour or so, then one of you can stand guard and I'll nap."

"I'll take that," Janusz decided, and promptly made to throw the waste from his meal on the bank.

"No, wait," Gabe said, throwing up a hand. "Give me that. We'll put it in one of the packages and weight it down in the middle of the river later."

"Ah, that is smart. Leave no means to track us." A mildly grudging Janusz handed over his trash and Gabe bundled it with his own. Franz was still eating, having learned the hard way at the monastery's guesthouse that eating slowly and not bolting his food resulted in better digestion…and better retention. Janusz stretched back out in the boat and was asleep in minutes.

Franz picked his way through his meal, growing sleepy as the food hit his stomach. At last he finished and handed Gabe the remains. The other man bundled it with the rest, then watched benevolently as Franz settled in for a nap.

***

Late that afternoon, Franz woke to find Janusz keeping watch as Gabe slept. He glared at the boy for a moment, then shook his head and returned his attention to their surroundings. Regardless of how little the boy trusted him at this point, apparently he was keeping a proper watch.

Another meal, this time of dried beef and hardtack, and Gabe wielded the paddle to push them off. A rock pulled from beneath the water near where they had drawn up served as a weight for the trash from their meals, and as soon as they got to deeper water, Gabe eased the bundle over the side. There was no splash, and the trash sank out of sight in the muddy water within seconds.

Together they pulled the camouflaged tarpaulin over the boat as they resumed their prone positions under it, and slowly they drifted out, past the islands and into the main channel once more.

***

As it grew solid dark, the boat floated past an island with a bombed-out village, then past a town with a port on the river. But with twilight well advanced and the reduced visibility it provided, the little boat was nothing but flotsam on the river, drifting down from what was left of Warsaw; when they had resumed travel after their midday break, there was considerable debris in the river of various types…including several bodies.

"What town was that, do either of you know?" Franz whispered.

"The island used to be a village named Kępa Ośnicka," Gabe murmured. "The town is called Plock."

"How do you know?" Janusz asked in a low tone.

"I used to work the river, before the war," Gabe explained. "I traded up and down it, and carried canned foods, lumber and coal on my boat. It is how I got into the resistance work. I know the stops very well…or I did." He shrugged slightly. "I suppose many will be gone, even if this ends soon."

"Where are we going?" Franz asked. "This is all still Nazi territory, right? Are we floating all the way to the Baltic?"

"Yes, it is all still held by the Nazis, though with the Russian advance, they are retreating back toward Germany," Gabe confirmed. "So they may not hold it long — I hope they do not — and it is arguable how well they are defending it. But no, it would do us no good to float to the Baltic; we would have to go all the way across it to Finland to find land that was free of both the Nazis and the Soviets, and there is no way this little boat can traverse the Baltic Sea. We would not survive."

"What are we going to do, then?"

"We debated that this afternoon while you slept," Janusz said, "during the time when I was awake to guard, and he was trying to go to sleep. I plan to continue north to Gdansk, and try to find a way to cross the Baltic to Finland."

"Whereas I have been called to Berlin by the resistance there," Gabe noted. "They wish me to help plan a regional recovery after the Nazis are defeated, so the Allies can hand over to us in a coordinated fashion across countries. It is a bit premature, but only a bit, I think. So at some point, we part ways, I suppose. I plan to debark somewhere around Bydgoszcz, though probably before we get into the town proper; the river turns hard northeast from there, and Bydgoszcz is the farthest western point of the river and therefore closest to Berlin. From there I'll go on foot to Berlin, hopefully behind the Soviet Army; the breeze bore the clanking of tanks in the distance this afternoon, while the two of you slept. I am no communist, but they are our best hope at clearing the road from this direction, though I hope the Americans and British beat them to Berlin."

"You will take the boy with you," Janusz declared, cold. "I do not want a Jew accompanying me, much less a child."

"You have not made the case that he is Jewish," Gabe pointed out. "You have only the tattoo…"

"Look at his face," Janusz shot back. "His nose, his eyes, his—"

"Are none of them guaranteed Jewish features," Gabe interrupted. "You have nothing save the tattoo to go on. Yes, he may be from a concentration camp…perhaps. But despite the tattoo being an Auschwitz procedure, there is no reason other camps, including some work camps, might not have experimented with it. The most likely camp from which he might have come is actually Majdanek — I have not heard if the Soviets have even reached Auschwitz as yet, but I know they reached Majdanek, though I gather from the friar that it was AFTER the boy arrived in Warsaw, so stick that in your eye — and all of the Jews were killed there last year. And that is only important to you, in any case. But whether he is or no, he is a human being, he is a boy, and he is alone. And it is obvious he has been mistreated. He is nearly a walking skeleton. Have some compassion."

"No! I care not. I will not take him with me."

Franz bit back what he had been about to say, aided by Gabe's subtle, gently restraining hand on his shoulder.

"I will be glad to take him with me," Gabe said then. "Franz, did you have a planned destination?"

"Just…west," Franz said with a shrug, turning to Gabe and ignoring Janusz. "Jakob told me to head west. To the Americans, he said. I can follow you to Berlin once it is freed, and keep going, I suppose."

"That will work," Janusz said, still cold and uncaring. "As long as I do not have to deal with you."

The darkness hid Franz' scowl.

"Sleep, son," Gabe said then, soothing, as he lightly rubbed the boy's shoulder, the gesture unseen in the dark. "You are safe here. There is little but forest ahead of us for some time. We are both wanted by the Nazis, and capture would mean our deaths, so you need fear no betrayal."

Franz tried to swallow his anger. Eventually he settled enough to sleep, listening to the water lap softly against the sides of the boat.

***

Once he managed to fall asleep, he slept through the night. His body was still exhausted from too many years surviving a concentration camp existence, and later, he assumed that Gabe managed to talk Janusz into allowing him to sleep while the two adult men kept watch.

They drifted past Włocławek in the wee small hours, and when the sun rose, they were a good ten miles past it, according to Gabe. The next marker would be when they passed the city of Torun on the northeast bank mid-morning. The river was narrowing and picking up speed, and was no longer braided, so they would have to be careful, especially since the river turned sharply west just before the city, and it was possible they could be driven up on the east bank and discovered.

"What should we do, then, to prevent it?" Janusz wondered. "Should we go ashore and portage across the curve?"

"I think I can manage to steer the boat without being seen," Gabe offered. "I have done this sort of thing a couple of times already, and it will be faster than a portage."

"Oh," Franz said in some relief; his anxiety had risen at the discussion. It would prove years before he learned to convert the undirected anxiety response to a usable adrenaline reaction. "Then perhaps this is what we should do."

"I hate to admit to it, but I agree," Janusz noted. "I suspect this is one reason why Gabryjel was placed with us."

"I think so, yes," Gabe said modestly. "I did talk with Commander Figlarz when the evacuation was planned. He tried to make certain that those who needed to get out had a way, and had one or more persons along with all the requisite skills to ensure success."

"Then this, we shall do," Janusz decreed, and Franz nodded.

***

As they approached the bend in the river before Torun, Gabe rolled onto his stomach and eased the paddle through a slot in the back of the shallow boat.

"Franz, you are in the front; can you see ahead?" he asked.

"If I shift a bit, I can look from beneath this cover," the boy replied.

"Do so, please, and help me by directing me."

"How?"

"We need to look as if we are drifting, without getting too close to the bank," Gabe explained. "I want to start out near the inner bank and gradually drift out as we go around the curve, but only go about two-thirds of the way across the channel. Can you help me?"

"Yes, I think so."

"Good. Let's get set. Tell me where we are in the channel right now, relative to the right and left bank."

"We are nearly in the middle," came the reply. "A bit right of center."

"Very good. Let me slowly shift us toward the left, then…"

*****

Janusz remained silent for the most part, but per Gabe's instruction, kept an eye out for any snags in the river. Franz gave soft instruction as to position, and Gabe used the paddle as a rudder and deftly but subtly steered the boat to give the impression it was adrift while avoiding the possibility of running aground.

From the point at which they started to actively navigate the river until they made it past Torun was about five miles, and the speed of the river made it an hour-long journey. It was a tense time, but all three males stayed calm and quietly relayed information, even Janusz.

As they progressed, Franz suddenly understood why Gabe had been concerned — this part of the river had been lined with breakwaters in an attempt to prevent the bends in the river's channel from becoming more extreme as erosion took its toll.

"Exactly," Gabe said, when Franz made a comment. "This part of the river migrated a lot in recent centuries, especially during flood season, so efforts were made to mitigate the tendency of the river bends to exaggerate from erosion. The breakwaters were part of that. But they create eddies in the current along the sides, and we do not wish to be caught in those. It would be virtually impossible to free the boat without revealing ourselves."

"How far do they go?" Janusz wondered. "The breakwaters, I mean."

"Intermittently all the way to the Vistula Dig-Through. You'll need to be careful. I'll make sure to leave the paddle in position for you to use it, even while lying down in the boat."

"What is that?" Franz asked. "The Dig-Through?"

"A canal that cuts through the delta, directly to the Baltic. Flooding caused problems, so in the last century it was decided to make the flow more direct. That way the ice is less likely to dam during spring thaws."

"Oh."

***

On the far side of Torun, the surrounding land was forested again, though there were no islands; there were an increasing number of sand bars, but these were badly eroded as a result of the Nazi destruction of the locks and dams on the river, and the rush of water that resulted. Most of the bridges had been blown by this point, as well.

They paused just before noon, finding a place where the trees deeply overhung the river's bank before grounding the boat beneath them. They made another meal off the Nazi iron rations, with Franz trying the turkey this time. The meals were largely lots of dense bread with a small tin of meat, and that not as good as the C-rations Jakob brought, but it was real food intended for soldiers, so it kept Franz going much better than the starvation diet he'd had in Majdanek whenever Jakob wasn't around — which had, unfortunately, been most of the time.

Again, he ate slowly, so he was the last to finish. Again, Gabe collected the waste, then rolled up his sleeve, leaned over and grabbed a large rock from the bank just under the water — it would be used as ballast to sink the trash once they pushed back into the channel, while the mud of the bank quickly filled in the space where it had been. Again, Gabe took the first watch, and Janusz was asleep before Franz could finish eating.

"Get some rest, son," Gabe told the boy kindly. "You and I will be getting off later tonight, and traveling on foot overnight. Are you up for that?"

"I think so. I will do my best."

"Good. Sleep as long as you can. I'll wake you when we're ready to go."

"What about you?"

"I'll sleep in a few hours, once Janusz is on watch. I've been treated a bit better than you have, so I can go awhile longer without the restorative of sleep."

This was not wholly to Franz' liking; he had a bad feeling about Janusz, and it had been increasing all day. He didn't like the idea of both Gabe and himself asleep at Janusz' hands. There was little help for it, however; Gabe apparently did trust Janusz.

So he bedded down in what passed for the bow of the boat, and was soon asleep, lulled by the lap of water, the soft chirp of birds, and the buzz of insects.

***

When Gabe woke him, Janusz handed two portions of dried beef and hardtack to Gabe, who passed one to Franz.

"At some point we are going to need to relieve ourselves," Janusz observed, "other than putting water over the side, that is."

"Likely not for some time," Gabe noted. "Typically, army rations — and that includes dried beef and hardtack — tend to, ehm, reduce that need. It's so you aren't needing to go in the wrong place, at the wrong time, or for the smell to give away your position."

Janusz winced, looking at the bar of hardtack on which he gnawed.

"Urg. Perhaps it is as well we have only been eating two meals a day."

"Yes. It also stretches the rations."

***

They set out near sunset. They wanted to arrive on the outskirts of Bydgoszcz around ten at night, when it would be solidly dark. That way, Franz and Gabe could make the river's bank without being observed — Gabe assured them that the area where he wanted to debark was sparsely populated, with forest nearby — and Janusz could then push off and resume his travels downriver.

"…And I already split the foodstuffs and added them to your packs while we were resting," Janusz told them. "I had nothing else to do, so I figured I might as well do it while we were safe. It would save time tonight, when we are close to Bydgoszcz and do not wish to be found."

"Good idea," Gabe decided. "Did you add some to Franz's also?"

"Of course," Janusz said, almost offended. "No matter what he is or is not, it is only fair."

"Of course. Thank you."

"Now we need to be silent until we get closer to Bydgoszcz, I think," Janusz said. "Bydgoszcz is a fairly large city, and we do not know when we may encounter people."

"True. And there will likely be Nazis in the city," Gabe added.

They headed downstream on their last leg together.

***

Chapter 6 — A Hard Go of It

It was nearly eleven when they finally grounded the boat on the western bank, practically in the bend. Bydgoszcz' riverfront was past the bend, and here the land was largely farm fields…or it had been, before the passage of the retreating Nazis had resulted in the deliberate destruction of the harvest. There would, Franz realized, be famine that winter. He sighed. *Not again,* he thought. *I would give an arm for one of Mamma's Sabbath challahs, or her chicken soup. Or just some fresh-baked bread.*

Gabe got out first, and hefted his pack and Franz' to the sandy bank. Then he gave the boy a hand, and Franz found himself back on terra firma. Janusz handed them one canteen each, and most of the water filters; with all the dead bodies in the water, he was loath to drink from the river, and the pair stood a better chance than he of being able to refill canteens as they cut across country. This had been discussed and agreed-to earlier; the fact that water was heavy and Franz was still weak meant he likely could not carry his share otherwise, in any event.

"Lie back down and I will spread the camouflage over you, then push you off the sand bar," Gabe murmured. Janusz nodded and complied, and with a good shove, the disguised boat moved away from the bank and back into the main channel. They crouched on the bank and watched until it was out of sight. Then Gabe turned.

"And now I want to do something."

"What?"

"Let us take stock, while we are still below the bank and fairly well hidden," Gabe said, teeth flashing dimly in what light there was as he grinned tightly. He hefted his pack in meaning.

***

It turned out that Janusz had not added any food to Franz' pack, and very little — certainly less than half, or even a third — to Gabe's pack. Franz still had all the food that Friar Antoni had given him, but no more.

Franz was dismayed, but Gabe began to laugh.

"What is the matter? Why are you laughing?" Franz asked, puzzled and upset.

"I'm laughing because I was warned not to trust him from the beginning," Gabe said, still laughing, but managing to stifle the sound. "Oh, he could be trusted not to kill us in our sleep, but on little else! So while he was asleep, I divided the food fairly, one-third each. Since you are still thin and weak, I didn't add yours to your pack, but I did add it to mine, and placed it all into a hidden compartment in mine. I left his share in the supplies bag, as he had no need for it to be in a pack…"

"Wait — you mean…" Franz said, hazel eyes widening.

"Yes. He took his fair share and put part of it into my pack. He shorted himself in the notion of shorting us!"

Franz clapped his hands over his mouth to cover the snort, then joined Gabe in stifling laughter.

***

They headed out immediately. Once they reached the top of the bank, Franz saw farmland spread out for a considerable distance, all of it food crops — mostly grain fields, but little of it was left untouched. Some had been harvested already, and what was left had been burned.

They followed the farm roads in the dark, walking single file, keeping to the central weed-and-grass-covered area and out of the dusty ruts, leaving less trace of their passage that way. A few lights off to the right indicated a village; they kept well away from it, as it was likely an outlier of Bydgoszcz and could have Nazis or Nazi sympathizers there. In about a mile, they crossed a couple of paved roads, then entered forested land, where they could be a little more relaxed about the possibility of being seen in the scant moonlight from the lunar crescent, as it was much less open, and the leaf litter precluded footprints. Gabe picked up the pace.

Franz kept up with him fairly well for a couple of hours. But by midnight, the pack on his back felt heavy and the straps had begun to cut into his bony shoulders; his feet felt leaden as well. He did the best he could, but soon Gabe noticed that the boy was no longer at his side, but lagging behind a bit. Over the next hour, that 'bit' increased to several feet, and then Franz began to walk behind him.

"Let's stop and eat some hardtack and have some water," Gabe suggested, moving to a rock outcrop under a tree and sitting. He patted the stone next to him, and Franz sat, then eased the pack from his shoulders with a stifled groan. "Heavy?"

"A little," Franz admitted, accepting the piece of hardtack and beginning to gnaw on it. "It hurts my shoulders."

"Mm. You don't have enough meat on your bones; that's part of the problem. Perhaps we can pad it a bit and that will help."

"With what?"

"You have at least one change of clothing, do you not? You changed into the camouflaged clothes the Home Army gave us, and you're still wearing them…"

"Um, yes. Oh! We can fold up a shirt or something and put it under the straps?"

"Exactly. I've done that before, when I was carrying very heavy packs; I'll see what I can do once we finish eating."

"Okay. Thank you."

"It's only right, son. I want to help as much as I can. You've been horribly mistreated."

"I still did better than some of the others. Including my family…" The boy's voice tapered off.

"Did any of them survive?"

"No. Most of them were dead within days. Uncle Eitan survived a little over a year."

"ARE you Jewish, then?"

Franz broke off eating and eyed the man. Gabe held up a hand.

"It doesn't matter to me either way, Franz," he said in an earnest tone. "But it would explain some things, and it would help ensure that I get you food that doesn't violate your precepts, if you are. I noticed," he said with some scorn, "that Jasicz put all the pork meals into my pack, and not so much of the chicken. Fortunately I had already distributed things more appropriately, so you will not go hungry. But we can perhaps buy additional food as we go, or scavenge it from the land."

"Ah," Franz said with a wry grimace. "Of course he did."

"Yes. Now, if you're Jewish, just so you know, I know Jews keep kosher, and they don't eat pork, but I don't know a lot more than that, so you'll have to help me."

"Okay. I can do that."

"So you are?"

"Yes. Pappa was a rabbi; so was Uncle Eitan. Pappa was training me to be a rabbi, too, so I know some. My last name is Levy; it's an ancient priestly clan. I haven't been able to keep kosher these last few years at Majdanek, though." He sighed in regret.

"Ah. How did you survive?"

He shook his head.

"Automotive skills my father taught me, a certain gift in that direction, quick wits, and my friend Jakob. Mostly the former; he couldn't be there a lot."

"I understand."

"I was able to fix the inspector's car when it broke down at the camp," Franz recalled, "and that meant I was useful to him. The commandant — whichever one it was at the time; they went through at least four while I was there, and half of them left when they were arrested — kept me around because the inspector was SS and outranked him."

"I see. Don't make the SS inspector mad."

"Yes. It also meant I ate a little bit better than the others — I got kapo food, mostly, but I wasn't a kapo."

"Kapo?"

"Um, funktionshäftling? The prisoners that…that worked for the Schutzstaffel, the SS? Most of them were, were as bad as the Nazi guards. A few were reasonably nice, but most weren't. I wasn't one of them."

"Oh, I see. They were currying favor with the guards?"

"Yes. But I promised Jakob I'd stay alive until he could free me, so I did what I could without…without doing wrong."

"Ah. And you are a man of your word."

"I try hard to be, yes."

"Where are you from originally? Lublin?"

"No. We had family in Lublin, and Father hoped to use the pretext of visiting for us to get out of Nazi-occupied lands. I'm not sure where he intended to go from there; I think he hoped to get to the Black Sea and across it, into the Middle East. Maybe even reach Palestine. I don't know how; the Nazis were in control the whole way. Mamma wanted to head west, toward the Atlantic, and try to escape to England or America, but Pappa thought that was too obvious. The Nazis were all over. There just…wasn't anywhere to go. We were from Leipzig, though."

"I see. Do you know what happened to your family home?"

"No. I've thought maybe I should go with you to Berlin, then continue to Leipzig to see. It is more or less along the way, if I remember right; it's been a while since I looked at a map. From there, I suppose I can decide what to do."

"True, it is, and I can see that you manage that, I think, even if I don't go with you myself. I have a map, and we'll look at it together later, and we can plan that leg of the trip."

"All right. That would be good. I remember maps pretty well…when I can actually see one."

"How is it that the friar said you were at the monastery before the Soviets had liberated the camp?"

"Jakob had, he had knowledge of the Red Army and knew what they were doing, so he and I planned for it. I had a — he said it was called a bolt-hole — and he…sent me word…to hide, or I could get killed. Or worse, dragged onto a train to another camp. Then, when the Nazis had deserted the place but before the Soviet army got there, he came and got me out, and… took me to Warsaw."

"…I see."

"Do you know Jakob?"

"No, but I know a bit about him. Mostly rumor. He is said to be a spy, and a damn good one. He is also rumored to be…something more. Or maybe something other is a better way of putting it."

"He is very good at what he does."

Gabe chuckled at the reply that both was and was not an answer.

"You're excellent at that, yourself."

"Thank you. I have had…experience."

"I expect you have, son. I expect you have."

The last of the hardtack went down, followed by some water from their canteens. Then Gabe took the shirts Franz extracted from his pack and fashioned pads for the pack straps, easing the pack back onto Franz' shoulders.

"How is that?" he asked.

"Better," Franz decided. "It does not hurt so much. There is already some bruising, but even that doesn't hurt as bad."

"Good. Let's see how far we can get. But let me know when you can't go any more, all right?"

"All right."

They set back out.

***

But by dawn, they had covered less than half of the distance Gabe had hoped to travel, though they were at least deep within the forest. Franz simply had no reserves to go that far, that fast. He never complained, and he never said to stop, but when they did stop, the boy all but collapsed beneath a tree, too tired even to shuck off the backpack. Gabe realized this was a problem, as it would be impossible for the exhausted Franz to keep watch for part of the sleep shift, and Gabe couldn't stay awake all the time to guard their camp while they slept and still

115

travel. Never mind how long it would take them to get to Berlin at this rate of travel.

He sighed, then crouched down, watching the boy. In his exhaustion and emaciation, Franz almost looked like an old man.

"Franz?"

"Yes, Gabe?" Franz opened his eyes.

"How old are you, son?"

"Um…" He stopped to reckon, and Gabe hid a wince; that told him as much as anything how much this lad had been through. "I'm fourteen."

"FOURT—?!" Gabe broke off, choking back the exclamation as much for Franz' sake as for safety. "I figured you for around seventeen. You're tall, and you carry yourself as much older. Plus you're thin after all you've been through, and that reads as older, too. I guess you've seen a lot."

"I have, yes. I have been beaten, I have had bones broken, I have been nearly raped and seen others raped. I have seen the naked dead bodies of my mother and sisters. I saw my older brother shot down in front of me and his brains blown out, simply for trying to defend me from a guard who was sick in the mind — he pissed on me from a watch-tower and thought it was exciting. I watched as my great-uncle slowly starved to death. I have had to break the bones in dead bodies to force them to fit into a crematorium oven. I have seen men and women shot and dumped into a mass grave, though I have not had to bury them. I have hidden in a small hole dug in the ground to escape detection. I have endured bedbugs and lice and fleas. Yes. I have seen things I never wanted to see. Many things."

"You said you worked for the SS inspector…as a mechanic?"

"Yes." Franz' eyes slid closed again.

"Did that mean you ate better than the others?"

"Once I reached that position, yes, a little. I no longer had to eat the nasty soup, but got bread for breakfast and dinner, and a vegetable soup with actual broth."

"What is the 'nasty soup' you mentioned?"

"I don't know what was in it other than some half-rotten potatoes and turnips," Franz noted, making a face but letting his eyes stay closed. "It tasted like it was made with weeds and rotten fish. And it was watery."

"Ugh."

"Yes."

"And they fed you that?"

"Yes. That was lunch."

"That was all you got for lunch?!"

"Yes. Breakfast was some sort of substitute for coffee — it didn't even taste like coffee — with no milk, cream or sugar, and dinner was a slice of coarse bread with a bare spoonful of margarine."

"And that's all they fed you?! All day??"

"Yes, until I became the Oberführer's mechanic. Then, as I said, I got bread morning and evening, two slices each, and a kind of vegetable stew for lunch that did not taste of weeds and dead fish, and had a thick broth. Sometimes for dinner too. And Jakob brought me C-rations when he could smuggle some in. I ate better than most."

"But you're still skin and bones."

Franz shrugged.

"The work was hard," was all he said. He thought for a few moments, then added, "I guess I grew up but not out."

He has a point, Gabe considered. *His initial growth spurt must have occurred and taken up all the excess calories he could give it. So he is tall for his age, and likely still growing, but he has little muscle and no fat, because he had no reserves to develop it.* He managed to avoid shaking his head. *He needs FOOD.*

"It looks like it," he said aloud. "Are you up for eating now?"

"Yes!" The boy sat bolt upright, eyes opening. "I am always ready to eat!"

Gabe stifled a chuckle — the boy had more than earned the right, after all, and the man wasn't surprised in the least — then gave him an iron ration with chicken meat, and took hardtack and dried beef for himself; after that little discussion, he had decided to give Franz as much of the more nourishing food as he could. *Fruit and vegetables would add nutrients he needs, but we haven't any at the moment. I need to rectify that, and soon.*

Once they had eaten and performed necessary bodily functions, Gabe pulled out a camp shovel and carefully buried their waste, disguising it with leaf litter, then looked around for a likely spot to hide a camp.

***

Since they were in dense woods, Gabe decided to travel in the daytime, so they slept until noon, then rose and ate some hardtack as a rude breakfast. Gabe was somewhat tired; he had kept more than one eye out when he could, and had not slept as much as he normally would have. But Franz had slept deeply and looked fresher, so the pair set out once more.

Late that day, they exited the forest to cross a short stretch of farm fields. Gabe gave the area a detailed scan with a pair of field glasses hidden in his pack, careful to cover them with a special thin cloth that would prevent reflections off the lenses. Then and only then did he lead the way across a narrow road and into the fields.

These had not been burned, as they were largely tobacco and not foodstuffs. This also meant they were tall enough to provide cover and an easy walk between rows. The fact that those rows were acutely diagonal relative to the road helped.

They kept going from one field to the next.

"We have changed direction, have we not?" Franz asked after a bit. "We are headed…slightly north of west? Isn't Berlin southwest of us?"

"It is, and we are," Gabe admitted. "But somewhere behind us will be the Soviet Army. They are likely to head straight for Berlin, so from Warsaw they will head due west. I want to bypass Bydgoszcz, then strike a river called the Notec. We'll follow it downstream; it arches around and empties into the Warta River, and that will take us to the Oder River, which forms the German border very near to Berlin. We won't follow it too closely, but there are lots of forests along it, and that will help us hide."

"Aha. And will provide fresh water, too."

"Yes, and we might even be able to fish, and get meat that way."

"Ah." Franz made a face. "As long as they are very fresh, I can maybe manage it."

"Ohhh, the rotten-fish soup."

"Yes." He shrugged. "I will try to eat it."

"I understand. I'll try to make sure it isn't too fishy-tasting."

"That is…appreciated."

***

Franz made it about the same distance as the day before; they kept going into the night and accomplished about eight miles, when Gabe had been planning on closer to twenty. But that plan had not taken into account Franz' physical condition, and Gabe realized he was going to have to do something to compensate.

So the next morning he pulled out a map and checked it, then ran through a few ciphered codes, and adjusted course.

This resulted in coming upon a small house in a tiny clearing in the woods off the fields, late that afternoon. On one side was a large pen where a dozen chickens scratched. Two sheep grazed in the small yard; a tiny barn stood behind the house. A goodly-sized garden was beside that.

"What?" Franz wondered, growing more alert as he recognized a house ahead. "What are we doing here?"

"Looking for help, and information," Gabe said. "This is a resistance member's house."

"Ah."

Gabe headed to the door and knocked, a slightly complex sound rather than a traditional *rap-rap*.

Moments later, the door opened.

"May I help you?" the housewife asked.

***

The front room was a combination sitting room/dining room/kitchen, with two rooms behind that — an office, and a bedroom/bathroom suite, though the plumbing was somewhat crude — and a lean-to off to the right. The furniture was fairly rustic, and looked handmade, but it was comfortable.

The housewife called her husband from the office, and Gabe gave the password, then introduced himself and Franz. She took one look at Franz and shooed him off to the dining table, sitting him down and going to the stove to fetch a bowl of stew from the pot simmering on the back.

Meanwhile, the husband and Gabe sat down in the nearby sitting area, so that the two resistance fighters could share information.

***

Half an hour later, Franz was blissfully consuming a huge bowl of hearty mutton stew replete with plenty of vegetables — potatoes, carrots, turnips, leeks, broad beans, mushrooms, squash, and red cabbage; lots of nutrients — with a thick slab of soft homemade brown bread beside it. Gabe watched with a benevolent smile as he turned to Konrad Hyjek, the Polish resistance contact in the area. His wife Iga, who worked with Konrad, was busy taking care of Franz, who soaked up the motherly attention.

"His real name is Levy; does he have papers that say something else?" Konrad wondered.

"Yes. Cristl. Frants Cristl."

"So you have a new friend?"

"I do, yes. He's been through hell, Konrad."

"I expect so, if he was in Majdanek and somehow survived."

"But he doesn't have much stamina."

"I wouldn't expect him to have much. So you probably need something to help speed things up if you're headed to Berlin with him."

"Yes, if you can come up with anything."

"As it happens, I have an extra hand cart, recently built. I made it myself, and I've refined the design. It's light and moves smoothly, but it's strong. I try to keep at least one on hand for refugees. If you can pull or push him, you're welcome to it."

"That might just work. He's not heavy. If the cart is light, we can throw him and both packs in it and go."

"It's not only light, I textured the wheels so they won't leave so obvious tracks. And it's been dry, so no mud to speak of."

"Then I think that's a yes, thank you."

"Good. I'll have Iga add a bag of fairly fresh food for you both. It'll be bread and dried meats — don't worry; I'll make sure she knows to keep it kosher, as well as the no-fish thing — and maybe some hard cheese. He can eat that instead of meat for some meals, and it'll pack some weight on him quicker. And maybe keep him full longer."

"That's a plan. Again, thank you."

"You have a way to go; you're going to need all of that," Konrad said, earnest. "If we can help you, we will."

"And it's greatly appreciated. What do you know of the relative movements of the armies? Has Berlin fallen yet? What does Hitler have planned?"

"Berlin has not fallen. However, Hitler is still in Berlin; no one is sure if he is bluffing or simply doesn't believe the Allies can reach there, or reach him there. It may be that that will be his downfall."

Both men drew deep breaths, then looked up to see both Iga and Franz watching and listening. Franz was still eating, however.

"Is he insane?" Franz wondered then. Gabe noted that the boy's manners were very good, and he swallowed and dabbed his mouth with a napkin before speaking.

"That is debated, and many in the resistance and the Allied contacts think he is, yes," Konrad noted. "Palsy has also been reported, and other symptoms of neurological disease; the Allied physicians are speculating possible Parkinson's palsy, though he tries to hide it in public appearances. There is also strong rumor that he is drug-addicted, and that this is affecting his thought processes. It may well be all of it. That is both good and bad, however. It means that he will likely waste what resources he has left, and quickly, but it also means he will not know when it is time to give up."

Franz screwed up his face in displeasure.

"No, it's not good, young Franz," Konrad responded to that expression. "And I have my doubts that you should continue to Berlin with Gabe, given your age and physical condition."

Franz' scowl grew deeper.

"So what have you heard is happening elsewhere?" Gabe asked, diverting attention from the very thing he had been considering.

"Mm. Let me think. We have not been sending out requests for information; we simply listen to the broadcasts already being sent and decipher them, so there is little danger of our being traced here. Oh, it is a good thing you got off the river when you did; there is a huge mess farther north, as the Red Army tries to push to the Baltic, and cut off the Nazi groups in the east…"

"But Janusz!" Franz cried. "He went on!"

"And if he keeps his head down, he might survive," Gabe pointed out. "He is not a fool. An antisemite, for certain, and not entirely trustworthy, but not a fool."

"Wait," Konrad interrupted. "Janusz Sasinowski? You traveled with him?"

"That's him, yes," Gabe confirmed.

Konrad shook his head.

"He's dead. That's already been reported. He was caught at Tczew — there are virtually no Poles left in the town; it's all German Nazis — and executed at once."

"How?"

"Someone saw him as he crossed under the Bridge, which is still intact, at least for now; he was apparently trying to steer a boat disguised as debris in the water. He was hauled out, identified, shot, and his body thrown back in the river."

Gabe glanced at Franz, who was extremely sober.

"We have to do better," was all the boy said.

"We will," Gabe reassured him before returning his attention to Konrad. "What else?"

"Mm, the Baltic offensive is being hard-fought. We're expecting a counter-offensive by the Nazi forces, most likely well north of here, from forces stationed to our west. We are in no danger here."

"Good. What else?"

"The American General Omar Bradley is running through France as fast as he can, headed for the German border; he is outstripping most of the German forces, but there is concern over his fuel supplies. Evidently a good bit of what he needs is being diverted to General Montgomery in the north, to judge by some of the reports I've gotten, and there's supposed to be a — pardon the pun — general dispute between Bradley and Montgomery."

"That's not good, either," Franz interjected. He was now stuffing a monumental amount of soft, fresh bread in his face, and Iga had produced a crock of sheep's-milk butter and a jar of honey to sweeten it. By this point, his face was both sticky and greasy from the honey and butter. Iga hid a grin, and fetched a damp cloth to put him to rights once he finished.

"No," Konrad sighed, "but it's the sort of thing that often happens in military situations between allies. Montgomery is British."

"Mmph," Franz grunted, unimpressed. He stuffed another huge hunk of buttered, honey-sticky bread into his mouth.

"So if the fuel holds out, Bradley might reach Berlin?" Gabe asked.

"I think that's a long shot, but possible. There are rumors Montgomery has something in mind for the Netherlands that might make for reaching Berlin faster, but if it happens, it won't occur for a few weeks yet. Something about a garden market, or the like." Konrad broke off to think. "Oh, and I'm sure you've heard the aircraft…"

"Yes, but not overhead."

"No. The Allied bombing runs are following a circuit to allow for maximum range," Konrad explained, as Iga got out a dish of poached pears and put several halves on Franz' plate, then cleaned his face of the honey around his shoveling the pears into his mouth. "Britain to western Russia, dumping bombs on Germany en route, refuel, Russia to Italy, drop bombs on North Italy, refuel in southern Italy, then Italy back to Britain, refuel, start it all over again. They're bombing hell out of Germany as well as the Nazi outposts in northern Italy. Many are making additional runs over Germany on their way back to Britain, if they can get the munitions in Italy."

"That explains that," Gabe decided. "I'd noted an almost continuous drone of aircraft to the south."

"Exactly."

"Anything else?"

"Not that I've heard. But if Bradley runs out of fuel during his attempt at what the Germans call a blitzkrieg, it's going to get messy quickly, and the whole Allied offensive will likely bog down."

"Mm."

"Yes." Konrad glanced meaningfully at Franz, who was focused on the poached pears. Gabe shook his head.

"I don't know," he murmured. "I'll need to think."

"We can't put you up in the house; not only is there no room, it's too risky. There are Nazi sympathizers in the village over that way." Konrad waved a hand westward. "But we have a good-sized underground bolt-hole a little way in the woods, and there are beds there. No one else is here right now."

"That will work. We can get some rest, maybe a hot breakfast if Iga doesn't mind, and I can work out what needs to be done."

"This is good. And no, I don't think Iga minds," Konrad said with a grin, watching his wife comb the boy's hair after giving him more bread. "If you'd like a hot bath, we can probably see to that, also."

"MUCH appreciated," Gabe agreed. "We haven't bathed since we left Warsaw. I hope we don't reek too badly."

"No, but I'm sure you'll like it. I'll see to it, then."

***

Eventually Gabe joined Franz — who was still eating — for a meal, as he continued to get as much information from Konrad as he could. Then Iga and Konrad prepared two hot baths — they had an indoor well pump next to the stove, plenty of firewood to heat water, and two tin tubs — and the travelers washed away the grime of travel in the little farmhouse's lean-to on the side.

Then Konrad took them back into the woods to the bolt-hole. It had been a hot summer day, even under the tree canopy, but the hidden underground room was deliciously cool. He extracted an armload of bed linens from a covered 'safe' or armoire in the corner and handed them to Gabe and Franz.

"It's just camp cots, I'm afraid, but I've been told they're far more comfortable than sleeping on the ground," he told them. "If you need them, there are blankets on the bottom shelf in the safe; since it's underground, sometimes it gets cool down here, even in summer. Gabe, I've shown you how to make sure the area is clear before emerging, so when you're ready in the morning, slip on in through the lean-to and we'll feed you a hot breakfast, then send you on your way."

"All right. Thank you so much, Konrad. And Iga, too."

"You're very welcome, my new friend."

Half an hour later, the bolt-hole was silent, and Franz and Gabe were sound asleep.

***

The next morning Franz woke tired and headachy. He had gotten cold during the night and had risen and fetched a blanket, but it hadn't helped a lot. He got dressed, shrugged into his pack, and followed Gabe out of the bolt-hole — putting the used linens into the basket by the door for Iga to wash later — and through the quiet forest to the little farmhouse. In the distance to the south, even at that hour, the drone of aircraft sounded.

Franz sat down at the table with Gabe and Konrad, while Iga cooked and brought the food to the table. There were scrambled eggs, thick slabs of sourdough bread slathered with butter and melted oscypek cheese, tart raspberry preserves, milk, and coffee. Given his emaciated condition, Iga prepared a mug for Franz that was half coffee, half milk, with a generous spoonful of sugar. The hot drink felt good on Franz' suddenly-scratchy throat. He ate well, though not with the previous night's enthusiasm.

"Not much for mornings?" Konrad asked him, smiling. Franz shrugged.

"Never really had a choice," the youth murmured.

"Are you feeling all right, son?" Gabe wondered. "This isn't like you."

"Felt better," Franz admitted. "Nose is stuffy. Head hurts."

The three adults glanced at each other in sudden concern. Iga promptly went to the boy and laid her hand against his cheek, then his forehead, and finally the back of his neck.

"He's warm," she observed. "I think he's feverish."

"That's not good," Gabe said. "There is no way he can possibly travel like that."

"I can travel," Franz protested. "I'll be fine."

"We'll see," Gabe said.

***

By the time they finished breakfast an hour later, however, Franz was worse. He sneezed violently three times and started to sniffle, then to cough. He sighed as if in pain, then slumped in on himself in the chair, seeming to doze.

"And he feels hotter now," Iga noted, lightly touching his forehead with her palm. "I think his fever is going up."

"There is an influenza coming out of the east," Konrad said. "Some think the Soviets brought it with them."

"Don't tell me it will be another Spanish flu pandemic," Gabe said darkly.

"No, no; not that many seem susceptible to this one," Konrad said, holding up a staying hand to settle the other man. "I know that Iga and I have already been exposed earlier this summer, and did not get sick. It is likely his run-down condition; the poor boy is nearly skin and bones. I'm sure he has little resistance."

"Konrad is right," Iga said. "This is exactly how Alfrid started a month and a half back. But he was only sick a few days; perhaps Franz will throw it off as well."

"Perhaps," Konrad said. "We can hope, for his sake. Gabe, what are you going to do?"

"I think we will stay here a few days," Gabe decided. "I'm loath to leave the boy after all we've been through together. I'd like to see him as far as Berlin at least, if I can."

"You won't make very good time right now anyway, between the Soviet offensive and the bombing raids," Konrad pointed out. "You may as well stay here and see how Franz does. We may need the extra hands to tend him, in any case."

"Does he need to stay in the bolt-hole?"

"No," Iga said. "Konrad has a back office for the farm; we can make up a cot for the boy in there opposite the desk, and I can tend him, and Konrad can still work at his desk. There is a doctor in the village who is, if not fully supportive to the resistance, then at least unlikely to turn us in; we have used him before, and he is discreet. And he need not know what we know about Franz."

"If anyone asks, he is Iga's nephew, recently orphaned, and traveling to meet his father's family who are fishers in Koszalin when he took ill. His travel companions dropped him off with us, then moved on," Konrad said. "There is enough resemblance between Iga and Franz that it will pass for the truth. It will be fine, even if he must stay here for an extended time."

"All right. I'll stay in the bolt-hole at night, or when it's not safe to be out and about," Gabe said, "and if he's not better in a week's time, I'll reconsider what to do."

"That will work," Konrad said, as Iga nodded.

***

But in a week's time, Franz was not better; he was worse.

"He's going into pneumonia," the village doctor said after he examined the unconscious boy. "His system simply doesn't have the reserves to fight this properly."

"Are we at risk?" Konrad wondered.

"No, no more than you were from your friend earlier in the summer," came the reply. "You are strong and healthy; he is neither. You say he was in hiding for a long time?"

"He was, yes," Iga said, glib with the half-truth. "My sister and her husband were part of the resistance. We tried to tell them to, ah, beware of their choices. It was not easy on their family at all, as you can see from his condition. The boy knows little, though; he's younger than he appears."

"Oh? I took him for late teens. How old is he?"

"Fourteen," Konrad answered.

"Really? That clinches it, then," the doctor said. "I had thought he might be an escapee from one of the work camps — in which case, I'd be obliged to report the matter. But he would never have survived a work camp at that young age."

"No, no," Iga said, distressed — though unknown to the doctor, it was at how close his guess was to the truth. "No, he is my sister's son. Mina and Wictor died in the Soviet offensive, not even by the Nazis' hand." She shook her head. "It is irony."

"It is," the physician agreed. "I can give him a shot of penicillin, and we will see how he does. Do you have garlic?"

"I do, quite a lot; we had harvested a small herb plot already this season and there are half a dozen braids drying in the lean-to, with two more and a piece, in my pantry." Iga beamed. "I make sure there is not only enough for seasoning food, but for any small medical matters that may crop up. What with the shortages…"

"Yes, yes, of course; I see, and that is wise. Good. Very good. Here is what I want you to do. Make a garlic soup and feed it to him; make sure to mash the garlic fine so that it is part of the broth. If you have onions, leeks or shallots, throw some of those in, too. It is folk medicine, but it is GOOD folk medicine. It will help the penicillin, and it will encourage the lungs to clear. When he is able to sit up a bit and eat, chicken soup will help clear his respiratory system, as well." He stood. "Apply cool compresses if his fever rises too high; I'll be back in a few days." He looked around. "Are we alone?"

"We are," Konrad said, conveniently omitting Gabe's presence hiding in the adjacent pantry. "Just you, me, Iga, and Franz."

"Good. I will try to get the boy as much penicillin as I can, though I will have to, ah, play games with the records, if you follow me; the Nazis in the area seem to think my medications are only for them and their forces, though that is NOT what my oath said. But I think he will need more before he gets better. The crisis should come sometime in the next few days, likely at night. And he has a long convalescence ahead of him, even if we can beat this influenza."

"How long?" Iga wondered, worried. She had caught the reference to a crisis in the boy's illness.

"Months," the doctor responded. He dug in his bag and extracted an ampoule and a hypodermic syringe with needle, commencing to load a dose into the syringe. "He does not need to be traveling in any event. The Soviets are moving west from Warsaw, advancing on Berlin in the south, and there is an active fight for the Baltic coastline in the north. You said the boy's father's family were fishers on the Baltic, yes?"

"Yes."

"Then he needs to stay here. He will be far too weak to travel in those conditions for some time. It simply is not safe. It would not be safe for your husband, here, and he is healthy." The doctor shook his head, and gestured Konrad to help him ease the boy's trousers waistband down, so he could pump the penicillin into Franz' hip. Iga moved to the other side of the bed and helped Konrad hold an unconscious Franz on his side while the doctor administered the antibiotic. Franz never so much as flinched. "There. No, given that location, there is no guarantee his paternal family will survive, either. I think it would be much better for the boy to stay here while matters…stabilize, one way or the other." He put away the hypodermic and ampoule. "I know you are kind to travelers and don't ask questions, but this boy is of your blood. My strong advice is: Keep the boy here for now. Even after he is well. No matter what happens, he will at least have family that way."

Konrad followed the physician out, sending him home with several dozen eggs, which were the barter price of Franz' care.

***

"Well, that wasn't what I was hoping to hear," Gabe said over the dinner table as Iga made a soup with an entire head of peeled garlic and a whole leek, carefully washed of grit, and even throwing a small chopped onion into the mix. "It sounds like the boy is going to have a hard go of it, even without the need to travel."

"It does," Konrad agreed, "and it sounds as if you both need to stay here for some few months. You have been called to Berlin to meet other resistance members and consult, yes, but there is no reason to get yourself killed, my friend, by walking into the middle of a battle like this. Let us be realistic — neither the Soviets nor the Nazis are friends of the real Polish government, which you represent. You help no one by getting yourself killed." He shrugged. "We have the room, we have the food, and Iga is an excellent cook…AND she is gifted with herbal treatments, even for serious ailments like young Franz."

"It will take all my skill this time," Iga murmured; both men heard.

"You don't think he's going to die, do you?" Gabe wondered, apprehensive.

"It is a possibility," she admitted. "He is very sick. But I will do all I can."

"As will I," Konrad added. "He deserves that much. Majdanek is in the middle of the villages surrounding Lublin, and no one there has done anything. Our people, and they did nothing to help."

"I know," Gabe sighed. "And that syn suki, Janusz, was as bad as any of them." (*son of a bitch*)

"I feel sorry for him now," Konrad agreed. "He is likely in a very bad place. But you are not, and we will care for you as well as your young friend. Please, let us."

"Yes. You are welcome to stay," Iga added. "If you go, you are likely to die. And that does no one any good, but especially not Franz. If I understood correctly, he lost everyone in his family in the camp. He does not need to lose a trusted friend."

"No, you are right; that is all true. And thank you for the offer." Gabe sighed. "Let me consider a while. I should like to see Franz turn the corner and start getting well before I left, in any case." He paused, then sniffed. "That smells good, Iga."

"I love the smell of cooked garlic," Iga responded with a smile. "And I am making a big pot of this. A cup for each of us will do us no harm."

***

The crisis came that night. Franz' fever began to spike very high; he tossed restlessly, moaning in pain, and the three took turns sponging him down to keep his fever under enough control that it would kill the pathogens yet not kill HIM. Whenever he showed even a semblance of wakefulness, Iga spoon-fed him the garlic broth. If needful, she shook him gently to rouse him in order to feed him.

By morning his fever had dropped, and he fell into a restful sleep.

***

It was over a week before Franz was awake and coherent, but by then, he had had another shot of penicillin from the doctor, and two whole pots of garlic broth from Iga. She used some of the garlic broth to make a delicious chicken soup with leeks and carrots and fed that to him, as well. And those, combined, were showing their mettle — Iga had a hard time keeping handkerchiefs washed for the boy, and had had to put a spittoon by the bedside for the crud he hacked from his lungs. Each morning, Konrad took it out to the edge of the woods and emptied it into the refuse pit, washing it out with a bucketful of water from the well before emptying that into the refuse pit also.

And upon discovering from ciphered radio transmissions that the Soviets were already between them and Berlin, Gabe decided to stay put until travel was safer.

***

Once he was strong enough to sit up — Iga provided plenty of pillows to assist — Franz began to EAT. He was pale, even thinner than he had been, and very weak.

"But the food is VERY good," he murmured to Gabe, who sat beside his bed often. "Iga knows how to cook. And she has told me to call her 'Aunt.' She is supposed to be my mother's sister?"

"Yes, that's what the doctor believes," Gabe said, "and he doesn't know I'm here, either. So yes, she is Aunt Iga and he is Uncle Konrad."

"All right. You have been an operative for long?"

"Since autumn of 1939."

"And it is nearly autumn of 1944 now."

"Yes."

"So five years."

"Yes."

"Can you teach me?"

"Teach you what?"

"How to be an operative."

"Why? The war is nearly over."

"There are always wars. I want to know how, in case I am needed."

Konrad, who had been listening from the door, pushed off the doorframe and unfolded his arms.

"I think Uncle Gabe and I can manage that, son," he said in a kindly fashion. "Let's find out what you know already, and we'll go from there."

***

It was more than a month before Franz was back on his feet and gaining significant strength, but this also came with a couple of benefits: He gained weight on Iga's cooking, he learned a great deal about spying and slinking about from talking to Gabe and Konrad and practicing the exercises they set for him, and the very light chores he was assigned around the small farm to help strengthen him enabled him to get out of bed for longer and longer times.

More, Iga sat down and taught the boy; he had not been able to go to school since entering Majdanek, and he was literate and very intelligent but lacking schooling on many subjects. Under her tutelage, he soon reached high-school-equivalent levels in what subjects she felt qualified to teach, though she could not teach him everything. Still, she managed to obtain books for him to read, and he devoured them, discovering he loved to read and learn. While he was in bed, he was reading unless he was asleep. Once he was back on his feet, if he was not working or sleeping, he usually could be found reading.

Most of it was nonfiction, but she also tried to introduce him to literature, and that was when he discovered a genre he would love for the rest of his life: science fiction. He eagerly read Verne, Wells, Doyle, Burroughs, London, Smith, and any others he could get his hands on.

It was fortunate, however, that Konrad and Iga had their own sources of food, and had stockpiled what they had; the destruction of crops, both deliberate in the Nazi retreat and accidental from battle, resulted in famine conditions to varying degrees through much of Europe. Grains and meats in particular were in short supply.

Elsewhere, the war was not going that well for the Allies. On the Eastern Front, the battle to reach Berlin was a slaughter for both the Nazis and the Soviets; despite the good start in eastern Poland and the Ukraine, the Soviets had yet to reach the city even by the end of the year. On the Western Front, Operation Market Garden in the Netherlands, led by British General Montgomery, was such a failure that the United Kingdom's First Airborne Division would never recover from their losses. The American General Bradley's forces had outrun their supply chain, and the Nazis looked to be repositioning to take advantage of the fact.

By the time winter arrived, Budapest was under siege, and the Battle of the Bulge had begun. There were horrifying rumors of massive raping of the women in cities the Red Army had conquered, and Iga no longer went out of the house; Konrad took care of any errands in the village, including visits to the little library for Franz.

As winter gave way to spring and Franz' 15th birthday approached, the tides of battle finally began to turn.

At Franz' suggestion, Gabe and Konrad created a hidden underground safe room for Iga, should any Soviet soldiers show up in the area. He helped where he could, and the work strengthened him.

After that, they began giving regular small chores to Franz, allowing him to work around the house and grow stronger. As he did, they gave him more and harder work, and he continued to grow stronger. When he began to do chores in the barn, then outside, he all but celebrated.

It would be late spring, and Franz would finally start filling out into the muscular body of a young man and no boy, before they could even think of leaving the little farm.

***

Chapter 7 — Go West, Young Man?

The Ardennes Offensive, called by some the Battle of the Bulge for its general appearance on strategic maps, fell apart as Patton and Montgomery struck the Nazi forces in a pincer move from north and south simultaneously. Casualties were high on both sides, but hurt the Nazis worse, as they were NOT a coalition of nations and lost forces they could ill afford to lose. They fell back toward the Westwall, called by the Allies the Siegfried Line, and tried to regroup; the Luftwaffe was broken by the defeat, and they had lost nearly a quarter of their fighting force.

The British Royal Air Force and the American Army Air Corps firebombed Dresden into ruins.

Seeing the Western offensive now moving inexorably toward Berlin, the Red Army initiated the Vistula-Oder Offensive, pushing hard through Poland toward Germany, driving the Nazis from the Polish cities as they went. In early February, they reached the Oder River, the border between Poland and Germany, scant tens of kilometers from Berlin. Only the fierce fighting by Germans in the border regions prevented the Red Army from invading Berlin itself.

But in April 1945, the press into Berlin resumed.

In the south, Budapest finally fell to the siege laid by Soviet and Romanian forces…though the reports of rape coming from that city were even more horrifying than before.

Unfortunately, the little farmstead hidden in the forest was not beyond these things.

***

Iga was cooking dinner for the men when unfamiliar hands caught at her waist and whirled her around.

A leering soldier in Soviet uniform stood there.

"Zdes' sejchas! Razve ty ne simpatichnyj!" he said. "Ja dumaju, chto u menja budet ty na uzhin!" (*Here now! Aren't you a pretty one! I think I'll have you for dinner!*)

"No, no, no! No, please!" Iga cried, as he grabbed her blouse and ripped. "Konrad! KONRAD! ANYBODY! HELP ME!"

Just then she realized she still had a cast-iron frypan full of hot grease in one hand. A quick wrist flip, and the hot grease doused one sleeve of the man's uniform, sticking and burning the skin beneath; it splattered across the side of his neck and face as well, and he yelled as the droplets of scalding fat created small but severe burns, blistering almost instantly. The follow-through of the frying pan narrowly missed his head as he ducked, glancing off the side of his head. He staggered, but did not release her.

Angry and in pain, he shoved her hard to one side, and she reflexively let go the hot pan as she fell to the wooden floor. He dove on top of her and grabbed for her head, trying to force a kiss on the struggling woman as his knees sought to push her legs apart.

Iga screamed.

***

Franz was just inside the forest from the farmhouse clearing, though out of sight behind a copse of trees. On the far side of it, there was a tree downed in the last storm, and he was using a hand saw and axe to lop off branches and cut it into lengths, preparing it to be chopped into firewood. Gabe and Konrad had been in the bolt-hole earlier, repairing it from a winter spent largely empty save for Gabe, who still slept there at night. When they finished, they headed out, the lad knew not where.

Suddenly Franz heard 'Aunt' Iga scream, then call for help. This was followed by a roar of pain — coming from a strange male voice. That was succeeded by an even louder, desperate scream from Iga.

All from inside the house.

He dropped the saw, caught up the axe, and sprinted for the door to the lean-to.

***

By the time he entered the house, however, he was using stealth. He crept swiftly but soundlessly through the lean-to and into the main room of the house, which also contained the cookstove and dining table.

There, on the floor, Iga fought off a dirty man in a Soviet uniform, as he sought to rip away her clothes and rape her. Her blouse was already torn, exposing part of her brassiere.

Briefly he flashed back to the image of his mother's naked dead body lying on the ground, her empty eyes staring at the sky, as several of the Nazi guards made crude remarks about what they would do to the body, given the chance.

Rage filled him. He switched the axe into his left hand. In two steps he was upon them.

***

A powerful backhanded swing with the back of the axe head knocked the man off Iga; he rolled into the middle of the room, ending up on his back, as Iga scuttled away on hands and knees as fast as she could, crouching in the nearest corner. He cursed, then looked up and saw Franz.

"Ty sukin syn!" he snarled, reaching for his pistol. (*You son of a bitch!*)

He never had a chance to draw it from its holster.

An enraged Franz, standing over him, raised the axe over his head in both hands and drove it down into the man's chest so hard the entire blade buried itself in his body. Blood splattered everywhere from the violence of the fatal wound.

The man tried to scream, but the damage to his lungs was too great; blood bubbled around the axe blade with each attempt he made. His arms thrashed frantically, but his legs remained still.

Within scant moments his terror-filled eyes clouded and glazed.

"Oh, dear God! Thank you, my dear, dear boy!" Iga said through tears; she now huddled on the floor against the wall in the corner. "He…he tried…"

Franz knelt beside his would-be aunt, putting an arm around her. "Shh, hush, Aunt Iga. You're safe now. He's dead. He'll never hurt anyone again."

Just then, Gabe and Konrad came in; they had been scouting the area toward the Notec River to determine how clear the route was to Berlin. They stopped cold at the sight of the dead man surrounded by his own gore, a hand axe buried in his chest, and Iga sitting on the floor, her clothes torn, being comforted by young Franz, who was spattered with blood.

"Son of a bitch," Gabe expostulated.

"That's what HE called me," Franz snarled, gesturing at the body.

"No. Never you, son," Gabe replied. "Never you."

***

Gabe cautiously examined the body, careful to touch little, while Konrad picked up Iga and carried her to their bedroom to settle her and change her clothes to undamaged ones. Franz came to stand over Gabe where he crouched. The bloody nametag on the body's shoulder read Кузнецов. *Kuznetsov,* Franz read without thinking, having picked up a certain amount of cross-language literacy in a place where prisoners were from all over Europe.

"I think we've managed to strengthen you rather well, son," Gabe said, his tone evincing mild surprise. "Near as I can tell, the blade is clear through the sternum, the heart, and well into the backbone. He wasn't going anywhere, and he didn't live long."

"No."

"You did well, Franz," Gabe offered, standing.

"Thank you, Uncle Gabe." Franz was still grim of face. "He was, was on top of Aunt Iga, trying to, to rip off her skirt and blouse, and…"

"And you stopped him. That's good. Is she all right?"

"Yes. I got here in time to stop it."

"Excellent. Are you all right?"

"I think so."

"Have you ever had to kill someone before?"

"No. Wanted to, many times, but was never in a position to do it."

"Are you going to have trouble later?"

"I don't know. Why should I? He was an evil man." He broke off, then added in a near-growl, "He reminded me of one of the concentration camp guards."

"Ah. All right. Get your things packed, and hurry. We'll need to leave before sundown. They'll be looking for this one — judging by the items in his pockets and the division he's from, he's a deserter, and probably a thief into the bargain — and we don't want to be here when they find him. Especially in this condition."

"Oh!" Franz' eyes grew wide. "What about Aunt Iga and Uncle Konrad?"

"We'll be leaving, too," Konrad said, coming to the bedroom door. "We hate to; this has been a good home. But we've expected to have to do this at any point during the war, so we're ready. I've already sent a special, ciphered signal to my network that lets them know we need a fast extraction, and they'll be here under cover of darkness to clear out the farmhouse of anything we haven't taken, including the food, herbals, and animals. For now, Iga and I will move into the bolt-hole and wait for our network. She's packing our clothes now; it won't take long. I'll get my banker's box with the paperwork, grab some of the foodstuffs, and we can go; we'll make sure to fill your packs, too." He came across to the pair, and took Franz' hand in both his own. "THANK you, son."

"You, um, you're welcome," Franz tried. "I wasn't going to let the bastard hurt her."

"She says you knocked him off her and halfway across the room with one blow, then planted the axe in him to the handle with the second blow."

"That's…that sounds about right."

"He sure planted the axe blade, all right. Go, Franz," Gabe said, headed for the lean-to door. "Go change and wash the blood off — you've got some splatter on your shirt, face and hair — and pack now. I'll fetch my things from the bolt-hole. We need to move fast."

"Give me the bloodstained clothes," Konrad said. "I'll get rid of them."

***

In less than an hour's time, the little farmhouse was deserted of all life save the flies swarming the carcass.

Franz never saw Iga and Konrad again.

***

By sundown, the pair had struck the Nortec River and headed downstream, careful to stay out of sight and leave as few traces as possible. Gabe surreptitiously watched Franz, strong and confident, as he shouldered his pack — laden with food and water — with no difficulty and kept up with the older man.

This will go much better now, Gabe thought. *I wouldn't have given a grosz for him surviving the pneumonia, and even less that he'd be this strong in six months. But youth, good food, fresh air, loving nursing from all of us, a willing spirit, and hard work do wonders.*

By dawn, they were eighteen miles downriver.

***

Franz turned 15 while he and Gabe were en route to Berlin. That same day, Gabe stopped at a hidden enclave with some resistance fighters; they gave the pair word that Berlin had fallen and Hitler was dead.

Franz thought it was the best birthday present he'd ever gotten.

***

145

They slipped into Berlin in early June. Much of the city was in ruins; there was looting and theft on all sides. The trick was to stay out of sight of the looters, the few remaining Nazi forces, and the Red Army…which meant, Franz came to realize, almost everyone they saw.

A wily Gabe, however, knew what he was doing: he headed straight for the rendezvous point. Well, as straight as a city in that condition would allow, at least. Franz simply followed, using all the stealth Gabe and Konrad had taught him in the last few months to follow his companion. It still took the better part of an afternoon to find the location, given conditions. Finding a fellow operative was even harder.

Finally they arrived at the spot as the light was fading from the sky; flickering light from all the building fires provided what little light there was. A man was picking through the rubble of a collapsed building nearby, and as they walked past, Gabe murmured, "Die gedanken sind frei." (*Thoughts are free.*)

"Aber wir sind nicht…noch," came the quiet countersign, and Gabe chuckled at the addendum. (*But we are not…yet.*)

"And the boy?" the operative asked.

"Is one of us. I'll explain later."

"Follow me, then. Only look like you're not following me."

"Right."

They turned and headed into the night, away from the city's center.

***

As they went, they passed a small group of Red Army soldiers outside the remains of a pub, busy getting drunk on the bottles of liquor from the relatively undamaged storeroom beneath. He overheard the conversation, and suddenly realized what they were discussing. He perked up and paid attention without looking like he was eavesdropping, as they casually wandered past.

"V konce koncov! U nas, nakonec, est' soüzniki, chtobj mj mogli delat' to, chto zdes' nuzhno!" (*At last! We finally have the Allies off our asses so we can do what is needed here!*)

"CHto? Vj imeete v vidu sdelat' ego chast'ü CCCP?" (*What? You mean make it part of the USSR?*)

"Da, konechno! Oni uzhe pochti dali ego nam." (*Yes, of course! They have all but given it to us already.*)

Franz listened closely, thankful he had seen fit to pick up a fair bit of Russian from the Soviet prisoners in Majdanek, but the rest of the conversation quickly degenerated into bawdy, drunken jokes and cursing. *It seems it's come in useful for something besides telling them to go the hell away,* he thought. *I need to tell Gabe once we're out of earshot.*

***

In the end, it seemed it didn't matter; the Allies HAD all but given the conquered territories to the Soviets. And the word of a fifteen-year-old kid didn't count for much when the diplomats had said their say, according to the resistance operatives. Hell, their contact noted, the word of fully adult operatives didn't count for much.

But the Polish and non-Nazi German resistance — some of whom were currently working together — wanted that same fifteen-year-old kid, especially after Gabe was done explaining a few things. Then the leader had some questions for them.

"Do either of you know anything about a Red Army deserter who was found dead in an abandoned farmhouse near Bydgoszcz a couple of weeks back?" the ring leader asked the pair…who promptly donned innocent expressions. "Man by the name of Kuznetsov?"

"No idea whatsoever," Gabe noted. Franz sensibly said nothing.

"Aha," the leader, Egon Klein by name, said knowingly, a smirk on his face. "I won't ask which. Judging by the muscles on the boy's arms, I don't need to. Good job; he was a bastard, by all accounts."

The three snorted, then laughed.

***

"No, that's fine," Klein agreed later, after a long discussion of how to ease them into the work. "Things are still very dangerous right now and there is little we can do as yet. I know the Polish Home Army wants the rightful government back in place on Polish soil, and the German resistance is trying to figure out HOW to put a rightful government in place, let alone who they can trust in the positions after…everything. But it's still pretty damn unstable as yet. Be damn careful, but go ahead and take Franz to Leipzig and see if there's any of his family left, and if his home survived. But," he added, growing solemn, "don't be surprised if there aren't any family members left, at least not there; the Nazis cleaned Leipzig out of Jews pretty thoroughly. And if the family home survived the bombing — big if — it might belong to someone else now." He shook his head. "We can try to sort that out eventually, if we get half a chance." He cocked his head. "Come back when you've checked it out, if you like, young Levy; we can find a place to use you in our organization."

"Thank you, sir," Franz said, shaking Klein's hand. "Depending on what I find, I may do just that."

The next day, still on foot but with fresh supplies, Franz and Gabe set out for Leipzig.

***

But large tracts of Leipzig were destroyed; unlike Dresden, the bombing in Leipzig had been conventional explosives, but the bombing runs had still produced firestorms in parts of the city. The destruction was nowhere near the scale of Dresden to the southeast, yet the damage was still severe.

Worse, the Jewish ghetto where Franz had lived as a child was completely burned out. No one in the area had the least idea if any of the Jews from that neighborhood even survived, though they knew that most had been shipped to Auschwitz; frighteningly few cared.

"And that bodes ill," Gabe noted. "All of it."

"Yes," Franz sighed. "I guess I really am alone."

"No, you're not."

"What do you mean? My whole family is dead."

"I mean I'm here. And I'm 'Uncle' Gabe, right?"

"Well, yes…"

"All right, then. Let's go back to Berlin and see what we can do to help Poland and Germany set up legitimate governments, shall we?"

Franz grinned, then sobered. "Thanks, Gabe."

"Thanks who?"

"Um. Thanks, Uncle Gabe."

"Good. I'm sorry about your childhood home, though."

"Me, too." Franz shrugged, a fatalistic response learned in Majdanek. "Let's go."

***

The Soviet occupation never left eastern Germany, Poland, Czechoslovakia, Ukraine, or any of the countries to the east that they had 'freed' during the war. In September of 1945, Gabe — and Franz — became operatives working for the legitimate government of several of these countries, alongside several other nations' intelligence networks, including the United

States and Great Britain, all cooperating reasonably well under the circumstances. When they were not actively on missions, Franz lived in a small apartment with 'Uncle' Gabe in Hamburg; it was not fancy, so it attracted no attention, and the presence of what appeared to be a widowed father with his son living in it aided their cover. Since their work always used false identities and often disguises, it was fairly safe; they only needed to ensure no one followed them home after a mission. By this time, and thanks to training given to Franz both by Gabe and their network, they were both adept at that.

Hamburg was being rebuilt rapidly after the carpet bombing by the Allies, and a significant Jewish enclave was forming there, though a large percentage in that enclave were migrants, emigrating from Soviet-held Eastern Europe on their way to either America or Palestine. Still, by choosing a flat on the edge of the Jewish sector, Gabe felt it gave Franz an opportunity to attend synagogue and mingle with people of the same religious beliefs. It also made it easier to shop kosher for their food; the older man had taken the time to learn what that constituted and pick up some classic Yiddish recipes, and found he enjoyed many of the traditional dishes of that cuisine.

The fact that, in that area, Franz went by Gabe's surname of Elhert helped their cover also, while not causing the local Jewish community to blink; they simply considered that Franz' widowed mother had likely married Gabe by way of hiding their Jewishness from the Nazis, and been successful at it. The fact that Gabe obviously cared for the boy was a point in his favor, as far as they were concerned.

Due to his youth — now that he had proper weight on him, he appeared even younger than he was, partly due to his time in Majdanek slowing his development, he suspected — Franz turned out to be especially good at the operative work;

none of the targets expected him to be any sort of intelligence operative. He spent the next several years as a 'street urchin' wandering the cities of Europe, usually acting as a courier, though sometimes he was sent to observe and obtain information on Soviet activities. Unfortunately, during this time, usually he literally was living as a street urchin; only when he was home in Hamburg did he have easy food, a bed, and clean clothes. But there were certain things he had grown used to in Majdanek, and if he could help others escape the Eastern Bloc countries, or work against those same regimes, he considered it worthwhile. Given the way they were ejecting and killing Jews and other 'undesirables,' they were, in his experienced estimation, no better than the Nazis. And he was in a position to know about THAT.

***

As consecutive birthdays passed for Franz and he continued to prove himself an apt agent, the various intelligence organizations began using him more and more on his own, rather than with Gabe, or with Gabe and other operatives. In order to facilitate this, he was taught to drive, and issued driver's licenses under several assumed names — and ages — that he used in his work. From time to time they made him sit out, however, in favor of intensive periods of schooling; he was therefore nearing the formal completion of his high school education, as the Americans called it.

He was also nearing his 18th birthday. Not that this made a great deal of difference; most European countries had an age of majority of either 20 or 21, so he was still considered a juvenile. Occasionally, however, Gabe or one of the Americans would hand him a beer without saying anything. He would grin and accept it without protest or comment, enjoying it with enthusiasm. As he grew closer and closer to 18, Gabe began offering him shots of hard liquor now and then, enabling him to learn what he liked and to develop a tolerance to it, partly for the work, partly for the sake of enjoyment. They never got drunk, and never drank in public socially, at least when off-duty; that was anathema to staying alive when one was doing intelligence work.

Noises started coming through various networks that something important was happening in the Mideast, and this resulted in a fresh influx of Jewish refugees.

***

"If they do create a modern Jewish state like all the rumors are saying, Franz, do you want to go?" Gabe asked one night when they were both home from missions.

"I don't know; I hadn't really thought about it," Franz replied. "I'm doing good work here, and I have 'family' here." He smiled at the older man. "I don't want to leave you."

"Well, that's the thing. I'd been thinking I might go with you. I mean, I know I'm not Jewish, but I can formally adopt you and then I should be able to go as your guardian…as long as we do it before you're officially of age."

"Oh! You'd do that?" Franz said, trying to hide the emotions the offer had created. "For me?"

"Of course. After the war was done with things, I don't really have any other family, either," Gabe pointed out. "And you thought your father was aiming for there as a final destination, you told me once. Want me to look into it?"

"I…think that might be good, yes."

"Okay, I'll have a look at it this next week. Or, well, when I get back from the next mission; I think I have to head out day after tomorrow, but I'll be back soon."

"I have a courier job, too."

"Where are you going?"

"Brussels, I think. Or someplace in that general area. You?"

"Headed east again."

"That's getting more and more dangerous, Uncle Gabe."

"I know. But I'm going to be ferrying out some more refugees, important ones this time. A scientist and his wife."

"Oh! That's even more dangerous."

"I know. But important."

"Just be careful. I have…a bad feeling about it." Franz frowned; he was starting to develop a kind of sense when a mission was about to go wrong, and the other members of his network were sitting up and taking notice.

"You know I'm always as careful as I know how to be," Gabe said, sober. "Especially if you say you have a bad feeling. I take it seriously, son, I really do. I have to admit, it's less worrisome now you're old enough to get around on your own. I don't have to worry what's going to happen to you if something happens to me."

"Aw."

Male hugs were exchanged, then Gabe rose and went into the kitchen. "Want a beer?"

***

Franz had turned eighteen during his courier mission, and was on the way back to Hamburg from Brussels when three things happened.

First, David Ben-Gurion announced from Tel Aviv that the modern state of Israel now existed.

Second, Syria, Egypt, Iraq, Trans-Jordan, and Lebanon attacked the new state of Israel virtually immediately.

Third, Franz got word that Gabe had been attacked inside the Ukraine, purportedly by an antisemitic gang, before he could get the scientist and his wife out of the country. Another agent, already in the Ukraine, had been dispatched to complete the job, and yet another was in the process of trying to spirit Gabe back to Germany, but would need help due to Gabe's injuries.

Franz immediately sent word to his network that he was diverting to the city of Lviv, Gabe's last known location in the Ukraine, to assist in rescue.

***

With help from Klein, who fed him information through classified means, Franz finally reached Lviv; it took him more than a week, thanks to the hornet's nest that the intelligence community had become in the region after the incident.

He found Gabe being tended by Inna Maslak, a Ukrainian operative working with their network. As he slipped into the passcoded flat — really a bolt-hole for intelligence agents — she met him just inside the door.

"Sobaki guavkayotʲ," he said. *(The dogs are barking.)*

"Dozvolʲtye myeni distati povodok," she offered the countersign. "You are Franz? His nephew?" (*Let me fetch the leash.*)

"Yes. What happened?"

"We are not sure," Maslak said, leading him toward a back hallway. "We think he was stabbed with…with something contaminated. Possibly viral, possibly radioactive…maybe both. The wound itself will not heal despite our best efforts, and… there are…other…symptoms."

Franz winced.

"How is he?"

"Not good," Maslak sighed. "He has been asking for you, however."

"Well, I'm here now. Let's get him home and get him well."

"I…I do not think…"

"Franz? Son, is that you?" came a weak, hoarse voice from a bedroom toward the back of the hall. "Are you here?"

"I'm here, Uncle Gabe," Franz said, stepping into the room...

...And stopping dead in horror.

***

If Franz hadn't known it was Gabryjel Elhert lying in the bed before him, he would not have recognized him. The man's face and hands were swollen, the hands lightly blistered and beginning to turn black at the fingertips. His lips were blue and likewise blistered, and he gasped and coughed and struggled for breath. The eyes were devoid of recognition, and as they roved the room, Franz realized that the man who had cared for him for years was blind.

"What the hell?!" Franz breathed. "Miss Maslak, what's wrong with him?"

"I'm dying, son," Gabe replied before Maslak could, his speech broken by pants, gasps, and coughs. "They...they got to...me. Not sure if...it's radiation or a...nasty virus, but according to...to the local network's physician, the symptoms indicate...maybe both. There's not a lot...anyone can do...except try to keep me com...comfortable until...the end."

"He's not contagious," Maslak murmured. "Whatever was on that knife was powerful, and it was targeted."

"It was...likely...engineered," Gabe explained, panting. "The radioisotope...would have to be...artificially produced...to be this hot. Probably powdered, for blood dispersal...through the...the body. Don't know about...about the biological part."

"I do; that was my specialty before the schools shut down during the offensive. It's why they sent me to help care for him. It was probably a biological weapon of some sort," Maslak added. "Likely intended for exactly this use — targeted introduction to a specific person, and unable to spread past that person. There are rumors in the intel community about Soviet developments like this. It probably was NOT radioactive, despite the symptoms; it would be too hot for the assassin to handle without killing himself, as well."

"I…I see."

"I'm so sorry, son. I wanted to take you…and go to Israel…together. You'll have to do it…without me…now. Promise me."

Franz moved to the bedside and knelt beside it, taking the puffy hand, trying not to wince as part of the skin sloughed away, exposing raw, oozing flesh.

"Promise you what, Uncle Gabe?"

"Promise me you'll go…to Israel. My gut says…says that's where you…need to be." He paused and coughed hard; blood came out in the froth, and Maslak bent over with a piece of gauze, gently wiping it away. "Promise me. PROMISE."

"…I promise, Uncle Gabe. I will do my best to get to Israel. And I will plant a fig tree for you there."

"That…that'll do…son." Franz felt Gabe squeeze his hand lightly; there was no strength in it. "S-stay with me a-awhile. It…I don't think it'll…be long now."

Franz glanced at Maslak, who shook her head.

"Of course, Uncle Gabe," Franz said, choking back tears and entering what he thought of as 'Majdanek mode.'

***

Gabe was right, as usual. A little more than four hours later, he slipped into a coma. An hour and a half after that, his heart stopped. Franz stayed with him, holding his hand, until the end.

"He told us what to do with…with his body," a gentle, sympathetic Maslak told the benumbed young man. "He'll be cremated and taken to the family cemetery in Poland. We'll see it gets done properly. If you like, we can send a small vial of his ashes to you, to take to Israel when you go."

"Thank you. That…would be appreciated," Franz said, almost wooden in his delivery, so hard were his emotions locked down. "Now I need you to do something else for me."

The nurse-operative was attractive and fairly young; she flipped her dark hair back and waited for the proposition she expected, in the young man's grief. The fact that Franz was a handsome young man by this point wasn't lost on her, either. But she wasn't expecting what she got.

"Get me all of the information available on the attack on Gabe, and let me see it," he said, voice tight.

Maslak nodded and stumbled out of the room, stunned.

***

Franz spent several days studying the information on the attack, then contacted Klein through the secure, ciphered line, and obtained all the available information on Soviet operatives in the region.

"…Yes, the scientist and his wife have made it out safely," Klein answered in response to Franz' other query. "The backup operative used the attack on Gabe as a diversion, and it worked, though it took a lot longer than they wanted, and they had to use a different route. Listen, I'm…so sorry, Franz."

"Thank you," came the almost-cold reply. "I'll head back in a week or so."

"What are you going to do in the meantime?"

"Ensure that what happened to Gabe doesn't happen again. At least through that agent."

"Can I talk you out of it?"

"No."

"Then I'll give it to you as an assignment. I was going to have that done anyway, I just hadn't thought about you being the operative."

"That'll work."

"…Be careful, son. And be certain." He paused. "If you target the right agent, their organization will likely do nothing; they'd consider it just retaliation, tit for tat, and their agent careless for letting you get to him. But if you target the wrong person, they'll retaliate on YOU. You MUST be certain."

"Always."

And Franz ended the call.

***

Franz spent another week going over the files and the evidence, making sure he was on the right track. When the modus operandi of a specific Soviet spy turned up, however, he knew he had found his target. A few more double-checks and another ciphered call to Klein confirmed it.

He went out that night, well after sunset, dressed head to toe in black, to include gloves and balaklava. He was gone for just over two hours.

When he returned around midnight, he stripped and showered; then, wrapped in a towel, handed the black clothing to Maslak.

"Burn these, please. Bury the ashes," he said, and ducked into the bedroom provided to him.

He was on the road an hour and a half later, headed toward the Czechoslovakian border.

***

It would be three days after that before the Soviet operative thought to have attacked Gabe was found dead, dressed in eveningwear, his neck efficiently snapped by what must have been a powerful agent, an expression of surprise on his face, well hidden in an alley off Lviv's famous opera district.

There were no witnesses.

It would be decades before anyone in the intelligence community was assassinated again via deliberate introduction of toxins during a stabbing.

***

He had made it through Czechoslovakia an hour and a half after leaving Lviv by dint of using a network-provided fake ID at the border checkpoint. And there had been no indication yet of any murder in Lviv; he was listening to Ukrainian radio news as he drove, to make sure. By the time the body was found — he had hidden it well — he intended to be in France, headed for the Riviera.

But he had a stop to make in Hamburg first.

The shortest route was through Prague to Berlin and thence to Hamburg, where he would disposition Gabe's personal effects with Egon Klein, then resign the intelligence position before continuing on, traveling south.

He crossed into East Germany around ten in the morning, using yet another fake ID at the border crossing. It was another two hours of solid driving to Berlin, but he would skirt the city and continue three more hours to Hamburg, assuming the checkpoints from East Germany to West Germany were not too busy.

He never reached the West German checkpoint.

While he was still en route, the Iron Curtain fell with a vengeance, and the Berlin Blockade began.

He was trapped in East Germany.

***

A grim Franz continued on to Berlin, but unsurprisingly, the bypass around the city was blocked by barricades and Red Army soldiers. So he headed into East Berlin, to the point of contact location for a western operative known to him, one Jarl Vogel. The contact point was along the Krausenstrasse near the intersection with Charlottestrasse, not so very far from the barricaded streets leading into West Berlin. Klein had evidently notified Vogel that Franz would likely show up once the borders were closed and West Berlin blockaded, for he was waiting, and got into the passenger seat when Franz pulled over.

Only then did he turn to the young man.

"Der Vorhang fällt," he murmured. (*The curtain falls.*)

Franz shook his head.

"Sie muss sich für den nächsten Akt erheben," he offered the countersign. (*It must rise for the next act.*)

"You realize this may take a while?" Vogel told the young man then.

"I know. But I made Gabe a promise," Franz replied. "It was the last thing he ever asked of me. I won't go back on that. I have to get into Western Europe to do it."

"…Understood. My sympathies, by the way."

"…Thank you."

"Let's go to a safehouse where you can stay. Turn right up here…"

***

Vogel placed Franz in a safehouse not far from the 'line' dividing East and West Berlin; it was a rather bleak attic flat in a largely unused house — a couple of operatives lived as 'roommates' on the first floor, but no one else — that would have been an easy walk of a couple of blocks to enter West Berlin. The problem was that the Soviets were not allowing anyone or anything INTO West Berlin, including supplies. One of the ways that was happening was by guarding, not only the city limits of West Berlin, but the border between East and West Germany. Which meant that Franz would be unable to get through to Hamburg unless they were able to devise a means that circumvented the current Soviet security measures.

And that was going to take some effort.

The attic was one room, with a twin bed in the left corner on one end of the gable. A tiny bathroom with toilet, tub, and sink had been added in the right corner. A small electric kitchenette was on the other end of the attic; a sitting area was in the middle, along with a small desk. There were windows in each gable end, but these had been covered with plywood to avoid Soviet spies seeing into the saferoom. The entry was a carefully-hidden pull-down staircase in the ceiling of the top hallway. It was all clean, but a bit dilapidated, with the drab sepia wallpaper and décor from the Edwardian period at the latest. Franz was secretly grateful for a flush toilet and indoor plumbing.

"Have you heard from Klein?" Franz wondered, as he and Vogel brainstormed in the sitting area all afternoon.

"Yes; as soon as the blockade went into place, he contacted me — and, I suspect, the other operatives in the area — to watch out for you. He did want to know what your plans were, though. I can pass that on in a coded form, if you like."

"That…might be good," Franz considered, thoughtful. "I know that if this takes more than a month, the rent will be due on the flat Gabe leased, so we need to handle Gabe's possessions. Is it likely…?"

"I would think so, I'm afraid," Vogel noted. "We have a stinking pile of horse shit, here."

"I can imagine. Are they trying to starve out West Berlin?"

"That's what it looks like. It's a kind of modern cold war siege. If they can get them to surrender or come over to the Soviet side, they think they can take the rest of Germany."

"Hmph."

"Yes."

"All right. Let me think," Franz said. "I might not be able to tell you today; I hadn't really thought past getting TO the flat, yet."

"Ah. Right," Vogel said, knowing. "Shock and grief will do that."

"It does," Franz admitted. "As much as I've experienced it, you'd think I'd be used to it by now."

"I don't think we ever get used to it. Not with those we love."

"Possibly not. But I can hope."

"I suppose. Well, let me go and find out the latest. I'll either come back or send you word if there's any change."

"Understood, and thank you. Meanwhile, I'll try to put together a plan for Klein to use in dispositioning Gabe's things."

"All right."

And Vogel left Franz alone in the attic safehouse with his thoughts and memories.

Too many of each, he quickly decided.

***

By the next day, Franz had a plan written out for what to do with Gabe's personal effects. Most of them went to various friends, and a few small things Franz intended to keep as a remembrance, the principal item being Gabe's compass. He still had the one Jakob had given him, for it was a work tool, but he wanted Gabe's as well, as a keepsake.

There was little of Franz' own in the flat, just some clothing for other seasons, and nothing that couldn't be replaced.

He was already wearing what little jewelry he possessed — a simple Swiss military-surplus wristwatch, more utilitarian than valued, the small compass Jakob had once given him, and his mother's wedding ring, which Gabe had ensured had a nondescript and unnoticeable stainless-steel chain to hang around his neck, long enough that the ring and the compass were both hidden inside his shirt.

"No change, and no ideas yet," Vogel said, after Franz handed over the list of items to be dispositioned. "I'll get this to Klein; we won't need to cipher it, I don't think. I expect we can gin up the transmission to look like just what it is — a simple death announcement with disposition of effects. And no one is going to care about that except the people sending and receiving it. I'll ask him first, though, in order to make sure."

"All right," Franz agreed. "If he can take care of all that, and just have a package of my things waiting for whenever I get there, that'll be good."

"He wants to know your plans going forward, though." Franz shook his head.

"I'm not completely sure, beyond getting into Western Europe. After that, I need to check on some stuff."

"Of course. It'll take time for you to figure out what to do going forward. You're grieving your uncle, and the mind doesn't work well at such times."

"…Yes." Franz sighed; it was true, but that wasn't the problem. Or rather, not the whole problem, or even the main part. How to do it was the problem. Still, he kept his thoughts to himself.

"All right. Stay here and rest, grieve, and do whatever you need to do. You'll be safe here, but keep your head down and stay out of sight. While you're resting, I'll get this to Klein, and we'll keep trying to come up with a way to get you out."

Franz sighed again as Vogel left.

***

The next day, the Western allies began the Berlin Airlift.

This was much to the satisfaction of both Franz and Vogel, because the situation in besieged West Berlin was already becoming critical; most cities did not have sufficient food for the population for more than a handful of days, if that, without being restocked from elsewhere, and West Berlin was no exception. It was arguably worse due to the presence of deserters and defectors from farther east.

Unfortunately, it did Franz no good…in several senses of the term.

The airlift was for WEST Berlin, and Franz was in EAST Berlin. It neither provided food supplies, nor gave him a way to get out. And along with the initiation of the airlift came a counter-blockade, eliminating trade between the Soviet Bloc and the western nations.

Food was rationed in East Berlin even before the blockade. As a result of the Western counter-blockade, shortages developed quickly and became more severe the longer the blockades went on. As 'a not-supposed-to-be-there person,' as Franz termed it, food and other consumable products such as soap or detergent were in even shorter supply than they had been before, by an ever-increasing amount. Vogel did his best to provide for the young man in hiding, but there was only so much to go around in typical Soviet-bloc countries, and this was even worse with the counter-blockade. Fortunately it was summer, or the search for coal and firewood would have been dire.

But it didn't begin to fill the cupboard of his saferoom.

Once more, he thought in discouragement, he was reduced to the barest amount of food and drink, his clothing going largely unwashed, though he rinsed them in the sink at least, even going so far as to scrub them in the tub on an old washboard Vogel found somewhere. Occasionally Vogel managed to bring powder detergent and Franz used it to wash body and clothes in the tub for as long as it lasted, which usually wasn't that long, even though he tried hard to eke it out. Sometimes Vogel brought a piece of bar soap, and that usually lasted longer, and was much easier on Franz' skin. But it was rare.

Summer waned; Vogel notified Franz that Klein had taken care of Gabe's effects, the apartment lease had been canceled, and there was a small duffel awaiting his arrival. It contained his own effects as well as Gabe's compass, as requested.

Autumn began; Franz was once again unable to celebrate the autumn holy days in any fashion save prayer. He was doing well to eat daily, though he fasted when appropriate. Vogel wasn't doing much better in that regard; he was sharing his ration with Franz, so neither of them had enough to eat.

Worse, as the year waned and the weather cooled, so, too, did the temperatures in their dwellings. And Franz only had his summer clothes.

He took to layering them, on colder nights wearing them all at once. Vogel managed to smuggle in a cardigan, a pair of dungarees — heavier and therefore considerably warmer than the lightweight linen trousers he had with him — an old-fashioned and almost-too-small wool-blend union suit, and an oversized winter coat, as well as a couple of pairs of woolen socks. The coat didn't fit, being substantially too big, but it all helped keep him warm, at least.

***

During Chanukah in December, close on Christmas, Vogel came to Franz.

"Klein has lined up a way to get you out," he said, "but we have to figure out how to get you into West Berlin first."

"Well, that's the trick, isn't it?" Franz pointed out.

"It is, but we have some options now that we didn't have before, I think."

"Talk to me."

***

A few days after the New Year, Vogel slipped into Franz' safehouse with a small backpack carefully compressed and hidden under his coat.

Inside Franz' room, he helped the younger man throw what little he had into the pack; the automobile in which he'd arrived had been 'vanished' by the resistance long since — it had been decided that if another was needed, it would be procured locally so as not to stand out. Once everything was in the pack, Franz slung it over his back, then put the big winter coat on over it.

"Huh," he grunted. "It fits, even with the pack."

"Of course it does," an exasperated Vogel said in friendly annoyance. "I'm not a fool! I knew we'd need to smuggle out what we could, and it would need to hide a multitude of Soviet sins. I planned for this, Franz. I didn't know HOW we were going to get you out, but I wanted to be ready when it happened."

"Oh."

"Exactly." They laughed. "Come on, now. I have something to show you, but we'll have to go onto the street. Act like you belong here."

***

They went down the stairs and out the back of the safehouse into a small mews between buildings, then slipped down the block before emerging from a side alley onto the street. It was dark, and they were dressed mostly in black and charcoal-gray clothing, save for Franz' jeans, which were still fairly dark blue despite washboard scrubbing. It was late enough that the street lights had been turned out to conserve resources given the shortages, and they traveled quietly for another block along the same street before turning left and moving toward the blockade.

About half a block away from the blockade, they turned down another alley and followed a mews until they reached the back of a particular house. Vogel made a gesture that translated as *in here*, and produced a key, unlocking the back door and slipping in quietly. Franz followed.

Inside, unsurprisingly, the house was dark. They moved down a hallway and ahead, a man appeared, dimly revealed by light from a window.

"Der Vorhang fiel," Vogel murmured. (*The curtain fell.*)

"Das ist uns egal," the man responded with the countersign. "This is him?" (*We don't care.*)

"Yes."

"Come with me."

The man turned and headed toward a side door. Opening it, he revealed stairs going down into the dark. He stepped into the stairwell, then produced an electric torch, directing it downward and turning it on.

"Come," he reiterated, and headed down the stairs, Vogel and Franz close on his heels. Vogel closed the door to the stairwell behind them.

***

The stairway led to the cellar. It was as dark there as it had been upstairs.

Until the man opened another door.

Suddenly there was light. It wasn't incredibly bright, but there were several lanterns — both electric and coal oil — illuminating two more men, and a large pile of dirt in the corner.

There were wooden slats piled in another corner, and several shovels and picks beside that.

On the right-hand wall, a large opening yawned.

"You dug a tunnel under the barricades," Franz whispered, understanding.

"Yes, and it comes out in the cellar of another house across the way," Vogel explained, keeping his voice low. "Klein ensured that another team was digging from there, and we met in the middle. It still took some time."

"We've already sent several out this way," the strange man said. "You two will be numbers four and five."

"You're coming, too?" Franz asked Vogel.

"At least for a bit," he said. "I'm going to try to smuggle back some supplies, this way."

"Aha."

"You'll have to crawl, and it's not a short tunnel," the unknown man said, handing them small electric torches. "Best get going. It's late."

"Go ahead," Vogel gestured to Franz. "I'll be right behind you. Just don't fart."

Franz snorted, then got down on hands and knees and crawled into the tunnel.

***

They were about two-thirds of the way along the tunnel, which was shored up with the brothers of the slats that had been piled in the corner, when a trickle of dirt signaled problems.

Seconds later, those problems manifested.

The roof of the tunnel partially collapsed, several large rocks pelting them along with considerable dirt.

Then something made a hollow thud.

Franz lunged forward when the collapse started, stifling a cry, and managed to avoid having his legs buried and trapped. He kicked free of what dirt did land on them, until he heard Vogel's hissed and very urgent, "STOP! Don't move."

"What's wrong?" Franz asked, glancing over his shoulder at Vogel, whose face had paled as he stared at something in the dirt.

"The collapse must have gone through to the surface, or pretty damn close to it," Vogel breathed, easing back. "There's a land mine in all this shambles."

"Farkakte, shit, merde, and scheiße," Franz cursed under his breath. (*'Shit' in Yiddish, English, French, and German*)

"Something like, yes," Vogel responded, carefully patting down his pockets, then producing a Soviet military surplus pocket-knife. "Try to stay still, as much as you can. I'm not sure yet if there's a trip wire in all this debris, or if it's pressure-based. But if any movement brings down more of the tunnel roof, it may not matter."

"What do we have?"

"How much do you know about such things?"

"A little. Not a lot."

"All right. My initial assessment is it looks like a PMD7 land mine, intended as anti-personnel. They're kind of hollow wood boxes with a charge inside. Usually you step on it and the weight pushes aside a pin and frees a striker that hits the detonator, and it blows. They CAN be rigged with trip wires also, but I'm not seeing one. I'm trying to survey it without touching it. Just hang on for a few minutes."

"Trust me, I'm not moving. Talk to me."

"Mmm." Vogel was quiet for a few moments, delicately probing the soil around something — Franz assumed the mine — with the knife blade. "Aha. That's…interesting."

"What?"

"The wood is partly rotted from the dampness in the soil, and I can move a piece of the wood and see some of the inside. Whoever laid this mine made a little error…or is a secret sympathizer. Instead of pulling the arming pin out, he snapped off the ring, by accident, probably. I think I can use my jack knife blade to wedge under the arming lever. That should prevent it going BOOM."

"Or it could make it go BOOM."

"If I don't do it right, yes. But I think I can do this. And I'm not seeing signs of a trip wire. Try to move very slowly down the tunnel about a body's length, if you can, without touching the walls."

"What about you?"

"Once I get this rigged so it won't blow, I'm backing out. I'll let them know we have a mine in the tunnel and we'll figure out something from there. You're on your own, Franz. Sorry about that, but I'm not going to try to crawl over this thing."

"I don't blame you. Okay, let me…" Franz started to ease farther down the tunnel, but a small trickle of soil began again.

"Stop! Stop!" Vogel exclaimed in a low tone, intended to carry to Franz but not through any opening there might be into the dark no-man's-land above. The last thing they needed was a Soviet guard cluing into their position. "If a rock lands on this thing, we're dead. Stay put and let me do this, then we'll both haul ass toward our respective ends of the tunnel when I give the word."

"All right."

It seemed to take forever. And he couldn't even see what was happening, which made it even more tense and frustrating. Franz listened intently as barely-audible metallic scrapes came to his ears.

"How is it—" he began.

"Shush. I gotta concentrate."

He silenced and continued to listen. A soft, slow grating sound was followed by a sudden, swift scrape.

"Shit," Vogel breathed. "It's not wanting to wedge in there, just slide out."

"Don't push straight," Franz suggested. "Use a rotating motion."

"What do you mean?"

"The back of the blade is wider than the edge. Use it like a wedge, and slide the edge in, then twist it to get the back of the blade wedged in there. Use the width, rather than the length. Just be careful that the blade tip doesn't contact anything it doesn't need to."

There was silence for a few seconds, then, "Oh! I see what you mean. Okay, let me see…"

More slow grating. Then the sound stopped.

Cautiously, Franz looked over his shoulder.

Vogel was easing away from the pile of dirt, his empty hands in the air.

"That's got it," he said. "Get ready to sprint for the far end of the tunnel."

Franz nodded, as Vogel eased his body to face away from the mine. They crouched in a runner's sprint position, dirty knees on the floor of the tunnel, facing opposite directions.

"Get ready…"

Franz lifted his knees just enough to run, careful not to bump the tunnel roof with his ass.

"Get set…"

Franz shifted his weight onto his fingertips and the balls of his feet.

"GO!"

He lunged forward, keeping as low as he could, sprinting toward the far end of the tunnel, still shrouded in blackness.

***

As he neared the end of the tunnel, a faint light shone in it. He didn't slow down, however, just kept going as fast as he could in a bent position, straight into the cellar of another house.

"Move move move!" he cried. "It may blow!"

There were several operatives in the cellar, and they all moved away from the mouth of the tunnel at Franz' warning. He himself straightened slightly and lunged to one side, hitting the earth floor and rolling aside.

Then they waited.

Nothing happened.

"Uh," Franz panted, remembering. He offered the password. "Ich ging unter den Vorhang." (*I went under the curtain.*)

"Mit unserer Hilfe," one operative offered the countersign. "Where is Vogel?" (*With our help.*)

"We were about two-thirds along when the roof caved in," Franz explained. "A mine — he said it was a PMD something — landed in between us. It didn't go off, but with the roof continuing to come down if we moved, a rock would have…"

"Right," the operative said, wincing. "So?"

"So he used his jack knife blade to wedge under the… arming lever? Then he headed back, and I headed forward, so he didn't have to crawl OVER it."

"Ah. Of course. All right; I'll call the far end and make sure he's safe there. Much as I hate the idea, we may need to blow this one and abandon it, then start over elsewhere. We got too close to the surface, I suppose. We're lucky nothing blew while we were digging, I guess."

"Meanwhile," another operative said, taking Franz' arm, "we need to get you out of here. You have a schedule to meet."

***

Getting around inside West Berlin was a breeze compared to East Berlin. The operative, who would only offer the code name B-thirty-two, led him out the back of the house — it was on the side opposite the barricades — and into the far street. They were across the intersection and down a block when suddenly an explosion sounded behind them, and Franz flinched and spun. B-thirty-two caught his arm.

"It's all right. They were going to do a controlled detonation of the mine and collapse the tunnel, then abandon the houses on each end. It's fine. Let's go."

"Where are we going?"

"Tempelhof Airport. It's the main landing site for the airlift operations. It'll be about dawn by the time we get there."

"Oh!"

***

At the airport, B-thirty-two reported to a man in an American officer uniform.

"Sir! B-thirty-two reporting with outbound cargo, per order three-G-nine-forty-eight."

The officer ran over a checklist, nodded, and checked off a listing. "Where is it?"

B-thirty-two grinned, turned, and indicated Franz.

"Uh, you know we're not supposed to carry passengers."

"He's not a passenger. He's cargo, per Rear Admiral Hillenkoetter, sir."

"Rear Adm…" The officer gaped for a moment before regaining his composure. "Right. Per the manifest, we'll put the special cargo aboard flight Bravo Foxtrot Nineteen; they'll be here in about twenty minutes. Pilot is Captain Bob Cranford. I'll have him notified he'll have a special cargo outbound."

"And the final destination?" B-thirty-two asked, glancing at Franz with a smile.

"Rhein-Main Air Base in Frankfurt."

Franz grinned.

***

Thirty minutes later, Franz was in the rear of the C-54 Skymaster cargo craft, already in the air and headed for Frankfurt.

***

At the air base in Frankfurt, as Franz came off the plane, he was met and escorted by two American military police and taken to a nearby hangar.

There, Egon Klein awaited him with an automobile. He gestured him toward the passenger seat, then personally got behind the wheel.

With a sigh of relief, Franz sank into the passenger seat and closed his eyes as Klein pulled away from the hangar.

* * *

Klein stopped at a small diner in Frankfurt, very near the base.

"Here," he said. "You're skin and bones, even under that huge coat. Gabe would haunt me the rest of my days — and justifiably so — if I didn't feed you as soon as I could. The American pilots all recommended this place. Said the food was good and coffee refills were free."

Franz settled in, ordering a farmer's breakfast — pan-fried potatoes with onions, scrambled with eggs, rosemary and basil, then topped with cheese, though he requested they hold the bacon garnish — black coffee, and orange juice.

It WAS good. Especially to a young man who had been half-starved since the previous June, and it was now January.

He fell asleep in the car when they left.

Klein let him sleep.

* * *

A week later, Gabe's small compass had joined Miriam Levy's wedding ring and Jakob's gift on the chain inside Franz' shirt, and a small duffel bag contained the rest of his worldly goods. Word had arrived that Jarl Vogel had survived the tunnel collapse and had managed his own escape as well, with Klein's remote assistance. Franz — now going largely by his last name of Levy, a sign of adulthood and respect bestowed upon him by his resistance network in the wake of recent events — had resigned from the intelligence operation and received his last paycheck containing a substantial bonus for avenging Gabe, as well as hazard duty pay.

Levy cashed it, withdrew what monies were in the joint bank account with Gabe, and bought a used car.

Then, upon Klein's advice, Levy headed southeast, modifying his original plan. He would cross the Alps through Liechtenstein and Switzerland, where they were slightly lower, then make his way toward Venice, Italy.

* * *

Chapter 8 — Finally!

As he traveled, not particularly rushing, he occasionally caught the odd tidbit of news.

The lifting of the Berlin blockade and the end of the Airlift. *About damn time.*

Vague rumors of the formation of an intel organization in Israel, which had survived the attacks by its neighbors at its formation. *Hm. Interesting.*

More rumors of a Soviet atomic bomb test. *Farkakte.*

Hearsay that Stalin's health might be deteriorating. *Good.*

The rise of Chinese communism. *Just damn great. Not.*

The formation of NATO. *Well, better than not. Pity it's needed.*

Truman in the White House. *This will be interesting.*

The start of the Korean War. *Damnation.*

Little of it sounded particularly good, nor inclined toward long-term peace. But none of it affected him directly, either. He kept going.

* * *

The used car Levy had bought made it out of Germany and through the Alps, almost all the way through little Leichtenstein, before it gave out. It had not been intended for heavy use in the mountainous terrain and in his haste to get under way, he had failed to reckon with the need to tune it to high altitudes. Unfortunately, with no tools to hand, let alone replacement parts, even with all his skills he couldn't repair it.

However, there were still abandoned vehicles from the war here and there, and after walking a couple of miles, he soon picked up another vehicle. But it had little in the way of gasoline in it, and it ran out before he reached a city where he might obtain more.

Unfortunately he had to dodge a couple of bands of brigands in the process; this part of Europe was still rather wild and prone to highway robbers and gangs of fascists that refused to acknowledge the war was over. That didn't help the fuel conservation problem, either. He finally found another abandoned vehicle, and this time he aimed for the nearest village he thought might have a petrol station, still dodging the roving gangs.

Thus he hopscotched around Leichtenstein, then into Austria and Switzerland, zig-zagging back and forth but gradually working farther south, for much longer than he wanted before he finally found the perfect vehicle.

It would need a bit of work first, however.

***

There was a junkyard near where the last car died some distance outside a little town called Mutten, and he went there in hopes of trying to find parts and fuel.

That was where he hit the jackpot.

***

It wasn't a standard junkyard as it turned out, but an old Nazi military equipment depot, long since forgotten, surrounded by a tall slat fence, and overgrown with weeds. There were no automobiles to be found there, at least intact ones.

What WAS there was an abandoned Panzer II.

Some time after the Nazis had essentially decommissioned the Panzer IIs in 1942, they stripped the turrets to recycle the cannons, installing them in defensive bunkers. This Panzer had apparently been sent south — along with most of the other equipment in the junkyard — in an attempt to aid Mussolini, but never made it that far, for reasons that likely had to do with command.

Levy fairly swarmed over the old tank, pulling away the tarpaulin shroud covering it which had protected the turret opening from the elements, as well as the armored vehicle as a whole. Much to his surprise, not only did it appear to be in reasonable condition thanks to the tarp covering, it had a full, topped-off fuel tank, properly sealed to ensure no degradation… AND the MG34 machine gun was still installed, and had three full ammo boxes in the back of the crew area. It was, he thought, arguable about what condition the powder inside the rounds was in; the Nazis had obviously originally intended to come back and head out in haste. *Likely some sort of blitzkrieg,* he thought. In the end, that lightning strike had not materialized, and when they'd cannibalized the Panzer for its cannon, they hadn't even bothered to check the gas tank.

If he could get it running, it would definitely be the biggest ride on the road, if not the fastest. It only moved at about 30 to 35 miles an hour max, but it ran on gasoline and had a huge fuel tank. If he could find a good car relatively soon — before the heavy armored vehicle could burn through it all — he could siphon all that fuel into containers and go a long way.

A quick check indicated that there was some sort of additive in the gasoline to ensure longevity, and while it wasn't quite as good as fresh-pumped gas, it would still fuel the tank's engine. He shook his head. *Well, He did it with the menorah oil in the Temple,* he thought. *I guess He can do it with petrol in a tank. It's said Adonai looks after children and fools. Arguably at this point, I'm both.*

Then he found the fuel station — well sealed and full to the top, so the volatiles in the gasoline had remained intact — and grinned. *Yes, definitely both,* he added to himself.

Levy dug around some and found the mechanics tools for the Panzer and a functional arc welder with some rods, then set to work.

***

It took some time, but he made sure the treads and wheels were in good repair, everything was properly lubricated, and the drive system functioned. Then he managed to find a truck hood — there were a few parts, but no complete vehicle — that fit the opening where the turret should be. He gathered up as many batteries as he could find and jerry-rigged them into a power supply for the welder. Then he fashioned a kind of crude hatch to cover the turret opening out of the truck hood, welded on some hinges, and attached the hatch. He didn't bother with a latch; his small duffel didn't make for much to steal, and there was plenty of room inside with just him and his duffel.

Last of all, he fed a belt of ammo into the MG34 and fired a burst at a nearby pile of discarded plate armor as a test. Not only did the gun not blow up in his face, the bullets put significant dents in the armor plate. He laughed aloud.

That'll do, he thought. He had no idea why he felt the need to check on the machine gun's function, but something in the back of his head insistently told him to do it. There were no other belts of ammo that fit, so he hoped if he had to use it on any highway robbers, the altercation would end quickly.

***

Once he got the Panzer up and running, he trundled it over to the fuel station. There, he broke the seal on the pump and topped off the fuel in the tank, then grabbed every fuel can in sight — and there were easily four big jerry cans — and filled them to the brim, then strapped them to the back of the tank, in the cargo space provided. Then he found the stash of jerry cans, and added over a dozen more, plus enough empties to hold half of the armored vehicle's fuel; it was far more than would fill the average automobile fuel tank.

And now I've got over a hundred gallons of petrol for down the road, he thought. *That's probably enough to get me to Venice and leave some over for barter. Depends on how much petrol the next auto burns, I suppose.*

Levy clambered into the tank, lowered the hatch, and rumbled for the road to Madesimo in Italy.

***

According to the maps Klein had given him back in Frankfurt, Levy crossed into Italy about fifteen miles down the road, as the tank trundled. His intent was to head for Milan, then turn almost due east to reach the port at Venice, via Verona and Padua; Klein had indicated that should be a reasonably safe place from which to debark, as well as a safe route to use in reaching it. Or as safe as anything was in Europe these days, given Soviet sympathizers, residual pockets of fascists, and remote areas with roving bands of desperados. Obviously he'd need to find an automobile before getting close to Milan; he didn't think cruising a tank into the city would go over well these days. It would cause far too much excitement for his safety. Still, he had a goodly way to go, so he was sure things would be fine.

He didn't even get close before excitement found him.

That was when he was glad for the tank.

***

The crowd in the tiny village blocked the road ahead. Levy debated about whether to take the smaller road around the village or see what was going on; it was certain that if he wanted to clear the mob — there were pitchforks and worse in the crowd — his revamped old Panzer was definitely going to be the way to do it.

Oh hell, he thought, as a certain feeling of foreboding hit. *Let's see what's up. Not like they can hurt me in my tin can.*

He moved forward. He wasn't sure what was going on, but he had a feeling he needed to see.

He was right.

There, backed against a stone barn wall, surrounded by pointed farm implements and a few long guns all aimed at him, was...

...Jakob Brahms.

***

Levy gunned the Panzer, running it right up behind the rearmost in the crowd, and making plenty of noise in the doing. Having run across a bullhorn at the junkyard and added it to the tank, he grabbed it now and activated it.

"WHAT'S GOING ON HERE?" he boomed in German; his Italian was rusty, but in this part of Italy, German should be readily understood.

The crowd had begun retreating in apprehension from the tank as it approached; now a spokesman stood forth. He acted brave, but Levy could see his knees shaking as he faced down the tank.

"This monster is a communist an' a wampyro," he declared in crude German with a distinctly rustic dialect. "He killed Luka, out on th' outskirts of the village. Drained him white, he did. Luka was one of us."

"And who might you be?"

182

"Giovanni Rizzo. I run the local chapter of Gli Italiani Contro Il Comunismo." (*Italians Against Communism*)

Hmph, Levy thought. *Bet it's a fascist group. Same song, different verse, but they're jealous as hell of each other.* "What is your charge against this man?" Levy demanded, while thinking as clearly as he could, *JAKOB!*

The vampire's eyes shot around. *Who are you?* he responded in kind.

It's Franz, Jakob!

FRANZ! You're alive! Oh, dear God, I thought…I thought…Warsaw! I was afraid you didn't get out in time!

I'll explain later. Get ready to fade, shift to your American form, and then RUN.

Run where?

Into my tank. They can't get to us in here. Not with the weapons they have.

An old Panzer? With a truck hood instead of a turret? I'm not even going to ask right now.

Good. Later.

Meanwhile, Rizzo was nattering on about how they had caught this stranger to their village walking down the main street right after finding Luka drained of his blood in his farmhouse outside the village.

"Shut up," Levy ordered then, and Rizzo gulped in midword and silenced. Then Levy lied through his teeth — about one thing, and one thing only. "This man is known to me, and he is neither vampire nor communist, nor communist sympathizer. Release him."

"We aren't gonna release him," Rizzo said, stubborn. "We're going to kill him, then cut off his head an' stuff his mouth with garlic. Like you do with any wampyro."

"You will release him, or else."

"Or else what?" Rizzo replied, defiant despite trembling legs, and the other villagers muttered, raising their various weapons, improvised and not.

Get ready, Levy told Jakob as he moved to the machine gun.

"Or else I fire," he said, allowing his face to show behind the MG34, which he pointed straight at Rizzo, whose eyes grew wide. The man stepped back a couple of paces.

"You're bluffing," Rizzo declared. "You don't have ammo for that."

Levy pivoted the machine gun to point at a cliff face a few yards behind the houses on the left; it was the base of an Alpine mountain, with the village in the valley; a mountain stream ran behind the houses on the right.

NOW! he told Jakob, as he let fire a short burst at the stone face.

The villagers had turned to watch the young man fire the tank's machine gun, flinching when it actually fired, as well as at the ricochets and rock chips that flew away from the bluff; that gave Jakob all the opportunity he needed. In a split-second he had vanished from view; several villagers fell over as if pushed out of the way, and Levy felt the breeze as the hatch opened and closed too fast to be seen.

Can you drive a tank? he asked Jakob, who had shifted from the Aryan German to the brown-haired American, Jake Abrams. The difference in appearance was substantial enough, Levy thought, that Abrams could have popped his head out of the hatch and the crowd outside would not have recognized him.

No, but I can handle the machine gun, Jakob replied.

Trade with me, then.

They eased past each other; there was not an incredible rush, as Levy had turned the gun back on Rizzo, who was now cringing and trying to ease away.

Just then someone looked back at the barn.

"HEY! Where did he go?"

"Cagare," Rizzo cursed. "This tank diverted us and he used the chance to get away. FIND HIM!" (*Shit; Italian*)

The mob broke up as everyone went hunting for Jakob… who was safely inside the tank.

***

Within moments the crowd had dispersed, and Levy put away the bullhorn.

"Why do they think there's a vampire?" Levy wondered then. "I mean, I can't imagine you doing anything like THAT. Not if the guy was innocent, anyway."

"No, he was, and I didn't, but there was one, just not me," Jakob summarized. "It's why I'm here. But they won't find him, because I already took care of him."

"Oh. So maybe we need to get out of here before they come back?"

"That sounds like a very good idea."

Levy put the tank in gear and they headed out at maximum speed.

***

Levy drove the Panzer while explaining how it came to be in his possession to Jakob, who laughed uproariously at the tale, delighted at finding his 'little brother' still alive and using his wits to good effect.

Then an extended conversation caught them up with each other since Warsaw. It transpired that Jakob had also been working as an operative, though in a different cell from Levy, which was how they had missed meeting.

"But I heard about the death of your friend Gabe," Jakob noted. "I just didn't know he was connected to you. I was actually the one to smuggle the scientist and his wife to the West in his stead."

"Well, no wonder it worked, then," Levy decided. "And yes, that…hurt. Gabe became as much family to me as you did, and now he's gone, too."

"What are your plans now, little brother?"

"Gabe was going to adopt me, and then we were going to emigrate to Israel together. He thought it would be a good place for us. He was on his last mission before we did that when he…when he died."

"You're heading south. Are you going to Israel on your own, then?"

"Well, I was, yes. I promised Gabe. Do you want to come along? I'd love to have you beside me."

Jakob drew a deep breath, then let it out in a sigh.

"I'd like to…but I can't," he murmured. "I'll go with you to Milan, but there I'll have to leave you."

"Why?" asked Levy, swallowing his disappointment.

"I have…other things to do." Jakob shook his head. "I'm not just acting as a Western operative, I'm sort of in the middle of cleaning up a group of…let's call 'em rogue vampires, for want of any better name."

"Oh. Was the one you killed in that village one of them?"

"Yes. I've got the advantage right now, and if I stop, if I go with you to Israel, then not only do I lose that advantage, I put myself — and anyone with me — at risk of THEM coming after US."

"Oh. Well, farkakte."

"Yes. If I get the chance, I might be able to visit you there later. I'll definitely tell some special friends of mine to keep an eye on you, if you don't mind."

"Are they vampires like you?"

"No. But they're just as powerful, probably a good deal more. And they're really good guys."

"Oh! Well, I won't mind a bit of that, I suppose."

"Good. I'll notify them in a bit. Where are we headed now?"

"In the general direction of Milan. From there I'll head for the port at Venice. My old intel cell chief recommended this route as being relatively safe, all things considered."

"Right. Then we'll need to get a car soon. I don't expect the authorities would appreciate an old Panzer rumbling into Milan. Never mind the imagery it conjures, the treads would tear merry hell out of the streets."

"No," Levy laughed. "I'd figured on that. But I want to get far enough away from the vigilantes for you to be safe."

"Thanks, little brother. They had enough shit there to do some serious damage, though I'm not sure they could have killed me. Now, if it had been night, different story."

"How so, 'big brother'?"

"They'd have had torches. Vampires and fire don't get along that great."

"Aha. Good info for the future, just in case I should run into any bad ones."

"Exactly; pin one in place, decapitate it, and burn at least the head, but all of it is better. That takes care of one."

"Ugh."

"Pretty much. Just don't ever do it to me."

"Never."

They changed the subject to lighter matters after that.

***

When they both adjudged they were far enough away from the village with the vigilantes, they started watching for abandoned cars. They eventually spotted a late-model Italian make on the side of the road with a flat tire and, as it turned out, an empty gas tank. Rather to their surprise, the spare tire was still in the boot.

"Do you suppose the owner just walked to a gas station a little while ago?" Jakob wondered.

"No, I don't think he went for petrol," Levy decided after a moment. "Look. There's dried mud splatters on the side next to the road, but not the other side. And there's a pothole over there," he pointed, "and the mud in the bottom matches the splatters, but it's dried up and even cracked. It hasn't rained around here in some time."

"So it's been sitting here abandoned for several weeks."

"Right. I think it's okay to claim it. I doubt the owner is coming back for it, for whatever reason."

"Could be stolen."

"Could be, but the Italian police would have found it by now and towed it away."

"You, my young friend, have a definite skill with logic and deduction. Remind me to tell you about a certain detective I once met in the Victorian era."

"Thanks, and I will." Levy grinned. "Let's get the tire changed, then fill the tank and load the jerry cans in the boot. We've got a way to go yet, and the day's getting on."

"Oh, this won't take long."

"Why not?"

"You have me to help. We'll be rolling in ten minutes. Move the Panzer off the road and get out the siphon hose; I'll have the car jacked up and the tire off by that time."

***

True to Jakob's word, they were already headed down the road in the newly acquired automobile fifteen minutes later, having both said a fond farewell to their previous heavy ride. The ammo for the machine gun was buried deep, under the tank.

Both men, it turned out, had an excellent sense of direction, and by late the next day they were nearing the outskirts of Milan. After stopping at a couple of shops and stores to acquire a small bag of clothing for Jakob — he had lost his own bag back at the village where Levy found him, and they had slept in the car the night before — they stopped at a small inn in a little village on the north side of Milan.

***

They checked in, received a key, and turned to the stairs with their bags.

Abruptly Levy froze for a split-second.

What's up, little brother? Jakob asked, hiding his startlement.

The man that just stepped up to the desk, Levy noted. *See him?*

I see him.

He was the Nazi guard who shot Eleazar in the head!

Damnation. I suspected I never found all of them. But I hoped I had. Come on, let's go up to our room before he sees us; he isn't likely to recognize you, but he doesn't need to see you staring. It might spook him.

But…

Don't worry — we can go slow. We can keep an eye on him while we go up the stairs; with my hearing, I can probably determine his room number as soon as the desk assigns it.

***

Once they were safely in their own room — it had twin beds and was comfortable and clean, if somewhat small — a very pale, scowling Levy, his hands knotted into white-knuckled fists, turned to Jakob.

"Did you get his room number?"

"I did."

"Good. What was it?"

"Why do you want to know?"

"Because tonight, after I'm sure he's asleep, I'm going to pick the lock, go in, and kill him."

"Are you sure you want to do that, Franz?"

"Why not?" a furious Levy demanded. "He didn't hesitate to kill Eleazar! I killed the man who tried to rape 'Aunt' Iga! And I killed the man who killed Gabe. And my cell supervisor was okay with that. He even made it a mission."

"But he never made it a mission to kill Eleazar's killer if you could find him, did he?"

That gave Levy pause; he didn't understand the point of the question.

"Well, no. It never came up. I thought you drained 'em all..."

"I hoped I had. But no. Let me ask you something else, then. Are you sure it's him?"

"I'm sure."

"One hundred percent? He hasn't changed at ALL since you were in Majdanek?"

"Well...there's been some changes," Levy admitted. "He's mostly bald now, and has more wrinkles..."

190

"Mm-hm. So you're not a hundred percent."

"Pretty damn close, Jakob."

***

"Listen to me, Franz. There is a very grave difference from carrying out an assignment to take out an assassin serving a despot, and murdering a man out of revenge. One rids the world of a menace, the other damages the soul. The same goes for stopping a rapist in the act. You do what you have to do to protect the innocent." Jakob paused and looked at Levy, his expression grave. "The boy I knew still had a pristine soul, for all he went through. The man I see in his place still does. Don't damage it for no good reason, little brother. The One knows who he is, and will see that he gets what he deserves."

He watched in silence while Levy processed that for long minutes, 'feeling' his roiling emotions. Finally Levy relaxed, unclenching his hands.

"All right," he murmured. "My father was a rabbi, as was his father, and his father's father. They wouldn't like it if I broke the sixth commandment, even to avenge Eleazar."

"Very good. As I said, God has ways of taking care of such matters."

"...Okay."

***

By way of avoiding temptation, Jakob had food sent up to them for dinner. Levy looked askance at the steak on Jakob's plate.

"I thought vampires only drank blood."

"Did you notice how I ordered the steak?" Jakob wondered with a grin. "Or that I put all the side vegetables on your plate? This steak is so rare, only a cow mooing would be rarer. I'm good."

They laughed.

***

Late that night, Jakob got out of bed and checked to ensure that Levy was sound asleep in his.

Then he went to the window, opened it, and eased outside, preternaturally clinging to the smooth stone wall of the building, before moving away from the window.

He was gone nearly an hour and a half.

When he returned, there was a trickle of blood at one corner of his mouth. He closed and latched the window, then swiftly ducked into the en suite bath, closing the door behind him.

Moments later, there was the muffled sound of a toilet flushing, followed by water running in the tap.

When Jakob emerged, his face was clean.

Levy roused briefly.

"Mmph? Jakob? That you?"

"Yeah, little brother, it's me. I was in the bathroom; the steak did cause some minor digestive difficulties. I'm okay now; go on back to sleep."

"Mmokay."

And Levy was sound asleep once more.

Jakob gave the young man a fond smile, then crawled back into his own bed and entered what he thought of as 'vampire sleep.'

***

The next morning when they emerged for breakfast, the little inn was swarming with Milanese police.

"What happened?" Levy asked the innkeeper as he came by their table to refresh the continental breakfast on the sideboard.

"It seems one of the guests last night was a former Nazi," the innkeeper explained, pausing with a pitcher in hand. "He was a guard at the Majdanek prison camp, 'cording to what I've heard. Apparently he committed suicide last night; he slit his own throat and bled out."

"Oh, really?" Levy wondered, shocked. "How do you know?"

"His throat was slit horribly; my daughter found him when she brought up the room service breakfast he ordered the night before, and he was on the floor in a puddle of blood. She all but fainted right there, but managed to get back downstairs and tell me, so I called the police, then put her in a room in the back with her mother, so she could cry an' whatnot."

"Poor girl," Jakob said, wincing in sympathy.

"Go on, please," Levy pressed, shooting a side glance at his companion. "How did anyone know what he used to be?"

"Oh. Right. The dead Nazi. All of his identification, from the concentration camp to now, was spread out on the bed," the innkeeper said. "He also had a passport under a false name, and a ticket to a berth on a ship to Argentina. Evidently he couldn't go through with it. Perhaps the memories were too great." He shook his head.

"Ah," Levy said, giving Jakob a surreptitious stink-eye.

"Finish your breakfast, Franz, and let's get on the road," was all Jakob said, as the innkeeper moved on.

***

In the car, Levy stared at Jakob, who had taken the driver's seat for this leg of the journey. When they were well away from the inn, the younger male spoke.

"So. Is your soul stained?"

"No. No more so than it ever was."

"Why not, then? Don't tell me you weren't the one to kill him. That one was too smug yesterday to have suddenly had remorse sufficient to kill himself overnight. And you knew which room he was in. Never mind a slashed throat would hide a couple of fang marks, and finish the job of bleeding him out."

Jakob drew a long breath and let it out in an equally long sigh.

"I wondered that myself, for a long time," he admitted. "Remember those special friends I mentioned?"

"Yes?"

"Well, some of them, you'd know as angels. I've already told Mike about you; he tends to stay in the Middle Eastern area anyway because of his assignment from Upstairs, and he said he'd keep an eye out for you."

"Mike," Levy echoed, then his eyes grew wide. "Micha-MIKAEL?!"

Jakob just smiled.

"I don't know for sure," he confessed. "He just told me to call him Mike. I know several of his pals."

"Farkakte, shit, mierda," Levy murmured. "Um, okay. Keep going. You had a point to this."

"Yes, I did. So like I said, I know several, and we've had some interesting conversations over the centuries. Like, since I have always tried to follow the One, why did I get…well, most vampires refer to the process as 'turned.' I never got a straight answer from 'em, but as nearly as I've been able to figure it from what I DID get out of 'em, I think I'm here as a kind of police and protector of sorts. And the turning was to give me certain tools and a weapon. At least, that's how I like to think of it."

"And…what? So you try to keep the vampire community on the straight and narrow, and protect innocents like I was?"

"Whenever I can, yes." Jakob shrugged. "Not just from vampires, but from evil in general. I still have a human brain, or, well, pretty close; to live as long as I have, and to do some of the things I can do, it has to have changed a little, I suppose. But that basically means they can't tell me everything they know. And even they don't know everything. Mike told me once that there's a special pedestal on the Other Side, and on it is a book that has a timeline of history — past, present, and future. And the angels refer to it when they need to know what to do next. But they're only allowed to look at the current pages and what came before that; only The One can look forward." He shrugged again. "So that's about as much as I've been able to figure out. And even that, I don't KNOW for sure. But I view it as kind of like your supervisor giving you the assignment to take out Gabe's assassin. As long as I do my due diligence to verify their sins — and I do — I take 'em out."

"But…they don't get a chance to repent? I mean…"

"Franz," Jakob said, earnest, as they crossed into Madrid proper, "I can't remember whether it's in the Torah or the New Testament, but there's a passage that says that there's God's children, and the Adversary's children. And it sort of indicates that the Adversary's children have already made their choice, and they're not GOING to repent."

"Oh. OH…"

"Now you're getting it."

"And the ones who were so vicious…"

"Were not going to repent of it. The fact that he had a berth on a ship going to Argentina told me that. Never mind that he'd kept his Nazi credentials…and the medal he was given for 'service above and beyond the call of duty.' Most likely by

Hitler's own hand, by the look. I left it all spread out on the bed, nice and neat, so the local gendarmerie could see who he really was."

"Farkakte, shit, merde, kacken, and more shit," Levy grumbled.

"Yup."

"So you 'policed' the gene pool, eh?"

"Exactly." He paused, giving Levy a sideways grin. "But I did have some digestive difficulties with the steak last night."

Levy stared at him for a long moment. Then finally he laughed.

Jakob laughed too.

***

Once they got through Milan and headed in the general direction of Venice, Jakob pulled over.

"I get off here, little brother," he said softly. "I wish I could go with you. But I'd only put us both in danger."

"Damn," Levy cursed, just as softly, his voice cracking slightly.

They got out of the car and extracted Jakob's bag from the back seat. He sat it on the ground by his feet, then held out open arms, and Levy went into them, as the two embraced.

"I've missed you," Levy admitted. "And now I'm going to miss you worse."

"I'm just glad I found you again," Jakob confessed. "I thought you were dead in Warsaw, and that I'd caused it by taking you there. I have felt like SHIT for that, little brother."

"Still..."

"I know. If I can, I'll swing by to visit when I'm done culling this group."

"Do, please."

"If I can, Franz. If I can."

And with a gust of wind, he was gone.

Sober and somewhat melancholy, Levy got back behind the wheel of the car, started it, and headed on to Venice.

***

After some negotiating, Franz sold 'his' car to a Venice local for a reasonable amount; it was a good car that he'd personally kept well-maintained during the last segment of his travels across western Europe, and worth the fifteen thousand francs the local paid him for it…along with the extra gasoline he had left from the tank yard.

Then a bit more negotiating earned him a berth on a freighter, complete with paycheck, headed from the port of Venice through the Adriatic and Ionian Seas into the Mediterranean proper, and thence to the Israeli port of Tel Aviv-Yafo.

He loaded his little duffel into the tiny cabin assigned to him aboard the *Roditore di Mare* and prepared to learn how to be a sailor.

***

The voyage from Venice to Tel Aviv normally took just over 8 days for a laden freighter, especially an older diesel like the *Roditore di Mare*. But her captain kept her shipshape, and he assured Franz that the ship could make it in that time.

Unfortunately strong storms were also relatively common on the Mediterranean, and one chose that week to form.

It was large and powerful, with a deep central low pressure core, not unlike what Americans would call a hurricane. There was little way to avoid it, so the captain gave the orders to batten hatches, go below if unessential to deck operations, and prepare to ride it out. Levy joined the other crew in securing the freighter, then he went below decks and secured his few personal possessions in his little cabin, broke out the antiemetic the ship's physician had issued to everyone, and waited.

Unfortunately they didn't have long to wait. And the rough seas just kept getting rougher.

Either HaShem wants to toughen me, or the Adversary wants to stop me, Levy decided, as even the most hardened sailors aboard the *Roditore di Mare* grew seasick at the tossing. *Or both. Either way, I have to just keep going. It isn't like I can get off at this point anyway. I'm beginning to understand the story of Yonah a lot better, though.*

The sounds and stench of vomiting were all over the ship, at least below decks. Levy took a dose of the antiemetic at the beginnings of nausea, and kept up the dosage per the directions on the bottle, thus managing to largely avoid vomiting…but not quite. At the height of the storm — the captain on the bridge used shipboard comm speakers to notify them they were moving through what passed for an eyewall — the movement was more than he could take, and he all but projectile-vomited into the toilet in the tiny head for a good five minutes. The ship steadied as they passed through the eye, then slammed into the rough seas in the far eyewall, and he gagged and heaved again, but he'd purged what little was in his upper digestive tract on the first round, and there was no more to come up except a bit of acid and bile.

Finally the seas began to calm as they passed through the worst of the storm. Levy lay on his bunk and rested, thankful it seemed to remain more or less still beneath him once again.

***

The crew emerged the next day mostly unscathed, though a bit weak and wobbly. There were a few that were in sick bay, and one of those had been slammed into a bulkhead by a sudden lurch of the ship and broke an arm, nearly shattering the radius bone, but the majority were in decent shape, if still a little woozy.

The ship, it turned out, was not in such good shape. The captain had chosen to drop the sea anchor and hold position once the ship emerged from the storm, until repairs could be effected. There were a few things that would require repair in drydock, but nothing that would prevent their reaching Tel Aviv.

In the end it took them almost two weeks to reach the Israeli coast; the storm had slowed their forward motion and blown them off course, and that combined with several days of repair meant an eight-and-a bit-day trip took twelve days and some few hours. Somewhere in there Levy turned 20, though he barely had time to notice.

But at long last the port city of Tel Aviv was in sight.

Levy breathed a sigh of relief as he helped tie up the *Roditore di Mare* at the docks.

An hour later he had his scrip and duffel, and he debarked the ship.

He had arrived in Israel.

***

Chapter 9 — Making Aliyah

Once Levy arrived in Israel, making landfall at Tel Aviv and registering himself as a new citizen, he discovered that things were not as good as he had hoped. The little country was overwhelmed with Jews making aliyah, largely from Soviet Bloc countries and similar regimes from which they had escaped. There was no place for him to even stay, no hotel room available in all of Tel Aviv or any of the surrounding towns and villages.

He had no connections there from which to search farther afield, and the number of available automobiles in the new nation was limited, so the prices on those that were available were sky-high. He couldn't find a taxi service that would take him farther than the bedroom communities around Tel Aviv, which were in no better shape than the metropolitan district.

With a sigh, he searched for a safe place to bed down on the streets of Tel Aviv.

He was a street urchin again at the ripe old age of 20.

***

He managed to eat decently for a while, but the pay from the freighter ran out all too soon, as did the monies from his and Gabe's bank account; the rate of exchange from lira to shekel wasn't as favorable as he'd hoped, so the sale price of the car burned quickly, too. Without an address he couldn't get a job, so he resorted not only to sleeping on the streets, but scrounging for food.

He found that the best place to find decent discarded food was behind the open-air markets, the Jewish equivalents to the Arab souk. Here he could find fairly fresh discards, and often the shop owners made them available for those like Levy who were trying hard to get by in their new land. He even made friends with several shop owners, who kept their discards expressly for him.

The best was the day-old bread, but occasionally he was able to get hold of smoked meats, or the odd fruit or vegetable.

Winter was difficult. But the climate around Tel Aviv was mild, and as long as he could find a place out of the elements, he could manage. Majdanek, after all, had been much worse.

***

The day of his 21st birthday, he overheard a conversation.

".,.No, I just wasn't thinking about the immigration situation," one man said to a companion in the small market. "So when Isaac arrived, he had nowhere to live. I felt dreadful. I kept him in my house as long as I could, but we don't have a spare bedroom, so he had to sleep on the couch, which wasn't long enough for him. He started waking with back and neck problems."

"What did you do?" the woman asked. She was of a comparable age and strongly resembled the man; young Levy decided they were likely brother and sister.

"Well, we started scouting out our options. I put out some inquiries," the man said, "and my boss told me that if he was of age and physically fit, he could go into the IDF and have room and board and pay for at least a couple of years, until he could manage to get himself set up on his own. So he did."

"Is he okay with that?"

"Very much so. He likes it here despite the difficulties, and wants to help protect the country."

"This works, then."

"It really does."

Levy moved on, looking for edible scraps in the dumpsters behind the market.

But as soon as he got half a loaf of stale bread in his belly, he headed for the nearest IDF recruitment office.

***

By the end of the work day, he was a duly sworn IDF soldier. He was given certificates for a hot meal that night, breakfast the next day, and a billet overnight, and would board a bus to be taken to boot camp the next morning.

***

He was sent to Bahad 4, usually known as Batar Zikim, for boot camp. It was in central Israel, not that far from Tel Aviv, in Camp Yigael Yadin, which in turn was part of Tzrifin — originally a British military base founded during World War I. It was also currently the only training base the IDF had. As such, it was very large; the reservation itself housed several different facilities, including a military prison.

Boot camp was a little harder than he'd expected. He had been living on the streets long enough for it to diminish his muscle mass a bit, and his strength was sapped as a result. However, given the current circumstances in Israel, the drill instructors understood the situation and made sure the recruits got plenty of sleep and all the food they could shovel into their mouths. It wasn't haute cuisine, but it was good solid food. The drill instructors also pushed them hard, but always seemed to ease up when their limits were reached.

By the time Levy graduated from boot camp, his musculature had filled back out and he was stronger than ever.

***

His mahlakot, or platoon, remained stationed at Tzrifin, at least for the time; in Israel, each platoon was broken into teams, or tzvatim, which might be individually assigned to different tasks. His mahlakot was on the small side, numbering only 35 privates or turaiim. Those 35 were broken into five tzvatim of seven turaiim with one rav turai — sometimes called a rabat or corporal — assigned to each team. The mahlakot overall was led by a segen, or first lieutenant, assisted by a rav samal, sometimes called a rasal, who was a platoon sergeant first class.

Unlike Majdanek, Levy found it to be a comfortable organizational structure; he knew to whom he needed to report, and what he needed to do on any given day — and he did it, and did it to the best of his ability. He was given room and board, and in turn, he helped protect the country he had decided to make his own, the only country that welcomed him because he was a Jew, not in spite of it.

***

That said, he was in a group of young men and women — women had been a part of the IDF since its inception, though in a separate division known as the Women's Corps — and that tended to mean hijinx ensued.

The celebration after graduating boot camp was rather raucous; all the newly-dubbed turaiim were given their first leave, and the local bars were hit hard. Much fun was had, some of it ribald in nature, and extremely well-lubricated.

Levy found it didn't take as many beers as he had thought to get rip-roaring drunk. He liked the sensation…

…Until he got up to leave the bar and head to the barracks.

His head promptly launched into orbit, and he staggered badly. He finally made it out the side door of the bar, into the adjacent alley.

That was when his stomach lurched and he grabbed for the wall to avoid falling.

Abruptly his gut seemed to explode, as stale beer and bile erupted from his mouth. He projectile-vomited all over the wall, two adjacent trash cans, and the gutter of the alley.

Suddenly his newly-assigned rabat, Noah Mayer, was there, an arm around his waist, pulling Levy's arm across his own shoulders.

"Here you go," Mayer murmured, as Levy swayed. "Never been shit-faced drunk before, eh?"

"N-no," Levy panted. "Never been drunk before, actually."

"We pretty much expected a lot of you to hit this point," Mayer noted. "It's standard after boot camp, I think. Part of the whole military experience. Let me get you back to the shuttle bus and we'll get you to the barracks and horizontal. Oh, and be glad you have tomorrow off; you'll have a hell of a hangover."

***

Mayer was as good as his word. Within an hour, Levy was in the barracks and safely tucked into his bunk, with medication for the latent nausea.

And he was right about the hangover the next day, too. Entirely too right, in Levy's opinion. The headache alone seemed enough to split his skull. Fortunately, the rasal and Mayer were ready with hangover remedies for the entire platoon, and after a few hours, Levy felt like getting up and going to the rec room to watch television.

After that, however, Levy made a personal rule: enjoy alcohol, but never to excess.

He kept that rule the rest of his life.

And Mayer became a trusted friend.

***

On Earth it was the year 1951AD when Pulgey Entiyti was voted President of the Pan-Galactic Coalition for a third ten-annum term. It was not completely unanimous — that never happened on ANY vote — but there were very few dissenting votes.

Except for roughly half a dozen worlds out of several thousand, there was general rejoicing across the galaxy at President Entiyti's continued governance. Even those half-dozen were no more than annoyed that their candidate did not win.

The cheerful potentate — who had not campaigned for the office, and fully expected another to take it — accepted the vote and resumed work on several trade agreements that were under way.

***

The next time Levy had leave and headed to the team's preferred bar, he only had a couple of beers, then left by that same side door that had seen him projectile barf before. He had just turned for the street — the alley dead-ended against another building — when it was blocked by a group of about four young Palestinians local to the area. Unfortunately they were known to be hostile, and suspected to be in search of a terror cell to join. Meanwhile, it seemed they wanted to harass the local soldiers.

"Anet lena," the leader said in Arabic, smirk growing to a grin as he saw that Levy was alone. "Anet lhem meyt." (*You are ours. You are dead meat.*)

Levy was still learning the martial art that would eventually be called krav maga, as well as several others, like karate and judo, and while he was learning fast, he wasn't at all certain he could take down four men at once. And since they were now advancing on him with wicked smirks, the leader having drawn a large knife, it was obvious they wanted an altercation.

Well, he thought, remembering his older brother with fondness, *let's give them one. Help me, Eleazar.*

Aiming the cry at the still-open back door, he yelled, "MARB!" at the top of his lungs, then stooped and caught up a loose cobblestone fragment from the alley pavement. (*Ambush!*)

Targeting the forehead of the leader, who was closest, Levy flung the cobblestone with considerable force. It hit hard, throwing the man backward, and ricocheted off, pasting the man beside the leader in the face. The leader went down on his back, unconscious but not dead; unlike Eleazar, Franz had not intended to kill. The knife clattered to the pavement. The other man, who had also drawn a knife, dropped it and grabbed his face — the stone narrowly missed his eye, and his brow was now bleeding into his eye profusely, the area swelling rapidly. Within seconds, between the blood and the swelling, he was unable to see from that eye. A quick kick to the knee on his blind side put him down for the count, howling in pain.

Levy lunged forward, drawing back his fist, and delivered a powerful straight punch to a third Palestinian's jaw, dodging the slightly awkward and wholly panicked knife slash meant for him from that same man, even as IDF soldiers poured from the side door of the bar, alerted by Levy's shout. They quickly grabbed the fourth assailant, immobilizing him as Levy came around with his non-dominant hand in a one-two combo, knocking the man to the opposite side. He staggered and went down, whereupon Levy applied a snap kick to the face that broke his nose and rendered him unconscious.

The last would-be attacker was currently being beaten upon by several IDF soldiers, even while continuing to attempt cutting them with his knife. One soldier took a minor slash to his arm, which drew blood; he, however, was more skilled in martial arts than Levy, being a samar, a sergeant first class. Enraged, he quickly disarmed his opponent as the other IDF soldiers backed off. Several quick combinations of kicks and blows put the man on his face; he hit the pavement hard and, the wind thoroughly knocked out of him, promptly passed out.

A ranag, a chief warrant officer, stepped from the group and approached Levy.

"Are you all right, son? Did they hurt you? You bleeding anywhere?"

"No, sir," Levy responded. "I made use of a loose cobblestone and what I knew from my martial arts training." He shrugged. "My older brother Eleazar once took out a Nazi guard with a rock, so I took a leaf from his book, as the saying is."

"Excellent! Where is your brother now?"

"In the bosom of Abraham, sir." Levy firmed his jaw; the memory still did him no favors emotionally. "The other guards at the concentration camp didn't take well to his killing one of their number."

"Oh. Damn. I'm sorry, son. But you chose a good man to emulate. I think your family must be descended from King David, by the sound."

"Well, sir, I'm a Levy, so we're more likely to be descended from Father Levi," he responded. "I'm afraid I don't know about any other links; my mother liked keeping up with it, and Father was a rabbi, so he was knowledgeable about our genealogy, But neither of them survived the first day at Majdanek. And I was too young yet for them to pass it down; I was in the camp nearly two years before I even reached my bar mitzvah. Not that there was much to it, but my great-uncle tried."

"Shit."

"Something like, yes, sir."

"Still, I think I'll call you David."

The other soldiers laughed, even as the local police arrived on the scene and began taking the miscreants into custody.

***

It was another hour before Levy finally made it back to his barracks; the police had taken statements from everyone, especially him since he'd been the original target. But he was worn out when he finally arrived at his bunk. It didn't take him long to prep for bed, strip to his shorts and t-shirt, and crawl between the covers.

He was asleep within minutes.

***

One of the female recruits he ran into a lot was a pretty brunette named Esther Aaronsen; her family was from Norway and had fled the Nazis. After a while, he asked her to go with him to the movies, and she accepted.

Their next date was dinner at a reasonably nice restaurant.

When he dropped her off at her barracks, he kissed her. And she kissed back.

Suddenly Franz Levy had his first girlfriend.

It wasn't particularly serious, but they both enjoyed being together.

They kissed a lot.

***

A few days later, a package arrived for him. It had no indication of who sent it, and he had no friends or relatives who might have done. He applied all due caution opening it.

Inside there was a box, and in the box, a long shirt of chain mail, an undershirt of soft leather, and a note. The note read,

> *Here you go, 'David.' I have a friend who likes to do medieval re-enactments, and he makes this shit. Wear this under your shirt the next time you go on leave. If they try to gut-punch you, they'll probably break a few fingers. I even had him do some special stuff to it to help make it cut-proof, not that chain mail needs much to do that. If they try to stab you with the point, it won't stop it, but it'll stop a slash, which is the technique those guys mostly use. Just be careful not to give 'em a stabbing angle and you'll be good. Oh, and don't forget your sling.*

Levy grinned wolfishly.

***

Three weeks later, coming out of the same bar — because it was THEIR hangout, dammit; the Palestinians wouldn't even go into a bar, as alcohol consumption broke Shari'ah law — the same group was waiting for Levy. They looked rather the worse for wear, with several black eyes and bruising still evident, and the guy whose knee Levy dislocated was not with them. But they came looking for trouble.

They found it.

Levy was indeed wearing the chain mail shirt with its leather undershirt beneath his fatigues. And he'd worn an old set of the fatigues, suspecting he might have another encounter, and less concerned the clothing might be damaged thereby.

He'd also acquired a western-style Y-shaped slingshot, as it required less room to utilize than a traditional Middle Eastern sling. This came out of a cargo pocket, along with a couple of shooter-marbles to use as stones — there were more marbles in the pocket — and he loaded a stone in the sling, then met their gaze.

Just then, he felt a slashing motion against his back.

He spun and let fly the stone. There was a thud, a grunt, and the fourth member of their group — apparently a replacement for Mr. Busted Knee — dropped unconscious to the pavement as the marble bounced off his forehead, very nearly between his eyes. Before the others could react, Levy was facing them again. Their jaws gaped wide.

"You — you are not hurt?!" the leader gasped. "Why are you not bleeding?"

"Because The One is on my side," Levy said with a smile. "MARB!" he shouted at the side door…

…And let fly three more 'stones' from the sling in rapid succession.

By the time the other soldiers could reach the alley, the wannabe terrorists were all unconscious, crumpled on the pavement, large lumps rising on their foreheads.

The ranag stopped, stared at the slashed shirt on Levy, the mail shirt glistening in the light through the slash, and the slingshot in his hand, then doubled over, laughing his ass off.

Levy just grinned.

***

After that, all the local Palestinians started giving Levy a wide berth.

"So can I come with you to the bar now?" Esther asked, when she'd stopped laughing after Levy told her what had happened.

"Yes, I think it'll be safe from now on," Levy decided, and grinned.

Esther started laughing all over again.

***

Upon finding out that Levy had been a member of the western resistance in Europe, and had been taught to drive by the other resistance members to include the ability to perform evasive maneuvers, Rabat Noah Mayer requested that Levy do a little teaching. He wanted to learn to drive like that, because he figured it would come in handy some day.

Levy conceded the point, and one weekend when they were both on leave, Mayer brought his car around and picked up Levy, and they drove to a defunct department store in nearby Rishon LeTsiyon. The car park for the store was fairly open, still well paved, and would provide a likely venue for driver training. The only negative was the rather deep ravine on the far side of the lot; a stream ran through it and there were fig and terebinth trees and scrub brush. The depth was such that, from the parking lot, one could look down on most of the treetops.

But since there was six feet of grass between the edge of the pavement and the edge of the ravine, they weren't worried.

"So how are we going to do this?" Mayer wondered.

"Well, I think the thing to do is for me to get behind the wheel and run a pattern that shows you what can be done, and then teach you how to do it," Levy suggested. "While you ride in the passenger seat and watch what I do."

"Run a pattern?"

"Yes. When the resistance operatives were training me, they put me through several set courses that taught the sequencing. You come out of this maneuver, then here's how you go into the next, and the next, and so forth. Once you get them down, they teach you how to swap up maneuvers. And I still remember them, and practice them every once in a while."

"All right…"

"Then I'll move to the passenger seat and put you behind the wheel, and I'll teach you how to run the pattern."

"Oh boy."

"Relax. It's not as hard as you think," Levy said with a grin. "I'd lay odds you have the pattern down by the time we're done. You need to watch your entry and exit speeds on the turns and spins, but that's the only real trick to it. I'll show you hand placement on the steering wheel and how to judge where you are in the curves and where to come out of the spins. Just don't tense up, or you can really overcompensate, and that's bad."

"…All right," Mayer said, still a little uncertain, and, Levy suspected, wondering what he'd gotten himself into. "Let's try this."

***

Levy drove through the pattern three times, increasing the vehicle speed each time, and Mayer picked up different things each time. Then they swapped places, and Levy had him drive through the pattern slowly several times, learning it before picking up speed.

He did well, learning the pattern almost as fast as Levy had as a teenager. It was when they sped up to full velocity that they had problems.

Mayer accelerated across the lot, hit the brakes hard, made the U-turn via fishtail. already accelerating out of the turn just as Levy had shown him. He repeated the process at the entry side of the lot, where he put the car into a full spin and a half and came screaming back toward the ravine side, where he intended to fishtail again, and return to the starting point.

But he mistimed the fishtail accelerations, and promptly tensed. That finished the matter.

The car did a full three-sixty even as Mayer hit the accelerator to attempt pulling away from the turn.

The vehicle shot across the remaining pavement, skidded across the grass as he tried desperately to slam on the brakes, and went over the edge of the ravine, as a wide-eyed Levy held onto the bucket seat and Mayer braced on the steering wheel.

Seconds later, they brought up with an uncomfortable bounce in the treetop of a thick, ancient fig.

"Shit," Levy said then.

"Too late; done did," Mayer replied.

***

Getting out and away from the car proved the hard part. In the end, they wound up easing away from the car onto the largest branches they could find and leaping the six or seven feet to the bluff, which was sloped enough to enable them to scrabble their way up the side to the parking lot. By the time they reached the top, they were dusty, dirty, scratched, and bleeding in a couple of spots.

"How are we going to get it out of the tree?" Mayer wondered.

"We call a tow truck," Levy noted, succinct. "And we call the lieutenant and let him know we're going to be late."

"Damn."

"Yes."

***

But when their superiors found out that Levy had been a resistance operative ranging across Europe in the aftermath of the war, they got interested instead of upset.

Within two weeks, Levy received transfer papers…into the Israeli Military Intelligence Directorate, commonly known by the Hebrew acronym/nickname, AMAN. Specifically he was transferred into the top-secret Sayeret Matkal, the special forces/ special reconnaissance unit…though he could tell no one THAT.

Two days later, Esther got her transfer papers to the naval training facility in Haifa; she would be putting out to sea soon after. Levy's first romantic relationship had ended.

A month after that, Mayer was killed by a suicide bomber while out shopping.

Levy managed to get leave from his training to attend the funeral, which was good because he was a pallbearer.

As he left the cemetery to head back to his billet, he sighed. He was getting tired of losing friends like this.

Then again, he thought, *'there is a time for every matter under the heaven.' Including death. So I'll probably never get rid of THAT.*

***

There was some intense training required to get Levy up to speed on the procedural aspect of how the IDF did intelligence operations, including paratrooper ops and special training with friendly Bedouin trackers, but in a matter of weeks he was receiving minor assignments within Israeli borders.

He also discovered chess, and the strategy behind it; he began to play whenever he got a chance.

Combining all of that with his experience in Europe, he quickly began to show promise as an AMAN operative.

***

One of the things the new operatives often did when they did not have an active assignment was to keep themselves honed by playing scouting and hunting games around the base at night. He was still at Tzrifin, but in a different part of the military reservation; it was big enough to give them plenty of opportunities to practice their techniques.

In the process, he started to find himself picking up on things that, at first glance, seemed almost psychic in nature, but weren't. This would one day be called by a Division One Agent his 'arachnid sense,' in a kind of homage to a comic book character that had yet to be created.

Like the time he felt someone or something was watching him, only to discover one of the guard dogs, who knew him because they had worked together during recent training, staring at him instead of barking…apparently expecting a skritch. Levy obliged.

Or the time he semiconsciously heard the soft footsteps following, and took evasive action before the other soldier had a clue he'd been detected.

But Levy knew he'd developed a new skill when he had the sudden sense of something WRONG, something BAD about to happen, and instinctively leaped backward—

—Away from a partly-hidden Palestine viper in the leaves and grass along the path, already in process of striking from its lair.

The sound of his personal-issue weapon firing rent the night, and military police and other AMAN operatives came running.

When they found him standing over the remains of the golden-tan viper, blown in two a couple of inches behind the head, no questions needed asking.

***

One of the things he was selected to learn was EOD, explosive ordinance disposal, and evertying that pertained to it. His instructor was a Mossad agent, since members of that organization had to have considerable experience. Ezra Gabai was a friendly sort, at least to Levy; he took the young man in hand, especially after finding out about his resistance work, and trained him personally, showing him all the ins and outs of handling various types of bombs and disarming them.

To have the kind of detailed knowledge and skill AMAN and Mossad both wanted him to have, they worked together for over six months.

At the end of that time, Gabai came to him.

"We need to talk," he said.

***

"Wait. And you want me to go along…as your backup?" Levy asked when Gabai had finished briefing him on a mission.

"That's right. The position is more observation than actual backup," Gabai said. "The higher-ups want you to get a feel for what it's really like to do the high-end missions, and you can be extra eyes, ears, hands…"

"Meaning what, exactly?"

"Meaning you can play nurse to my surgeon on disarming any explosives we find, and back me up when I take out the bomb maker." Gabai paused. "Wait. Your chain of command does know about the takedown of your friend Gabe's assassin, right?"

"Um, no, actually…"

"So you told me, but no one else?"

"No one else was supposed to know. The resistance cell leader knew, but nobody else in the cell did. Or anywhere else. And until I told you, I'd kept it that way."

"All right. Good. I haven't betrayed your secret, though I might have let on that you knew more about that sort of thing than they knew."

"That's fine, I guess." Levy shrugged. "I just didn't want anybody coming after me for it. Especially when the cell leader — he was actually the regional lead, in addition to my cell — sanctioned it."

"That'll work, then. Okay, so let's go over the details of the mission…"

***

Jabalia was a Palestinian refugee camp in the outskirts of Gaza, near the north end of the Gaza Strip. It was near Checkpoint Erez, one of the key ingress/egress points for Palestinian workers in Israel.

Jabalia was also one of the hot spots for terrorist activity in the region.

Maadin al-Khatib was the prized centerpiece of a fedayeen cell headquartered in Jabalia, and whose members largely worked in Israeli territories. Al-Khatib was a rather skilled maker of improvised explosive devices.

It was the job of Team Alef — made up of Mossad agents Ezra Gabai, Kalev Berg, and Yarden Fein, and IDF AMAN Rabal, or Corporal, Franz Levy — to ensure he never made another IED.

***

It was a bit over forty miles from Tzrifin to Jabalia. Yarden Fein drove the team down from the base to Checkpoint Erez in a civilian Willys station wagon, and Kalev Berg would drive it back; meanwhile, Berg rode shotgun. While they were inside the Strip, both would function as reconnaissance and sniping; surveillance had already been performed before Team Alef was put together.

Gabai napped on the way down; it was well after dark when they left the base after picking up Levy, and he would need to have his wits about him once they arrived at their destination. Levy was also supposed to nap, but found himself a bit too keyed up to do so.

It wasn't long before they all were.

***

They were halfway to the checkpoint when a mortar shell impacted the road directly in front of them, but did not explode.

Fein executed some deft avoidance maneuvers, the likes of which would have impressed Levy had he not been grabbing for whatever would hold him in place within the vehicle. Berg had instinctively braced himself in the front passenger seat, the result of years of training coming in handy. Gabai, however, woke to being violently thrown about the back seat, eventually ending up in the floorboard when the station wagon finally came to a stop. It rocked briefly, but did not turn over.

"Verdammt," Berg cursed. "Everybody in one piece?"

"Ugh," Gabai groaned. "I'm still checking body parts."

"What he said," Levy agreed, as he helped Gabai crawl out of the floor and back into the seat.

"I'm getting us out of here," Fein said, shifting the car back into drive. "Just because the damn thing hasn't blown up yet doesn't mean it won't."

"No, and I'm going to call it in," Berg agreed. "We're far enough away for a call to be safe, especially if it's ciphered. And we don't need civvies getting blown to bits." He pulled out a radio as Fein got them back onto the road and under way.

"You don't suppose that was aimed at us, do you?" Levy wondered.

"Doubtful," Gabai decided. "Nobody but our immediate superiors even knows about this, and half of them don't know our destination."

"Sheer dumb luck," Fein affirmed. "I'm not smelling any foul odors, so I assume we won't have to reupholster the car."

"No, it happened too fast," Levy offered with a wry grin. "We might have to pull over and take a piss, however."

"Now I'll agree to that," Berg averred as he put away the radio.

***

While Team Alef had defusing experts with them, they also had a schedule to meet, so Berg called his lead and let him know there was an unexploded ordnance embedded in the road; he was assured that the local police jurisdiction would be notified and barricade the road until the mortar round could be detonated. Which, in turn, likely meant the road would need to be reconstructed in that section; Berg began planning a new route back.

"Which," he pointed out half an hour later, during the by-then-mandatory piss stop in the shrubs by the roadside, "is probably a good thing anyway, given tonight's job."

"It is," Gabai agreed. "I'm good with it."

"Me too," Fein noted.

They all turned to Levy, who was still emptying his bladder.

"Um, me three, I guess," he said with a shrug. "I didn't know I had a vote."

"Of course you do, Franz," Gabai declared. "You're part of this team; you get input."

"Okay. Then can I make a request for the future?"

"Sure."

"Next time you lot take me out on one of these, remind me beforehand not to stop off for mess coffee first, so I can stay awake. Damn, I'm never going to get rid of all this…"

They all laughed.

***

It took longer than they'd planned to get to the checkpoint thanks to the unexpected nigh-disaster and ensuing physiological responses, but the guards there had been notified to expect them, though not why, or who they were; they knew only to let them through, then back out, no matter what ruckus ensued in between.

The Willys rolled through the gate and into the Gaza Strip.

***

The area outside the checkpoint was largely farmland or open field; the area inside the boundary was heavily populated. Most of the buildings in the area were of cinderblock construction; some of the masonry work was rather slipshod, as if it had been put up in haste. There were few street lights.

Fein eased the Willys station wagon into the neighborhood where al-Khatib lived. There, he hid it in the shed that had been arranged for it; their undercover contact emerged from hiding.

"Is the garage available for the night?" Fein gave the sign in Arabic.

"Only until the morning," came the countersign. "Go. I have this."

Berg and Fein slipped away, into the darkness.

Gabai and Levy tucked little earpieces into their ears and activated miniature microphones hidden in the collars of their tunics, then waited until a tiny red light lit on Gabai's radio, which was itself set to silent mode; any comms would come in through the earpieces. He touched Levy's shoulder.

"Let's go," he said.

***

Team Alef was in typical Palestinian dress for summer — loose trousers, tunics, and keffiyehs — with a bit of makeup here and there where needed. All four were also fluent in the local dialect of Arabic, and they walked quietly through the streets toward their stations.

As the escape driver, Berg was closest to the vehicle; he took up a position on a rooftop overlooking al-Khatib's house

221

and watched for anyone coming or going. At this time of night, there were no obvious lights visible in the windows; a few faint orange glows showed where some sort of nightlight might be, but no shadows moved across them.

He pulled a long case from beneath his tunic and proceeded to unpack a sniper rifle on a bipod.

Then he pulled another, smaller package and set a small explosive device on the side of the building below his position.

Only then did he press a special button on his silenced radio; it would light a tiny red button on Gabai's radio, signaling him that he was in position.

Then he put on a small headset and hooked it into the radio.

***

On the far side of al-Khatib's house, Fein set up his position as well in much the same way: on a rooftop overlooking the target house, he determined there was no one out and about, and all lights within the house were out. The sniper rifle on a bipod came out, and the little explosive was attached to the wall beneath his overlook.

Then he, too, keyed the special button on his silenced radio, and donned his headset.

***

Gabai and Levy wandered down the street in front of al-Khatib's home, moving slowly and casually, murmuring to each other in Arabic from time to time. As they passed the house, they slowed. Moments later, they heard Berg in their earphones.

"All clear."

Seconds after that, Fein added, "Ditto."

They turned down the dark side alley toward a shed separated from the other buildings.

***

The shed where al-Khatib made his explosives was a metal prefabricated structure, and it sat on short stilts, with three steps up to the door. It had a padlock on the door, and no windows, and it should have been a cake walk for them to get inside.

Unfortunately, halfway down the dark alley, Gabai stumbled on a loose stone and nearly fell, grabbing the nearby wall with one hand, barking his knuckles badly in the process. Levy spun and grabbed him, keeping him from hitting the ground. He stifled a hiss of pain.

"What happened?" Levy breathed, as Gabai leaned heavily on him.

"I think when we dodged the mortar in the car, I got banged up more than I thought," Gabai whispered. "I'd been noticing my left hand was starting to swell, and dragging it across the concrete blocks just now didn't help it one bit. And now I think that rock just finished off my ankle. I don't know if I can even get into the shed, let alone scale the wall to his room."

"Shit," Levy murmured. "Do we need to scrub?"

"Near Side copies," Berg's voice murmured in their ears.

"Far Side copies," Fein added. "DO we need to scrub?"

"No," Gabai decreed. "I'll talk my, ah, my son through it."

"Me?!" Levy hissed.

"You. You're well able to do any of this. I'll be there for the hardest part."

"Al'ama," Levy cursed quietly in Arabic. (*Damn*)

"Calm down. You've had the training for all of this. Work with me."

"…All right. What's next?"

"Get me to the shed. Then help me get up the steps into it."

***

By the time they got into the shed — the padlock was surprisingly basic, and Levy had no trouble picking it — Fein and Berg were keeping eagle eyes on the area so the pair would not be disturbed; there was no way Gabai could run if swift escape were needed. This meant 'Code Black' was in play: any interlopers who showed on the scene would be sniped.

"All right," Gabai said in a more normal tone, though he kept his voice low despite the closed door; they didn't need passersby overhearing a conversation from what should have been an empty shed. "Do you remember the plan?"

"Scout out all the completed IEDs and all the nearly-completed explosives, wire them together, and attach a remote detonator," Levy replied. "In the dark."

"Good. Yes, in the dark. It's easier than you'd think. You'll be doing the wiring, because this hand won't deal with the fine coordination now, I'm afraid," Gabai pointed out, holding up a hand that was starting to swell rather badly by that time; bruises and some barked skin — though no blood — showed on the knuckles. "There's a piece of lumber over here that looks like the right length for me to use as a makeshift crutch; let me grab that and I'll help you look for the devices."

"I copy. Begin search?"

"Begin."

They took opposite sides of the shed and began the search.

***

After about half an hour, they had an organized cluster of improvised bombs sitting on the central work table, and several large incomplete devices and components were laid out next to them. Gabai handed Levy his tool roll.

"Remember to use that stylized method of wiring; we want this to look like that rival fedayeen group once they find the bits."

"Got it," Levy replied.

It took Levy about another fifteen minutes to wire everything together in the fashion desired, then five more to attach a detonator Gabai brought along that would be triggered by a special radio signal.

The pair slipped back out of the shed and locked it behind them. They would trigger the detonator once they returned to the car. Better yet, as Gabai told Levy, they would trigger it after they had passed back through Checkpoint Erez.

***

"Checking in," Fein's voice murmured in their ears, keeping the conversation in Arabic.

"The gift is wrapped," Gabai responded. "Readying to visit the family."

"Copy."

"Weather status?"

"All clear on the south."

"All clear on the north," Berg chimed in. "Getting late, though. Need to hurry."

"Understood," Levy answered.

***

"Okay, son," Gabai said, avoiding using Levy's given name, which was patently not Arabic, "you have the correct window sighted?"

"Top floor, right hand?"

"That's the one. I have a couple of things you'll need to help you along," Gabai noted, producing a couple of small bundles from somewhere in the folds of his tunic. "Here. Strip down to the skin suit, then put on these booties and gloves."

"I guess it's good you made me fit up as if I was going to do it," Levy said, obeying the Mossad agent. "At least I'm ready to do this."

"Exactly. You always go in with backup plans, just in case. ALWAYS. You're my backup plan."

By this point, Levy was standing in a snug matte black bodysuit, a small tool belt slung at his waist. He pulled the cowling, currently scrunched around his neck, up and over his head and face, and instantly became a shadow. He accepted the two small bundles Gabai proffered, unrolling them to produce a pair of flexible booties with embedded crampons on the balls of the feet, and gauntlets of similar design, save that the crampons covered the palms and fingers. All of the crampons were angled backward and slightly hooked. Donning them and strapping them firmly to ankles and wrists, he turned toward the cinderblock wall.

The specially hardened crampons bit into the cinderblock with relative ease, and Levy cautiously scaled the wall. It felt awkward; he was hanging from his hands and feet, but he was strong enough to hold his position, and he kept climbing.

It took him nearly twenty minutes to go up the three stories to the top floor, then work sideways to the designated window. There was a faint orange glow, indicative of a night light in the room; it made it at once easier and harder. He leaned over cautiously, trying to ensure that no light behind him would silhouette his head and make a target for someone wielding a gun inside. Peering through the window, he ensured that the only occupant was al-Khatib — who was a widower, hence the lack of mate in the bed — and he was asleep.

Facing the far wall, at that, Levy thought. *Which gives me a bit more advantage.*

"What do you see?" Gabai asked in his ear.

"Solo. Asleep," Levy replied, succinct. "Facing away."

"Good. Like I showed you, then."

Using the specialized crampon on the tip of his index finger, Levy quietly drew a large circle on the glass, then used a suction cup on the back of the gauntlet to tap and remove the section of glass. Reaching inside, he unlatched the window and silently raised it, allowing himself entrance. The circle of glass was placed on a dresser to await departure.

Tiptoeing over to the bedroom door, which was almost closed, he peered into the hall, careful to avoid being seen. The hallway was empty. He locked the door from the outside, then eased it closed, turning the knob to latch it without the telltale click.

Then he moved to the bed and drew the special semi-automatic pistol that Gabai had issued him for this mission, a matte blued Fratelli Tanfoglio 9mm in a hidden holster on his tool belt. He extracted the silencer from its pouch on his tool belt and screwed it onto the pistol. Picking up the extra pillow and putting it around the gun by way of additional insurance — there should be no one else in the house, but he was taking no chances — he put two rounds into al-Khatib's head.

The body spasmed once, then slumped. A quick check of the carotid pulse confirmed: al-Khatib was dead. He holstered the pistol.

Then he pulled a small explosive device from the tool belt and placed it on the floor beneath the bed, directly under the body. He flipped a switch to arm it, then went back to the window and out, snagging the disk of glass as he went.

***

On the wall, he closed the window, reached back through the opening and latched it, then carefully cut out the entire pane. He took it and the original circle and sliced them into fragments, which he then put in a special bag and tossed down to Gabai, who proceeded to use the same stone which had tripped him up earlier to quietly crush the bag's contents, then carefully dump them on the ground beneath the window, even as Levy came down the wall on the opposite side of the window from where he had ascended.

On the ground once more, he doffed the crampon gauntlets and booties and tucked the cowl back down around his neck, then donned his Palestinian clothing once more. He moved to Gabai's side — who was still using the makeshift crutch to get around — and they quietly headed down the alley and back the way they had come.

***

Back at the station wagon, Gabai sent the 'all clear — withdraw' signal to Berg and Fein. Berg arrived first, being closer, then Fein.

They climbed into the station wagon, nodded to their embedded contact who had stood guard over the vehicle while they performed their mission, and headed for the checkpoint.

***

Once the car was out of the Gaza Strip and in Israeli-controlled land, Levy turned to Gabai.

"Now?" he wondered.

"Now." Gabai nodded, and handed Levy his radio.

Levy removed a cover on the top, then pressed the hidden button thus revealed.

Behind them, quadruple suns lit the night, and four adjacent conventional-explosive mushroom clouds rose, one considerably bigger than the others.

"Exit one bomb maker and his lab," Gabai noted.

***

The first place they went was to the Mossad physician so Gabai could be properly seen-to.

There, they discovered that he had a nasty ankle sprain, nearly a tendon tear, and severe bruising and sprains within his left hand, as well as the abrasions. The doctor could find no indication of any bone breaks or anything more severe, but it explained the pain, swelling, and lack of flexibility that had required Levy to take over.

And Gabai declared that he had graduated his training.

***

At that point, and after his superiors received Gabai's classified mission report, Levy was considered a full-fledged operative for AMAN and a possible fill-in for the Mossad.

He stayed busy for the next few years.

He was content.

Alone, but content.

***

By this time, Levy had a fairly stable personal life, and was making good money doing what he considered was good work, protecting his chosen nation from those who had sworn to destroy it.

So he went to a real estate agent in Tel Aviv and arranged to buy a small house outside of Rishon LeTsiyon, basically a bedroom community to the south. He spent his leave time here, occasionally inviting friends over for meals or similar social activities.

The back yard was rather bare, but that was fine: he knew what he intended to do.

He went to a landscaper and purchased a fig tree.

Then he dug a hole in the corner of the yard and planted it. In the bottom of the hole, before he put in the tree, he emptied a small vial of ashes. Then he filled in around the roots.

"There you go, Uncle Gabe," he murmured, as he watered down the loose soil around it. "Just like I promised you. Sorry it took so long."

Then he planted flowers around its base in honor of his family.

He told no one, but the next time his friends came over for a cookout, they raved at the beauty of the little garden oasis.

***

In late May of 1956, Levy turned 26. He was a Rav Samal, a decorated sergeant major in the IDF's AMAN; the rank was usually abbreviated 'rasal.'

In July of that same year, Levy was called into his commander's office.

"Rasal Levy, I'd like to introduce you to Noam Katz. He's with Mossad Merkazi le-Modiin ule-Tafkidim Meyuhadim. He wishes to speak with you."

Then, rather to Levy's surprise, Major Eckstein rose and left his office, leaving Levy alone with Katz.

"Please sit down, Rasal Levy," Katz said in a pleasant tone, indicating the visitor chair next to his own. "You are coming up on time in grade, as well as your periodic determination whether or not to continue in the IDF, and I have some options to discuss with you."

A curious Levy sat.

***

Within two months, he was no longer in the IDF, but working for the Mossad's Caesarea group. It was rumored that he was part of the Kidon, the ultra-secret urban legend of a special unit responsible for assassinating enemies of Israel, but he always just smiled and shrugged if another agent asked him.

Unknown to him, he was given the nickname of 'the Jewish Ninja.'

Privately, his superiors decided the moniker fit.

***

Chapter 10 — Spooks

Levy spent the first few years in the Mossad helping to eliminate attacks on Israel from neighboring states. This included the Egyptian-held Gaza Strip, the West Bank, and the Golan Heights of Syria, so it required infiltration and a fluent knowledge of various dialects of Arabic. But by this point, Levy had demonstrated a talent for languages and a skill for blending in, so those were not issues.

Some went easier than others, however.

*****

In 1958, there were a series of rocket launches from the Golan Heights in Syria across the Jordan River into northern Israel. The pinnacle of irritation of Israeli officials was reached when the principal hospital in the region was struck and damaged so badly it would need to be torn down and rebuilt, leaving the area without emergency and surgical facilities.

Several Mossad agents were sent to scope out the area from which the rocket launches were originating; Levy was assigned the area around Mount Odem. With the addition of a beard prosthetic — most agents who went undercover stayed clean-shaven to allow for quick changes to such — he was inserted under the guise of a Syrian merchant, one Salah

Mahmoud; this enabled him to wander around without attracting undue notice.

***

It didn't take long, or a great deal of detective work, to locate the fedayeen cell; overconfident, they simply left the rocket launcher on the roof of their building, going up to set the targeting and launch.

Levy felt his detective abilities were wasted on the mission.

Still, he did his due diligence and snooped out the members of the cell before reporting in.

It was right after that when things went sideways.

***

"No, this one is in the clear," Levy, still in disguise as the Syrian Salah Mahmoud, told his Mossad contact in Za'urah, in the modest, thick-walled Arab-style house provided for said contact. The village was on the far side of a cluster of villages on the slopes of Mount Odem, one of many extinct volcanoes in the Golan; his target was in Seif, elsewhere on the slopes of the volcano. "No small children, only teens of some age, and all of them part of the ring."

Their relationship was, in public, that of a merchant and his distributor; Levy had been invited to dinner, with a discussion of business to follow. Dinner was over, and now the business discussion was under way.

They sat in the room he'd designated as his office within the house. It was a stucco'ed room with dark wood furnishings in a distinctly Middle Eastern style, with tile inlays here and there, and wicker accents. The desk stood under the one window, with bookcases on either side, and a small table with two chairs for providing mint tea to guests; this latter was where Levy and his contact currently sat, sipping on the aromatic warm beverage — welcome in this especially cold winter. The window above the desk overlooked the modest courtyard in the center of the house, and despite the time of year, it was open to provide some fresh air; the female agent serving as his wife in the subterfuge had made a supper dish of fish with lots of onions, leeks, and garlic, and while it had been delicious — Levy could attest the fact — the strong smell lingered.

"What about the women?" Akeem Hussein asked; it wasn't his real name, but in the Golan in 1958, using a Mossad agent's Jewish name got him killed.

"They are, if anything, more extreme than the men," Levy noted, setting down his cup of tea. "Several of them, and of the teens, are in training to be suicide bombers. Never mind the rocket launcher — occasionally under camo, but usually not — on the roof of the house." He shook his head. "I haven't decided if they're just that overconfident, or that stupid."

"The neighborhood?" Hussein pressed.

"This is a clan of sorts, an extended family unit," Levy explained, pointing to the map on the table. "The entire block and all of the surrounding buildings are occupied by this one cell. They're ALL fedayeen."

Hussein sat back in surprise.

"So one run will take them out?"

"It should, yes. Or enough to break the cell," Levy noted. "With no collateral casualties. Whereas the rockets they're firing are hitting hospitals, orphanages, nurseries…"

"And deliberately so," his contact said in disgust. "They're TARGETING those hospitals and orphanages."

"I know," Levy said with a nod. "I was able to listen in on their plans, and what they'd set for the next targets."

"What?! How?"

"The women gossip in the souk. And I am a merchant."

"Humph. Eich hafn az ze al filn en gehennim," the other man growled, keeping his voice low to avoid anyone else hearing Hebrew. (*I hope they all rot in hell.*)

"It would serve them right," Levy agreed in similar tone. "Still, that judgement belongs to HaShem."

"You are right, meyn khaver, but I can hope," the contact offered with a wry grin. (*my friend*)

"Can't we all?" Levy offered, bone-dry, and they both laughed, though the sound was grim. "Well, I'll get the marker on the target building. You notify Headquarters."

"I will."

Levy slipped out by the back door, vanishing in the darkness.

***

It was only about a mile between Za'urah and Seif, and the terrain, while hilly, was relatively flat, so close to the mountaintop. It was also largely wild, and with Damascus the largest city some fifty miles distant, there were few cars. So Levy walked.

He did not take the road; he didn't want that kind of potential visibility. But he paralleled it, keeping to the Odem forest for as long as he could before slipping through the mountain scrub brush.

It was cold on the mountain; winter was coming, and it was night. The moon was waxing gibbous and gave a reasonable amount of light for foot travel, when it appeared between the scudding clouds. The seasonal rains had stopped for the time, though the ground was muddy and wet and the air was damp. The temperature hadn't hit freezing, but it wasn't far from it tonight, and the wind on the mountain was biting.

To combat the weather, Levy wore traditional Syrian clothing intended for winter: loose woolen trousers, less structured than European; a kaftan, likewise woolen for the winter and loose enough to hide some interesting equipment underneath, and a dark hooded cloak. On his head was a white taqiyyah topped and largely hidden by a red and white checked keffiyeh or gutrah. The hood of the cloak went over all. His feet appeared to be shod in traditional leather shoes, but even the most stringent Muslims in the area tended to use galoshes over them during the rainy season to prevent ruining expensive leather in the mud. Levy, being no fool and having some experience with the matter, opted for rubber rain boots that looked like leather. They also made for much quieter footsteps.

The end result was fairly warm and dry, especially when he added long underwear and woolen socks under all.

With the addition of special pockets and pouches, it also effectively hid weapons, lockpicks, and all the other equipment of a skilled Mossad agent.

***

Har Odem, or Mount Odem, known to the Syrians as Ras al-Ahmar, was one of a series of ancient volcanoes that lined the Syrian-African Rift Valley, and which had produced the Golan Heights in geologic history by dint of extensive basaltic lava flows. The Mount Hermon range nearby, however, was mostly uplifted limestone. In any event, there were plenty of caves and deep canyon-like valleys where people and animals could hide. The seasonally-abundant rainfall and the remains of once-extensive forests meant the area held substantial wildlife. So it boded Levy to remain aware of his surroundings, even in the dark. Just because he wasn't followed by a human didn't mean he couldn't be killed by an animal.

So he heard the soft but distinctly squishy footsteps shadowing him to the left, despite their being slightly downwind of him. The distance indicated that whoever shadowed him was on the road, mucky though that was — it was one reason he had not used it; the trail he would leave was too obvious. He paused and scanned the ground before him, as if searching for his next step in the dim light. The footsteps paused. He resumed; they resumed.

Farkakte, he thought. *Someone's following me, no doubt. Have I been found out? Will I even make it to finish my mission? Was someone listening in the courtyard?*

Considering his position, Levy continued to ease through the brush.

He had gone roughly another five hundred feet by his estimate, when he became aware of something else.

***

The kynokephaloi were a kind of mythological cryptid, reported to have been seen on many continents, but most common to the Middle Eastern region from Greece around to North Africa, and as far east as eastern India and the Andaman Islands, though the island population was apparently now extinct. The name came from the Greek κυνοκεφαλοι, and the word meant 'dog-head.' They were reputed to have roughly humanoid bodies comparable in size to humans, but canid heads; some said that the Egyptian god Anubis had been a kynokephalus, and Greek myth featured the creatures in a couple of instances.

In some cultures they were said to be civilized, and historical figures from Marco Polo to Christopher Columbus had reported them. One legend even held that Saint Christopher had once been a kynokephalus, only assuming full human form after his conversion to Christianity.

More often, however, they were considered bloodthirsty creatures, not so much different from a werewolf, and fierce fighters, even warriors in the more intelligent, cultured tribes.

There had been legends of them in the area of Israel for a long, long time. The limestone areas allowed for caves which wildlife used as dens, and occasionally even the lava flows showed ancient flow tubes that could be used in similar fashion. Kynokephaloi were supposedly not averse to using them the same way.

Levy's IDF unit had seen a group — a pack? — of what they could only describe as kynokephaloi one night during his early training and deployments, before he had been assigned to AMAN. The encounter had been 'near distance,' no farther than about fifty meters but no closer than about thirty, and the soldiers could hear and see them fairly plainly by the crescent moon's light; night vision goggles had provided a bit more detail, including the clawed 'hands' and the teeth of a large predator. They had heard the things snuffling and growling in the dark, and smelled a peculiar kind of pungent, sharp, wild-animal stench from them.

And they were patently hunting.

More, they appeared to be trying to follow the soldiers' spoor, what little they'd left; fortuitously they had been training in evading search dogs, and this seemed to also elude the kynokephaloi.

Just in case, however, the unit commander ordered everyone to climb into the trees as quietly as possible. The creatures did not appear able to climb, and they could, he decreed, observe from there. Given the creatures' actions and reputations, none of them had been stupid enough to approach that night; the unit had spent the night in the trees, and the kynokephaloi had finally lost interest and wandered off, apparently in search of an easier-to-acquire dinner. The unit commander refused to report the incident, and no one in the unit disobeyed.

Levy had been curious enough to investigate the area the next day, however. He had found strange footprints that were very humanoid but possessed of large claws, and tufts of coarse fur with a downy underlayer caught in the brush, the likes of which he had never seen. There was a small cave opening nearby, and the prints led to its mouth; he did not approach closer.

It had been an experience he never forgot.

***

So when the breeze brought that same peculiar, acrid, almost-but-not-quite wild-animal smell to his nose as he attempted to make his way to Seif, he was instantly aware of what it was, and that it was close, and upwind.

Which meant that it was on his right, as opposed to the human on his left.

Then he heard the faint snuffling. A soft, growling whine floated to his ears. It was hunting.

It was hunting…him.

Sonuvabitch, he cursed to himself. *Assassin on the left, monster-thing on the right. And me in the middle, being hunted by both. Some days I do hate this job.*

He began to think harder and faster.

***

Levy kept his cool but picked up the pace slightly. Since both entities already knew he was there, he used only minimal stealth. If he could get another hundred and fifty meters, he should be able to act.

The footsteps on his left likewise picked up the pace; the snuffling kept up as well, but did not come closer…yet.

Levy kept going until his target was in sight.

Then he broke into a sprint, moving swiftly into and across the muddy, unpaved road, choosing his steps carefully.

There was a startled exclamation from the left, and a slight snort of surprise from the right, then the sound of mushy thuds and crashing brush…

…As Levy jumped onto the big newly-fallen branch from a recent storm leaning against the rock that he'd seen as he walked to Za'urah that afternoon, and used the green wood as a springboard up into the wild carob tree from which it had fallen. Grabbing limbs, he swiftly hauled himself higher into the tree, its evergreen leaves concealing his form…

…Just as a Syrian man appeared on the road…

…And a huge, black-furred kynokephalus crashed out of the brush.

The man screamed in a combination of terror and ferocity, and pulled a hidden hunting knife as the kynokephalus charged.

***

Levy waited a full ten minutes after the kynokephalus dragged his dead prey away to its den, then he shinned down the tree trunk. He produced a small flashlight from a hidden pocket and verified that he left no footprints in his sprint across the road; he had specifically chosen large rocks as stepping-stones over the expanse of mud. Satisfied, he turned to slip off into the darkness…

…And froze in his tracks.

A huge five-foot-long Palestine viper, disturbed from its cool-weather lethargy by the fight at the tree's base, was coiled to strike.

Farkakte, al'ama, l'enfer, he cursed to himself in Yiddish, Arabic, and French. *Frying pan, meet fire. (Shit, damn, hell)*

***

It took twice as long as he had anticipated for Levy to reach Seif; after he pinned the viper to the ground in mid-strike with a well-placed throwing knife only a couple of inches behind the head, not-coincidentally severing its spine in the process, he waited for the snake to die. Then he retrieved his knife, wiping it on a handy leaf from the carob tree before returning it to its hiding place.

He moved away from the dead snake some fifty feet… then quickly found a convenient rock outcrop as his knees decided to refuse to lock out.

Well, experienced or no, an assassin, a kynokephalus, and a viper all targeting me specifically and trying to kill me inside a half-hour is gonna do things to the adrenaline, I guess, he considered, as he sat and worked at calming down and preventing the shakes that threatened. *That was one hell of a fight between the Syrian and the dog-head, but the Syrian never stood a chance. One good swipe of the thing's claws gutted him like a cow in a slaughterhouse. Better him than me, though.*

It took fully half an hour for him to settle enough to proceed with a decent degree of alertness.

***

Finally he arrived at Seif. It was past midnight and nothing was on the streets of the village, so there was little to impede his progress except the possibility of a stray dog barking.

A REGULAR dog, he thought, taking extra care to avoid attracting the attention of ANY canid.

He approached the house that was the headquarters for the fedayeen cell, slipping to the side through a narrow alley.

There, he slipped off his rubber boots and socks, tying the laces together and hanging them around his neck before stuffing the socks inside. The cobblestones of the alley were cold and damp on his bare feet, but this way he could feel with them, and use his toes.

He turned to the stucco'ed wall; it had been poorly maintained on this side and there were pits and holes where the stucco had spalled away from the underlying laths.

Using these as hand-and toe-holds, he began to scale the wall. The fact that the alley was extremely narrow enabled him to chimney a good part of the way.

On the second story, he found a likely spot and activated, then tucked away a special bit of electronics in a particularly large, deep pit in the stucco.

He got down the same way he got up.

Then he donned his socks and shoes, and the Jewish Ninja slipped away.

*****

The next day an Israeli squadron of MD 450 Ouragans overflew Seif. They fired a full volley of Matra air-to-ground missiles, modified to home in on the device that Levy had planted on the side of the primary building the night before.

Moments later, that section of Seif was missing.

*****

From the peak of Har Kramim roughly two miles north and on the far side of the Druze town of Buq'ata on its slopes, 'Salah Mahmoud' stood with a tiny but powerful pair of field glasses, looking south.

Suddenly the mushroom clouds of conventional explosives blossomed in the distance. Several secondary explosions appeared, bright along the horizon; apparently the rockets stored on the rooftops had cooked off.

'Salah Mahmoud' smiled, tucked away the field glasses, and headed down the mountain toward his waiting extraction.

"Mission accomplished," he murmured as he got in the ancient, battered car.

"I never doubted it," said 'Akeem Hussein.' His 'wife' — a physician, there for emergencies — sat beside him. "Let's go."

***

In early December of 1959, having more than adequately proven himself in the Caesarea group, Levy was assigned to Operation Garibaldi and sent to Argentina. He spent the next six months shadowing one Adolf Eichmann; Nazi hunters Simon Wiesenthal and Lothar Hermann had together managed to identify the Nazi officer several years earlier, and the Mossad had spent the intervening time slowly gathering evidence that Wiesenthal and Hermann were right.

It was Levy's job to follow Eichmann's every move through Buenos Aires while the Mossad and the Israeli government prepared for the capture; should Eichmann show indication of flying, Levy's mandate allowed for assassination and extraction. He worked closely with Zvi Aharoni as the latter investigated Eichmann further and after only a few weeks, Aharoni had confirmed Eichmann's identity without doubt.

"Yes," Aharoni told Levy. "Keep up with him. Do NOT let him get away."

"Are we not going to simply extradite him?" Levy wondered. "I mean, I've never been to Argentina, but…"

"No. It would do no good, and might do great harm," Aharoni explained. "The Argentine government remained neutral throughout the war, refusing to declare war on Nazi Germany and exporting goods to them, until the outcome of the war was obvious. Then, and only then, did it 'declare war' as everyone else was mopping up. THEN they accepted fleeing Nazis into their country! Argentina is known for refusing, ignoring, and otherwise flouting such requests. They might even warn him so he has a chance to flee. I don't have proof of that, but I don't have proof against it, either."

Levy scowled.

"I see. Does he need to be taken down, then?"

"No. At least not yet. There are political considerations to deal with. I have it to understand that Ben-Gurion is carefully considering what to do in the matter."

"What do you think will happen?"

"I suspect he'll be spirited to Israel for public trial, if all goes well."

"Hm," Levy grunted. "Well, I'll be glad to help."

"I'm sure you will," Aharoni chuckled.

***

Levy found himself concealed in brush at the edge of an open field along Calle Garibaldi in San Fernando de la Buena Vista, a suburb of Buenos Aires, on the evening of May 11th, 1960. As Eichmann wandered by, a disguised fellow Mossad agent met him.

"Señor, ¿tiene un momento?" Zvi Malkin asked. (*Sir, do you have a moment?*)

Suspicious of the stranger, Eichmann stared at the man for a moment.

"¿Qué? ¡No! ¡No!" he cried, and spun to run. (*What? No! No!*)

Levy leaped from the brush and blocked Eichmann's path, even as another agent joined him.

In moments the three younger men had subdued Eichmann, who was by then in his 50s and not in the best of shape. They moved him to a waiting car, where he was bound and gagged, placed in the floor, and covered with a blanket.

Then they headed for a safehouse.

***

"No, Franz, we're going to do this right," Rafi bar Eitan — the Mossad agent leading the operation — said, as they stood in the front room of the safehouse and discussed the man imprisoned and under guard in the cellar. "The prime minister wants every proper step taken. We need that evidence to take him to trial."

"But we need to find Mengele too, Rafi!"

"Not this time. He's gone already. He was gone before we ever got word to pick up Eichmann. Probably someone tipped him off at some point, or maybe he just never lights in one place for long. That trail is cold, and we need to move with Eichmann."

"Farkakte, shit, mierda, and stront!" Levy cursed. "Very well. Tell me what you need me to do."

"We're going to need you to go out and verify some things for us," Eitan said.

"All right. Give me a list," was Levy's answer.

***

A week and a half later, between Levy's work and that of a couple of other Mossad agents, they had all the proof they needed; the team smuggled a sedated Eichmann aboard an El Al flight to Israel.

Three days after that, Eichmann was confined by Israeli forces on Israeli soil, and Ben-Gurion announced his capture to the Knesset.

A few days later, a certain 'Jewish ninja' hit the milestone age of 30.

Franz Levy moved on to his next assignment.

***

In the Earth year 1961AD, Pulgey Entiyti was elected to his fourth term as President of the Pan-Galactic Coalition.

By this point, there was essentially no dissent, and no other being would consider running against him; he was too greatly loved by the people of the galaxy, and for good reason. Under his administration, more treaties and agreements had been signed than in all the three millennia of the Coalition's prior existence. Unless and until he chose to resign or retire, the position was effectively his.

In later years, a certain cheeky female PGLEIA Agent from Earth would term it the 'Pax Entiyti.'

***

Over the next several years, Eichmann was put on trial, convicted of crimes against humanity among other things, and executed.

Levy kept up with it around various missions, which largely consisted of more excursions into Palestinian territories and surrounding countries, hunting down terror cells and either serving as the point man on a custody team, or as an assassin to take them out.

He was very successful at both.

On a couple of occasions, he served as special bodyguard to this or that notable figure, sometimes political, sometimes not, sometimes Israeli, sometimes not. He served well in each instance.

Until, a few months before his 35th birthday, in late 1964, he was sent to Brazil.

São Paulo, to be specific.

***

There, he worked closely with Yaakov Maidad, a Mossad agent with whom he'd worked on the Eichmann case. Maidad was attempting to get close to one Herberts Cukurs, the so-called 'Butcher of Latvia,' so that they could do much the same thing they'd done with Eichmann. The only question was to what country he'd be remanded for trial.

When word came down that they would get no help from either the West Germans — who were not interested in prosecuting — or Brazil, the Mossad agents realized it was Israel or not at all.

And given the man's crimes against humanity in general and Jews in specific, 'not at all' was unacceptable.

***

It took time and considerable effort, especially in disguising Maidad, but eventually Maidad became Cukurs' 'business colleague,' a supposed airline mogul from Vienna, Austria called Anton Künzle.

"Franz?" Maidad said, coming to his fellow agent in the bolt-hole in which he stayed. It was mid-February of 1965. They had been in São Paulo for five months.

"Yes, Yaak?" Levy said from the makeup table where he removed his disguise for the evening.

"I'm about to go forward with the plan. I think we're ready."

"Headed for Montevideo, then?"

"Yes. If we can get him out of Brazil to Uruguay, it will be much easier to 'export' him to Israel. You stay here and keep an eye on Cukurs and ensure he does not flee."

"I can do that. Then follow on behind him?"

"Yes, on the same flight, if you can. Assuming he takes a commercial flight and doesn't fly, himself."

"Point. I'll have to act fast, either way."

"You will. I'll see what I can do to expedite matters, though. If I send you both tickets on the same aeroplane flight, it should take care of the matter."

"All right; that'll work. You head on and set things up. I'll be there as soon as I can get there behind Cukurs."

"Good. I'll see you there."

***

It was another couple of weeks before a ciphered message told Levy that the team was ready and the rendezvous with Cukurs had been arranged. To ensure that Levy had no problems, the 'company' wanting to work with Cukurs and expand his business into Uruguay did indeed send him a plane ticket for the journey…and sent one for Levy, as well.

Levy packed his things and got ready; he was keeping an extremely close eye on Cukurs, and emerged from his concealment near Cukurs' apartment to catch another taxi as the former Nazi took one to the airport in São Paulo.

At the airport, Levy blended into the crowd at the gate and boarded the plane to Montevideo some eight passengers behind Cukurs.

The plane made good time, and landed in Montevideo fully half an hour early.

***

There were two Mossad agents waiting at the Montevideo airport: one to meet Cukurs and one to meet the disguised Levy. Both of those agents were heavily disguised, as well.

Levy was whisked ahead of their target, to a beige brick house in a remote suburb that Maidad had rented under the guise of Künzle, and which would be the rendezvous point. The house had been rather drab and unfurnished, but Maidad had rented furnishings suited to look relatively posh and to liven up the décor. The furniture was in place when Levy arrived, but little else was. Maidad and his assistant Caleb Asshur were running around frantically trying to get everything ready.

Unfortunately, due to the early flight, Maidad did not even manage to fully don his Künzle disguise before the car arrived with Cukurs.

The team constituted only five men, including the drivers, Levy, Maidad, and his assistant Asshur; since Cukurs was approaching his 65th birthday — almost ten years older than Eichmann had been — the team expected the apprehension would be relatively easy.

They were wrong.

As soon as Cukurs recognized that several of the men sported Jewish features and that Maidad had been Künzle, he lashed out, fighting furiously. Judging by some of his shouts, he had followed the Eichmann trial some years before, and recognized that he was headed for the same.

In the course of the ensuing fight, most of the furniture in the room was overturned and several lamps were broken. Levy aimed a lunge for Cukurs' legs, attempting to take him down, but the Nazi kicked him in the chest, knocking him aside. Levy gasped and slumped, trying to regain his breath and almost unconscious; the pain was considerable and intense.

He roused when he heard one of the drivers scream and hold up a bloody hand; Cukurs had nearly bitten off one of the fingers. The other driver grabbed for a hammer that had been left on a nearby cupboard — Maidad and the fifth operative, Asshur, had been trying to hang pictures, among other things, before Cukurs' arrival to make the house seem lived-in — and swung it viciously at Cukurs' head; the man went down instantly upon impact.

Levy hauled himself to his feet and turned to Samuel Fredman, the driver whose finger was nearly bitten through. He headed into the kitchen and got some coffee stir-sticks, kitchen twine, and clean cloths, then he carefully splinted and bandaged the wound until Fredman could be seen by the Mossad physician who was always nearby for these missions…though never in the same place as the apprehension, lest something go wrong and the physician be killed or injured too badly to be of use.

By this time, Cukurs, who was not dead but severely injured — blood and some clear fluid, most likely cerebral fluid, was streaming from his ears and nose — was trying to talk, pleading for his life.

"Pleassse! Po-potatoes! Jus-jus' jam listen t-to me! Le' me 'splain! I w-wasss ordered t' do 't! Wassss Eich-bread! Jam! Lots of jam! Magadasskim! Manj…M-my life was post! I-I had t'!" he stammered, speech slurred, intermittent word salad evincing the damage to his brain.

Abruptly blood gushed from his nose and he grabbed his head, which now had a severely depressed section where the hammer had struck.

"He's not going to make it to a doctor, is he? Let alone to trial," Maidad murmured to Levy.

Sick at the sight, Levy merely shook his head.

"Take him down," Maidad ordered.

Levy nodded and pulled his primary concealed weapon; his backup, a reliable little Beretta 21A, was tucked in an ankle holster. But the backup was a .22LR, and this weapon, a 9mm Beretta Model 1951, was more certain to end Cukurs' suffering, and do so swiftly. *Which is,* Levy thought, bleak, *more than can be said for what HE did to the Jews in Riga.* He extracted the silencer from a hidden pocket and screwed it onto the pistol, aimed at a now-whimpering Cukurs' forehead, pulled the trigger twice, and put two rounds into Cukurs' brain. The man dropped like a sack of flour.

Abruptly Levy was elsewhere.

***

Assigned to the litter detail, young Franz scoured the area of the yard near the closest lookout tower; the Nazi soldiers tended to think it funny to throw out their meal waste around their posts, then watch as the prisoners alternated between trying to eat the scraps and putting the inedibles into their burlap sacks for disposal. One perverted bastard even thought it was funny to relieve himself on whoever was below the tower on rubbish detail.

Unfortunately his latest victim was young Franz.

Franz leaped away, between the supports, up under the tower proper, and tried to wipe away the urine…

…Just as a roar of outrage erupted nearby.

"YOU DAMN BASTARD SON OF A BITCH! THAT'S MY LITTLE BROTHER, DAMN YOU!!"

And suddenly his big brother Eleazar was running toward the guard tower, as the laughing guard fastened his uniform trousers.

Franz spun when he heard the shout from a familiar voice.

"ELEAZAR!" he cried. "Oh, Eleazar! I'm so glad to see—"

Eleazar bent and scooped up something from the ground, then made a throwing motion.

The powerfully thrown rock soared upward, striking the perverse guard, who was wearing a uniform cap rather than a helmet, squarely in the temple. The guard staggered, his rifle clattering to the deck of the platform. Then he pitched over the rail, plummeting to the ground more than a story below, and laid there, his head canted at an odd angle.

The other two guards swung their weapons around and opened up on Eleazar.

The young man staggered as blood spattered out from his body, but he stood upright, proud and determined.

"Feh! Geh in drerdt, shtikl'ch drek!"

One of the guards shifted his aim and put a bullet through Eleazar's head. A red mist exploded outward behind him.

He dropped like a stone, a round, slightly singed hole in his forehead, and most of the back of his head missing.

***

Levy spun and sprinted for the back door, instinctively holstering his weapon as he went. He slammed through it and onto the small verandah in the rear. There, he hung over the rail and vomited into the shrubs of the landscaping, then leaned heavily on the rail, panting.

After a few minutes, Maidad came out.

"Franz, are you all righ—?" he began, then caught the soured smell of fresh vomitus. "No, obviously you are not all right. What's wrong? You've seen and dealt death before…"

"Flashback," Levy panted.

"Want to talk?"

"Not particularly."

"I'm still waiting."

Levy sighed. Maidad outranked him in the organization and was the team leader into the bargain; it was the same as an order. And he understood why.

"Flashback to Majdanek," he admitted then. "I watched a Nazi guard shoot my big brother in the forehead, the same way. With pretty much the same results. Only…messier."

"Ah. That explains a lot," Maidad decided.

They were silent for a time, while Levy regained control of his digestive tract. Finally Levy offered comment.

"This job plotzed with a vengeance." (*blew up; Yiddish*)

"It did. And I'll take responsibility for it."

"You shouldn't. If Hoffman had maintained control instead of viciously stoving in Cukurs' head with a hammer, we might have completed this mission the way it should have been done, instead of having to put him down like the dog he was."

"Maybe. But I should have had a bigger team, with weapons drawn. He caught on faster than I expected, and was stronger than I thought."

"The team wasn't ready; the plane came in much earlier than it was expected."

"True. But that's still my fault. I should have had a plan for the driver if that happened. And I should have had the house ready yesterday, and myself ready this morning. Unfortunately, the furniture delivery was late, and…" He sighed.

"Your call on that. I still think we could have done it. Listen, if it's all right with you, I think I'm done with this job."

"Yes, he's dead now; we just need to figure out what to do next. *I* need to figure out what to do next. You can go, if you like. Where are you going to go?"

"Home."

"Israel?"

"That's home now, yeah."

"Tel Aviv?"

"Yes."

"Make sure you aren't too direct."

"Of course. I've been doing this awhile."

"How old are you, Franz?"

"Mm…be 35 in May."

"Hm. Maybe you're getting a little too old for this part of the job? Not that you aren't good, but the older we get, the more we…introspect." He shook his head. "For that matter, I am, too. I'm starting to give real consideration to getting out of the field work so much."

"Point. I'll give it some consideration on the way home."

"Do that, meyn khaver."

***

Montevideo to Brasilia, to La Paz, to Quito, to Caracas, to San Juan, Miami, then New York. From thence to London's Heathrow, to Rome, and finally to Tel Aviv. From Tel Aviv it was a short drive to his house outside Rishon LeTsiyon.

Franz Levy was home.

The next day, he filed a request to be transferred to the Collections department.

The transfer was approved immediately.

***

Chapter 11 — Falling Apart

Levy got a couple of days off once he arrived back in Israel to allow for acclimating to the time zone, for which he was thankful; he'd flown over half the planet to get home. Unfortunately by the end of that time, he realized he was unwell.

He piled into the bed with several blankets and made sure the phone in the bedroom was on the nightstand, along with his newest acquisition, the transistorized TV remote; the console TV was next to the dresser, opposite the bed. He added a big, just-opened box of tissues, and climbed into bed.

Then he all but passed out.

***

When Levy didn't report for work for the second day after his supervisor Yaakob Falkenburg knew he was supposed to come back to work, Falkenburg got worried. It wasn't like Levy, and he was concerned that something was wrong. Given the nature of their work, possibly seriously wrong.

He called the small flat that Levy kept in one of the Jerusalem bedroom communities, but no one answered. That wasn't entirely surprising; he knew that Levy thought of the house near Tel Aviv as home, and the flat was just for convenience. So he called the Tel Aviv house. And let it ring.

It rang for nearly two minutes before someone answered.

"Mmh. He-hello?" a groggy, hoarse voice grated.

"Franz?"

"Yeah."

"Are you all right? You should have been at work two days ago."

"Uhn. What day is it?"

"Thursday."

"Oh farkakte. Sorry. No. Not all right. Sick."

"What's wrong?"

"Um. Flu?"

"You sound really hoarse."

"Uh-huh. Throat sore. Concrete in head an' chest. Aches. Chills. Headache."

"Sounds like the flu, all right."

"Yeah. Think so." There was a long pause on the other end of the line.

"Franz? You still there?"

"Uhn. Oh! Sorry, Yaak. Kind of out of it."

"It seems so. Listen, my current lady friend is a physician. Let me talk to her and I'll see what we can get you to help you feel better and get well."

"Soun's good. Lissen, Yaak, goin' back t' sleep now…"

"Okay, Franz. Get some rest."

There was a click, and the dial tone resumed.

Falkenberg pressed the hook switch in the cradle and held it for a couple of seconds, then let go and dialed Dr. Talia Yitzhak.

***

"Yes, it sure sounds like the flu, all right," Yitzhak, Falkenberg's current romantic interest, noted. "Not much you can do for that, these days. Did he take his vaccination last fall?"

258

"I doubt it. He was already in Brazil, monitoring a target there at that point, I think."

"Oh. Well, that explains it. And you say he just got back less than a week ago, and used the usual technique of hopping all over to disguise origin and destination?"

"Yes."

"That's probably how he got it, then. He picked it up from a fellow traveler in those flying tin cans with recirculated air."

"Oh. Shit."

"Yeah, but it is what it is. Listen, if you can get him some aspirin, some decongestant, and — you'll think this is stupid — some chicken soup, and make sure he drinks fluids until he floats away, he'll be on the road to feeling better. Make sure the fluids are mostly water, and nothing caffeinated; those will dehydrate him, and if he's as feverish as he sounds, he's already practically boiling water out of his body."

"Right," Falkenberg said absently, scribbling the instructions on a notepad on his desk.

"Listen, do you need to postpone dinner tonight while you go see to Levy?"

"Would you mind, Talia?"

"No, Yaakob. I kind of saw that one coming. Your friend and top operative is ill; you need to go make sure he's okay. And since I'm a doctor and healing is what I do, I'm fine with that. Yell if you need me to come help."

"You're the best, Tal. Thanks. I'll ping you as soon as I know something. If he's hallucinating or something from the fever — and it almost sounded like it on the phone — I'll call you from there. If you know where you're going, it's not hard to find his place."

"Right. I'll wait to hear. Like usual."

Falkenberg winced.

"Okay, honey, talk later."

"Later, Yaak."

He hung up, tore the note off the pad, and headed out.

***

Some time later, Falkenberg showed up in Levy's house.

The two men had become trusted friends over the years, and being his supervisor, Falkenberg had been trusted with a key to the house. This way it would be taken care of while Levy was away on a mission, which often took months if it was a Nazi hunt such as his most recent one.

The house wasn't especially large, but it was nice, well built and comfortably furnished. There was a slight old-European air to the furniture and overall décor — light wall paint and the occasional wallpaper; dark, fairly ornate wood on the overstuffed, tapestry-upholstered furniture and shelving — and Falkenberg often wondered if it resembled the home in which Levy had spent his childhood.

The Mossad supervisor had a couple of bags of groceries in his arms, and he glanced around the bedroom.

The room was reasonably spacious, painted in pale blue, with a double bed and dark cherry dresser, chest of drawers, and bed. A small console TV stood next to the dresser, directly across the room from the bed. Light blue sheets clad the bed and wrapped Levy's sleeping form; a quilt in blue toned star patterns topped the sheets. It resembled an heirloom, but looked too new for that.

There were no pictures on the walls. The master bathroom door opened next to the television. The window opposite the room's entrance looked into the back yard, and the flourishing little oasis Levy had created there.

The TV was off, though the remote lay in the bed, on top of the covers. The nearby wastecan was full to overflowing with used tissues, but there was no sign Levy had had anything to drink — no glasses, mugs or bottles were anywhere in the room. A quick peek into the master bathroom revealed indications that the toilet had been used several times since Levy had returned home, but not recently. Falkenberg shook his head. *That's gonna be some bad dehydration,* he thought. *I might have to ask Talia to come over with an IV just to rehydrate him.*

Then he set to work.

*****

In short order, using disposable surgical gloves he'd picked up at a pharmacy, Falkenberg had emptied all the trash in the house into bags and set it on the street for pickup. A quick change of gloves for fresh ones ensued before he put a just-opened box of tissues near Levy, and moved the TV remote to the nightstand. A brand-new carafe with matching glass was filled with water and set on the nightstand as well.

Then he sat on the edge of the bed and carefully woke Levy.

"Mm? Wha?" Levy said, regaining consciousness, though it was obvious he was woozy.

"Here," Falkenberg said, and shoved a thermometer into his mouth, then timed it on his wristwatch. Levy blinked in surprise but cooperated. Four minutes later, Falkenberg removed the thermometer and looked at it, then tisked.

"A hundred and two and a half," he noted aloud. "When's the last time you had any water, Franz?"

"Uh, I dunno," Levy replied, seeming confused. "This morning?"

"What day is it?"

"Um…Monday?"

Falkenberg took a deep breath. Levy blinked again.

"NO," Falkenberg said, firm. "It's THURSDAY. Do you mean to tell me you've not eaten or drank anything in FOUR DAYS?!"

"I…dunno. Maybe."

Falkenberg poured a glass of water from the carafe, then shoved it into Levy's hands, as the sick man pushed up in bed. "Here. DRINK. No wonder your fever was high. Here's hoping your kidneys still work right." As Levy sipped at the water, then began to chug it, Falkenberg extracted several pills from bottles into a dose cup. He topped off Levy's water glass, then handed him the dose cup. "Here. Down the hatch."

"What…?"

"Aspirin for the fever, and a decongestant. Do you have a cough?"

"No…"

"Okay, good, because I forgot the cough syrup. If you develop one as things start to clear, I can go get some."

"All right." Levy knocked back the pills, then continued to drink, and Falkenberg kept refilling the glass as long as Levy wanted water. When he was finally sated, the big carafe was almost empty, so Falkenberg took it into the bathroom to refill it.

"That's better," he murmured. "Weren't you thirsty before now?"

"Yeah, but I didn't feel like hauling it out of bed to get anything."

"Ah. I expect you're hungry, too, then."

"Um. Yes and no."

"What do you mean?"

"I mean my belly is empty, but I don't have any appetite."

"Chicken soup with matzoh balls? It's canned, but better than nothing. And I kind of like this brand; it's better than most."

"That…sounds like it might work."

"Have you been nauseated?"

"No, just too tired to bother."

"All right. Let me go in the kitchen and heat this up. Stay put."

"Um, well…"

"'Well' what?"

"Might need to hit the, uh, bathroom after all that water…"

"As dehydrated as you likely were, I'll be surprised. But if you do, go. It means I got you rehydrated. Just yell if you get wobbly and I'll take the soup pan off the burner and come running."

"Okay."

***

In fairly short order, Falkenberg had food and more water inside Levy, and after about an hour, Levy finally did have to get up and relieve himself. He wore only a pair of boxer shorts, a holdover from IDF days, and Falkenberg helped the still-weak man get to the bathroom, then stood behind him and steadied him while he emptied his bladder. Then he helped him back to bed.

Fetching his overnight kit from his vehicle, Falkenberg spent the night on the couch in the den, ensuring his friend was on the road to recovery, feeding him, refilling the carafe periodically, and ensuring he took medications to ease the flu symptoms.

By the next morning, Levy was drinking water and taking his medications on his own, as well as urinating regularly and walking without aid.

Pleased, Falkenberg showed him where everything was, sat a couple of extra boxes of tissues on the dresser, made breakfast for them both, washed up the dishes, then departed.

***

Unfortunately, the crud left in Levy's lungs didn't want to come out readily, and as the flu departed, bronchitis arrived.

A brief call to Falkenberg resulted in his arrival with another person in tow — Talia Yitzhak.

She gave the man a quick once-over, then gave him a pill bottle containing ampicillin, with instructions on how often to take it.

"Now drop your shorts," she said, reaching back into her medical bag.

"Excuse me?" Levy almost stammered, hazel eyes wide.

Yitzhak pulled out a hypodermic and ampoule.

"I'm going to give you a shot of the same antibiotic in your ass, to get you going faster," she explained. "You don't have to drop 'em completely if you don't want to. Just pull the waistband down far enough for me to put this in the gluteal muscles, and you're good."

"Oh," Levy murmured, and complied.

"There," Yitzhak said, disposing of the used hypodermic in a sharps container in her case. "Keep drinking water, keep taking the decongestants and eating well, and hack that crap out of your chest. Spit it in the toilet if you can." She paused, then wondered, "Have you had pneumonia before?"

"Yes," Levy answered, "back during the end of World War II. I wasn't long out of the concentration camp, and evidently the Soviet Army brought a strain of flu with them, and…"

"Aha. Yes, that makes sense," she said. "You're already halfway to pneumonia, by my judgement, but if you've had pneumonia, it seems to make you more predisposed to getting it again on down the road."

"Lovely."

"Yeah, but as long as we watch out for it from here on out, we can keep you from doing this again. And next time, no matter where you are, get your flu shot."

"Right."

***

After that, Dr. Yitzhak dropped in regularly to check on Levy during his recuperation.

As the shit hit the fan in the wake of the botched apprehension of Cukors, Falkenberg stayed incredibly busy; he never was able to make up the aborted dinner date with Yitzhak. Or, for that matter, schedule any others.

Once Yitzhak had signed off for Levy to return to work, she invited him to a homemade dinner at her place.

Not knowing about Falkenberg's interest — he had been too feverish to catch the 'lady friend' remark — Levy accepted.

***

En route to Earth to see how they stood and whether they should remain quarantined or not, the *Hsshth*, Pulgey Entiyti's personal flagship, encountered an unexpected distress signal. It was in an unknown language…which was odd, in this sector of space. More, the signal appeared to be actively jammed. Abruptly it cut off and did not resume. A quick message to Entiyti in his stateroom resulted in a decision to respond at maximum speed. Entiyti promptly hastened to the bridge.

But well before they reached what triangulation said was the source's location, they encountered something else.

265

"Who the ardrub is that?" the captain of the flagship wondered, even as Entiyti emerged onto the bridge. "I have never seen a ship of that configuration before."

"Nor have I, my friend," Entiyti agreed.

"It is in none of the registries, sir, milord," the helm officer noted. "It is apparently from an unknown race."

"It appears so," the captain decided. "Open a comm frequenc—"

"Incoming communication, sir," Ii'k'ee og Rr'nk'ii, the Deltiri communications officer currently on duty, noted.

"On speaker," the captain ordered. "Translation."

"On speaker. Translation."

"...You will surrender immediately, or face the consequences," blared on the bridge speakers in Galactic standard, which happened at this point to be Korian. "Repeat, this is Captain Krrk Twwwd of the Arctin. You have entered our space. You will surrender immediately or face the consequences."

"What the sllthshht?" Entiyti wondered. "THEIR space? We are in Territory Three. That has been Coalition space for many centuries."

"FIELDS UP! BRACE FOR INCOMING!" the helm shouted.

Suddenly the area around the *Hsshth* was filled with missiles and weapons beams. The *Hsshth* shook, but sustained no damage.

"Fire, milord?" the captain asked Entiyti.

"At your discretion, Captain," Entiyti said, trying not to snarl.

"Open fire! Helm's discretion!"

But in the split-second between the cessation of the unknown ship's attack and the *Hsshth*'s response, a small tender, looking rather like a crude lifeboat, detached from the other ship, headed generally toward the *Hsshth*.

"BELAY THAT!" the captain cried. "Helm, what's that? Is it an escape pod?"

"Sir!" comm officer Ii'k'ee exclaimed, one hand to his forehead as he 'read' the situation telepathically. "Yes! It is a lifeboat, and there is one being aboard, fleeing for its life!" He paused, checking instruments. "Yes, there goes the emergency message!"

"Extend force fields around that lifeboat and lock on tractor beam! Bring it around to the aft hangar deck!"

"Done, sir!" Helm replied.

Almost before the helm could extend the shields, the other starship opened fire on the tiny lifeboat. But Helm was swift, and the weapons did not reach the little craft.

"Sirs, the entity aboard just passed out from fear," Ii'k'ee informed them, his voice very quiet. "He seems to have expected to die."

At that point, realizing the escape pod was beyond its reach, the hostile craft opened fire again on the *Hsshth*, and continued firing.

"Notify me once the pod is safe in the hangar," the captain ordered, glancing at Entiyti, who nodded approval.

"Let me know, as well," Entiyti added, "because I wish to meet this being."

"Sirs, it is safe in the hangar," Helm added moments later.

"Good. OPEN FIRE! Weapons free!"

The *Hsshth* opened all weapons on the hostile craft.

Moments later, it was so much gas and dust, dispersing into open space.

***

The comm officer notified the Linguistics Department and Security, and a Deltiri linguist and a security detail including several guards dressed in burgundy and black uniforms joined Entiyti just outside the hatch to the hangar deck. They waited until the deck was fully pressurized, then entered.

"Milord Entiyti, I am Hh'c'p og Mm'bl'l, serving today as your translator; the entity within is still unconscious, and may need medical assistance," the Deltiri noted. "I am contacting sick bay with a request for a medical triage team."

"Excellent," Entiyti said. "Meanwhile, let us see what we have."

The security detail joined with the hangar deck crew and together they managed to figure out how to open the escape pod without damaging it.

Inside was a diminutive being with red skin and large, somewhat pointed ears, patently unconscious.

Moments later, Dr. Werfer Eretigen, Entiyti's personal physician and an old school chum, showed up with a team of medtechs and a gurney.

"Well," he murmured, upon seeing his patient, "he'll have plenty of room in the gurney..."

Entiyti stifled a wry chuckle.

"Any idea what species it is?" Eretigen asked.

"None."

"Hm. Not sure what setting to use on the medscanner, then. Well, it looks a lot like Indak, except for the skin color. I will try Klateen, for now."

The others watched as the Draconan physician knelt and carefully scanned their visitor. Eretigen adjusted several settings on the scanner, then took another reading. A few more tweaks, and a third reading.

"Aha," he said. "I think that got it. He is not Klateen, but he is similar." He rose to his feet and turned to Entiyti. "Milord, he appears to have been beaten rather severely, but is not in danger of his life. I recommend we take him to sick bay quickly. More, I recommend Indak tend him. We will likely need the Deltiri translator to accompany," he added, glancing at that being, "but I think we have a survivor of…whoever was in that ship. I cannot think they were the same as this one, however." He gestured at the little red being. "He shows high levels of what passes for fear hormones. He was trying to get away?"

"That is what it looked like, yes," Entiyti confirmed.

"All right. Let us make him conscious and comfortable and healing, and then perhaps we can determine what just happened."

"Go."

***

Indak and Eretigen worked together on their patient. Indak was of a comparable size to their patient, save he appeared to be much older, and had a brick-orange, almost terracotta, skin tone, long white hair, and to judge by the still-closed eyelids on their patient, smaller eyes.

"But many similarities there are," Indak told Eretigen. "Heal him, we can."

"Do it," Entiyti ordered. "The only answers we will have for what just happened are in his mind. It IS a him, yes?"

"Yes, yes, male he be," Indak confirmed. "Recognize I the genitalia when him strip did we."

***

It took around a quarter-hour, but soon a battered little alien was sitting up in bed, looking around himself with big yellow eyes. Entiyti and the others tried various languages, but the little red creature merely shook his head. Entiyti waved over Hh'c'p, and the Deltiri nodded and moved beside the bed.

Seconds later, Doron's eyes opened even wider; he blinked several times, then nodded. This went on for several minutes, then Hh'c'p turned to Entiyti.

"He says his name is Doron, sir. He comes from the Edeptis system on the Outer Arm, and he is what we would consider a combination physician and engineer, though he considers himself a healer. He is apparently adept at inventing new medical procedures and equipment, and he was a prisoner aboard the other ship. He says he was aboard one of the first explorational ships from Edeptis, when it was attacked and captured by the other starship. They were apparently after him and his skills and knowledge, because they wasted no time slaughtering the other crew, and destroying their ship. It was likely their emergency call that the bridge picked up." He paused, then added, "He does not know who or what they were. Some sort of avian race, he believes, but he had no clear view of any of them."

"He was the only survivor?" Entiyti said, horrified.

"He was, sir. I can see the events in his mind. He is rather traumatized. He was also beaten in an effort to get him to tell them of his inventions, and he refused, because he uses them for good, but he could see how some of it could be used by them for, as he put it, 'very bad things.'" He paused, then added, "He also says thank you for saving him. He believes us to be good beings, despite our — to him — fierce, frightening appearances."

Entiyti pondered briefly. "Can you facilitate a conversation between us?"

"I can."

"Please do."

***

Doron, I have someone who wants to talk to you, Hh'c'p told the little being.

Oh? Who it be? Doron replied.

Hello, Doron, Entiyti said. *My name is Pulgey Entiyty. I am a Draconan of Emdali, and I am the President of the Pan-Galactic Coalition. Welcome to our space, and my flagship, the* Hsshthh, *or* Winged Dragon.

A dragon you are, then?

Of sorts. A friendly one, however. My people prefer peaceful interactions among the galactic peoples.

Good that. Unsure was I about where landed I.

No, you are safe here. I may look fierce, and we took care of those who captured you and killed your crew in a distinctly fierce fashion, but we are not always fierce. Only when it is needful. We will look after you, tend your wounds, and feed you well so you heal. Then we will see about getting you home, though we have not heard of your system before now.

That good is, too. Doron sighed. *Not feed me did they. Hungry I.*

Then we need to ascertain what you eat, and provide it.

Is thankful, I. Is maybe helps the healers of yours, when healed I.

If you so choose, that would be welcome and much appreciated. But you are not obligated. We do not charge for helping someone in need.

Aw. Is more thankful, I. He sighed again.

Milord Entiyti, he is getting tired. He needs to rest, Hh'c'p said.

Very well. The big Draconan smiled, and Doron smiled back. *I will leave him to rest and be fed properly.*

Doron sank back into the pillows as Entiyti left the room, and Indak and Eretigen began working on his wounds.

***

Franz sat down at Talia's table, and she produced a platter of smoked salmon with cream cheese, capers, and bagel toast slices for the appetizer.

"Uhm," Levy said, trying to figure out how to explain. "Talia, hartsenyu, I, uh…" (*dear heart*)

"Don't you like lox?" she asked, realizing something was wrong and noting the direction of his gaze. "I don't keep strict kosher, but I thought all Jews liked lox."

"I…" Levy sighed. "In Majdanek, the drek they fed us tasted like rotten-fish soup…"

"Ohhhh," Yitzhak murmured, suddenly understanding. "Well, I'm not fond of fishy fish either, but I like this stuff. It's smoked, really well smoked, and it tastes more of the smoke curing than of the fish, I think. Would you at least try it? Just a taste?"

"I…can do that," Levy agreed, getting a small piece of toast, spreading it thickly with cream cheese, then topping it with a scant spoonful of capers, before adding a thumbnail-sized flake of the salmon. With a little hesitation, he shoved it in his mouth and chewed hastily. Partway through, he slowed down, considering. Finally he swallowed.

"You're right. This isn't fishy," he declared. "It's…I think I might like it."

Then he reached for more.

Talia smiled, pleased.

***

The pair were watching Levy's favorite television show later that evening, a relatively new science fiction series that would become extremely popular in later years, eventually spawning a film franchise and several spinoff series. When it was over, he admitted to her, "You're going to think this is stupid."

"What?" Talia wondered.

"That green slave girl? That look was sexy as hell."

"Oh, really? You thought so, did you?"

"Yeah. Kind of stupid, I know. But there's something really cool about it, you know what I mean? She's alien, she's unique, she's — well, I guess she's not unique THERE, but… she's different. Exotic, sort of."

"Okay, that's interesting. I can see your point, though. I guess I hadn't thought about it like that."

***

The next evening she invited Levy back over to her place. They had a very nice dinner that she home-cooked expressly for him and then Talia disappeared back into the kitchen to put things away. There was the sound of dishes being loaded into the dishwasher — a device that was a bit uncommon in Israel as yet, but which, as she was a busy physician, saved Talia cleanup time, so she had sprung for one. Then things grew quiet as Levy watched TV — she had told him she didn't want his help when he offered — and waited for her to come out.

After a good ten minutes, Talia came out.

Except it wasn't quite Talia.

She was wearing a skintight, green, crotchless unitard, green gloves, a green wig, and green Halloween makeup. Somehow, she had even managed to have the 'rug' match the 'curtains.'

She slunk by him, casting him a seductive glance, then went into the bedroom, leaving the door open.

273

Levy's hazel eyes dilated and grew wide, and without a word, he rose and followed her into the bedroom, closing the door.

Neither Mossad agent was seen until the next morning.

***

When Levy reported to his supervisor the next day, Yaakob Falkenburg noted the smug, cat-that-ate-the-canary look on his face…and sighed to himself.

He's a damn lucky man, he thought, stifling the jealousy. *She's got it all. Beauty, brains, strategic smarts, and patch-it-up ability. I had hopes in that direction myself, but I guess I'm too late. Never mind too damn busy. Because in many ways, he's got it all, too. And now he has her. He'll be damn near unstoppable in the field now. Though maybe we can finally look at pulling him in from ALL the field work if they get serious. Which will be a good thing. He's getting a little long in the tooth for a field agent, not that he's that old yet. But he's getting on towards forty AND is a concentration camp survivor, and this job is for kids in their twenties that haven't already been through hell and out the back door. So…yeah. Bad for me, good for him and for the organization. I'll start working out a plan to ease him from the field work and into an administrative job, maybe a leadership role.*

But things didn't quite go according to plan.

***

They had been lovers for over a year when Levy caught another cold, and like usual, the cold went into his chest and settled there. Inside two weeks, he had severe bronchitis. Yitzhak decided to treat him yet again, having treated him for all the others.

"This is the fourth bout of bronchitis you've had in the last six months, Franz," Yitzhak told her patient. "Never mind the gastrointestinal problems, the headaches, the intermittent joint aches we've been treating for over a year now — off and on, pretty much since I've known you, honey. I think it's high time we need to do some testing; I'm sure you were exposed to some nasty shit in Majdanek."

"Whatever, Talia," Levy sighed. "Just give me something to get rid of it, please. The coughing interferes with undercover work. Not to mention the lowered energy levels. Either one is apt to get me killed, at this rate."

"Which adds to my argument that you need to retire from the field work, honey. Not just the really intense stuff; ALL of it. The weight loss won't do, either, Franz," Yitzhak told the Mossad agent. "What's wrong? You usually eat like a horse after a long day in the field."

"I don't know," he sighed again. "Seems like I just get full sooner. I don't want as much."

"Yes, let's get some tests run," Yitzhak decided. "I don't like the sound of this."

"All right," Levy said, mildly exasperated. "THEN can we go out to dinner, like we planned?"

"Of course, Franz. I've been looking forward to it; you always know the best restaurants. And you KNOW I love the company, sweetheart."

"Good," Levy said, satisfied.

***

But it wasn't good.

"...No, Franz, I'm sorry," Yitzhak said softly a week later. "I've been consulting with my colleagues, and there's no doubt — you have advanced lung cancer that is already starting to metastasize to your stomach and liver."

"So that's why I haven't been hungry," he breathed, shocked. "What caused it?"

"Do you have a history of cancer in your family?"

"No. Well, I don't know for sure, but I'm pretty certain not. When they weren't being killed by Nazis, my family members tended to live to old age."

She sighed.

"Then we think it is most likely what you were exposed to in the concentration camp," she explained. "You would have been exposed to low, nonfatal but constant levels of the Zyklon B, which may not have caused the cancer — or it may; but it certainly didn't help, even if it didn't cause it. And it probably contributed to some of the other problems, like the gut issues and the liver jaundice. Then there are all the combustion products of burning bodies…did you not tell me that the crematoria ran constantly?"

"They did," a somber Levy confessed. "And depending on wind direction and weather, it was not uncommon for my clothes to be covered in soot just by being outside, but especially if I were assigned to clean out the crematoriums that day. Which I was, early on." He shrugged. "And it wasn't like we had changes of clothing, or any real way to wash them regularly. So once it was there, it was there for a good while."

"Ugh," Yitzhak grunted, letting her displeasure show in her face. "Demonic bastards."

"No argument there, Talia." He paused, staring at the floor. Then he looked back up at her, and there was something of pleading in his eyes. "Isn't there something we can do? Surgery, radiation, chemo?"

"If we'd caught it a year ago, perhaps," she murmured. "Even six months ago, maybe. When you first started having the bronchitis episodes. But…not now."

"Why?"

"Those all require things be at a much earlier stage, Franz," she explained. "Surgery needs it to be all in one lump, preferably in one organ. Radiation needs a discrete target. You don't have either of those now. And different kinds of tissue require, at the very least, different strengths of the chemo, sometimes different KINDS of chemo. And they don't always play nice together. Plus, chemotherapy works because tumor cells are slightly more susceptible to toxins than normal cells. It's a delicate balance of killing the cancer cells without killing YOU. The farther along you are, the sharper that balance, and the harder it is to find and maintain it." She drew a deep breath. "We discussed it and…we think it wouldn't work, Franz. We'd be at least as apt to kill you as the cancer, and there's no guarantee we could get the cancer."

"So…nothing?"

She shook her head. "I'm…so sorry."

"How…how long have I got?"

Yitzhak averted her gaze from the almost desperate hazel eyes fixed on her face. "Six months, max."

"Six—?!"

"Max. I'm SORRY, Franz. So, so sorry."

They were silent for several minutes, as Levy absorbed the situation and Yitzhak waited to see if he had questions.

"It is what it is, then," Levy murmured. "I'm dying."

"…Yes."

"Then let's do this," Levy said, sliding off the exam table and down to a kneeling position. "I love you. Talia, will you marry me? Make what time I have left happy by being my bride? I'll retire from the Mossad, you can take extended leave; we'll sell our places and buy a big house on the beach outside Tel Aviv…" He gazed at her with shining eyes. "Say yes, my love."

There was a long silence, as Yitzhak stared down at the earnest man. Then she closed her eyes and turned her head. A tear spilled through knitted lashes.

"I…I'm sorry, Franz. I…I can't. I just…"

Suddenly she spun and left the room in haste.

Levy, still on his knees, stared after her in wide-eyed, heartsick shock.

***

"He's dying?" Levy's supervisor in the Mossad, Yaakob Falkenberg, said in surprise, when Dr. Yitzhak reported to him first thing in the morning two days later. "My best agent, and he's got maybe six months?"

"I…I'm afraid so," Yitzhak said, very pale.

"What are you two going to do?"

"I don't know what he's going to do."

"I didn't say him. I said 'you two.' You've been seeing each other, haven't you? You're lovers."

"We were…but not any more. I should have never agreed to examining him back when he had that bout of influenza. Or," she added, "I should have looked a damn lot closer."

"So…you broke it off?"

"I had to, Yaakob," she whispered, dark eyes tearing, though they did not overflow. "I…I can't deal with watching him…die."

"I suppose you want to be reassigned? Someplace away from here, maybe? For, say, about six months?"

"If…if at all possible."

"Does he know?"

"He…sort of. He proposed…and I declined."

"Ah." Falkenberg thought for a moment. "Hm. Maybe it's as well, then."

"Is that all, sir?" Dr. Yitzhak managed a brief return to formality.

"Yes, Dr. Yitzhak, that's all for now. I'll arrange a transfer for you."

"Thank you, sir." She turned toward the door, then paused. "Um…could you do something else for me?"

"I can try. What?"

"Can you…explain to Franz?"

"I'll tell him watching him die would break you."

"That…will work."

And she was gone.

*****

When Levy showed up in Falkenberg's office five hours later — it was early afternoon — he, too, was pale.

"I assume you've seen Dr. Yitzhak's report?" Levy asked. Falkenberg noted the formality with which he addressed the woman Falkenberg knew he'd hoped to marry one day. He stifled a sigh.

My best agent, and a good friend, and it's all gone to Gehennem in a handbasket for him, he thought. *After Majdanek, surely he deserved better than this, HaShem.*

"I have," Falkenberg said aloud, keeping his tone quiet. "I'm sorry, Franz."

"I'm hearing entirely too damn much of that," the agent said, growing annoyed. "I'm not dead yet, and I'm not an invalid."

"What do you want to do?"

"Give me a job. The most dangerous one you've got out there."

Knowing his agents quite well, Falkenberg was already prepared for that one.

"Suicide mission?"

"Beats hell out of letting the cancer have me." Levy shrugged. "Lets my death at least be useful."

"All right. Have you been following the situation between us and Egypt over the Suez Canal?"

"The blockades and closures? I have."

"Good. Then I won't have too much briefing to do..."

***

It didn't take that long. Levy had been moved to the Collections department of the Mossad roughly a year and a half earlier; he had been deemed an excellent agent but getting too old for the most intense field work. There was no denying that the body slowed as one grew older, despite the best training, and Levy had been a thirty-something in a twenty-something world.

Now, however, Falkenberg assigned him to the Metsada department and sent him off, on assignment.

He was headed for Suez.

It was May 27th of 1967.

***

Chapter 12 — Meetings

Tired of the ongoing problems accessing the Suez Canal by ally and trading partner as well as their own military and commercial shipping, the Israeli leadership had finally decided to pre-emptively strike Egypt in an effort to gain control of the canal passage.

Volunteering for what was almost certainly a suicide mission, a grim, hopeless Levy went ahead as an embedded intelligence agent to feed information back to Mossad headquarters on what was most vulnerable and what routes to use to gain access to the southern end of the canal.

He was still there and still sending back information when the Six-Day War began.

***

He slipped around the town of Suez as the sun set, looking for the most likely position from which to gain control of the canal proper in that region, which was the southern end of that water route. His stress level was high, because he fully expected not to live out the night…and that was as he wished it. All hell was about to break loose within the hour; the Israeli Defense Force would be arriving soon, and the Egyptian army was already positioning itself to meet them. Still, he had a mission, and he intended to see it done before the end. Not knowing when nor how the end would come, however, was… difficult.

He had just completed his mission, signaling back a likely site for a strategic command post, along with three secondary sites and recommendations for how best to gain control of the southern end of the Canal passage. This information got a thumbs-up from Headquarters, and the verbal commendation that he had done excellently, and was a least as good a strategic planner as the general commanding this particular column advance. He couldn't deny that gave him a warm fuzzy.

But it was time to find a spot where he could either survive this shtik drek, or do as much damage on his way out of this life as possible.

Then he spotted someone he was surprised to see.

Damn, he thought, as he watched the stranger wandering around a small courtyard with a central fountain. *Whoever that is, they aren't Arab of any flavor; the skin tone is too pale, and that blond hair isn't from around here. And the camera around his neck clinches it.*

For a split second, he thought it might be Jakob in his German persona, but once he got a good look at the face, he realized it was a stranger; he had not seen Jakob, nor any sign of his friends, since he'd left Italy.

He watched from cover for several minutes, verifying his initial conclusions of ethnicity by observing the strange individual; it would not do to mistake an implanted Egyptian agent, on the lookout for Israeli spies, for a tourist. *Then again,* he considered, *I had the sense to apply a bit of makeup, a wig, and native clothing before leaving my flophouse this morning, so I wouldn't stand out so. That's no blond wig on that mensch, though; that's real hair. With no headgear, you can't really disguise a hairpiece on a man that well. Not that short, at least.*

By the look of him, he's British, Norse, German, or maybe American. And a couple of those are on our side, anyway.

From time to time, the stranger raised the camera and took pictures of some of the detailed tilework on the fountain, occasionally running a light hand over it as if in a certain awe of the handiwork involved.

No, Levy concluded, *if this is an embedded agent, I can't see the logic. This idiotic mensch needs to get the hell out while there is still time. And it looks like it might fall to me to do that. Unless I can think of another way. Fast.*

Just then, a dull, clanking rumble from the west told him the Egyptian military was already on the move with heavy armor. It only took a second or two for the experienced Mossad agent to realize they were headed his way…and close. Too close.

Shocked and concerned — and out of planning time — Levy ran toward the trapped tourist.

"What the hell are you doing here?!" he exclaimed in glib Arabic. "We have to get you out of here! The Egyptian army will be here in just a few minutes, and the Israeli army maybe five minutes after that!"

"I do not understand," the obviously puzzled tourist replied — in English. "Is not English the common tongue here?"

Without pause, Levy immediately switched gears.

"We have to go, now," he said in emphatic, fluent English. "You're in the middle of a war zone, and both armies are moving. They'll converge here in minutes!"

"Oh dear," the blond tourist said, oddly formal, brows furrowing. "I did not mean to do that! I thought I should be clear by the time that happened. I do not want to take part in a war! Can you help me? Can you lead me out?"

Levy didn't hesitate; his personal moral code had been forged in no less a fire than Majdanek, and it was adamantine.

"I can try," Levy declared. "Follow me."

***

But before he could even turn, a sudden squawk of sound from somewhere nearby coincided with a sudden odd… FLICKER…in Levy's tourist. He recognized the sound as some inexperienced nitwit trying to initiate radio jamming and causing feedback in everyone's comm-sets, loud enough to hear at a small distance. He felt sure the entire unit was now half-deaf and cursing out the young private.

The squawk diminished in volume, finally silencing...

...And suddenly the blond tourist was gone, and a towering, dragon-like being stood in its place.

It was bipedal and tall, the dragon — somewhere between eight and nine feet, Levy estimated, though it was crouched a bit to make it closer to a tall human in height — possessed of beautiful silver-white scales, rough and spiky in places like the elbows, smoother in others. Black horns stood out across its head, and as Levy watched, they flexed slightly. So too did dark-gray, leathery, bat-like wings on its back, partly unfurling.

The being was clad in black, close-fitting vest and leggings, and its splayed, claw-like, four-toed feet were shod with tall, flexible black boots in what Levy judged to be some sort of leather, formed and shaped to the foot, with straps and laces here and there to close them properly. At that observation, Levy spared a quick glance upward, revealing that the hands, likewise, were four-fingered and possessed of substantial claws, though otherwise they resembled human hands save for scales instead of skin.

Its legs were configured very differently from a human's, and it walked mostly on what would be considered the toes. It had thick, long, powerful thighs, short, nearly nonexistent calves, and the heels pointed upward, rather like a cat's, though there was no dewclaw such as might be found on a feline.

An equipment belt was slung around its waist, with several bits of equipment Levy recognized — a flashlight, a canteen, a basic multipurpose knife…and something that resembled a large black pistol, but with a far more substantial frame, hung at his right side. Another, smaller pistol-like object hung at his left side, but did not remotely resemble anything found on Earth, except perhaps in some science fiction film.

The broad, flat face wore a shocked expression, the coppery-orange eyes wide in surprise.

"Farkakte, verdammt, merde, and shit!" Levy exclaimed, stepping back, astounded. "What the hell?!"

"Giissht hiigeessht," the dragonlike being said at almost the same time, in a tone that sounded like cursing. "Forgive me; the electronics of the approaching forces have apparently disrupted my solid holographic disguise."

"It's…that WAS really you," Levy stated in wonder, recognizing the voice of the blond tourist issuing from the dragon's mouth. "This is what you truly are?"

"It is," the being admitted. "I did not wish to frighten anyone on Earth. But I was tasked with coming here by no less than the Ennead. Not, I suppose," he continued with a sigh, "that you know what that is."

"You're definitely not from Earth, then," Levy concluded, mildly off balance mentally as he decided he was suddenly living in a real-life science fiction story — science fiction had been one of his favorite genres, along with mysteries, ever since Aunt Iga had introduced him to them — but he was determined to hold it together despite the alien being's imposing appearance, never mind the advanced weaponry on its belt. Fortunately, that same genre love gave him the wherewithal to do so proactively. "Where are you from, and what are you doing here?"

"My name is Pulgey Entiyti, I am from the planet Emdali, and I am a Draconan," the creature elaborated. "As I am the President of the Pan-Galactic Coalition, what you would consider the galaxy's government, I was here on a little fact-finding mission, attempting to determine if Earth is yet ready to join. I wanted to get a first-hand look at what is currently considered the most contentious disagreement between nation-states on the planet." He looked around with bright orange eyes that glowed like flame. "I appear to have chosen the wrong place to conclude my mission, however; I will soon get TOO close a look, it appears. And by the sounds of the heavy machinery being moved nearby, I may not be able to return to my spacecraft." He shook his head in what seemed aggravation. "Haarg is going to be angry, and rightfully so; he told me not to do this personally."

"Bodyguard?" Levy wondered, and the dragon nodded.

"A bit ago, I was watching a small child playing with her stuffed dolly…she was so innocent, having so much fun, even as her parents prepared to evacuate the area…" He sighed. "In my delight, I lost my situational awareness, and now I am trapped." His shoulders slumped, the leather-like wings behind them drooping in despair, even as the flexible black horns seemed to wilt. "And now you are going to kill me."

***

Levy paused, watching this…Draconan…and listening to his explanation.

He's just here on a fact-finding mission, a kind of prediplomatic mission, he thought. *He's not a saboteur, nor yet a provocateur, like I feared for a moment. Not five minutes ago I saw that girl go by with her parents as they fled the approaching conflict, and she was clutching a rag doll, so he's telling the truth. Besides, my gut says he's legitimate. And by now, my gut is pretty damn good. Not for much longer, but for now, at least.*

He looked around, trying to judge where the approaching Egyptian forces were, relative to where he knew the Israeli forces intended to enter Suez, and made his decision.

"No, I'm not going to kill you," he told Entiyti. "It's not like I haven't had a nonhuman friend before, and he was more trustworthy than many of the humans I've known. No, I'm going to do my damnedest to get you out of this mess. No sense in a pre-diplomatic first contact going south on my account."

Entiyti perked up, his horns erecting with the hope of rescue, and he shook his head with what Levy took to be a half-smile.

"And you are?"

"That's not important right now. Call me Franz."

"Very well, Franz, my new friend and benefactor," he said. "I will trust you. Tell me what to do."

"Where is your spacecraft, and how far away is it?"

"Over there," the Draconan pointed south, "hovering over the open water, about what you would call a kilometer out from shore. It is a shuttle to my cloaked flagship in orbit. I will need to get to a beach where it can land, or at least hover over the surf. I do not mind getting wet, and I can swim."

"Farkakte," Levy grumbled, thinking hard and fast. "They're going to be watching the water, and there's next to no cover along the shore there, especially after the bombing runs. This could get complicated."

"What do you suggest?"

"Keep low and come with me, and hope it's dead dark by the time we get there," Levy said, and turned, Entiyti close on his heels.

***

The pair slipped through back alleys, the ruins of buildings, tiny little lanes, piles of rubble, and mews on their way to the waterfront, Levy doing his best to avoid the recon scouts he knew both sides would have put around their forces — after all, was he not one of those scouts? Unfortunately, even his own side was likely to fire on a dragon, and ask questions later. Meanwhile he watched the sky grow darker and darker, thankful for what cover it gave the pair, one of whom was far more obvious in these environs than he could have wished.

But when they got near the shore, they found that 'next to no cover' had become NO physical cover left at all, thanks to an Israeli air raid only the night before which had destroyed all the trees and buildings left standing along the shoreline. There was not even any rubble; everything had been flattened.

More, there was a flanking move under way by the Egyptian army to attempt cutting off any amphibious attack, and it was coming straight down the shore road from the west. Two Jeeps in the lead, surrounded by at least one platoon of infantry soldiers, were closely followed by a single T54-3 and a pair of T34-85 Soviet-style tanks, with the T54 in the lead of a rather motley collection of armored troop carriers, and the T34s bringing up the rear.

"That's not good. Do you have a means of contacting your ship?" Levy asked Entiyti, even as he scanned the area in all directions and stared out to sea for a moment. "Could they land in the clearing over there? And how much damage will it take if one of those tanks fires on it?"

"I do, they can, and likely none," Entiyti replied. "But the tanks cannot hit what they cannot see, in any event."

"Meaning?"

"The shuttle has a full, active cloaking capability. And force shields."

"Aha," Levy said with a wry grin. "I don't know how any of that works, but I know enough to know that you have some serious technology there."

Entiyti's responding grin was toothy and wolfish; he said nothing, however.

"All right," Levy said, briefly checking a device in his pocket. "I'm not showing any signs of the jamming signal that interfered with your disguise. Can you bring it back up? It would definitely help in getting you out of here unnoticed..." Levy brought out a special radio device, aimed the directional antenna out to sea, and tapped a code into it.

"Let me try," Entiyti said, pulling a small device from a hidden pocket of his own and activating it.

Suddenly the blond human tourist was back.

"Good," Levy said with a grin. "Contact your ship and have them come in and set down. I've also spotted an Israeli frogman team just offshore and I've sent them a clandestine signal, so I might get backup, but I still need to provide a diversion for you to run across that open space to your ship."

"How do you intend to do that?" Entiyti wondered as he produced a far more sophisticated communications device than Levy's radio, keyed in an emergency rendezvous code, then set the locator beacon.

"Not sure yet," Levy said, keeping an eye out in several directions. "Probably a suicide end run. But a galactic president is worth it, don't you think?"

"What?! Why would you sacrifice yourself??"

"Do you know what cancer is?"

"I do, yes."

"It's in my lungs and already spreading. The doctors aren't sure what caused it, but it seems to be environmentally caused, rather than genetic. They think. Anyway, it's too far along to stop; they can't cut it out, they can't burn it out, and they can't poison it. There's nothing they can do, and I'd rather help you get out than let the cancer have me." Levy shrugged. "Didn't figure to make it through the night in these circumstances, anyway. Let me know when your shuttle is on the way."

A soft beep sounded from Entiyti's comm device, and a slight whirring sound came from overhead.

"It is here," Entiyti said. "Landing in progress."

"Good. I'm going to do my best to focus their attention on me." He gestured at the Egyptian forces, just entering the road over the breakwater. "After I break from cover, count to ten and then sprint for your craft. If HaShem — um, the Creator God — blesses me, it'll be over quick, and maybe I'll even see you again one day, in His tabernacle."

Before Entiyti could reply, Levy sprinted into the road.

***

The Draconan watched in astonishment as, from somewhere, Levy produced an Uzi and opened up in rapid-fire and incredibly accurate semi-auto mode on the advancing Egyptian forces, which were mostly foot soldiers and unarmored Jeeps in the lead; a couple of tanks brought up the rear, but were not yet in position to do much. One tank led the armored vehicles, and it was the only one Levy appeared to be really worried about.

***

Levy was indeed concerned about the T54, but not overmuch; he knew its strengths and weaknesses and intended to make full use of that knowledge.

After so many years in service, he was one of the Mossad's top agents, known for his speed and accuracy with any sort of weapon in hand; within seconds, Levy took down the two

290

lead vehicles and most of the platoon of infantry soldiers backing them up on foot.

He glanced over his shoulder at Entiyti, then roared, "Go! GO!"

***

Entiyti turned and sprinted in the direction his comm unit told him his spacecraft lay...

...Just as several Egyptian bullets slammed into Levy.

Levy staggered, gasping, and dropped the spent Uzi before pulling several grenades from wherever he'd produced the Uzi.

***

One grenade went into the cluster of soldiers trying to bring him down, reducing them to shredded body parts.

A second went under a third Jeep, which rose several feet in the air, flinging out the dead bodies of its driver and passengers, as well as pelting the area with automotive parts and shards of the bonnet.

He held a third grenade for a split second, until the lead tank's commander popped up to see what the hell was happening. A throw that would have put Levy in major-league baseball contention dropped the grenade through the opening after the tank commander ducked back down, but before he could get the hatch closed.

Moments later a double detonation sounded, with the second being larger than the first, as the grenade detonated the fuel and ammo within the tank. The hatch blew off and the top half of the commander — minus arms — tumbled out in a spray of blood and offal as the tank's turret shot almost straight up a good thirty or forty feet. It came down on the armored personnel carrier immediately behind the tank, a Sorokovka BTR-40;

the tarpaulin roof of the Sorokovka provided no protection whatsoever from the massive turret, and the vehicle fairly crumpled to the ground from the impact. There was no sign of movement from the Sorokovka.

Hmph, a satisfied Levy thought, fighting through the pain and blood loss. *Two for one. Not bad for one grenade.*

***

Just then, the Israeli frogmen swarmed the bank, coming out of the Red Sea at speed in response to Levy's message, and moved between Levy and the remaining Egyptian force as they freed their weapons.

One of the frogmen knelt and slung something off his back, producing an RL-83 Blindicide rocket launcher and unfolding it. His buddy deposited a waterproof bag beside him and opened it, extracting an anti-tank round. The first frogman quickly loaded the rocket launcher with the round, aimed it at the side of the rear tank, and fired.

The rocket turned out to be a shaped charge; the round cut a hole in the T34's armor like the proverbial hot knife in butter. Screaming came from inside for a few seconds as the round incinerated the crew.

Abruptly the tank sped up, continuing to move forward, though now at a slight angle. It encroached on the T34 in front of it and banged into its rear, pushing hard, as the other T34 driver struggled to control his own tank.

Suddenly the rogue tank exploded as the ammo inside cooked off. The turret flew off, cartwheeling away and taking out two unsuspecting personnel carriers, and incapacitating part of a third.

The turret, in turn, ripped off part of the front armor, which slammed hard into the rear of the tank in front. One track slipped off the drive sprocket of that tank, and a piece of shrapnel pierced the engine compartment. It stalled, even as the tank crew bailed; sparks were coming from the engine compartment, and smoke began to trickle out of the hole. Frogmen picked off the crew as they emerged.

The original tank finally stopped, its wreckage now spread across the road, the burning hulk set squarely across it.

In destroying the T54, Levy had rather effectively stopped the progress of the line — they were single-file to accommodate the road width — and now the frogmen, in taking out the T34s bringing up the rear, had ensured the surviving mechanized forces in between were trapped; the substantial remains of a building blocked their off-road ability inland, and the water came up to the road shoulder on the other side.

Heh, a watching Levy chuckled to himself. *They aren't going anywhere. Except to the morgue. The frogmen are mopping up the operation.*

Pain lanced through his torso, and he felt dizzy.

Uh, he grunted to himself. *Speaking of morgues, I think I need to find a nice quiet spot to die.*

***

Bleeding badly by this time, Levy had enough strength left to turn and hobble out of what remained of the battle, holing up in an alley off the beach, where he would be sheltered from further gunfire. He slumped to the ground and scanned the beachfront for signs of the 'tourist.'

By that time, however, Entiyti was aboard his personal shuttle, and that cloaked craft had lifted off. The dying Mossad agent listened as a soft hum rose, then faded into the distance.

Success. One last mission…that no one on Earth will ever know about, I suppose.

Levy collapsed and passed out.

***

"NO," Entiyti all but roared. "We are NOT going back to the *Hsshthh*! This human was not frightened of me, he HELPED me! He saved my life at the cost of his own! I will not leave him if it is in my power to save him now."

"But sir," Grassh Foorg, the shuttle's pilot and himself Draconan, said. "He was hit with many projectiles. Surely he is dead now."

"Perhaps. But perhaps he is not so dead that our newest physician cannot revive him. We must at least try."

"Ah. Point. I had forgotten the little red one. Well, let me see if I can find his signature," Foorg decided. "We can try to catch him in a tractor beam — the shuttle's tractors are not so strong as the *Hsshthh*, and thus should not harm him — and I will carry him to a place out of harm's way so we can bring him aboard, milord. Then we will rush for the *Hsshthh*. Does this sound like a workable plan?"

"Yes, because we will need to get him to that strange little physician while there is still time for the physician to work his miracles. Do it."

"Consider it done, Milord Entiyti."

***

The shuttle *Llaagaarsshti*, or *Heaven Sent*, made quick work of finding Levy in that back alley, though they had to wait a bit while the Israeli amphibious team's medic checked him out. It seemed to the two undetected watchers that the medic considered the Mossad agent either dead, or close enough to it as no matter, with no triage really possible.

The pair of Draconans watched as the comm officer called something over his radio, then the team quickly moved Levy's body into a more hidden location and headed inland. As soon as they were out of sight, Foorg caught Levy's body in a tractor beam, lifting it off the ground and extending the shuttle's cloak around it. Then the pilot headed for a peninsula extending into the Red Sea a few tens of miles to the southeast.

Right behind them, and called in by the frogmen, a flight of IDF 101 Squadron's Mystere IVs came in hard, strafing the recent scene of battle, then bombing it to hell and back.

***

The *Llaagaarsshti* arrived moments later at the peninsula the pilot had selected as their target.

There, he carefully deposited Levy on the ground, then landed the *Llaagaarsshti*. Unstrapping, he directed the Galactic President.

"Look in the aft port stowage, lowest rack, and get out the medical kit and the antigrav gurney," he said. "I will go see what his damage is. Meet me outside with the gurney."

"On it," Entiyti said, unbothered by the orders; Entiyti had accepted the position of Galactic President to help make things better, not for the ego-boost of the position. Besides, the pilot knew better where everything was, anyway.

Within moments the two Draconans had gently lifted the smaller human into the gurney, strapped him down, and towed him back into the shuttlecraft. While Foorg flew, Entiyti wielded the medical kit's contents in a furious attempt to plug the holes in Levy's torso — the wounds were still bleeding, indicating the heart was still beating.

Then they were streaking through the night sky, headed for Entiyti's flagship and a faint chance to all but bring Levy back from the dead.

***

Dimly, Levy was aware of snippets of conversation.
One conversation was in modern Hebrew.

"...No sir, I can't save him. I doubt a full-up emergency suite could, at this point. They nicked the descending aorta. He'll bleed out, most likely even before a surgeon could open him up enough to reach it."

"Pity. This is Agent Levy?"

"Judging by our briefing packet and the ID code Comms said he sent, I'd say so."

"Well, he was expected to be a casualty; it was a likely suicide mission, he knew it, and volunteered anyway."

"Why?"

"Nobody outside his chain of command really knows, and those who do aren't talking. It's a farshltn shame. He's a damn good agent by all accounts, and I for one was hoping, but it is what it is." (*damn; Yiddish*)

"Yes, sir."

***

There was a brief moment of darkness, then Levy's ears worked again. He felt chilled despite the desert air.

"...Orders from higher up say to come back for the body. Hide it behind the rubble so the enemy doesn't desecrate it and move out."

He felt himself gently lifted and carried a short distance, then laid down once more. It hurt despite their obvious care and reverence, but he had no energy left to groan.

Soft scuffling was followed by silence, as Levy lost consciousness again.

***

When he woke this time, it was with the feeling of movement beneath him, and a soft, sibilant language he did not understand being spoken over him. He felt very cold and decidedly breathless.

(...Yes, he is still alive. You did well, Lord Entiyti, to stop the bleeding with the special packing and add saline to his circulatory system.)

(The medscanner indicated that would work, though I fear it left what little blood he still had in him rather…dilute.) There was a pause. (I was shocked at how much he had lost. There was blood everywhere, poor being.)

(Yes, but the quad-ox compound helped to compensate for the oxygen transport. I show decent brain function. He — ah! He is conscious, though probably very groggy. Speak to him, milord.)

"Franz? My friend Franz? Can you hear me? It is President Entiyti. It is your friend Pulgey."

Levy managed a faint groan.

"Good. Do you recall saving me? Getting me to my shuttle?"

Levy got out another groan, but it was weaker.

"Very well. We are going to see about using what, to you, would be very advanced medical techniques. They will save your life, in many ways. Is this acceptable? Grunt once if yes, twice if no."

Levy, sure he was hallucinating prior to death, still managed a very deliberate, single grunt. After all, he considered, if this WAS real, he wanted to live.

Another voice interjected.

"I here, Entiyti Lord. This human be?"

"Yes. He is just conscious, and is able to respond in a minimal fashion."

"Good. And approves he gives for procedures?"

"He has. Are you ready?"

"Yes, ready I be. Go we, hurry hurry."

"Excellent. Please, sir, proceed."

Levy dimly felt something pressed to the side of his neck. There was a soft hiss, a cool sensation on his throat, and then darkness descended again.

Ah, hallucinations. I thought so. Ha'Shem, welcome me into Your tabernacle, was his last thought. *I want to see my family again.*

***

Yaakob Falkenberg sat in his office late into the night, tensely waiting for the phone call he expected to come.

At one in the morning, Tel Aviv time, the phone rang. He jumped, instinctively glanced around to make sure no one saw the moment of weakness, and answered.

"Falkenberg."

He listened for long moments.

"But what was he doing?"

He listened even longer.

"So other than giving the frogmen a chance to make it ashore, and stop the flanking maneuver, you don't know? No, of course that isn't likely to have been the only reason. He was my top agent, and he was always thinking a dozen steps ahead, and several layers deep. All right. Well, it is what it is. No, you may not ask why. Thank you."

Falkenberg hung up and put his face in his hands, struggling with a host of emotions, some of which he hadn't expected. After all, he'd worked with Levy for some years now, and often talked strategy and planning over drinks at one or the other's home. If any person in espionage could be said to have a real, trustworthy friend, he had had one in Levy. And the reverse had also been true. But now his friend was gone, and he himself had utterly failed to come up with a way to help, other than to expedite that death.

Finally he pulled himself together and sat up straight.

One more call to make, and then I can go home and drink myself into oblivion, he thought. *Damn, but I'll miss him.*

***

Dr. Talia Yitzhak, in her new apartment in Tiberias on the western shores of Lake Kinneret — what Gentile Christians usually called the Sea of Galilee — sat in bed in silken pajamas, staring at the bedside telephone in the semi-darkness. She had already cleared her schedule for the next day, just in case, but she was tense and anxious. She knew what was likely going to happen this night, and she did not want the news. But she had herself almost guaranteed this night would happen. And that, she would regret to her dying day. *From what Yaakob told me, I think I hurt him worse than the cancer diagnosis. I should have been stronger,* she berated herself. *I should have stood by him. Should have found a way to give him what he wanted. Then at least I could have been Mrs. Franz Levy, his widow. But no, I was too much a coward. Fool that I am.*

The phone rang, interrupting her self-castigation, and she jumped, then grabbed for it.

"Dr. Yitzhak. Yaakob, is that you?"

"Yes, Talia. It's Yaakob."

"I'm listening."

"He was shot down in Suez, on the Gulf shore, creating a diversion to allow a group of frogmen to make landfall against a flanking force of Egyptian infantry and armored." There was a pause. "He's…gone."

"Oh, dear God…"

"I know, Talia. I'm hurting too. I'm sorry."

"Th-thank you, Yaakob," she breathed into the phone. "I…we'll talk later."

"It was fast, Talia. Not much pain. No lingering, like the cancer would have done."

"I…I know."

"…I'm here if you need me, Talia."

"Not…not yet." Her voice broke. "Later, Yaakob."

"Okay. But remember: I'm here. In whatever way you need me. Just say the word and you have a shoulder. Meantime, try to get some sleep, honey. Good night, Talia."

"Good night, Yaakob."

She hung up.

Then she flung herself across the bed and wept violently. All night

***

She didn't show up for work the next day.

Nor the day after.

Nor the day after that.

By the end of the week, she had been declared missing.

Two weeks later, Dr. Talia Yitzhak was found in bed in her apartment in Tiberias, a gunshot wound to her temple.

A brokenhearted Yaakob Falkenberg made the funeral arrangements.

***

Chapter 13 — Surprises

Much to his surprise, Levy woke up naked in a soft bed, his body carefully covered with blankets. He was deliciously warm.

What the hell?! he thought, startled. *I should be dead. I...*

Abruptly a memory surged back.

'...Come back for the body. Hide it behind the rubble so the enemy doesn't desecrate it and move out.'

Farkakte, verdammt, and merde! he cursed. *Did the Egyptians find me? Maybe the wounds weren't so bad they couldn't patch me up? They'll be pumping me for info! Maybe even torture! I need to figure out how to get out of here!*

He flipped back the bedclothes, intent on getting up and finding clothing to slip out of the hospital.

Instead he froze, staring down at his own torso.

No bullet wounds, he thought in shock. *Not even scars! What the hell did they do? Not even the Americans could do this!* He paused, thinking. *Maybe I'm in Shehaqim, the third heaven? I would not have thought Sheol to give me a...*

He stopped, then eased out of bed and padded across the small hospital room on bare feet; the floor was cold, and appeared to be some sort of metal. But he headed straight for the sink and the mirror over it. There, he got his third shock.

His thirty-seven-year-old face barely looked twenty-one.

Shit, he thought, shocked. *What the hell happened to me? I died…didn't I? This MUST be Shehaqim…*

***

Just then, a short, red-skinned being with yellow eyes toddled into the room, and Levy spun.

Well, THAT doesn't look like an angel! he thought, wry, and wishing for at least one of his personal weapons…which were, of course, nowhere in sight. Nor, for that matter, were his clothes.

But that was when he saw the gentle smile on the creature's face, and the soft look in its eyes. *Or maybe not,* he changed his mind.

"Greetings!" the little red being said. "You much much better feeling must be."

"I…I am," Levy admitted. "Um, excuse the lack of clothing…"

"No, no, fine that be," the little being waved off the apology. "Clothing soon come. My name Doron be, I Edeptis from, and I physicians one of working you on, per intense request of Entiyti Lord President. I here to you examine, if to see, um, regenical process successful was." He walked over to the bed and patted it in invitation.

"Regenical?" Levy moved back to the bed and sat. "Do you mean regeneration?"

"Um, yes, be that it. Please to excuse Englishes mine," the little physician said, seeming to flush a dark red. "Entiyti Lord to me gave the, um, 'binary language translationer' for the Englishes, but not long times to review it, have I. Busy you heal, I, and get not it until after here you. Busy, busy. No study. Understanding me?"

"Yes, I understand you." Levy offered the little being a smile, and Doron returned it, though he seemed a bit shy to Levy. "So I'm…where am I?"

"Entiyti's ship aboard, you be. Sick bay, is."

"Aha. Now I get it. I got him out, so he got me out."

"Yes, that way is." Doron nodded as he used the bed controls to lower it to his height, then he produced a device and scanned Levy from head to toe. "Oh, good very, is."

"What's that thing?"

"Medscanner, it called. You condition, read it. Galactic standard use is."

"Farkakt, I knew he said the medicine was more advanced, but damn." Suddenly the memory of the alien conversation returned; he remembered giving permission to be worked on, and gratitude washed through him.

"Yes, yes, advanced we be, is Earth compared," Doron said, and smiled again, more openly this time. He made Levy lie down, then carefully and gently palpated his abdomen. "Tender? Hurt not?"

"No, it feels fine."

"Good. Is lucky you, is."

"Yes, but..." He sighed.

"Wrong what?"

"I'd rather have died fast from the bullets than waste away slowly from the cancer."

"Oh. No, no. No cancer. All gone bye-bye."

"What?! It's gone? I'm healed?"

"Yes, yes." Doron fairly beamed this time. "Franz all well, long live now. Younger, even. You see mirror?" Doron gestured at the mirror in which Levy had been looking at himself when the diminutive physician had entered. "You see younger?"

"Um, yes? By a good bit, actually…"

"Is process part. Is to remove cause cancer, is make young to before cause cancer."

"Uh..." Levy paused to parse that one. "So…to heal the cancer, you had to regress my age to before I was exposed to whatever caused it?"

"Yes, yes. Right that."

"Well, damn," Levy said blankly.

Doron grinned.

***

After donning a special garment that Doron had brought to him — with considerable help from a Draconan nurse in the donning, for it was a complicated piece of tailoring, with lots of hook-and-loop straps — Levy sat in the hospital bed and thought.

Well, it apparently wasn't anything at Majdanek, when all is said and done, he decided. *Because if I'm now around 20 physically, and they regressed me to that age to get past whatever caused the cancer, then it was something I was exposed to in my early to mid-twenties that caused it. Not, I suppose, that something in Majdanek might not have set me up to react to the something. Maybe. Or not. Something on the streets of Tel Aviv? Maybe in my IDF days. Wait. Could it have been when Gabe died? A possible radiation source, and the virus…but it was targeted, it shouldn't have contaminated ME…huh. I guess I'll never know for sure.*

He pondered that for a bit, but had no answers; he simply had no idea what could have caused the cancer. He shrugged to himself.

In any case, I'm well, and I appear to have a long life ahead of me after all. Now I just need to figure out what to do with it.

***

"No, it would be difficult for us to return you, Franz," Pulgey Entiyti said some time later, when he came by to check on the human. Levy's room in sick bay was larger than he might have expected, but with the big Draconans aboard, he supposed it made sense; Entiyti was currently sitting in what Levy had considered an oversized visitor chair…until Entiyti sat in it. "I am afraid we simply cannot risk returning you to your original life, in any case."

Levy was still clad in that snug jumpsuit the nurse had helped him don; it seemed to be comprised largely of elastic and something like the rather esoteric Velcro recently developed on Earth for NASA, but it covered the important parts while allowing the physicians access to whatever parts they wanted to check, intubate, catheterize, or otherwise probe. He sat up in the bed while Entiyti sat in that very large visitor chair at the bedside.

"Well, I can sort of see that," Levy noted. "I leave the battlefield dying several times over, nearly forty, and come back completely healthy and looking barely old enough to buy a beer."

"Exactly. We might, I suppose, come up with a way to place you elsewhere, with a new identity, but I need to know a bit about you, first. That way my staff and I can figure out where to put you."

"Oh, I understand," Levy said with a grin. "You need to know more than just my first name."

Entiyti let out a roar of laughter. "That would help, yes."

"I take it Earth failed the test?"

"What?"

"It's not ready to be accepted into the galactic government yet?"

"Oh. No, not quite. It is getting there, but I think patience is required for a bit yet."

"I see."

"Now, about that name and background, Franz..."

"Uh, well, all right, but there's something I need to do first."

***

An awed Levy sat in an antigrav 'wheelchair' pushed by Entiyti, and stared across the bridge of the *Hsshthh* at the display screen.

The big room was not unlike that depicted on a certain science fiction television show currently broadcast out of America; Levy was a huge fan of the show and had watched the latest episode shortly before making his way to Suez for what was to have been his last mission. It seemed — if Entiyti was to be believed, and Levy did — that the set designer was, ahem, not from Earth, so it stood to reason, he supposed.

But this one was no TV set, it was real. And manned by creatures that could not possibly be humans in rubber suits. And the starfield on the display screen looked nothing like the stylized version depicted on that show — it looked REAL.

After having been introduced to Draconan Captain Guurth Abergari, he sat and watched the bridge crew work for a good twenty minutes, utterly fascinated.

Finally Levy nodded, and Entiyti pushed the medical transport chair back toward one of the bridge doors.

***

But instead of going back to the sick bay, Entiyti took him to a comfortable lounge.

"Here," he said. "This is covered with an armored shutter when we are in danger, but this is our observation lounge. I come here sometimes when I need to think. You are looking out into space, Franz." He pushed the chair up to one of the huge viewing ports, and Levy gazed out, directly into deep space, for the first time in his life.

In the near distance he saw a little blue marble, with an even smaller silver marble nearby. A bright star shone some distance farther away, yellow-white with a hint of green; smaller disks could be seen scattered here and there in a roughly linear arrangement against a background of stars. Arching up from behind the star was the familiar Milky Way.

After a moment, Levy realized his jaw was hanging open, and he closed his mouth. He found, however, that he couldn't wipe the shit-eating grin off his face. He was utterly delighted with his predicament.

"All right," he said then. "Thank you. There's no doubt this is real, and no Egyptian simula..." He broke off mid-word and shook his head. "I don't even know how they could simulate this."

"They cannot," Entiyti said. "Not even your Americans could. Not with their current technology. Though I had it to understand they will be trying to reach your Moon in a few more years."

"Damn," Levy breathed, glancing at that tiny silver marble.

"Do you trust me now, trust us?"

"Yes!" He turned his gaze back to the Moon. Entiyti noticed.

"We can take you there if you like, but we would have to be careful," Entiyti said. "Your Americans are likely to succeed — though, unknown to them, the Soviets have essentially failed already — and they would not need to see YOUR footprints already there." He grinned; it was a mischievous, if toothy, expression. "But yes, we can. After all, it would not really diminish their accomplishments, which would be to reach it under their own power, with their own ingenuity."

"We could?" a shocked Levy almost stammered. "You mean, you'd—? And I could?"

"Would you like that?"

"I'd love that!"

"Let me see when Doron will release you, or at least permit it with assistance, and it will be arranged."

***

Two days later, with Haarg Draang, Entiyti's chief bodyguard, and Dr. Werfer Eretigen, Entiyti's personal physician, carefully escorting him on either side, a space-suited Franz Levy became the first human ever to walk on Earth's Moon. He was in a medical power suit, it was the lunar farside, and their footprints were carefully erased with puffs of nitrogen after they ingressed, but it was still a first.

None but the crew of the *Hsshthh* would ever know.

And Levy was all right with that.

***

"...And so that's my whole story," Levy finished the verbal biography, which had only waited on his confirmation that he was indeed on an extraterrestrial spacecraft and not being set up to obtain information. "It really doesn't matter where you put me, because I don't have anyone left to care, really."

"What about this physician, the one you asked to espouse you?"

Levy averted his face.

"She said no."

"But she may have done so only to avoid having to watch you die, my friend."

"I'm barely 21 physically now. She's in her late 30s. I don't think it'd work." Levy chuckled, but it sounded strained to Entiyti.

"We could ask Doron to reduce her physical age as well."

"No. I don't…I think it might be as well to move on," Levy said, keeping his face averted. "I…I would have thought she would care enough to, to stay with me through it, to help me get through it, but..." He shook his head. "No," he said, more firmly. "No, I learned in the concentration camps not to care so much. Not to let anyone that close. I should have trusted my lessons in that regard."

They were silent for long moments, as Entiyti realized that Levy had been deeply hurt by his love's rejection, especially in such dire circumstances.

"You saved me, you know. In so doing, you may well have altered the history of the galaxy."

"Huh. Hadn't thought of it like that. And I'm not really even used to thinking of you as a galactic leader; you were someone that needed help, and I was in a position to help."

"And for that, I am more grateful than you will ever know."

"The feeling's mutual, you know. I'm not dying now."

"True."

They fell silent once more.

"I have an idea," Levy said then.

"What?"

"I had a chance to talk to Haarg and Werf when we were suiting up for the moonwalk," Levy explained. "Haarg said he was your chief bodyguard."

"And so he is."

"That implies you have a group of bodyguards."

"I do. The Entiyti Bodyguard Corps, they call themselves; I am seriously considering making the name official. Nearly two octads of hand-picked warriors who have pledged themselves to my protection. It is a longstanding tradition of the leader of my clan, which I am, but this is the first time in Emdalian history that the corps has ever had more than Reptoids and Draconans in it."

"Do you take volunteers?"

"We do, but they must pass rigorous testing."

"As soon as Doron releases me, put me through it. I want to sign up."

"What, and not return to Earth?"

"When I can explore the galaxy? Why should I return?" Levy said, his face lighting up, hazel eyes fairly glowing golden. "There's nothing there for me anymore, anyway. This…this, I could get into!"

"Well, then," Entiyti said, chuckling. "Based on what I saw on Earth, it sounds like I have myself a new bodyguard. I will notify Haarg, and he, Werf, and Doron can consult on when you will be ready."

***

It was a few days yet before Levy was ready to endure 'rigorous testing' of any sort; the space suit in which he'd walked on the Moon was an enhanced suit, known as a 'power suit,' to aid his movements — after some weeks in the regeneration pod, neutrally buoyant, he was still a bit weak for strenuous activity. Meanwhile Doron performed medical testing and a bit of physical therapy, especially as regarded Levy's lungs.

While that was occurring, Entiyti assigned Levy quarters aboard his flagship — quarters not far from his own stateroom — and sent a couple of crew members to Levy's old flat on the outskirts of Jerusalem, and his house near Tel Aviv, to fetch what few things he didn't want to lose. There wasn't much; a childhood spent either in a concentration camp or on the streets of Europe meant he'd learned not to collect 'stuff.' There were some personal weapons, a couple of small keepsakes from friends, his mother's ring, Gabe's compass, the compass from Jakob, and his clothing, and that was it. Soon he was putting his clothes in the wardrobe of his quarters, placing the weapons in the personal armory safe of those same quarters, and positioning the keepsakes in sight on the corner desk. The ring went on a chain around his neck, then tucked into his shirt, out of sight.

"And now I'm moved in," he told Entiyti that evening over dinner together. "Though the closet and the weapons safe were…strange…"

"Bigger on the inside than they looked from the outside?"

"Exactly."

"Small, specially-engineered space warps," Entiyti explained. "I will have our ship's engineering officer provide you some reading material if you have an interest."

"I do, but I might need a bit of mathematics tutoring," Levy said, flushing in embarrassment. "I don't exactly have a bachelors degree, though the coursework I got working in the Mossad came close."

"Oh? As knowledgeable as you seem to be?"

"No. When half your youth is spent in a concentration camp and the other half on the streets of Europe, and the early years of your adulthood on the streets of Tel Aviv, then you joined an organization as…tight…as the Mossad, there's neither time nor money for higher education."

"Do you even have a…what is it called…a high school diploma, I think?"

"I do have that," Levy admitted, flushing deeper. "Though it was issued after testing when I joined the IDF."

"IDF?"

"Israel Defense Force. The Israeli military. I was a soldier for a while."

"Ah. Not to worry, my friend," a soothing Entiyti said, pouring after-dinner drinks for them both as they sat in the living area of his quarters. "We can provide a more generalized reading experience on the science and technical matters for now, and we can also provide those higher education courses if you wish them. Paid for as a member of my guard corps, of course." He shrugged as he handed Levy his glass. "We have universities of our own, after all, and most of the courses are available for remote study, so you will not even have to physically attend. And you will need to pick up a few more languages, I suspect. Of the not-Earth variety."

"I'm loving the sound of this," Levy decided, sipping from the glass. His eyebrows shot up in surprise. "Oh! Is this Laphroaig Scotch?"

"It is. Twenty-five-year-old cask strength, diluted a bit with water to decrease the burn. Do you like it?"

"It's got the Laphroaig taste, but it's far smoother and subtler than anything I've ever been able to afford," Levy admitted. "Yes, I like it a lot. Thank you for sharing."

"Well, there are certain advantages to working for the Galactic President, after all," Entiyti said with a smirk. "You'll find that there is a fairly brisk galactic business in the finer Earth liquors; they are well made and popular with the, ah, the…I think the Americans call them, 'beautiful people' of the galaxy."

"Ha!" Levy laughed. "But if Earth isn't supposed to know about the Coalition, then how…?"

"Those not from Earth who have moved there to live must make a living too, eh? Especially those who might be there as advance scouts, reporting to us on Earth's development. And so sometimes they set up a galactic trade," Entiyti explained. "Earth entertainment is extremely in demand, and as a result the latest fads on Earth tend to quickly spread throughout the galaxy. Bacon is also quite popular."

"Eh, that's one I can't do," Levy said.

"Oh? Why not?"

"Remember my explaining about Judaism...?"

The resulting conversation was long and in depth. Entiyti was fascinated.

***

By the time Levy was ready for the bodyguard testing, Entiyti had explained the more common pieces of weaponry to him, as well as the structure of the Coalition.

"So it's a representative republic, and the main representative body is somewhere between the American Congress and the British Parliament?" Levy confirmed.

"I believe so," Entiyti agreed, only mildly uncertain. "Likely closer to the Congress than to Parliament, in that all the representatives are elected, but regardless of standing at home, all are referenced as Lord or Lady whoever…or, in the case of certain species, such as the Ke!endarians, who do not acknowledge gender, or the Xemlon, who have four genders, we use whatever equivalent title they deem appropriate."

"And then there's this Ennead..."

"Yes. That is the major deviation from any of the representative bodies on Earth. Given how many inhabited planets are in the galaxy, Franz, and some of those, such as Emdali, have more than one sentient species which must be represented, well, the General Assembly can get very crowded.

It is currently housed in the largest single room anywhere in the galaxy! That took some engineering, let me tell you! But for the more contentious debates, it is next to impossible to keep order in the Assembly, as you might expect. The Ennead, sometimes called the Council of Nine, is elected from within the General Assembly to review certain items of business, often handed up to the Ennead during debate in the General Assembly. The Ennead can act on its own for certain things, usually to do with galactic security, and for others, they come back to the General Assembly with a recommendation, which is then voted upon in the Assembly. And I lead both groups, the Ennead and the General Assembly, since the Ennead is really just a subset of the Assembly."

"Well, that all makes a certain amount of sense, I suppose, milord Entiyti."

"No, no, no, Franz, let us not do this," Entiyti protested. "At least not in private."

"What did I do?" Levy wondered, perturbed. "Did I give offense?"

"Not in the way you think, my friend. And after saving me on Earth, you ARE my very trusted friend. I want you to TREAT me as a friend."

"I'd like to think that's so on both sides, but..."

"But?"

"I'm going to work for you, at least I hope, if I can pass the testing. You can't have favorites, and I can't be that familiar."

"Oh, sssllltth ssshhiissh ttthhssiiss asssshh hiiisss geessht! Of—"

"Wait, wait, wait," Levy interrupted, hazel eyes widened. "What the hell did you just say?"

"Oh," Entiyti said, expression momentarily blank. "I said, 'Damn it to the sixteenth level of hell.'"

"Oh. I need to learn that one; that was…pithy. I didn't know hell had sixteen levels."

"Heh. It does on Emdali, if not on Earth."

Levy snorted. "Okay, go ahead. What were you about to say?"

"Ah, yes. Of course I have favorites, Franz," Entiyti declared. "Everyone does. The problem comes when you start CHOOSING favorites, when you start showing a difference between those you know well and those you do not, in official business situations. In any given group, any sentient is going to find that there are some to whom he can relate, and others that are nice enough, competent enough, but with whom he has nothing in common. Even those with whom we 'do not hit it off,' as you humans say. As long as I do not shuffle off onerous duties on those with whom I have nothing in common — and I do not, and do not plan to start — then there is no problem. And I have never had anyone in my employ complain."

"Huh. Okay; what is it you want me to do?"

"My friends call me Pulgey." The Draconan paused meaningfully. "My CLOSE friends call me Pul."

"All right…Pul."

The Draconan grinned toothily. Black horns relaxed across the silver-white head.

"That is much better," he decided. "Now, let me see how well you picked up on details of the proto-cyclotron blaster from our last conversation..."

***

It took a while for Levy to gather all the information he needed to pass the testing. Some of it was easy; Entiyti's people had already gleaned enough on Levy to pass his background check before Levy was even conscious after being rescued, though it had been difficult without his full name.

315

The results of his regeneration meant he was physically fit and had no illicit drugs in his system…not that he had ever been prone to using such.

Likewise the sick bay was able to verify his fitness level, which was quite high, since as a Mossad field agent he'd made sure he stayed in prime condition; his life — and others' — could depend upon it. It only took a few days, roughly a week, for his body to regain its familiarity with gravity after weeks — almost an Earth month — of neutral buoyancy, and with it came that high fitness level. He had immediately asked if there was a fitness center aboard and been introduced to it by Draang. Workouts commenced the same day.

A surprisingly quick session with a Deltiri bodyguard — the Deltiri were a telepathic race, and that alone was new in Levy's experience — resulted in his being declared mentally fit AND not a security risk.

A full-body scan by Dr. Eretigen ensured he had no identifying body markings…aside from the fact he would be the only human on Entiyti's bodyguard staff, that is. It seemed the tattoo from his days in Majdanek had been mildly affected by the regeneration bath, and while it was still there, it was deemed not obvious enough to be a problem. This suited Levy, as he despised the thing, and he semi-jokingly threatened to get his arm injured just so they'd have to put him back in the bath and get rid of it.

Haarg Draang put Levy through the written exam, which was a broad test to gauge Levy's general knowledge and awareness.

Then he put Levy through a threat recognition simulation, which also served to demonstrate Levy's strategic planning capabilities, as it turned out.

***

"What's this?" Levy asked, as Draang led him into a large room, empty except for a control panel next to the door.

"This is a simulation room," Draang explained. "It is one of the first of its kind, and it is still in development; there are some technologies we need for it that we are still negotiating to obtain. But it will depict a scenario for you as if it were real. This test is a puzzle; you must figure out what is going on, and what to do about it. I will stay here at the control panel, but you will not be able to see it or me."

"What's my task?"

"You are en route to Pul's location. He has summoned you, but it is not an emergency summons, or even a priority one. It is, however, optimal if you show up at SOME point." Draang handed him a small device, somewhat larger than a deck of cards. "This will lead you to his location…among other things. The real object has security and to spare, including cyphered signals, so assume it cannot be hacked. Stolen is a different matter." He paused, then added, "Anyone you take down in the simulation, whether lethally or otherwise, will disappear from the field. So be aware of that. If you render them unconscious, however, the strategic computer may simply choose to bring them back in at a different point, as if they had regained consciousness."

"Okaaaaay. You gave me back the equipment I had on me when you…well, Pul…the collective you, brought me aboard. Is that fair game to use?"

"It is. It is why I gave it to you when I did."

"And what am I supposed to do in this simulation?"

"Whatever you see fit, once you ascertain what you think is happening."

"And that's as much of a heads-up as I get?"

"Yes."

∗∗∗

Suddenly it was dark except for a few scattered lights. Levy was standing on a street in a big city at night; towering high-rises, taller than any found on Earth, clustered around him, their tops disappearing in the dark night sky. The construction material looked like stone — perhaps granite of differing shades and textures — but given the height, he suspected it was a veneer, and the underlying construction was made of something much stronger.

It had been raining, for the pavement was wet. He seemed to be in a narrow side street, though not an alley; vehicles of some sort traversed a larger street a few tens of meters to his right. Neither Draang nor the control panel were visible anywhere.

He shrugged, glanced at the device in his hand, then turned right and headed toward the main street.

***

When he reached the street, he checked the device again, and turned left, headed down the street. It was late, and while there was traffic, it was sparse, and mostly of the supply truck variety, though he had to admit that they were considerably different than what he was used to — there were no wheels, for starters; apparently they were hovercraft of some sort, and stayed a couple of feet off the ground when in motion, or when stopped at an intersection. Given his recent introduction to the medical wheelchair with a built-in antigrav unit, he suspected that was the case for these trucks also. A few were visible parked along side streets or in alleys, and these sat directly on the pavement.

He glanced about, taking in the detail of his surroundings, and realized he was in the high-rise district of some alien city. The architecture was somewhat unusual, but in general it wasn't too different from any of the big cities of Earth he'd traversed, save for the building heights. There were no power lines or other infrastructure hints visible, and he assumed that, as many Earth cities were starting to do, the infrastructure had been placed underground.

Levy kept going, periodically glancing at the tracking device to make sure he was on the path.

***

Halfway down the block, he became aware of light footsteps a short distance behind him, perhaps ten meters, if that. They didn't sound like human footsteps, but then he wouldn't expect them to do so; there was probably no human avatar in the simulator. And there were no other pedestrians in the area that he could see.

He considered for a bit, then paused to look in a shop window — it seemed that street-level shops were common in cities across the galaxy — and the footsteps behind him stopped. He desperately stifled a snort.

Shades of Agatha Christie or something, he thought to himself, still trying hard not to laugh. *That's about as cliche'd a response as I can think of. But it's also pretty universal. Still, it's telling. I'm likely being followed. Let's find out.*

As he reached the next intersection, he took a quick glance at the gizmo in his pocket, then quickly cut left, even though it said to go straight. Moments later, the footsteps also turned left. He checked the device again, exclaimed, "WOOPS!" and, glancing both ways to ensure there was no traffic on the side street, he quickly jaywalked across the street, headed back to the main street, and continued on.

A shadowy figure, now on the far sidewalk of the side street from Levy, turned and went back to the intersection, crossing the street there. The footsteps behind him picked up the pace until they were once again some eight to ten meters behind.

Hm, Levy thought. *I'm nobody. They're after Pulgey. Whoever 'they' is. Are? Whoever. Now, they could steal my tracker gadget, or they could just follow me right to him. Or they could kill me and take the gadget. But Haarg said Pul was in no rush, so I can take my time figuring this out.*

Eyeing the vehicular traffic in the main street — which had picked up significantly — he selected a brief break in the suddenly-heavy traffic and jaywalked again, sprinting across the main artery before his tail could react. Then he ducked down an alleyway and into a mews.

Once there, he knew he was out of sight, but it remained to be seen for how long. And if the tail had an accomplice, he might not be out of sight to it. And it only made sense to assume there WAS an accomplice. They wanted the galactic president, after all.

So he found a tight space between buildings — one that none of the other bodyguards he'd seen would fit into, so he had to assume that it was unlikely his pursuers would, either — wedged himself in the gap, and began to chimney upward.

***

He went up several stories, until he could access a mezzanine balcony. Slipping from shadow to shadow, he used this to double back along his route, until he could get a good look at the being that had been following him. He was still several stories up, so he decided to make use of his Mossad gear. Pressing his way into some landscaping shrubs to hide his form from any potential observers, he pulled out a special set of glasses and donned them, turning a small, unobtrusive knob on the temple. This enabled a telescoping set of lenses and mirrors, and he zoomed in on the being that had followed him, who was currently standing in the mouth of the alley down which Levy had ducked earlier.

It was a loosely disguised Kydeen — a human-sized, bipedal, intelligent koala creature — looking around in some confusion, apparently wondering where the human had gone. Moments later it was joined by a werewolf-like being; Levy thought it was a Tekulan, based on his tutoring sessions by Entiyti. Abruptly he started in recognition: there was an amazing resemblance to the kynokephalus, and he wondered if there had been Tekulans on Earth long ago, and the kynokephaloi were their descendants. He decided to discuss it with Entiyti later, and returned his attention to the meeting below.

A brief conversation ensued; Levy read the lips, but it was not a language with which he was familiar, and he couldn't tell what was being said. He did, however, pick up 'Entiyti' several times in the course of the conversation, so that told the tale to him…especially when the pair pulled out weapons and checked them.

Mm, he considered. *I can't prove it, so I can't shoot 'em outright. BUT…I might be able to put 'em down for the count for a bit. Where's that thing Yaakob gave me…?*

In moments, he was extracting a compact, collapsible-stock rifle from a hidden pocket of his suit coat, unfolding it, and loading it…with darts.

I guess we'll see if Earth tranquilizers work on these guys, he thought, taking aim. *If they don't, they're gonna be pissed off. Or maybe really sick.*

One soft hiss was followed by another; the Tekulan dropped within a couple of seconds, and the Kydeen only took a few seconds longer.

Two nonlethal takedowns, he thought. *Not bad. I can't guarantee that's all of 'em, though. If this is really an assassination attempt, and there's more than one, then there are likely several; a coordinated effort of some sort. So I need to assume I'm still being followed, and act accordingly.*

Just then, a flash of dull red light caught his eye, off to one side. Instinctively he ducked deeper into the shrubs, and looked closer…but saw nothing. Another flash out of the corner of his eye, and on the other side, told him what to do.

Using averted vision, he was just able to suss out a grid pattern in what he assumed to be a near-infrared laser system.

There ARE more, he realized, *and they're trying to map out my location. Which likely isn't a good thing, especially for me. Time to move, Franz, before you become a target.*

He was still a bit thin after the whole cancer scare, though his full, rather substantial-for-his-stature strength had come back with the better absorption of his food, and this now stood him in good stead — he could fit into places that none of the other bodyguards could, because in the main and for obvious reasons, they were fairly burly. Though he was himself quite muscular, Levy was never going to be a burly man, because he didn't have the frame for it, especially after spending his formative years in Majdanek. But, he considered, this meant he could go places more muscular men couldn't, without being in the least weaker than they.

So he hit his belly among the shrubs and wormed his way through them and into the building. The door had been locked, but the device Draang gave him served an additional purpose — as he neared, it vibrated in his hand, the door clicked, and it unlocked. *Well, Pul said there were advantages to working for the Galactic President, and he wasn't joking,* Levy realized. As he passed through the door and it closed behind him, he heard another soft click as the door latched once more, and the device vibrated lightly to serve notice that it was responsible.

Once he was inside and hidden in the deeper shadows inside the building — on this level, it was a shopping plaza after hours, though other floors had darkened offices he'd seen through the windows as he climbed — he paused to consider while he folded up the stock of the dart gun, tucking it back in his jacket.

All right. They're after Pul, he thought. *I mean, they COULD be after me, because human. But this is a bodyguard test, so they're more likely after Pul. Besides, it was his name I read on their lips, not mine. I have a gadget to lead me to Pul. So they can either kill me and take it, and go right to him — not a good plan for me, for several reasons, notably being I'd like us both alive — or they could simply follow me to him. Also not a good plan. I don't know where the rest of them are, and they have those disguises, not to mention cloaking…or didn't Pul say they hadn't miniaturized it to personal size yet? Okay, so no cloaking. But definite disguises, since I never saw the guy with the laser grid system. And I don't see why, if those disguises can make Pul look like a six-foot blond human man, they couldn't make these zin fun a hur look like part of a wall.* (sons of bitches)

So there's a couple things I can do: I can destroy the tracker. Except Haarg said I needed to show up for Pul eventually. Aha. Eventually is the key word. Which means the other thing I can do is to lead these momzers on a megillah of a chase. So keep the tracker, Franz, just keep it out of sight, and go anywhere EXCEPT where it tells me Pul is. (bastards; long, long story)

He eased over to a window and peered down at the street.

The Kydeen and the Tekulan were gone.

Surprise, surprise. Get your tuchus in gear before you lose it, Franz, he thought, and headed for the nearest door, utilizing the shadows to his maximum ability.

Which was considerable.

***

Before he left the shopping plaza, however, he discovered another of the gadget's abilities: A detailed map. Studying the layout of the mall, he slipped into a party supply store using the tracker's secondary abilities. There, he nosed about until he found several things he wanted, tucking them into pockets. He could pay for them later, he supposed, if this were happening in the real world. Or maybe it would go on an expense report; that sort of thing had yet to come up in discussions with either Draang or Entiyti. But for now, he needed them to keep himself and his detail — namely Galactic President Entiyti — safe.

Moments later, he was headed for the catwalk to an adjacent building.

***

Evidently his pursuers had lost track of him inside the shopping mall; there was no sign of surveillance as he crossed the skywalk into the next building. This suited him just fine; the longer he had to get away from where they were looking without being detected, the more apt he was to be able to drop the subterfuge and just head for Pul's location.

Even so, he took his time making his way, keeping above the streets and looking for less-direct routes to get him where he needed to go. If that meant dog-legging, or zig-zagging, he did so. If it meant doubling back, he was okay with that.

But it was not to be. Suddenly he saw the same dull red flash out of the corner of his eye as he traversed an open plaza on the twenty-eighth floor between two buildings.

"Mm-hm," he hummed knowingly to himself.

He pulled a thick, stubby cylinder out of a pocket, then pressed a small button on its end and threw it into the air.

There was a loud *POP*, and suddenly the air was filled with glittery confetti. It caught in the turbulence between buildings and spread out into a huge cloud of laser-disrupting chaff, even as a grinning Levy darted for the far end of the plaza.

Several more attempts to map his location were met in similar fashion; he didn't know WHY they were trying to grid his position, but he could imagine several options, none of which were good. He kept thwarting them with the chaff from the alien version of a cracker, but they were going to give up on that soon, and he hoped he could catch whatever came next.

So rather than wait for them to try something different, HE tried something different.

A quick check of the gadget in map mode showed him a Draconan haberdashery shop nearby. He let the tracker unlock the door, slipped in, and ensured it was locked behind him while he sussed the inventory. He caught up a dark cloak and threw it on over his shoulders, put up the hood, and slipped out the back entrance the same way he'd entered the front.

Now he blended into the shadows even better, and the matte black material he'd chosen would tend to absorb the near-infrared gridding laser's light rather than reflecting it back; he needed to remember for the future that the sheen of most high-quality menswear from Earth was not always a positive.

This enabled him to get a little further away from his pursuers. He went down to the street level and hunkered in an alley off the main street, watching the antigrav vehicles move past.

Just then, one of the large trucks trundled up beside him from the rear and paused, waiting for a break in the traffic to turn out into the street. Levy got a good look at the structures underneath; seeing plenty of room and several items that looked like handholds of some sort — possibly for workers on the truck's motive system — he didn't hesitate. Within seconds, and before the truck could pull out into traffic, Levy was underneath. He doffed his cloak, swiftly rolled it and strapped it to his back, then grabbed the handholds, slipping his feet into another pair farther back. He pressed close to the undercarriage of the vehicle...

...And they were off.

***

Given the antigrav field, it proved to be easier than Levy had expected to hang on to the undercarriage and ride the truck through the city.

Here, he was completely hidden from anyone not literally lying on the street, watching under the vehicles, and as this wasn't something he expected most operatives to do, he figured he was in good shape, at least for the time. He had no idea where he was going, but the antigrav field helped keep him in position, so he had a hand free to check the map on the tracker.

Well, at least I'm not going the opposite direction, he decided, *even if I'm not headed quite in the right direction. If I ride this long enough, I can get far enough away from the search center that, by the time they've figured out I'm no longer in their perimeter, I can probably get to Pul.*

He settled in for the ride.

***

After roughly half an hour of riding beneath the truck, it slowed and looked to be turning into another alley.

Likely arriving for either a dropoff or a pickup, he thought. *Time to bail before the driver spots me. Of course, I couldn't see if there WAS a driver; this might be a drone. Even completely automated. Still, I'm not going to risk it.*

The turn was slow, as the big vehicle navigated the transition between smooth street and less-kempt alley pavement. Once it was well into the alley, Levy let go and drifted gently to the ground, as the truck moved on, deeper into the alley. He rolled onto his belly and looked ahead; there were several loading docks ahead.

He grinned to himself, donned the cloak again, and disappeared into the shadows.

***

The tracker said Pul was in the building just ahead of him. A cloaked Levy hurried toward the door, having detected no sign of anyone shadowing him in some time. *Almost there,* he thought. Still, he remained alert and aware.

Which was a good thing.

Abruptly a red dot appeared on his chest.

"Shit," he cursed succinctly, and brought up the object he'd been carrying in his left hand, quickly adjusting its angle.

The small palm mirror reflected the targeting laser back along its path; a slight flick of his wrist resulted in a suddenly-stifled scream somewhere in the near distance overhead. *Even alien eyes don't like lasers,* he thought in satisfaction. Given the aliens in question were simulations, he wasn't too worried about permanently blinding an ally.

Levy darted through the door of the building and into the adjacent stairwell, taking two stairs at a time as he ran upward.

Eight floors up, and with no sign of pursuit, the tracker indicated Entiyti was nearby. Levy exploded through the stairwell door, ran to the indicated apartment door, and the lock clicked open as the tracker buzzed in his hand. He pushed through, the mirror having been replaced en route by his Mossad-issue Beretta model 21A .22LR, which he kept in an ankle holster.

Pulgey Entiyti stood beside Haarg Draang, both of them standing over the simulation room's control panel.

The rest of the simulation faded away.

Entiyti began to clap, as Draang grinned broadly.

***

"That was impressive," Entiyti told Draang later over drinks in his stateroom. "Thank you for allowing me to be a small part of the simulation, if for that reason alone."

"He did excellently well," Draang declared. "That was not only situational awareness, that was strategic planning."

"It was," Entiyti agreed. "I would say we can consider that one simulation to have passed both tests. Do not you think?"

"I do," Draang said with a nod, and sipped his whiskey as Entiyti settled back in his armchair.

***

Thanks to Entiyti, when it was time to demonstrate his weapons proficiency, Levy had enough information at least to recognize the various weapons with which he was presented.

They were set up in a special compartment aboard the *Hsshthh,* one which had heavy armor AND force fields on all four walls, deck, and deckhead. It also had simulated live targets, using something the crew called 'solid holograms.' Levy remembered that Entiyti had referenced his disguise with the same term, and made a mental note to find out more.

"So, Franz," Draang said, "in THIS simulation, there are no 'friendly' targets. When I initiate the simulation, I want to see how fast you can eliminate each target with the weapon you are carrying. This is an enemy battle situation. Does that make sense to you?"

"Entirely," Levy averred.

Draang kindly started with Earth weapons — a handgun, a rifle, a shotgun, and an Uzi. As one of the top Mossad agents, these proved no problem; he'd already demonstrated his abilities to Entiyti in the diversion that enabled the galactic leader's escape, after all. Now he needed to demonstrate it to Draang.

When the Earth weapons had been duly and rapidly utilized with considerable aplomb, he was presented with a moderately-sized ray gun, followed by a very large projectile weapon — Levy recognized the large pistol Entiyti had carried in Suez — and a much smaller ray gun, which had been the smaller, strange weapon Entiyti had carried.

Fortunately Entiyti had already let Levy handle each of the three advanced weapons, using his own personal carry weapons to do so; Levy had yet to fire one, however. He had asked many questions of his new friend and absorbed all of what he'd been told to the best of his ability…which was pretty damn good, all in all.

So when the Winchester & Tesla death ray was handed to him first, and the 'active' area went live, Levy didn't hesitate: He put the small ray gun into 'grenade mode' and tossed it into the middle of the target area, doing his best to center it among the targeted non-beings, then dove behind the nearby backstop.

There was a loud chirp, a flash of light, and a booming shock wave, loud in the confined space. When the wave reflections dissipated, Levy rose from his shelter, to find Draang all but smirking, a wide toothy grin on his dark-green, scaly face.

"That was well thought," Draang said, taking the human's arm in a friendly fashion. "You have been talking to Pul, I see."

"You call him Pul?"

"Yes. He prefers to be on close terms with most of his bodyguard corps. Not all of the guards are comfortable calling him out so familiarly, and he allows their comfort level, as they choose. But I have worked with him some years now, and have grown fairly close to him." He cocked his head. "He has asked you to call him thus, as well?"

"He has. I think he feels obligated because of what happened in Suez."

"No, that is not how he thinks, Franz. Because of what happened in Suez, he knows you are a being of honor, and worthy of his trust…and friendship. So he offers them to you."

"Oh. I see now. I was…a little hesitant to call him that, when he invited me."

"You should not be. He means it, and wishes you to do so." Draang smiled. "I would wager he did not so much ask as demand, if I know him at all."

"Sort of, yes."

"Good. Do so, if you wish. But do not feel obligated, yourself — he would not want you to. Now, let us move on to the proto-cyclotron blaster…"

***

The proto-cyclotron blaster, Levy decided, was somewhere between a shotgun with adjustable choke, and the Uzi, but closer in size to the Uzi, though lighter. The beam could be spread wide, or choked down to a very narrow diameter, only about the size of a pencil.

But, Levy mused as Draang set up for the next round of testing, the wider the beam, the weaker it would be; it would take time to kill enemy attackers, and time was usually a luxury one didn't have in a firefight. If it were possible to ramp up the power of the beam, that would compensate, but there was no time for that now. He'd have to talk to Entiyti about the possibility later.

So instead he choked down the beam as tightly as it would go. When the simulation went live, he stepped out from behind the backstop, pointed the weapon, depressed the trigger, and swept it across the room twice, back and forth. The simulated combatants dropped in multiple pieces, fading away once they were 'killed.' In seconds the room was empty.

If Draang had had eyebrows to raise, he would have, Levy decided from the look on the Reptoid's face.

"Pul did NOT teach you that," the bodyguard noted. "I have never seen him try anything like it, even in training."

"No, but he told me a lot about the weapon, and I've been thinking about its strengths and weaknesses," Levy admitted. "I thought a scything action would work better than a beam spread."

"And you are correct. Widening the beam weakens it."

"Is there any way to…well, damn," Levy broke off.

"What?"

"I don't know if you've ever heard the Earth term, 'hot rod,' Haarg."

"I have not. Perhaps to heat something that is not normally heated, if I judge by your context and the definition of the two words?"

"More or less, yes. Colloquially, a hot rod is an internal combustion engine vehicle that's been modified to run hotter than spec," Levy explained. "I was thinking..."

"Ah! You are wondering if there is a way to 'hot rod' a blaster," Draang realized.

"Exactly."

"Most likely. We will go into the weapons repair room later and work on that."

"I'm game."

"Good. You are doing well, my friend. Very well. We have one last weapon, but it requires a certain amount of caution, especially for one your size."

"Ah. That'd be the rail gun, I expect. Lord Entiyti — uh, Pul — showed me his."

"You expect correctly. It is large, but even so, the mass of the frame does not fully offset the recoil in any wise, so be careful. It kicks like an ooog. And that is for someone my size, and I have somewhat on you in the matter of mass."

Levy accepted the massive weapon. Having hefted Entiyti's, the weight did not surprise him, but he did choose to wield it with both hands. *Think of it as a big Uzi and use it on semi mode,* he considered. *But take your time, Franz; this thing's going to kick like an angry ass. A BIG angry ass. A really DAMN big angry ass.*

When Draang initiated the live simulation, Levy remained behind the backdrop, sniping with the rail gun and using the backdrop heavily as support.

Pop -pop -pop -pop...The rail gun fired repeatedly and swiftly. The magnetics meant that he could, if he chose, fire it even faster than the Uzi, for there was no physical mechanism to cycle. And he knew it would also operate in full auto mode, but until he had more experience with it, Levy was not remotely about to attempt THAT. The recoil of the first shot resulted in the pistol practically over Levy's ear and pointed at the deckhead, as it was. He was glad it had not smacked him in the face.

But in the end, it was as effective in the Mossad agent's hands as the Uzi, and within seconds, all of the simulant enemy was down. He slipped on the safety, which amounted to diverting the current in the rails, and carefully laid the weapon aside as Draang approached from the observing station.

"My compliments," the big Reptoid said. "Given your smaller stature as compared to myself or Pul — though Draconans are lighter than Reptoids to allow for the flight function; still, humans are even lighter because of their smaller stature — I would not have been surprised if the first shot had put you on your tailbone. But not only did you control it quite well, your timing on all weapons was among the top of our guard corps. I would very much like to know more about this Mossad for which you worked; they trained you most excellently."

Levy grinned.

***

"How did he do, Haarg?" Entiyti asked his chief bodyguard from the privacy of his stateroom, late that evening.

"Truly stellar, Pul," Draang told the galactic leader over their drinks. "I know you said he did an amazing job of covering for you against the advancing Egyptian forces on Earth, but now I think I see what you mean."

"Did Grassh think to obtain a video recording of the event? On Earth, I mean."

"I do not know, but now I think I want to find out."

"And so where are we in the testing?"

"Finished. He passed all the testing with plenty of room between him and failing — sssshttt, he bested most of the Corps. He is going to make an excellent bodyguard for you, Pul. I have made some effort to introduce him to the rest of the Corps in the course of his testing, and he has charmed them all. He is a diplomat in addition to being a warrior."

"Even better news." Entiyti paused, thinking. "Haarg..."

"Yes, Pul?"

"When Arcphlim Bulurg was killed in that airlock accident back on the Kydeen transfer station, you lost your second, did you not?"

"I did, Pul," Draang said with a sigh. "That Kydeen was a good male, and would have been an excellent successor when I retire from the work. But..."

"But now you have no one in the position, do you?"

"I do not. Of the few in the Corps who have the tactical and strategic abilities, they are either approaching time to rotate out themselves, or do not wish the responsibility of leading the Corps. And generally speaking, those who do not wish it rarely have the temperament or general wherewithal to do so, anyway."

"True. Perhaps you should take Levy under your wing," the president suggested. "He seems to have a good head on his shoulders for such things, he has experience germane to the position, and he certainly seems excited about working with the Corps."

Draang looked at Entiyti with wide eyes.

Then, deadpan, he declared, "Reptoids do not have wings."

Entiyti growled in his throat and slapped his chief bodyguard on the shoulder before they both burst into laughter.

***

"You're joking, right?" a dumbfounded Levy asked when Draang broached the subject. "You're just now bringing me on — you're having to measure me and tailor brand-new uniforms to fit me — and you want to know if I want to be your successor?"

"Yes, Franz," Draang said from behind his office desk aboard the flagship. "Sit down and let me explain."

"That's going to be some damn big explaining," Levy said, doing as Draang said, but shaking his head.

***

"Farkakte," Levy said, when Draang was finished. "So you're telling me your hand-picked guy died in an accident last year, um, I mean annum, and nobody else wants the job? Is it that hard?"

"Not really, I do not think," Draang said. "It is simply timing that leaves me without a second. Either those who might do the job are close to retirement and do not wish to postpone it, or they are not interested in…I think you humans call it, 'moving up the ladder.'" He shrugged. "Of those, they like what they do already, and do not wish to add to it, for various personal reasons. In most cases, this is because they do not have the mentality for it in any case, and are self-aware enough to realize it."

"So you're checking with me? Without my ever having stepped into the job yet?"

"Actually, you have," Draang pointed out. "You nearly gave your life for Pul on Earth. The shuttle's pilot was able to obtain video of the entire sequence of events, including your turning mid-confrontation to shout at Pul to move his tailbone onto the shuttle, when he was frozen in place, watching you."

Levy flushed.

"Seemed like the thing to do at the time," he muttered.

"Of course it did. And that is the sign of someone who is good at guarding the safety of others. You have the skills and the knowledge already; we need only work you into our formations and strategic movements. And what I have seen indicates you have an excellent strategic head of your own, and may end up adding to our plans and strategies. And if that is the case, then I need to train you personally, because you are currently my best and most likely successor. If you are interested and willing."

"What's involved in the job?"

"Just what you have already seen me do. I set up the schedules and shifts, I interview candidates, put them through the testing; I do the paperwork, and I lead the team. I work closely with Pul to determine what he needs to do, then sit down and work out the safest way for him to do it, make a plan for the team, and ensure that plan is properly carried out. Oh, and I am his personal taster. Are you familiar with that kind of duty?"

"You mean checking for poisons and such?"

"Exactly."

"Mm. I've heard of such things, but never done them, myself. Besides, we're still figuring out what I can and can't eat of your food..." He cocked his head. "The sick bay indicates that most of it should work, but some of it might not be suitable, and could even cause problems."

"True. But not all of Pul's chief bodyguards have been from Emdali, so there are established protocols for that." Draang shrugged again. "Should you find yourself in this chair and unable to do that particular part of the job due to species incompatibilities, you simply invoke those protocols, select a Reptoid or Draconan from the Corps — or take a volunteer — and they become the chief taster."

"Aha." Levy paused, thinking. "So okay, right now you just need a backup, right?"

"I do, yes. If you do not want the job in the long run, this simply becomes a short-term workaround."

"And you've already talked to the rest of the Corps?"

"I have. And showed them the shuttle video from Earth. They were pleased that we seem to have recruited so astute a bodyguard, let alone the next chief bodyguard." He met Levy's eyes, then added significantly, "There were no protests."

Levy thought a bit longer, but he could see no negative consequences. He liked all of the Corps, and they seemed to like him. If they had no objections to him stepping in and immediately taking the number two slot, then why not see how it went?

"Okay," he said. "Let's try it and see how it goes. We can always reassess at a later date."

"Done. Pul will be very glad to hear it; he likes you, and this was his idea."

"It was?!"

"It was."

"I'll have to tell him thank you, then."

"I already have."

***

Thus began Franz Levy's tour in the Entiyti Bodyguard Corps. He absorbed Draang's training adroitly, and within a couple of months began to be of immense assistance to the big Reptoid, both with the paperwork and in handling the other guards.

"And as if that were not enough," Draang told Entiyti one night when he reported to the galactic president, "he is positively formidable in any sort of combat. This 'Mossad' truly trained him well. He says he trained in a number of 'Oriental martial arts,' including something new that they were planning to call 'Krav Maga' when once it became public, and that he learned through all of it how to use his opponent's mass against him. And so he can; he does so in a frighteningly swift fashion. He even put me on my back twice during training."

"What?! You??"

"Me. Even with the size difference. And if someone puts a weapon in his hand?"

"Yes?"

"Duck. The enemy is going down."

"Oh! That formidable?"

"Every bit, Pul. Every bit."

"And he is already functioning as the assistant chief?"

"Yes, and the other guards consider him a dear friend already. He has a dry wit that is apt to leave one in sudden

337

laughter five seconds after he has moved on, and he is..." Draang broke off and chuckled.

"He is what?"

"He has a positive talent for cursing. What I know of Earth would scarcely fit in a teacup, but I do have some knowledge of several of the languages. He curses in multiple languages, often in the same curse, and Pul, he is picking up the curse words from the native languages of the entire corps! When he gets annoyed at something, the air around him fairly turns green!"

The two males, Reptoid and Draconan, burst into laughter.

"Oh! I cannot wait to hear THAT!" Entiyti panted through spasms of hilarity.

"I have no doubt you will!" Draang chortled. "And sooner rather than later!"

***

Once Levy was duly and properly settled into the bodyguard corps and deemed in prime condition, Doron approached Entiyti.

"Entiyti President Lord, is wanting me home to go," the little healer requested. "Is grateful am I for rescues, and for to fix Levy sir, but is homesick I."

"Of course, my friend," Entiyti replied, smacking his palm across his face. "Of course. We should have done that sooner, but the timeline on reaching Earth in time to report back to the Ennead...I hope you can forgive me."

"Is not to forgive," Doron said, patting the bigger being's hand lightly. "Is RESCUE me, when colleagues mine survived not. Saved me, you. Is much grateful I. Time extra is problem not, especially when to recover the Levy sir could I. And better to learn the Englishes time next I will! Swear I this!"

They both grinned, and Entiyti leaned across his desk to a small switch.

"Entiyti to bridge."

"Speak, milord."

"Captain Abergari, Lord Doron of Edeptis wishes to return home. Can we fit that into our itinerary at the earliest possible opportunity?"

"Since you already sent your report to the Ennead, we are in no rush to reach Aleancë, milord. It is a significant diversion, as Edeptis is on the Outer Arm and Aleancë much closer to the core, but one we can easily accommodate."

"Do so then, please."

"Very good, sir."

"And there we are, my friend," the big Draconan told the small Edeptan. "Next stop, your homeworld."

"Oh, good very is that," Doron sighed with a smile.

***

Draang and Levy began to plan for a public appearance by President Entiyti upon their arrival at Edeptis; Entiyti strongly wished to petition the planet to join the Pan-Galactic Coalition.

The planet was not a member of the Coalition, nor had it been known to the Coalition prior to the *Hsshthh*'s reception of the mayday call from the ship on which Doron had been. Unfortunately they had not been in time to rescue the others; the pirates had chosen to destroy the ship before any but Doron could safely board the emergency rescue tenders, then take the little healer captive. It was Draang's considered opinion — shared by Doron, as he discovered — that the pirates had been after Doron specifically, given his consummate skills as a physician and medical engineer, and this had been why they had fought back so viciously. But it could not be proven, and he said little about it, even to Levy.

In the end, however, the visit never happened: There was a vicious attack by persons unknown on the transfer station around the Dendroid homeworld of Viridis. It was in Division Six, and Edeptis was closer to Division Twelve, but as president, Entiyti was being recalled to the Coalition capital world of Aleancë effective as soon as he could get there, for security purposes.

So Doron was placed aboard the *Llaagaarsshti*, which Levy now discovered was a heavily armored and armed interstellar shuttle, very nearly a corvette but with more passenger capacity, speed, and range, and this was aside from its extensive and powerful force shielding and cloaking systems. Several of the *Hsshthh*'s standard security guards attended the little healer, and Entiyti saw him safely off.

Much to Levy's disappointment, he was unable to say goodbye to the little alien who had saved his life; his shift duties had him elsewhere at the time of Doron's departure, and he was unable to schedule to meet him after going off duty for the evening on his previous shift.

It would be decades before they renewed their acquaintance, and their lives would be very different.

***

Chapter 14 — Things Get Hairy

Upon arrival at Aleancë, the Bodyguard Corps accompanied Entiyti into the capitol building, to his office. The building was gigantic, as it also housed the full Council room and most of the representatives' offices, as well as the Ennead chambers.

"And because he is the Coalition President, he has quarters there as well, suited to entertaining dignitaries, so it is fairly large," Draang told his new second, who was all but gawking at his first visit to another world; knowing it would be a culture shock, Draang had made sure Levy knew he was off-duty, but expected to accompany them and familiarize himself with the layout. "More, we have a barracks near his quarters, so we are close if we are needed."

"Are we on duty 24/7?" Levy wondered. "Um, 48… however many…?"

"Essentially, yes, in shifts," Draang answered. "Though we usually have a slightly smaller detail when we are here, since there are also guards assigned by the Ennead on him. We work together; I will introduce you to them later. Pul also wants me to make sure I give you a tour of the chamber rooms after we get him settled."

"That sounds great!" Levy enthused, trying and failing to hide his excitement.

***

Levy mostly watched the process, at Draang's instruction, while they settled Entiyti into his quarters — which quarters indeed comprised a very large and luxurious suite, suited to a galactic leader — and his formal office, likewise large and stylish.

Then the Entiyti Bodyguard Corps settled into their barracks, taking turns to ensure that Entiyti was guarded at all times.

"Now," Draang said then, "let us go…I think you call it, 'sight-seeing.'"

"Yessss," Levy all but purred.

***

The Ennead chambers were fascinating with their considerable symbolism, and the Great Chamber of Representatives was so huge, it was awe-inspiring. Levy was intrigued by the architecture and materials engineering that allowed so gigantic a room to stand with so little obvious support.

But the sight that stuck with him the longest was when a humanoid female walked into the Great Chamber — which was at that time empty, as the Council was not in session — and moved to one of the council consoles.

She was tall for a humanoid female, very shapely, and extremely graceful; her formal robes draped over her body almost lovingly, clinging and flowing like a living thing. Even from the podium where he and Draang stood, Levy could see her smile at something, and it seemed to light up the huge chamber.

But it was her complexion that caught his attention.

She was GREEN.

From head to foot.

Her hair, her skin, her nails. Even her eyes, he thought, squinting to try to bring those small details into focus. *Just like a certain character from that science fiction TV show from America. Only she's obviously NOT wearing body makeup. And she's even more beautiful.*

He thought his heart skipped a beat for a moment. He surreptitiously put a hand to his mouth in case he was drooling.

"Um, who is that?" he managed to ask in a more or less normal tone of voice.

"Who?" Draang asked, following Levy's gaze. "Oh. She must be getting ready for the next session; I did not think anyone was supposed to be in here today, or I should not have brought you yet. That is Lady Teela Krimnet, the elected representative from the Kor system. This is her first term of office, but likely will not be her last; she shows great promise and great heart for serving her people, just as much as her deceased mother did, and Pul has taken her under his wing as one of his protégés. I would not be surprised," he considered, "if she is appointed to the Ennead in her next term. But maybe she will wait a bit."

"So she's smart as well as beautiful."

"She is, yes. Many have noted that fact." Levy didn't see the grin Draang was trying hard to hide.

"Can you, um, introduce us? I'd like to talk to one of the representatives..."

"I just bet you would," Draang breathed, stifling a laugh.

"What?"

"Nothing. I was debating over how to accomplish it. You see, I do not know Lady Teela personally; I have never had occasion to meet her. I only know her by sight and reputation. Perhaps at some point, you can ask Pul to introduce you to some of the representatives. He sometimes has what I think are called 'cocktail parties' in his suite."

"I might just do that."

***

But Entiyti had no such gathering planned in the current circumstances, given they were under tight security.

Levy stifled a sigh of disappointment.

***

Upon the return of the *Llaagaarsshti* from Edeptis, the swift shuttle landed in the hangar deck of the *Hsshthh* in dry dock above Aleancë, and the security guards debarked. Shuttle pilot Grassh Foorg stayed behind, however.

"No, there is something wrong with the Alcubierre drive," he told Hangar Control over the comm. "I want to have a look."

"Do you require assistance?"

"No, I do not think so," Foorg decided. "I know enough of the systems to be able to open the hatches into the drive compartment and determine what is wrong. I may need assistance repairing it, but that remains to be seen."

"Very well. We await your problem report, and will have mechanics at your request."

Foorg unstrapped and went to the aft, opened a hatch, and moved into the lower deck, which was essentially a maintenance deck.

***

Ten minutes later, a loud scream cut the atmosphere in the hangar deck, followed by a small explosion in the aft of the *Llaagaarsshti*.

Automated fire suppression systems engaged, and emergency personnel ran toward the little spacecraft.

***

341

"Damn," Levy murmured, as Draang and Entiyti practically gaped in horror. "So there was a problem, the warp glitched, and it killed Grassh?"

"Fairly effectively," *Hsshthh* Captain Guurth Abergari reported. "The fluctuating warp fairly shredded the poor ssllitthhssshht. We had to identify the remains genetically." (*bastard, Reptoid*)

"Sssshttt," Draang cursed. (*shit, Reptoid*)

"Sssllltth ssshhiissh ttthhssiiss asssshh hiiisss geessht," Entiyti cursed. "He was a good pilot, and a good male."

"Agreed," Levy said, very subdued. "What kind of condition is the shuttle in?"

"Not good," Abergari admitted. "It has been towed out of the hangar deck and will be in dry dock for repairs for some weeks. The feedback from the explosion in the drive fried the navcomp and several secondary systems."

"Unn," Draang grunted. "That is unfortunate."

"It is. More, it wiped out entries from the recent mission before the records could be downloaded into the archives."

"But…no one else knew how to get to Edeptis," Entiyti realized, expression blank. "We were going to add it into the galactic map once we had those records. I had hoped to convince the system to join the Coalition. And Werf wanted Doron to conduct a seminar on the regeneration process."

"That…may take a while, milord," Abergari replied, wry.

***

Matters had finally settled down after the attack on the Viridis transfer station by a group that the Pan-Galactic Law Enforcement and Immigration Administration had concluded were pirates, since there seemed to be no particular system involved, so security for Entiyti was ramped down a few notches.

345

As a result, an invitation came in from Exinul in the Luyten's star system to attend a special banquet in honor of their recent signing to the Sydys Concordat and joining the Coalition, subsequent to an attack from non-Coalition planet Durkera in the Procyon system, which the Coalition helped them fend off.

Entiyti graciously accepted. Captain Abergari quickly arranged for a new shuttle and a new pilot; both were swiftly vetted and determined secure. Draang and the rest of the bodyguard corps prepared for the journey to Exinul.

***

Everything proceeded smoothly upon the *Hsshthh*'s arrival at Exinul, and most of the bodyguard corps and Entiyti himself donned powered exosuits for the banquet; Exinul was a super-Earth and possessed gravity nearly two and a half times the usual for most Coalition worlds. Their atmosphere was breathable, however, and so the suits were only needed to assist the wearers against the planet's gravity.

By contrast, the Exinulans were short, stocky, muscular beings with mahogany-toned skin, elephantine feet and legs to ensure stability, pincer-style hands, short cylindrical heads set on thick necks, slits for mouth and nostrils, funnel-shaped holes for ears, and eyes with a permanent nictitating membrane to protect them from the harsh light of Luyten's Star, their system's sun. The result was a species that moved comfortably, even gracefully, in the high gravity.

Entiyti, surrounded by his bodyguards, which included both Draang and Levy, was duly introduced to the Exinulic planetary president, B'uria Vrukhur; while the planet possessed many nations, those nations had cooperated in the wake of multiple incursions by the Durkera fleet to create a planetary council. It had been this council that reached out to the Pan-Galactic Coalition for assistance.

Now the Exinulic President escorted Entiyti to their seats in the banquet hall; most of the planet's nations had at least representatives in attendance, most of whom were the nations' leaders. They stood and applauded as Vrukhur and Entiyti mounted the slight platform for the VIP table, their chief bodyguards following closely.

Levy took his position just behind the platform, which was fairly low due to the gravity; in an emergency, he fully expected to be able to leap to the top of the platform easily, especially with the aid of the exosuit. However, since this was a friendly gathering, he didn't expect an emergency. The rest of the corps spread out over the hall as the guests found their seats, and Indak, who had come along in case of medical problems from the different cuisine, crouched near Levy.

In the back corner, the chefs who had prepared the banquet put the finishing touches on the plated food, and the waiters organized themselves for the huge task.

***

The Exinulans had carefully ascertained the nutritional needs of Draconans, and their meal was expressly designed to be consumed by Draconans, Reptoids, and Exinulans.

The first course was thissslan soup with croutons and kooossheess, a kind of cheese made from the milk of Emdalian cattle; the end result was not unlike French onion soup, though thissslan was more like asparagus than onion. A nice Exinulic purple wine was served alongside. The bowls were placed in front of Entiyti and Vrukhur; Draang and the Exinulic bodyguard both tasted soup and wine, then waited a couple of minutes. When neither showed any sign of harm, they nodded, and Entiyti and Vrukhur partook. At that point, the waiters served the rest of the banquet hall.

"Get Franz a small cup of this," Entiyti murmured to Draang as he ate the soup. "I know he cannot eat it now, but I think he will like this, and it should be safe for humans."

"I'll talk to our waiter and have him set aside a portion for the guard corps," Draang agreed. "It will be a nice treat for them."

"Very good."

***

The second course was arsssluuk salad with a kind of Exinulic sharp cheese and edible flower petals from the most common flower on Exinul; it had been previously checked for Draconan allergies and tested negative. This time a yellow wine was served as accompaniment.

Again, the two bodyguards tasted the salad and wine, waited several moments, then nodded to their leaders, and the waiters began serving the rest of the hall.

***

The third course was a kind of souffle, delicately flavored with some sort of herbs, and glasses of Emdalian ssrrg wine.

This time, however, when the bodyguards tasted it, while the Exinulan guard was fine, within seconds Draang began to choke and gasp. His green scales paling, he fell to the floor. Entiyti immediately pushed away from the table, kneeling beside his friend and chief bodyguard, even as Levy called out orders to the guard corps and leapt to the top of the platform, Indak close behind.

Indak knelt on the opposite side of Draang from Entiyti, whipping out a medscanner and running it over the prone form. He muttered some sort of curse and yanked out a hypodermic syringe; it had no needle, but used osmotic pressure to force its contents into the body. If placed over a blood vessel, the medication entered the bloodstream. He promptly pumped a HUGE dose of the medication into Draang. Immediately, and with Entiyti's help, he began performing a kind of CPR on the downed Reptoid.

"Come on, Haarg," Entiyti whispered to his unconscious friend. "Come back to us."

Meanwhile Levy, unable to help Draang, stood protectively over the trio, his blaster out, and watched the banquet hall with a hawk eye.

As a result, he spotted one of the chefs trying to slip out the rear door of the hall.

"CORPS! CONVERGE!" he shouted. "STOP THAT BEING!" He pointed at the door.

Before the chef could get more than a hand on the door, he was on the floor, tackled by Agoboo Bobogoo, a Lambda Andromedan guard. Agoboo wrapped all six tentacles around his quarry, who by that time was going nowhere, powerful Exinulan or not; Lambda Andromedans were not lightweight, nor weaklings, themselves.

"Take him to the brig on the *Hsshthh*, maximum security; initiate interrogation, and wait for me there," Levy ordered.

Half a dozen guards placed the chef in restraints and led him out of the hall. A dozen more held the rest of the chef and wait staffs at gunpoint. The other guards surrounded the platform, facing out, weapons at the ready.

"I am so, so sorry," a horrified President Vrukhur repeated. "I do not know how this happened. I do not know."

"It's all right, Madame President," Levy said then. "We believe you. But there may be a faction that doesn't agree with joining the Coalition. Or there may be an embedded agent from your enemies. Or something else, even. Do you have a location where the staff may be held safely while we get to the bottom of this?"

"They are all under suspicion?"

"For now they are, yes. We'll know once our Deltiri interrogators question the one I had taken to our ship."

"Of course. Do you trust me and my guards to execute it?"

Levy scanned the other being, bringing to bear what would eventually be called his 'arachnid sense.'

"Yes. Do it. Now."

Vrukhur stepped out of the way and conferred with her chief bodyguard. Within moments, the rest of the Exinulan guard contingent had formed an armed guard to escort the banquet staff from the room. Two of Entiyti's guards went with them; the rest spread out to guard the exits.

***

Just then Indak sat back.

"Gone is he," the little healer said in a mournful tone. "Nerve agent of a sort it was, in the food. Stop it could I not."

"No, no, no. But President Vrukhur's guard did not grow ill," Entiyti noted, voice choked.

"It must have been placed only in your food, Pul — uh, milord Entiyti," Levy said. "Aartung?"

"Here," the Erikian bodyguard said, moving to Levy's side.

"I need you to put the food and drink from Lord Entiyti's dinner place into forensic bags and take them to the sick bay on the *Hsshthh*. We need to find out what was in it as soon as we can. Maybe we can throw Haarg into a regen bath like Doron did me."

"Cannot we," Indak said sadly. "For sake of Lord Entiyti, on you the procedure perform would Doron after what him happened, but loathe was he to us teach it. Not in danger would he put us from those who him captured. Them he feared greatly. And now reach him we cannot."

"Well, farkakte, shit, merde, argdun, and glagaram," Levy cursed quietly, kneeling beside the being who had been his friend and superior. "I swear, I have a death curse on me or something. Haarg, my friend. Too soon. Far too soon. You'll be missed, my friend. Greatly."

"He will, indeed," Entiyti agreed, his voice breaking several times.

Levy patted Draang's chest very gently, then stood.

"Rrslig, you and Harfek stay and see about bringing Haarg's body back to the ship. The rest of you, prepare to immediately escort Lord Entiyti back to the *Hsshthh*. GO."

They went.

***

"Sir, we found this in his pocket when we searched him," one of the bodyguards said as Levy entered the brig. The guard handed him a small dropper vial, carefully bagged. The bottle was half-empty.

"Huh," Levy grunted, studying the labeling. "That's a nerve agent, all right. That was one of the first things poor Haarg had me learn. Farkakte. Do we know where he got it?"

"Not yet, sir," the guard replied. "We notified the Deltiri translators, who are also certified to interrogate if need be, and one is on the way."

"Good."

Moments later, the same Deltiri Levy had already met, Hh'c'p og Mm'bl'l, entered the brig proper.

"Good to see you, Hh'c'p, just not under these circumstances," Levy said.

"Indeed, my friend, indeed," Hh'c'p agreed. "This Exinulan is the one I need to interrogate?"

"He is," Levy confirmed. "Someone tried to kill Pul. Indak says it was a nerve agent, and here this vial of nerve agent turns up in this guy's pockets…AFTER he tried to leave the scene of the murder."

"Oh dear. Mmm. Yes. Let me see what I can determine…"

***

Half an hour later, Hh'c'p reported to Levy, Entiyti, and Captain Abergari in the bodyguard corps' ready room.

"He is indeed the one who poisoned Lord Entiyti's portion; it was in the wine. No one else was involved in the plot," Hh'c'p informed them. "Apparently he lost his spouse in a relatively recent attack by the Durkera, prior to the Coalition's intervention with more advanced technology. He is rather deranged from the grief, and seems to blame Entiyti for the Coalition not intervening soon enough to prevent that death. Never mind that his planetary leaders did not contact the Coalition until AFTER that event."

Levy and Entiyti smeared hands down their faces at the same time.

"So he's not right up here?" Levy wondered, touching his temple.

"Not at the moment, no," Hh'c'p confirmed. "I have notified the Doctors Indak and Eretigen of this, and they think he should be evaluated by someone specializing in post-traumatic stress. Such an expert may be able to treat him and make him well."

"Meanwhile, poor Haarg is dead," Entiyti grumbled, grieving and angry.

"Oh no! I had not heard that," Hh'c'p exclaimed, shocked. "Oh no. That is…dreadful."

"Yes," Levy murmured. "I hate it like hell. He was a good friend, and an excellent leader for the corps."

"You will do as well," Captain Abergari declared.

"Ah. Well, I can certainly fill in until Pul gets someone with more experience to put into the job," Levy agreed.

"You are backing out, Franz?" Entiyti asked. The black horns seemed to wilt across his forehead.

"No, Pul. Just pointing out that you can do better for a chief bodyguard."

The black horns stood straight up. Entiyti started to speak, but Captain Abergari held up a clawed hand to interrupt the discussion before it could become contentious.

"May I suggest that there are more important actions that need to occur now than that particular discussion? You can resume it later, and 'hash it out' as the humans say, between you at that time."

Levy and Entiyti looked at each other, then nodded.

"Point," Entiyti said. "Go do what you need to do, Franz. You have the information to proceed now."

"Gone," Levy said, leaving the room at speed.

***

In short order, the rest of the banquet staff were cleared and released; Entiyti met with Vrukhur in a quiet discussion of events; the perpetrator, one Moban Gluk, was formally transferred into Coalition custody. He would be taken back to Aleancë for a hearing, though he would likely be declared innocent by reason of mental impairment, and treated.

Meanwhile, Draang's body had been brought aboard the big flagship; it would be transported back to Emdali for a family memorial and interment. Dr. Eretigen would accompany it; he had only come along on recent excursions because Entiyti had had a nasty recent bout of intestinal infection shortly before the Earth exploration. But he had just gotten word his mate was expectant from before he had left, and as there was the likelihood of complications, he was needed there. Indak would resume his position as chief medical officer on the *Hsshthh*.

And the *Hsshthh* departed Exinul under the special running lights mandated for a funeral cortege.

***

Once the *Hsshthh* was well outside the Luyten's Star system, Eretigen accompanied Draang's body aboard the shuttle *Aarg'sshiibeekk Ksssht*, or the *Devil's Bane*, whose running lights had been likewise modified. Gurgev pilot Gabia Ruus would see them safely home to Emdali.

The Entiyti Bodyguard Corps — the name now formalized by Entiyti himself — gave one of their own an honored sendoff, as the sleek black coffin made its way through the *Hsshthh*'s corridors toward the hangar deck, Levy, Entiyti, Eretigen, Abergari, and two of the guards with the most seniority serving as pallbearers. A final salute took place in the hangar proper by the entire Corps. All but Eretigen emerged from the *Aarg'sshiibeekk Ksssht*'s hatch, and Ruus entered.

Moments later the hatch closed; a special force field came up between the honor guard and pallbearers and the shuttle, then the force-field outer hatch was dropped, and the *Aarg'sshiibeekk Ksssht* shot out of the hangar bay with the venting atmosphere.

Haarg Draang was gone.

***

"...No, no, no, Franz," Entiyti told him in his stateroom over drinks several evenings later.

The lights were dimmed in the main chamber of the stateroom in respect of the melancholy mood. The pair relaxed in the comfortable sitting area, Levy curled in an overstuffed armchair, Entiyti on a chaise longue. An end table stood between their seats, suitable for temporarily discarding drink glasses and supporting a lamp, the only light in the room. Entiyti continued.

"You were Haarg's second. It only makes sense. This sort of thing is what he was training you to do, in case something happened, Maker forbid, only now it HAS happened. You have the skills and abilities and the mental capability, and the entire Corps knows it. And approves, let me add."

"They do?"

"They do. I talked with them, WITH Haarg before he…he died, in a casual environment. A couple of the guards are using this opportunity to retire, which means you will need to recruit a few new guards, but the rest expressed relief that there was someone of your talents ready to step into the role." He smirked, then added, "And a couple of those were glad it was not them stepping into that role!"

Levy paused and held up a finger to hold, setting his drink aside; he swallowed, then let out a monumental snort of amusement.

"You didn't pressure anyone? Nor Haarg?"

"I swear by my family crest," Entiyti said, holding up one clawed hand. "No one was pressured or coerced. That is not my way, in any case, as I should think you would know by now."

"Well, not deliberately, no. But you're an important person, Pul. You can be intimidating without ever knowing it."

"I know. And Haarg and I made sure to make them feel relaxed and welcome when we talked to them. Much as I am doing with you now, in fact."

"Oh, really?"

"Really. More, I informally polled them yesterday. None of them want someone else to lead them. They want YOU, Franz. They know you, and they trust you."

"All right, all right," Levy sighed. "I accept the promotion to chief bodyguard."

"Good. It is about damn time," Entiyti rumbled, wry. "I will announce it tomorrow morning at the Corps briefing, and notify the captain as well. He can notify the rest of the crew. Oh, and I will send word back to Aleancë."

"That works. All of it."

"Now, you are aware that the Oord have requested a diplomatic meeting, and soon?"

"Yes, but I didn't see the rationale. What do they want?"

"Something about marauders that have been attacking their shipping. I do not know more than that, as yet. But they are looking to ally themselves with the Coalition, and I am looking to convince them to JOIN the Coalition."

"I see. So that is where we are headed next?"

"We are, yes."

"Do you have the schedule and the layout?"

"I do, for they sent them to me only a few hours ago. Do you wish me to forward them to you?"

"Please. I'll start setting up a plan for the guard corps."

"Consider it done, before I retire for the night. You can start planning in the morning."

"Terrific, Pul."

***

Chapter 15 — Oh Dear

The pair stood in Entiyti's quarters aboard the *Hsshth*, the Winged Serpent. Levy helped the galactic president prepare himself for an upcoming diplomatic social event — the first of the negotiations with the Oord — helping him choose suit colors and accessories.

"...You are sure you do not mind, Franz?" Entiyti asked the human. "I do not THINK it will be dangerous this time, but still…after what happened to Haarg…"

"I'm your bodyguard, milord Pul," Levy responded, sincere, though teasing the boss that had rapidly become a trusted friend. "If part of that is being your food tester, then that's what I'll do. Just give me a heads-up about anything that's apt to give me problems as a human and not a Draconan, or when there's a real possibility of…repercussions, let's say."

"Given we — my crew, my bodyguard corps, but me in particular — do not know so much about human digestive systems as yet, I will do my best," Entiyti promised. "On all of it."

"Well, so far, I do fine on Emdalian foods, so I should be okay," Levy pointed out.

"True. Are you ready?"

"Yup. These are the Oord, yes?"

"That is correct."

"Okay, making sure I got the species correct, just in case. I'm still kinda new to all this interstellar stuff, remember."

"All right. Let us go, then."

***

The little diplomatic cocktail party went well — the few attendees as well as the cook and wait staffs had been VERY carefully vetted well in advance, after what happened on Exinul — and Levy preceded Entiyti, sampling some of everything he put on his plate, and sticking close by his side. The rest of the bodyguard contingent spread unobtrusively around the room, and somewhat to Levy's surprise, more than one of the visiting ambassadors expressed comfort at the subtle but patent protection.

"Usually the other side finds it obtrusive, bordering on offensive," he murmured to Entiyti, mildly puzzled. "At least in my experience, which is mostly on Earth, but…"

"Well, in this case, the Oord asked for this meeting," Entiyti responded in kind. "Something about marauders on the fringe of their territory, and they felt the Coalition would provide for watching each other's backs."

"And it would," Levy agreed. "They aren't Coalition members, then?"

"No. Not yet, at least. I've been nudging in that direction, and this gives me the opportunity to nudge a bit harder, because certainly it would be easier to accomplish what they wish if they were in the Coalition. But not as yet."

"I get it. I wonder who the marauders are. Did they say?"

"No, they did not," Entiyti noted. "I am not sure they know. There are so many possibilities — rogue factions from Coalition worlds, nonaligned planets, raiders from — as you call it — the Large Magellanic Cloud…there is little telling. At least without more information than we currently have to hand. Perhaps several with overlapping territories."

"True. Oh," Levy said, watching what Entiyti put on his plate. "What's that?" He pointed to a particular vegetable crudité on the potentate's plate.

"Ah, that is thisssslan," Entiyti explained. "You have had it in soup, and liked it. This is the raw vegetable form, for…what is the Earth term? Horse doofers? It comes with an excellent dip…"

"Hors d'ouvres," Levy corrected, hiding a grin with great difficulty. He took one of the spiky veggies off Entiyti's plate and munched it. "Mm. A stronger flavor than the soup, but it's very good. Rather reminds me of an Earth food called Brussels sprouts, though it's shaped more like asparagus."

"I thought you would like it." Entiyti's eyes twinkled, almost mischievous; Levy noted it and wondered, but hadn't time to ponder it when Entiyti's attention was diverted. "Oh, there is the Oord prefect; I should go speak to her."

"I'll follow your lead, my friend."

"I do like that," Entiyti murmured, heading for the prefect, Levy in tow. "It is quite nice to consider my chief bodyguard as one of my most trusted, dearest friends. They have always been trusted friends, but you and I…we 'click,' as you like to say."

"I rather like it, too, Pul."

***

But he didn't like it later.

It seemed that, unlike cooked thisssslan, where the cooking broke down the cell walls, human digestive tracts did not deal well at all with raw thisssslan stalks.

The first Levy realized that problems were looming was when he arrived back in his quarters late that evening and

359

reached for his usual nightcap…and set the decanter back down, unopened. Moments later, his disturbed belly let out an alarming howl, followed by a loud and very prolonged gurgle.

Seconds after that, he found himself sprinting for the head in his quarters, stripping off his uniform trousers as he went.

He barely made it onto the toilet before the explosive diarrhea hit.

***

As the Entiyti Bodyguard Corps — what there was of it currently — assembled the next morning in their ready room, everyone wondered where their new chief was.

"It is not like Franz to be late to the morning call," Rrslig Kuur, a formidable Reptoid, noted, puzzled, even as Lord Entiyti wandered up; he sometimes sat in on the morning briefings so as to provide background information on upcoming events. "Even before he was made chief, he was never late to the call. He was usually early."

"Perhaps milord knows," Aartung Gwig, an Erikian guard assigned to the Corps, considered.

"Knows what?" Entiyti asked, tuning in to the conversation.

"Chief Levy is not here, and no one has seen him," Kuur explained. "And that is not like him at all."

"Mm. Have you called his quarters?"

"I just pinged his comm," Kuur noted. "He did not answer."

"I will go see what is wrong," Entiyti decided, horns crossing in concern. "Perhaps he is ill. Kuur, can you handle matters until we have Chief Levy on his feet?"

"I can, milord," the Reptoid declared, squaring broad shoulders.

"Good. Let me go find Franz."

***

The door of Levy's quarters was locked. But as the focus of Levy's job and his boss, as well as the feeling between the two males that they were rapidly becoming the best of friends, Entiyti had been given all permissions to enter Levy's quarters some time back. He put in the code and the door opened; Entiyti stepped through...

...And reeled back at the stench.

"What in the name of the Maker...?" he gasped. "Franz, are you in here? Are you all right? What on Emdali happened?"

"I'm here," Levy's weak voice responded from somewhere in his quarters, "and I'm alive. But I rather wish I weren't."

"What is wrong?"

"Judging by…by what came through…in the wee small hours…last night," he panted, tone wry, "raw thisssslan isn't nearly as good for human digestive systems as cooked."

"Oh dear. Is that the reason for the smell?"

"I'm afraid so. It was…bad. I nearly passed out at one point, just from the stench. Never mind the intestinal cramps, and the feeling that my gut was being sandblasted on the inside."

"Where are you?"

"On the floor of the head. Naked. With a damned raw ass. But the head needs to be hosed down and sanitized, I'm afraid. For that matter, so do I..."

***

By the time Entiyti got Levy more or less upright — the human had to hang onto the nearest towel rack to stay that way — and hosed off in the shower, then wrapped in a clean robe and reclining on the sofa, the truth had come out: Pulgey had fully expected Franz to have some mild problems with the thisssslan, based on the reactions of similar humanoids in the galaxy, and had played what he expected to be a slight prank on the being he was coming to think of as his best friend, almost a brother. He had, however, never expected Levy's reaction to be so violent, or so prolonged.

"And for that, I must beg your deepest forgiveness, my friend," Entiyti sighed. "I only expected some indigestion. I swear unto you on all I find holy, I did not expect nor intend harm to come of it."

"Ooof," was all a drained Levy managed in response for a long moment. Eventually he continued, "It's okay; you didn't know. But Pul, I think I probably need to get to sick bay. I'm badly dehydrated at the least, and my intestinal lining probably needs a bit of treatment, if I judge by the feel of things. Never mind my ass, which feels like it got burned completely off."

"True…" Entiyti shook his head. "I have initiated the emergency decontamination in the head, so all should be clean and sanitized when we get back. Let us head to sick bay, Franz."

Levy rose from the couch, still wrapped in nothing but the robe, a thick, soft kind of not-quite-terrycloth; even his feet were bare. He took two steps forward before his legs buckled.

The much bigger Draconan caught him before he could hit the floor; then, shaking his head, scooped up the smaller human male and personally carried him to sick bay.

***

It required a couple of days in a hospital bed with an IV for the sick bay on the *Hsshth* to straighten out Levy's gut — the mucosal lining was all but gone in places, fairly scoured away — and get his rather badly dehydrated body back into a semblance of normal. And several more days before they would let him back on duty. But they eventually managed it, with the assistance

362

of several medications which Doron of Edeptis had introduced to them, and which they simply added to the IV.

Entiyti had continued with the diplomatic mission, Rslig Kuur serving as the temporary head of the bodyguard corps. But the pairing did not have the rapport that Entiyti and Levy had, and both were somewhat relieved when Levy was back on duty once more…though the medical staff refused to let him be Entiyti's food tester ever again; Kuur was stuck with that job.

***

Over the next several weeks, Entiyti discussed the incident with Levy, who was more than a little embarrassed by the whole matter.

"No, no, Franz, please do not feel badly," Entiyti soothed. "No one had any idea it would affect you like that. It was dreadful, and I am only glad it did not cause permanent damage."

"That would make two of us, Pul," Levy agreed, rueful.

"But I must admit to some curiosity about this Earth vegetable you said tasted like the thisssslan," Entiyti confessed. "This 'Brussels sprouts,' I believe you called it?"

"Yes. They're quite good, and the thisssslan reminded me a lot of it," Levy said. "They're usually cooked, though not always. And not everyone on Earth likes them, but I do."

"I see. Well, you know thisssslan is one of my favorite vegetables…"

"Yes, which is why your little prank worked so well."

"Oh, do not remind me, Franz," Entiyti said with a wince. "I wish to the highest heaven I had never thought to do it. So at any rate, I am quite curious to try some Brussels sprouts. Do you think we might possibly manage to acquire some, that I might taste them?"

"I don't know, Pul, but I'm willing to try, I guess," Levy agreed. "Let me get with the comms officer and I'll see what can be arranged."

"Excellent. Tell Boogop to contact Athanasios Tsukalos; he is one of our embedded observers. I expect Athanasios can manage a clandestine shipment."

"Right."

***

The lead communications officer of the *Hsshthh* knew several of the embedded Coalition agents placed on Earth to monitor the planet's development, including the requested Tsukalos. It was no difficulty for her to contact the Zumbirian male and request a small shipment of the vegetable be sent via courier to rendezvous with the flagship.

Upon taking possession of the package, Levy grinned to himself.

***

Levy arranged for the Brussels sprouts to be properly steamed, lightly drizzled with balsamic vinegar, and served with Entiyti's lunch as one of the vegetable sides the next day.

"Ah! I like this very much," Entiyti said, sampling the unfamiliar vegetable. "It tastes delicious. Not unlike the thisssslan, yet…different somehow."

"I'm glad you like it," Levy noted with a smile. "It does taste a lot like the thisssslan, doesn't it?"

"Yes! And this must be the Brussels sprouts of which you spoke?"

"It is. I think that properly steamed Brussels sprouts are a delicacy."

"I should have to agree with you."

"I thought you would."

"We may have to arrange for regular deliveries from Earth," Entiyti decided, eating his luncheon with enthusiasm.

"Take it easy, there, Pul. Slow down. I don't want the same thing to happen to you as happened to me. I can't guarantee you won't get a bellyache."

"I have not the time, my friend," Entiyti explained. "You know I must go to meet the Kirlyn right after lunch."

"Ah yes, that's right," Levy said, standing at the ready nearby as was protocol while his friend and employer ate. "That trade negotiation begins this afternoon, doesn't it?"

"It does, and it will be…difficult," Entiyti reminded him. "Their atmosphere is quite different, and our ship does not readily accommodate their environment suits. So we will be forced to go to them in ours. It is why the sick bay did not want you taking part; they are worried you are not yet recovered enough from, ah, 'thisssslan poisoning,' as it were, to spend long hours in an environment suit."

"Well, that's fair," Levy agreed, as Entiyti polished off the last of the Brussels sprouts; everything else on his plate was gone as well except for some gravy. "Ready, Pul?"

"I believe so, Franz."

"I'll walk you down to the hangar deck and the suiting rooms."

"Excellent."

***

The longer Entiyti sat in the diplomatic conference with the Kirlyn aboard their ambassador's flagship, the more distressed he became, as apparently his last meal disagreed rather violently with him. His normally silver-white scales began to turn a kind of ashen gray with the increasing malaise.

Then the rumbling started.

Oh dear, he thought. *That cannot be good.*

But it was when the gaseous byproducts of the consumption of vegetative matter to which he was unused began to make its presence known that he realized he might be in trouble.

Despite his best efforts, the gases passed from his digestive tract into the suit by the usual orifice, with little to no ability for him to prevent it, given the increasing pressure in his gut. Worse, the suit's scrubbers failed to remove it from the atmosphere. The longer this went on, the sicker he became, because the odors were foul and nauseating…and thoroughly mingled with his breathable atmosphere. It turned out they were also tinted.

And he wasn't entirely sure that gas was the only thing coming out of that particular orifice.

Fortunately the suit's components apparently muffled the sounds, sufficient that no one noticed.

Unfortunately, since the gaseous emanations were indeed tinted, he could not keep it a secret.

"Milord Entiyti! All you all right?" the Kirlyn ambassador exclaimed, noting his pallor and the wisps of vapor through the visor of Entiyti's helmet. "You are pale! And the air within your helmet is turning…green!"

"Are you under attack, milord?" one of the bodyguards asked; Entiyti was too ill to note and identify the face inside the space suit helmet.

"Oh no! Someone is attempting to poison President Entiyti again!" the ambassador exclaimed in horror.

"Uh, no, no, my friends, it is quite all right," Entiyti attempted to calm the ambassador, despite feeling as if he might disgorge his pedal claws. "I fear I am, ah, a bit under the weather and am feeling decidedly…off. It may be, um, as well that I return to my own ship. We, we are working on negotiating the fine details by now, are we not?"

"Yes, milord."

"And the Coalition diplomatic corps representatives are on top of matters?"

"Of course, milord," the chief negotiator for the Coalition averred. "All is well in hand."

"Good; I had no doubts. I simply wanted to ensure I was not needed. Forgive my indisposition, but is everyone all right with the notion that this negotiation can proceed without me for an hour or two? While I go back to my stateroom, lie down and recover?"

"Yes, milord, but are you sure everything is all right? Do we need to summon a physician?" the ambassador wondered. "I have it to understand your personal physician normally travels with you…"

"No, no. I suspect that something disagreed with me at my last meal," Entiyti tried to explain, now wondering if this was how matters had begun with Levy…and whether this was for a similar reason. "But no matter; it is nothing serious, it is simply a bit…off-putting. I will return in a few hours, and all will be well if I simply lie down awhile."

"By all means, then, milord, do so," the chief negotiator said. "We shall manage just fine here."

***

Entiyti rose and left the conference, headed back to the airlock connecting the two ships, accompanied by his bodyguards. As soon as the bodyguards at the airlock were signaled, they prepared it for his passage; without delay, he stepped into his flagship with some considerable relief.

Fortunately the changing rooms for environment suits were nearby for logistical purposes, and the airlock had been chosen for that reason. As the gastrointestinal urgency ramped up, he scurried rapidly into the changing room.

Immediately techs began removing the suit, and he urged them to all speed as matters in his gut began to come to a head.

"Hurry hurry hurry, now now NOW now now," he began to chant, and they rushed through their task. But when they removed his helmet, they released the by-now-somewhat-concentrated and very noxious fumes. The techs staggered back, gasping; one turned and threw up.

"Oh! Has there been a malfunction?!" another asked, shocked.

"NO, WE DO NOT HAVE A MALFUNCTION! NOW NOW NOW NOW NOW!" Entiyti ordered in a stentorian tone.

Swiftly they removed the space suit, revealing a nude Draconan, who promptly sprinted for the nearest head, even as the techs exclaimed in dismay over the condition of the suit's interior.

***

Franz had been notified of Entiyti's early return, and he hurried down to the changing room, arriving just in time to see Entiyti's naked posterior disappear through the door of the head, as the door slammed shut.

This was shortly followed by a loud roar of distress, which immediately preceded numerous disgusting splattering, bubbling, flapping, and motorboat sounds emanating from behind the door of the head.

Biting his lip nearly bloody to avoid indiscreet laughter, Franz made a mental note: *Head doors aboard the* Hsshthh *should be checked for soundproofing henceforward.*

***

The next day, after sick bay treated Lord Entiyti for mild dehydration and a perturbed digestive system — though admitting Levy had had it far worse — and before he returned to the negotiations, Entiyti came to the bridge in order to ensure that his communications requests for certain items not usually to be found on a starship would be unheard by the rest of the crew. Especially a certain head of bodyguard security.

What the bridge crew also heard were certain mutterings of retaliation, followed by the transmission to a request recipient that, "This means war!"

After Entiyti departed the bridge, Captain Abergari put his face in his taloned hands.

"Maker help us," he grumbled, "this will either be one of the greatest friendships in galactic history, or the death of us all."

"Embrace the power of AND, sir," Ii'k'ee, at the communications station, intoned fatalistically.

The rest of the bridge crew sighed acknowledgement.

Author Notes

These two beings — the man who would become Director Fox, and President Pulgey Entiyti — have become the two most popular of the secondary and tertiary characters in the *Division One* series. Some time back, I began speculating about the possibility of a spinoff series detailing their adventures from before *Division One* existed. As you can see, I decided to run with it, though it took me a long time to get it written. Welcome to the *Blood Brothers* series in the *Pan-Galactic Coalition Universe*.

Things have not gone great in Casa Osborn since the last *Division One* book was released. My beloved husband and cover artist, Darrell Osborn, died suddenly in December 2021, and I spent most of 2022 just trying to keep my head above water and keep the household going — said household now consisting of only myself and my cat, Elrond Half-Siamese.

I swear, when Darrell departed, it felt like he took my whole heart and half my brain with him. It turns out there is such a thing as widow's brain, and it isn't a good thing at all. It was a long time before I could coherently string words together on paper, and I'm still not very good at it, nor am I very good at working out detailed plots; this particular book was a bit easier, since it largely followed historical timelines and all I had to do, for the most part, was figure out the order of certain historic events, then plug Franz into them.

I managed to put out a couple of longish short stories or short novelettes, depending on your definitions, by way of attempting to write; *Get Off My Lawn* and *The Gingerbread Cat* were well received. So I kept trying to write longer forms. This is the first novel length story I've written and COMPLETED since Darrell died, and it's been a bit of an experiment to see if I even still could. I owe Richard Weyand the next book in the *Section Six* trilogy of the *EMPIRE* series, but that's a dyed in the wool spy novel, and that's gonna take some serious thinking…which my brain is only now starting to do, more than a year after the worst day of my life. I already have a good bit of certain key sections written, but trying to figure out the middle is going to be the hard part. Y'all please be patient with me; I'm doing my best. I'm just hoping my writing mojo comes back in full.

To that end, let me thank beta readers Jim Woosley, Evelyn Zinn, Randy Jones, Troy Logsden, and protégé Tony Thompson (who's also beta reading this). These guys tell me if I did a halfway decent job of this, or if I'm totally off in the weeds. Apparently I was reasonably successful.

As for replacing my cover artist and layout man, I think I did okay. Dimitri Walker did a bang-up job on the cover for *Get Off My Lawn*, then sent me the finished painting, which is already framed and waiting to be hung in my house (which is undergoing post-mortem declutter and rearranging, which is also SLOW when you're handicapped, so it's a long way from finished). And Tiffanie Gray turns out to know exactly what software Darrell used, and can do a fantastic job replicating his style. And she knows how to use the software to do print layouts. I could use the layout software a bit, but I was not the expert he was; besides, it resided on Darrell's laptop, and he didn't leave any password lists, so I can't even access it now.

For those who keep up with my mom, she fell and broke some ribs last fall, and we had a scare that she might have had congestive heart failure (she didn't). But she's gone downhill after two broken ribs, two serious bouts of UTIs, and a possible bout of covid. She went back in the rehab facility and thence to a nursing-care facility. Didn't help that pretty much the entire family, including me, came down with either covid or flu right after Thanksgiving.

Oh, and my HVAC system died in the middle of that horrid frigid cold we had mid-December of 2022. Kitty Elrond and I ended up huddling together under several blankets, and me in two layers of clothing, to keep warm one night, while I prayed that the water pipes wouldn't freeze and burst (they didn't). I ended up having to replace the whole thing except the ductwork. THAT was an expensive proposition, complicated by needing to move a whole buncha stuff to enable the attic unit to be removed and replaced.

Yeah. 2022 was HARD.

Anyway, I'm doing my dead-level best to find ways to move on, to keep writing, to maintain the legacy of Darrell's beautiful artwork, and to keep kittiboi and me warm and fed and healthy. If you're so inclined, send up a few to what the galactics call the Great Maker for me that I get there soon, and that my family does well.

Moving on…

~Stephanie Osborn

Huntsville, AL

Jan 2023

About the Author

Stephanie Osborn is a former payload flight controller, a veteran of over twenty years of working in the civilian space program, as well as various military space defense programs. She has worked on numerous Space Shuttle flights and the International Space Station, and counts the training of astronauts on her resumé. Of those astronauts she trained, one was Kalpana Chawla, a member of the crew lost in the Columbia disaster.

She holds graduate and undergraduate degrees in four sciences: Astronomy, Physics, Chemistry, and Mathematics, and she is "fluent" in several more, including Geology and Anatomy. She obtained her various degrees from Austin Peay State University in Clarksville, TN and Vanderbilt University in Nashville, TN.

Stephanie is currently retired from space work. She now happily "passes it forward," teaching math and science via numerous media including radio, podcasting, and public speaking, as well as working with SIGMA, the science fiction think tank, while writing science fiction mysteries based on her knowledge, experience, and travels.

For more, or to subscribe to Stephanie's newsletter, go to her website,

http://www.stephanie-osborn.com/